I0760425

Grave of a Fiery Poison

Book 1.5

Monica Shantel

GRAVE OF A FIERY POISON

FEATHERS & FLAMES
BOOK 1.5

MONICA SHANTEL

Grave of a Fiery Poison

Copyright © 2026 by Monica Shantel

All rights reserved.

No part of this publication may be reproduced, distributed, or transmitted in any form or by any means, including photocopying, recording, or other electronic or mechanical methods, without the prior written permission of the publisher, except as permitted by U.S. copyright law. For permission requests, contact [include publisher/author contact info].

The story, all names, characters, and incidents portrayed in this production are fictitious. No identification with actual persons (living or deceased), places, buildings, and products is intended or should be inferred.

Book Cover by Monica Shantel

Illustrations by Monica Shantel

Map by Monica Shantel

ISBN 978-1-960696-16-8 (Paperback) 978-1-960696-15-1 (Hardcover)

First Edition

To those who have been struggling and giving it your all when you can't anymore.

You deserve your happy ending, too.

AUTHOR'S NOTE

This book deals with heavy themes, including violence and gore, attempted sexual assault (two incidents), topic of sexual abuse of a minor, and mention of losing a parent to cancer. There is language throughout, as well as sexual content in a few chapters, all cracked door. Please keep this in mind to decide if this book is right for you.

"Naera" 11/12/25

"Matthew"
11/13/25

GREAT HALL
MATTHEW'S OFFICE
GARDEN /COTTAGE
HEAVEN

Prologue: Copper

Ayden

Massive—ruffled in wariness—her wings folded behind her as she skipped up to the apartment. Her eyes darted between buildings. Angel could never be too careful, unless it had been because I rejected her and dared to put her in a vulnerable position.

People were coming home from work or doing errands, dragging themselves through the brutal necessities just to get by in this life. They checked their cars for lost items. They yelled at family members to hurry and get inside or to help them carry bags in. Whatever it was, nobody paid any attention to my hot guardian angel strolling by with caution.

Maybe a Mormon town wouldn't call for question anyway.

My gaze didn't waver for a second, even as she put more distance between us—my stomach churning from the risk. In another instant, she disappeared. Her cloaking ability. I despised it most of the time when I couldn't see her, but I hoped in this case it would keep her safe from him.

Angel wasn't in any *real* danger. Liam couldn't hurt her anymore, but that didn't leave me worrying any less.

I'd never felt this way before.

Something deep within grew. Warm, and fuzzy, like those fizzy candies you'd try as a kid. It made you feel funny but the curiosity piqued and you wanted to hold onto it for longer. With that came an immense need to protect. I'd never been the protective type, given my tragic childhood and the horrors I experienced. I could never save myself from *him*, so I'd never tried to look after anyone else since. I didn't want that burden of keeping someone else safe from my corruption.

However, this had been innate. As if I had never experienced being exposed and helpless at all. What a lie.

Or maybe it was because of that memory that I'd had a bigger desire to ensure Angel never felt hopeless at all.

Snickering, I forced down that urge. Wasn't that her job? Wasn't she supposed to be *my* saviour?

I shut my eyes, my head falling back against the headrest of the driver's seat.

She ripped the car door open, and I popped open an eye to catch the silly woman in her antics, but the passenger door remained shut. "Angel?" My brows furrowed as I twisted toward the back seat. "Fuck," I muttered.

Liam's grin widened as he pressed the tip of his blade into my neck, other fingers digging into the fabric of the seat, right behind my shoulder. "Where's Elli?"

Elli? Did this bloody wanker call her *Elli*? Who the fuck did he think he was?

"You don't get the privilege of even uttering her name, dickhead," I growled.

He wiggled a finger at me. "You don't get the privilege of telling me what to do when I'm the one with the knife to your neck." His eyes roamed the parking lot. "Spying on me, eh? Is there something I should be aware of?" He leaned in, his dragon breath choking me out. Shit, that was an insult to dragons.

Carefully, I turned my head away, forcing down the fire beneath the surface of my skin.

"Let's wait here, shall we?" A command more than a question. Even his voice was nauseating.

"I got nothing!" she shouted. When I glanced her way, she came barrelling toward the car. She yanked the door and fell into the seat. "He covers his tracks too well." Her gaze met mine, and all that light had been snuffed out. I could strangle Liam right here if I could just get that bloody knife from him. He'd taken everything she ever cared about.

"You didn't think I thought of everything?" her *murderer* chuckled.

"Liam, you don't have to do this," she pleaded.

His eyes snapped from me to her. "I do," he smacked his lips together and my lips curled up toward my nose. He couldn't appear anymore repugnant if he tried. "You're going to mess up everything if I don't." He sighed. That deceitful, pitiful twat.

"If you do this, we'll make sure you pay in every way possible and it's going to be so much worse than prison, *or* death row." Her big blue eyes glassed over. If he made her cry, I'd rip his own eyes from his head with my bare hands.

Her fingers wrapped around mine, and she squeezed. "Ayden, look at me." I peered at her to find her stuck like glue, her mind racing as she fumbled the words. "Don't let him get to you. That's his game."

I swallowed whatever fear I'd been displaying before, promising her.

As her fingers slipped between mine, her voice softened. "I love you, Ayden Dyer."

Fuck, why couldn't I just say the same in return? Why couldn't I get my damn tongue to cooperate so I could swear my life to her? A cruel world devoured a pure soul like hers, and I crushed her spirit far more than they ever had. I was her living nightmare.

Was that why I wouldn't tell her I loved her far greater than flames did oxygen?

Liam's chuckle ripped through whatever dreams we had left. "How cute." The knife slid across my neck with ease, a sting overwhelming every thought. I choked on the blood that poured, clawing at my throat as I tried to curse him. If I could grab Angel and tell her a thousand times over that she was the dead therapist I needed all along, I could go peacefully.

I just couldn't say anything.

"No!" her voice croaked as tears spilled down her cheeks. She nestled her face in my neck. Fuck Liam. I'd torture him when I got the chance, and I'd stick to that threat. "Come back to me."

But I'd let her down.

For a moment, I feared I ended up far below.

But when the light blinded me, I knew that it'd just been God finding His own joke in this. Maybe He had a sick sense of humor, too.

I couldn't say I didn't admire Him for it.

I was given no time to question the white wings that hung on my back as screaming tore me out of my shock. I'd been right where they left me—bleeding. A corpse.

Only now I wasn't so...battered—and left for the world to kick around some more.

I stood outside the car, catching a glimpse of my body.

"This is for killing the man I love," she cried.

I yanked open the back door to find my Angel forged of chaos, heartbreak, and murder. She'd plunged his own weapon into his body countless times. It couldn't have been counted as self-defense because she was already dead, but she came to my aid. I'd never hold that against her. He wrenched her entire world from under her feet.

She stumbled out of the back, feet slapping the road on her way out. "He deserved it. I swear he deserved it." She lifted her gaze, looking right through me.

Then, she twisted her neck to catch the twitch of his finger.

"He did, Angel. He deserved to meet karma," I reassured her, wrapping her in my arms, burying her in my chest, and pressing a soft kiss to her temple. The scent of rich roses radiated off her. Freshly bloomed on spring morning shortly after the rain had stopped just for the sun to come out from beyond the clouds. "He deserved to die for every heart he broke, and *every* life he stole."

Then I was torn from her—my safe haven. I'd been ripped from everything comforting I ever knew.

They forced me to my knees. Chained me. Grabbed me by the hair and ripped my head back.

Whatever the fuck their names were, they lifted a needle filled with black liquid, brought it over, then injected it into my neck. I yelled out as it burned through my soul.

Fighting against their restraints, the searing left behind the shell of a heart.

This drug devoured my morals and everything I'd worked hard for in the last few months.

As I curled forward, I grunted, smacking the sizzling cement. But that wasn't what threw me off—no.

It was the realization that the cement didn't burn me at all. Hot, sure, but it didn't char my form or leave open wounds. What the fuck

did they do to me?
"He's ready."

Shrieks pierced the sky, consuming every inch of the forest. I pushed harder—faster—my skirt bunched up in my fists as I sprinted after the fallen angel to the highway of Hell.

Levi.

"Ayden!" I screamed as a branch slapped me and I tumbled to my knees. "Let him go!"

That damned smirk on Levi's face grew. He had Ayden by the throat, nails digging into his soul. "There are no happy endings around here." He jumped down the stairs that had opened up in the earth, pulling Ayden behind him.

"No!" I scrambled to my feet, nearly tripping, darting over just as the portal swallowed them whole.

My entire world shattered at that moment. The moment Ayden disappeared from my arms. The moment he'd been taken by a fallen angel. The moment the man I loved had been dragged to Hell.

After his brutal demise, his apartment would be cleared out and put up for rent as if his memory hadn't tainted the walls of that structure. Anyone who had been bold enough to consider living where a man's life spiraled downwards would still be haunted by such nightmares to come.

Not of my doing—no—but of *his.*

His taste still lingered on my lips, but his scent began to fall away from my form the way they'd torn him from my soul. What had my heart been without his? Nothing but yellow police tape that reminded the public to keep their distance.

I became caution.

As hard as I tried to keep my mind from wandering, it conjured up all the terrifying things they'd inflict down below. The scorching heat that forever blended with a stinging nobody could shake. An itching you couldn't suppress. Bugs scurrying under the skin. Boils and blisters.

I had to do something. I had to save him.

Again.

And yet, nowhere to turn to. That had been my fate. Not his family, nor mine. Nor Selene. Not a single person was available for me to confide in, allowing me to spill all my darkest fears.

What would become of Ayden? All alone, begging for me to save him the way he did months ago. Only this time I could not come to his rescue. I could not take on his pain the way I had when I first fled.

How could I get down there and haul him out without getting caught?

Sure, angels could not be killed. I had already hit that *lovely* milestone in my lifetime.

However, we were at great risk of harm when we were at the mercy of Lucifer himself. It was not a place any angel or sane human wished to be. My boyfriend was going to be chained up and tortured endlessly until he bled out on the stones, burning like a strip of bacon in the morning sun. Reliving that kind of pain was a far worse fate than death. But these days, much more than met the human eye was far worse than the shut-down of a body.

"Don't look so glum, Elli."

I whipped around to face the man who always managed to bring my world crashing to the ground. "Don't you dare call me that, Liam."

He tilted his head. "Why, is that not your name?"

Eliana Bree Wilson.

A name I kept hidden from Ayden for months. A select few still knew it, and Liam had been no different. Still, I did not wish to hear my name leave his lips. Ever. He turned it *poisonous*.

And the next words made me want to murder him all over again. "I think I could help you, Elli."

Narrowing my eyes, every buried emotion slithered from the cracks of the graveyard in my bones. "What makes you think you could be of help to me?" As he opened his mouth to respond, I cut him off. "No, actually, what makes you think I'd even *accept* your help? You murdered my best friend. You murdered me. You murdered the man I love and now that he's been kidnapped by your friends, you think you can waltz around with an offer? In what delusional world do you think I'm going to ever team up with someone as vile as you?" I spat.

He took a step closer, his gaze focused, unwavering, and he said, "Because it's simple. Ayden is trapped in Hell, and I'm the one person who has an *in* with Lucifer himself."

I admitted I'd stab him all over again. I would have loved to be given the chance and make him feel the way he forced on me just thirty minutes ago.

Terrified. Feeble. Fraught.

"Why?" came out in a whisper.

His eyes gleamed. "Why what?"

To prove to him I wasn't afraid, nor did I allow him to have the power, I closed the distance until our faces came within inches. "Why do you want to help me save the very man you just ripped away from me only a half hour before?"

"I don't have much time." He glanced at the sky, his form flickering.

I'd been reminded that his body was once lying in Ayden's car, bleeding out. He was supposed to be dead, yet here his soul stood. Blood poured from his abdomen, but not a drop truly stained the earth below our feet.

Was he dying? If he did, would I watch him be sucked down to Hell?

"Your lack of time and piss-poor decisions are not my burdens to bear, Liam. The day you slit Selene's throat, you lost all of my respect."

His lips curved up in one corner. "Did I? Don't be so sure about that. You were all over me. I could see it in your eyes." He lifted his hand, his fingers brushing my chin. "You're just upset that you weren't smart enough to catch on before I tore you from your body."

I opened my mouth to curse him out, but before I had the opportunity, his soul disappeared. Wherever he went, I couldn't be entirely sure. I didn't see him get yanked into the rotting soil, nor did he float away. Regardless, I yelled out to release all pent-up rage inside me.

I remembered that week leading up to my death so vividly, and I had never once seen Liam as a potential date. I'd never been attracted to him.

Falling to my knees, I clawed at the grass, pulling out clumps as I laid my soul bare to the forest floor in hopes I'd be able to hear him from under the crust. "Ayden, I'm coming for you."

In what universe had it been fair that I found love only to lose him to Hell? To Liam? To Levi?

None.

Not an ounce of it made sense.

Slowly rising to my feet, my wings fanned out behind me as I screamed at the sky. Every tragedy that painted my name would go down in history, and I'd be the one to set the world on fire if it meant I'd finally have him back in my arms.

If I had to unleash the monsters of Hell, so be it.

It wasn't going to end like this, and I'd be damned to ever accept a fate where the man I loved suffered at my hands. All because he'd had the bitter pleasure of meeting the very beast who'd taken everyone I'd ever cared about.

No more nice girl. No more Eliana Wilson, or Angel.

For him, I'd do whatever it'd take.

I wandered the clearing, but the portal never opened. I inspected every rock and branch for some secret trick, yet nothing. Fire spread through my veins every week that passed in which Ayden suffered their wrath.

If someone had asked me to take their life, I wouldn't have hesitated. Not for a second, in fact.

The venom that traveled through my soul bled out through the crevices of promises once kept—now disintegrated. I'd beg for forgiveness once I was certain he was safe in my arms.

I hadn't spent nine months fighting for his soul just to succeed and lose it all in the span of thirty minutes.

Despicable, and that's exactly what the fallen angels were.

Nothing about me felt the same, but it still felt pure. Pure of hatred.

We'd been told never to hold that amount of fury within us, but I could certainly spare enough of it for the very creatures who'd done nothing but leave my afterlife in shambles.

He'd been the petals without a flower, and I a stem without a chance to ever bloom, shielded by darkness. Together, we made up a whole rose.

That was why I *needed* him. He allowed me to flourish in the light.

My petal torn from my stem.

A piece of me gone.

The only soulmate ever made for me stolen.

Eliana didn't get second chances. Finding him even in my death had been simply a miracle. To receive it all to then lose it? Unspeakable. I'd never find another Ayden, nor would I want to.

Once upon a time I swore never to fall for him. He'd been nothing but trouble.

It turned out I reveled in disorder. I was a guardian angel, and I'd be nothing without it.

But breaking promises seemed to be something I'd been a pro at. It'd be a lie if I didn't admit that, and now that the truth became crystal clear, I'd wear that like a badge.

It'd be what fueled me to bring him back.

The fallen angels hadn't been careful enough, and because of their carelessness, they'd feel whatever I'd been bottling the past nine months while dealing with Ayden's incessant insults.

I would hate to be them.

But more importantly, I'd hate to be Ayden. I had been him when we were tortured in Hell. When the flames licked our souls and left permanent trauma. The sorrow written in his eyes as he saw the destruction he caused by walking the path he had. The bloody strikes against his back as he cried out, trying as hard as he might to bite back the cries. He had wanted nothing more than to be strong, to prove to me who he was. Not weak, but rather in charge. He believed he deserved such torment. He took it like a man should have, and that had been the moment in which I truly hated him and admired him all in one breath. He proved not only his strength, but how much I loved him and ached without him by my side. Choosing to walk away after our injuries healed was the hardest decision I had to make.

For us, I made it.

Because without me, he realized how deeply rooted his cravings for me went.

I'd grown on him the way he'd fused to my soul.

So this time around, I'd save him again. I'd take great pride in being his guardian once again.

Nothing was sweeter than revenge, best served with the scorching of a woman's rage.

Ayden taught me well.

My downfall.

Also my mentor.

And Liam? The asshat truly believed that I'd team up with him. Never. Not in a million years, nor if everyone vanished and he was the only human left.

Human—if he stayed that way.

Given his current state, everything had been on the line.

I'd never lose sight of Ayden, either. Being immortal gave me all of eternity to fight for him. Nothing to truly hold me back except the monstrous beings Lucifer called his pets.

His bright green eyes stuck in my mind, begging me to save him. He could argue that he didn't need rescuing because it wasn't his role to be the damsel. Once he'd become vulnerable to me, he proved that to be a facade. He'd always put on that front so nobody saw the broken man shouting for someone to hold him tight. To kiss his head and promise everything would be okay.

Now he didn't believe it ever would be.

I'd let them take him. I'd allowed him to go.

As the vexation towards them grew, so did the resentment of my own failures.

Ayden Dyer was *mine.*

They couldn't have him. They couldn't have his laughter, nor his smiles. They couldn't taste his sweets, nor steal the beating of his heart. Everything he did, it had been made for me. I'd go down there and when they witnessed a glimpse of what I was capable of, I'd tear them apart and relish their pleas. I'd never show them any mercy.

They gave me all the permission in the world when they took my other half.

I'd run my fingers through his hair again. Stroke his beard. Savor the taste of white chocolate raspberries lingering in every kiss.

I'd marry him and give him all of me if he'd allow that.

One thing was always certain, despite how hard he tried to deny it and how hard he fought.

Ayden Dyer belonged to me and nobody else.

Not Sunny. Not Liam. Not the fallen angels.

Having everyone believe he was never mine had been the biggest mirage we put on for the world, but we all knew down in the dark corner of his heart, he had never been anyone else's.

Like honey, I'd be *dripping* from his teeth.

Even in Hell.

They couldn't take what was mine and live to see the nightfall.

I'd never allow it.

And for that reason alone, the world would burn in their wake.

I grumbled as I lifted my fist to knock. I supposed I'd be a little courteous. She never did anything wrong, but I'd remind her that he was mine.

The door creaked open to reveal soft hazel eyes and messily braided hair. *Damn me,* she was adorable even when she crawled out of bed. Was I so sure I needed her help to find Ayden?

"Elena!" I'd forgotten for a moment about the fake name I went by.

Well, I couldn't correct her now.

She opened the door wide before her fingers wrapped around my wrists and tugged me into her arms. "You're back! I didn't do anything wrong, did I?" Her brows knitted together while she pulled away from me.

Shaking my head, I cleared my throat. As if I needed to... "They took him. You have to help me."

"Who? Who took who?" The gears clicked into place fairly quickly. "Ayden? Did someone take Ayden?"

She had no idea he was murdered. How the hell did I break that news to her?

Forget manners and morals.

Time was of the essence here.

"Damnit!" I rubbed my eyes. "Listen—and I apologize for not giving you time to process this—Ayden was murdered." Her hands slapped against her mouth. "Lucifer and his Legion kidnapped Ayden. They dragged him to Hell, and—" And then realization hit me. What would Sunny be able to do from here? She was merely a human with no connection to Hell or any way to get in and out. She had no access to the supernatural world. I had been grasping at straws. A desperate attempt, and a poor one at that.

I'd managed to crush a woman's hopes and dreams. For what, exactly?

"He's...dead?" her words came out barely above a whisper.

After the way Sunny had contemplated her own worth yet poured her soul into Ayden, I knew now why I stood before her.

If I didn't keep her at my side, the fallen angels would use him against her, or even her against him. And if I was truly unlucky, *them* against me.

"You're not safe here. You should come with me."

"What does that even mean?" Sunny cried.

I grabbed her wrist and dragged her from her own home. Where? I couldn't be entirely sure. But when we arrived, I'd know.

As we trekked through the woods, I found myself standing in front of the portal down to Hell that once existed, where my precious Ayden had been taken. "There." I pointed at the rock. "This is where it happened."

Her eyebrows drooped towards the center as her irises filled with worry. "Where...Ayden died?"

"No. Where they took him. Levi. Lucifer. All those, and excuse my French, fuckwads. Damnit." A small sob ripped through me. "I don't know what to do. Liam murdered Ayden right in front of me. He wanted to watch me suffer. He wanted me to beg for mercy. He wanted to take back control because even if he can't hurt me, he can *hurt* me. Then he tries to offer his help? No, that's not important." I waved my hands around with the shake of my head. Then, I pinched the bridge of my nose. "I need to get him back. If I don't, there's no telling what I'm going to do."

Not cry. Not scream. I'd tear the world apart. I'd lose my sanity. I'd succumb entirely to the darkness for all the joy it stole from me time and time again.

"I don't understand." Confusion laced through the hairs of her eyebrows, weaving its way before absorbing into the wrinkles forming between them.

"Ayden and I are together now. That's the truth, the full story. But if we don't stop yapping, he might not stand a chance at surviving what they have in store."

"Understood" came out just above a whisper.

A part of me shriveled up at the thought of hurting Sunny. Mortified, even, that I could callously say such harsh words without a second thought. Time was *still* sensitive, however. I could rectify my transgressions down the line. What I could not go back and do was reverse what they'd inflict on an angel in Hell.

"What do we do?" she asked with more steadiness.

What *did* we do?

"We..." My gaze trailed back to the rock as I conjured up ideas. Talk to Matthew? God? The Thrones? Maybe. I'd keep those ideas on the back burner. They'd be more of an *if-we-need-to-do-this* kind of plan.

We were on our own for now.

"We find the portal. We find a way into Hell," I finally answered.

"We?" Her voice jumped up a pitch.

"Sunny, I can't do this alone. Don't chicken out on me now."

Maybe I'd been ridiculous and selfish to ask her at all. To ask her to risk her life for a man she loved but could no longer have. To flaunt our relationship in her face. To dredge up all the horrible memories that drove her to suicide in the first place.

Wow, I was abominable.

"I need someone. I *can't* do this alone," I repeated.

My gaze darted around the area. My throat closed in. My chest tightened, and that heartbeat I hadn't experienced in over a year and a half, it pounded in my ears.

If Sunny said no, I couldn't force her.

Begging for her to aid me was far more humiliating than anything else. Far more than confessing my love to Ayden after he'd chosen her.

And months later, he picked me. He picked me up off the ground where I'd stumbled along the way after trying to move on from the imprint he left on me. I never had, either. His grip had been far too tight. Rightfully so.

My Ayden Dyer.

The terror slithered up every inch of her body, squeezing right at her heart. She wore it openly. "I don't think I can. I'm sorry."

Part of me urged myself to tell her she didn't need to apologize, but I couldn't get my lips to part. My tongue swelled, and that damned lump formed. Instead, I spun on my heel and pushed myself off the ground as I disappeared up into the clouds. I wanted to be anywhere but here, in existence.

As I hit the fluff, I skidded to a halt with my hands balled into fists and teeth gritted.

The sight of all the other angels boiled my blood—knowing they got their happy endings while mine had been taken.

I couldn't stay here.

Dropping from Heaven, the grass flattened beneath my feet. The edge of the forest looked over the city as a warning of what was coming. Of what *I* could do, what I might have done for Ayden's safe return.

Sitting at the edge of the cliff, my feet dangled. Before me, a black feather floated. I snatched it with a scowl. "You're going to suffer to no end. I'll make sure of that."

Vengeance was no pure trait to possess, but I had always justified it by reminding myself that Lucifer and his minions deserved relentless torture. I could hardly be vengeful for ensuring the villain paid for his crimes. Hell for eternity. What went around came around.

I'd do it to protect him. I did what was best for him.

Why did the guilt still gnaw away at my insides?

"Ayden, I will find you," I whispered to the earth. "I'll drag you back here myself. I will never stop searching, never stop fighting, until you're safe in my arms. You can count on me."

The grass shivered in the wind as if Ayden had heard and responded the way he knew how.

It was silly of me to imagine, but I needed any sliver of hope that he was okay. For our sake, he had to be okay.

"Please, God, let him be okay."

Pleading could only do so much these days. We wouldn't need to do it at all if the afterlife had been a lick of fair. Ayden had been taken by the fallen angels. I had once, too. Were any of us truly safe?

We had been promised such things.

And now...

Now I wasn't so sure.

I was expected to never stray from this path, and I hadn't.

Well, not entirely true.

I'd fallen for a human man.

But if that had been so sinful, why had they told me about it? Was it *to warn me not to do it?* Why give me Ayden at all? *To tempt me? Test my strength as a Virtue?* Why did God wave the sin away when we confessed?

Had he been used to poison me?

Was this all some twisted game?

Hundreds of questions and not one answer to satisfy me.

I could almost hear them screaming at me to go to Matthew for help. What would he do? He had never been very eager to aid any situation, and he'd only truly been there in Hell as a last resort.

Would he care to look for Ayden?

I despised the thought myself, but I had to consider it. Did anyone in Heaven care for Ayden's soul? His well-being? Or had saving him just been to protect *their* reputation?

I feared I was on my own.

Standing up, my eyes grazed the city below.

As if the sky were a film—my eyes the lense—charcoal clouds rolled in. Lightning cracked open the veil, thunder shaking the world before me. On cue, rain began to pour.

"Do You sense it?" I asked in a low voice. "Do You sense the shift, the balance faltering? An angel—a changed man—has been ripped from his paradise. Certainly You must know what has happened. Nothing goes under Your nose unnoticed."

The next explosive noise came as my answer.

He knew.

But what was He going to *do* about it?

Water poured right through me, but I'd hoped it would soak me in the cries of the innocent.

I hadn't been that lucky, or blessed, whichever one came around these days. They were mocking me. Hell, Heaven, the earth. The entire universe had been laughing in my face and what could I do?

When more lightning struck down, it glowed a vibrant orange

rather than cool white with a subtle aura of lavender.

I stumbled forwards, nearly plummeting off the cliffside. "What does that mean?"

It couldn't be good, right?

"What does that mean?" I screamed at the sky.

Nobody answered, as usual.

I chalked it up to my imagination when the next strike had been the most normal color known to man. However, I was no man, and certainly not living.

Because even if it had been real—and I hadn't been losing my mind—no way would angels above or below be that concerned with another being dragged to Hell. Unless my sanity had gone when I was tortured in Hell months ago.

That dragged up far more questions.

Could only the supernatural realm see it?

If humans could, why had I never seen it before?

Were we the only angels stupid enough to get kidnapped by Lucifer and his Legion?

If it was because of the event, why was I only seeing it now?

What exactly did it mean?

Or was I truly just seeing red, clouded by the impending doom?

An icy breeze fanned across my backside, slipping through strands of my hair. Then, "Questioning your sanity, *Angel*?"

Clenching my jaw, I dipped my chin down at an angle, towards him. "You don't get to call me that, Levi." I always despised it when he did.

"What, you don't like it?"

I whipped around, jabbing my pointer finger to his chest. "You're a fallen angel! You have no right to take everything from me then use *that* nickname as a weapon."

The corner of his lips tugged upward as he towered over me.

"Because I'm a fallen angel? Is that so? Are you so sure that's the reason?" He tilted his head. "Or would it have anything to do with a certain man you've dared to fool around with?"

I scowled. "We have never fooled around." The love Ayden and I had was real. He swore he'd wait for me. We'd never even gone that far.

He hummed, eyes scouring the buildings painted behind me. "If I were you, I'd be careful insulting fallen angels."

"Or what? What more can you fucking take? You've ripped everything from me, Levi. What more is there to lose?"

Selene. Ayden. Parents that never loved me, and being brutally murdered by the very man who had also killed my best friend. I'd been the foolish woman too distracted to notice.

"Oh, you poor thing," he said with a mocking frown. "Little do you know just what else we've already burned."

I lunged forwards as he fell back with a throaty laugh. "See you around." With that maniacal grin, he shot into the sky. I decided against going after him, since it'd do me no good.

I needed to get down to Hell somehow. Without them stopping me.

I *needed* to save Ayden before they stripped him of everything he ever was.

HADES

Levi's words replayed in my head.

"Questioning your sanity, Angel?"

The only sense that he could have asked that in was about the bolt of fire that struck the sky. He saw it, too. I hadn't imagined anything, which meant it had to mean *something.*

I wasted no seconds flying over the treetops before landing in front of the portal. I expected to stand and wait around, or to have to search for a hidden key or some way to open up the cave underground.

I had not anticipated that it would open up *for* me.

A trap, of course. I knew that.

I'd happily fall for it though.

Rushing down the stairs, my bare feet smacked the hot cement. They began to blister, but I brushed it all off. It had been nothing compared to the crack in my heart growing considerably.

In fact, it matched the rage that festered inside me.

I marched through the halls with the blood of my enemy worn with pride, and my head held high.

As Levi rounded a corner with a click of his tongue and shake of his head, I scowled. His gaze roamed my form as if to judge me for whatever wrongs I'd committed. I beared no shame. "Come to rescue your pet?" With a furrow of his brows, tilt of his head, and darting of his eyes up to the stalactites, he pursed his lips. "No, I think *you* were always the pet."

I opened my mouth to respond, but he beat me to it, "Isn't that right, Ayden?"

My heart leaped up into my throat, choking me out.

Levi twisted his body back towards the hall as Ayden showed himself, wearing a solemn expression.

I willed my feet to move, but they disobeyed. My tongue lay thick in the back of my mouth as I let out a strangled cry. Everything in me refused to rejoice at the sight of my love.

Something had been off, like the way you'd dream of a place you visited every day where instead your brain warped the perspective and shifted things just enough without alerting you that it'd been a nightmare.

Before me stood the poison in my veins. My nightmare in which terror seized my voice.

Ayden Dyer wavered, and where bright wings once hung in triumph of his victories, was now a constant reminder that we would never be from the same world.

"What's that expression for? Don't you love the new look?" Levi asked with too much ridicule lacing his tone. "I prefer it. In fact, I think it fits all his life choices quite nicely."

Finally, I managed to step towards Ayden who stumbled back. "Don't, please," I pleaded. "Don't do that."

He didn't listen, and I had him against the wall in seconds.

"You're terrified of me, Angel," he croaked.

I wished to tell him he was wrong, but that'd be a bold-faced lie we both saw right through. How had I been expected to handle all this otherwise?

"What have they done?" I reached up without even thinking, running my fingers over the black feathers, curling them over the radius.

Real.

Not in my head.

Whipping around to face Levi, I shouted in his face as I stormed over, shoving him into the stone wall. "Why is it so hard for you to just leave us alone? Are you in love with him or something?"

He faked a gasp. "What, you mean you can't love your little boyfriend now that he's one of us?" When I dropped my arms, he closed the gap between us. "Say it. Just say the words. Rip off the bandage. It'll hurt so much less once you do." He laughed. "Dare I say you might even like it!"

I swallowed. "To satisfy you? Never."

"Don't look so glum." He grabbed my shoulders, twisting me to face Ayden. "He's still intact."

The words spilled out like sludge from a sewer, "He's a fallen angel!"

Regret washed over me almost as soon as they left my lips.

Levi, however, had been pleased by the confession. Out there in the world, making this an inescapable truth we couldn't shy away from.

"You two have a lot of catching up to do." He twirled his finger before disappearing beyond the cavernous arch.

Ayden shoved his hands in his pockets. "There's no way to reverse it. I know that's what you're thinking about." His jaw clenched as he turned his chin, refusing to look me in the eyes. "It's permanent, Eliana."

Eliana.

He'd used my actual name.

It didn't prepare me for the sting in my heart, nor the tear in his.

"Not everything has to be permanent," I let out quietly. "I can talk to Matthew. God. I can go to the Heavenly Court and we can get this fixed. You were wrongly kidnapped and..."

"Every time I try to do something good, it backfires. Why try? Why fight the inevitable? All I'm good for is being malicious. That's all I'll become. I don't deserve better. I told you that from the start!" he shouted. His eyes glassed over, voice trembling. He wanted to be angry, but Ayden had only been able to conjure up pure desolation.

I ached to comfort him. I desperately wanted to promise he was going to be okay but I was having a difficult time believing that myself.

"I'm certain Heaven is laughing at us right now." He ran a hand down his face, forcing a dry laugh. His eyes shifted across the rocks and then he redirected them to the fiery pits. What did he see but his demise?

"Ayden," I started, "please, listen. I can't guarantee how this ends. What I can guarantee is that you'll always have me. I will always love you. Do you understand that? I'm not going anywhere." I sauntered over to him, slipping my fingers in his. "Ever. You have me until the end, and if you go down, I go down with you."

He shook his head. His gaze fell on our hands as he said, "No. No, I would never want you to give up everything for me. You've worked far too hard to get what you have."

"And yet I will give it all up for you in a heartbeat" came out in a whisper.

"Angel, don't. Don't say that." He ran his tongue over his bottom lip. "Why are you so willing to give it all up for my sake? I don't deserve your love."

"I lived my entire life alone. I begged for anyone. Friends. Family. A partner. All I ever got was a friend, and then she was brutally murdered. And you know what happened next?"

"You trusted him, and he turned around to kill you, too," he mumbled, stroking his thumb over my cheek.

A nod. "He did. But after everything, I still became a guardian angel. I met you. I'm never going to *regret* that. I'm willing to give it all up for you, Ayden, because that's what you've done for me. That's what love is. If I can't have you, then there's no reason for me to be here. If I cannot be happy after my own death, then there bears no reason that I matter at all. I've done everything right, and if I cannot get my happy ending after all of that..." I swallowed my sobs before they reared their ugly cries.

"For you to believe that there's no point, that you keep getting sucked into a cycle of corruption, it hurts to hear you feel that way. I want to help. The way I know how is to devote my afterlife to you. I'll stand by you every step of the way, and when I'm needed, I will protect you. You deserve my love. You always have. You believe you don't matter, but you mean everything to me. I won't let you love me more than I love you in return." I fisted his black collar. "If you so much as *think* I'll leave you to fight this alone, you're sorely mistaken. I'll be damned because I'm not going anywhere. You can't *make me.*"

His hands slid up into my hair. "If you stand by that, you can't go back on it. This is a binding promise. You can't just say '*my bad*' and undo the damage. You know how much trouble you'll be in for fraternizing with a fallen angel."

My gaze roamed every detail—every inch of his face. "I know." I placed my palms on his chest. "But if they can't be understanding as to what truly happened to you, I don't want to associate with anyone so heartless. Empathy has always been my only redeeming trait. You, Ayden Dyer, can simply call me a casualty if that's what I must be."

With his eyes firm on my lips, he rushed in without another thought as if he had stolen the last breath from my lungs.

A hint of sugar laced my tongue, and I could almost grasp what else bonded this kiss.

Before he ripped himself away from me as if I'd been the burner he accidentally touched, turned on to full heat. "You might be okay with condemning yourself, but I can't do that to you. I'll never do that to you, Eliana."

He hadn't intended my name to sound like a swear, but it had.

At first, I assumed he said it to hurt me, but I knew now he had only used it to try and separate us for my own safety.

I didn't want him to protect me. That was my job. I could take care of myself just fine.

I balled my fists at my side. "Are you trying to go back on this? You said so yourself, the damage is done. Why would you make sure I want this only to think *for* me? I don't want you to control my decisions!"

"We're far under the earth. They haven't seen us down here. Nobody has to know." His eyes darted to the stalactites and slid across the ceiling. "You have a chance."

"A chance?" I choked. "A chance at what?" I spat. "A chance to go back up there and get fucked over?" His eyes grew the size of saucers. "You have no idea what awaits me. I can assure you that He doesn't turn a blind eye. He knows exactly what's happened down here. If you think I'll ever find someone else to love, you're mistaken. It took me over twenty years and my own murder to find love, and now you want to pretend you're protecting me? I'm not too good for you. You don't deserve worse. In case you've forgotten, you had earned your place before they turned you into one of *them*."

"I'm the first human to become one." When I didn't respond, he stepped closer. "Yeah, I know. I know that I'm an anomaly, but I also know that fallen angels were once guardian angels, the kind only born in Heaven." Another step. "But I'm not a guardian angel, am I? So how? Why me?" The gap was snuffed out as he backed me into the wall. "Because of you, Eliana. Because you are, and I was your guardee. They've been targeting you since you first became one. They want you. Being with me is handing you over to them on a silver platter. You don't want me to protect you, but you don't get to make *that decision* for me. I am undeniably in love with you, and I'll never be able to live with myself if I let anything happen. If you didn't want my protection, you never would have let me fall in love with you. You never would have returned when I begged you to."

A shiver slithered through every bone, every muscle, and every limb in my soul.

Slipping my fingers under his black button-up, I noted the tension in his neck. "If you're so sure, then have a swell time trying to resist what you want. You could never deny me even if you staked your life on it, and you *have* done that before." I brushed them over his stomach, earning myself a low groan at the base of his throat.

Then I pulled my hands back to myself and slid out from between him and the sizzling stone. "I've lost too much despite doing everything right." I narrowed my eyes. "I'm no longer the perfect angel everyone wants me to be." I turned on my heel and left Hell.

Time to come up with a new plan.

As I passed low branches with vibrant green leaves, I swung and took out some of nature with me. Maybe it'd been a little harsh, but my wrath ran deep. Between the fallen angels turning him into one of them, and Ayden having the nerve to tell me I couldn't be with him.

"Just you wait," I hissed. "You won't be able to resist me for an eternity, Ayden Dyer. And I have an *eternity* to make you fold."

Nothing interested me aside from creating a new plan. He didn't want me around, and all I wanted was to fuse myself to his ribcage. To be the black feathers upon his wings. I wanted him to carry me with him wherever he went.

Storming into Matthew's office, I slammed my palms on his desk as he shot me a warning. "Ayden has been kidnapped and..." I didn't know what. "He's been turned into a fallen angel." As to how, I couldn't be sure.

He folded his hands, locking his fingers together. "And I suppose you want me to make an exception."

"No, I want you to reverse it, Matthew!" I screeched.

He stood from his seat, fingers pressed against the top of the steel desk. With narrow eyes, his face fell dour. "Eliana, you won't speak to me that way. I require respect at the very least. I've done nothing to deserve less."

My teeth chattered as I bit back my words. "And what have I done to deserve this? Is this punishment for Justin? For Ayden's death? You tell me I'm going to fall in love with him, yet I'm the one being punished because even if I fight it, it's not enough. You told me. You still gave him to me. God gave us the green light! And when he finally makes it to Heaven, he's ripped away and turned into one of them. I—" The words caught in my throat as I stumbled back.

He opened his mouth to speak, but I shook my head as a lump formed in the beginning of my throat. "Now you're going to tell me there's nothing you can do. There's no cure. God can *do anything.* He can simply go down there and take Ayden back and reverse it, and you're going to tell me He won't. Why?"

Matthew didn't say anything this time. His gaze faltered, vanishing in the end. He hadn't been prepared for that. No, because something untraceable flashed in his eyes before I could catch it.

Chagrin, maybe?

A grave show of emotions that he rarely ever allowed anyone to see.

Matthew was meant to be the strong one—an Archangel people could look up to and learn from. He was never meant to display any sort of weakness.

But I didn't categorize empathy as such.

It humanized him, and we could use a lot more of that given how many angels were once human.

Clearing his throat, he glanced back up at me. "We saw what happened on your visit. We've had to propose a plan." He gestured towards the medium oak door as it creaked open. "Meet Naeva."

I whipped around to face a woman far more beautiful than anyone I'd seen before. Dark, perfect curls with one strand out of place, yet it'd been intentional. Full lips. Round, chestnut eyes. A skin tone kissed by the sun as if she'd resided right underneath the big, bright, and burning star.

And her dress had been as if someone had picked out a silk curtain and draped it over her shoulder before cinching it around her waist, the skirt stopping just below her knees.

But her wings—although white—had been much smaller than any angel I'd seen around before.

"Naeva here is..." Matthew trailed off.

"Cupid," she finished with a soft smile. "Heaven's version of Cupid." What a honeyed voice she possessed.

Matthew gave a curt nod.

"Why is she here?" I forced that lump down my throat, hope scratching the surface.

He stepped around his desk. "We've decided to help you with your situation."

"How?" I asked, skepticism sinking its teeth in me.

Naeva rushed over. "Allow me." She smelled of cotton candy, which had been a scent I never expected from a love...angel?

I followed her out of his modernized, plain office. "How do you plan to help?"

She fluttered her plentiful lashes. "The way a cupid helps best, of course."

Narrowing my eyes, I swiped my tongue between my lips, wetting them. Or trying. "Ayden's a fallen angel. Can you reverse that?"

We entered a small room, dingy yet bright at the same time.

Naeva sent me a frown. "No. Unfortunately we cannot do anything about that. But what you did was wrong. It was a cry for help, and I can fix that for you."

"Are you bringing him back or not?"

She slowly shook her head. "You cannot see him again. He's the enemy now."

Of course I'd been right. He saw what we did—the kiss. I hadn't kissed Ayden, no. He only saw me kiss a fallen angel, despite knowing exactly why and what happened days before that.

She twirled her fingers. "It's not punishment, Eliana."

"It feels exactly like punishment," I mumbled.

"You deserve love."

"Yes, and he's currently suffering in Hell."

She dropped her head for a moment before pressing her lips into a line. "I can't do anything about that, but I can turn things around. I can ensure you find love again."

"I want Ayden."

"He can be a man you know. It'd be acceptable to love him."

"I don't want anyone else," I seethed.

Lifting her feet, she fluttered around the room, grabbing something from a top shelf cluttered with colorful bottles. "Let's see..."

Vines dangled from the ceiling and plants decorated every windowsill made of light red bricks. Soft sunlight spilled through the glass.

A lovely cottage filled to the brim with the most peaceful remnants of human life.

"Why? Why me? Why now? Why have I never heard of you before now? Why isn't God letting me just wallow and suffer?" I asked, forcing back all of the vengeance.

When she landed back on the floorboards, she smiled. “Well, I usually come out in dire circumstances. We don’t particularly enjoy interfering with free will and the fate of things. This is considered a dire circumstance.”

I turned my head away, doleful. “Because I kissed a fallen angel.”

“Precisely.” She hurried over to a quiver, grabbing arrows. When she paused, she glanced at me. “Eliana, please. We’re doing this to restore the balance of our world.”

“Restoring it would be seeing what they did to him and making an exception!” I threw my hands up into the air, snagging a finger onto a potted plant hanging from the ceiling and bringing it crashing to the floor.

“That’s not plausible. He’s a fallen angel. It runs deeper than just appearance now. He’s going to crave chaos and devilish choices.” She slowly approached me. “Please.”

“Stay away from me!” I stumbled back into a window. I didn’t understand why they couldn’t just reverse the effects.

She let out a small sigh. “I’m not the enemy here. I’m simply doing my job.” She reached down to clean up the soil and rehang the plant. As good as new. As if it’d never made a mess in the first place.

Just like they were attempting to do to me, to remove my pain and pretend I’d never been heartbroken at all.

“Which makes you the enemy,” I said with as much sourness as I could muster up.

“Come,” she said as she waved me to follow. “Now I can’t pick anyone still living, for obvious reasons.” She dipped the tip of her gilded arrow in the dark red liquid. “But you can pick anyone else.” She wrapped her gentle fingers around my wrist, dragging me out to the main courtyard. “I know you’re questioning if this makes them obsessive. No, it doesn’t. It doesn’t alter anything about them except their feelings for you. It enhances the attraction.”

"Stop." I ripped my arm away. "I don't want this. I want Ayden!" Birds chirped and I fought back the urge to tear them from the sky.

Naeva shot me a solemn look. "Please, stop fighting it. We can't do that."

Forcing the lump down my throat, I shook my head. "Have you ever been in love? Of course not. You couldn't understand how deeply rooted that is. He's the thorn in my side but also the entire flower. I cannot let him down. I can't just forget about him and move on. That's not how love works," I hissed. "But you wouldn't care, would you? Cupid has always had a hard spot for unrequited love."

"You have me confused with the Greek and Roman versions. I'm certainly no god. I'm an angel, and one of a kind. A secret from everyone, really, until I'm needed to set right what was wronged." She brushed her dark, tight curls from her eyes. "Pick someone. I can't keep begging."

I waved her off. "Then stop."

She turned to face the other angels roaming about, lifting her arrow and pulling it taut against the bowstring of her matching gilded bow. "Can't do that, Eliana. Pick."

"No."

"Pick one. I don't know your type."

"Ayden Dyer. No less than him."

"There are plenty of English angels that look like him." Her eyes slid my way.

"Not with his personality, or his family, his love for baking. Not his green eyes, or his unending love for me."

"The love part," she began, "we can fix. That's why I'm here."

I shouted, "It's not the same!"

"Pick someone."

Naeva didn't flinch nor appear stressed by my resistance. She carried too much patience, and I wanted to break her down. I needed her to be on *my* side.

I took a step forwards. "Someone?"

"Yes?"

"You said, '*pick someone.*' You didn't tell me to pick a man."

Why had I always been so nitpicky, the kind of woman to hang on every word and the meaning behind them?

She lowered her arrow a bit, shrugging. "It's just a word, Eliana." Then she pointed the dripping tip at the crowd. *"Pick a man."* She shot me a look with a snort. "Better?"

I faced forwards, scanning the faces when they landed on someone too familiar. "What the hell is he doing here?" Shock. Agony. Terror. Whatever I named, it coursed through my soul until every last crevice of me was full to the brim of it.

"Who?"

I pointed, choking on his name. "Liam."

Swinging her arrow, she gasped. "Oh! Good choice." She let it fly.

"No!" I yelled, grabbing her bow with wide eyes, the arrow embedding itself in Liam's shoulder. He groaned a bit, rubbing away the pain as the weapon of choice faded into nothing, never having existed at all, at least to anyone but us two. "Naeva, what did you just do?" I sucked in air.

"You picked him." Her brows knitted together.

I swallowed as I clawed at my throat. I didn't need air, but I couldn't seem to replicate anything else. I couldn't *breathe* all over again. "He's the man who killed me and Ayden."

With a tilt of her head, Naeva chewed her bottom lip. "This might be able to be reversed."

"Do you promise?" I asked in a scathing tone.

"I said he can't be living." She swept her arm from Liam's right to his left. "He's technically living. I do tend to get carried away at times and act before I think."

"Is that *so*?" I'd burned a hole through her gaze.

Liam glanced at himself before meeting our eyes. Mine of disdain. Hers jeering. "I'm not sure how much longer I'll have. They're still keeping me on life support, but..."

"But what?" I spat.

He gulped down some air. "But I'd been teetering on a deal with the Devil. Selling my soul. If I do, I live. If I don't..."

Was it so wrong of me to scream at him that he deserved such a horrible fate?

Naeva shook her head as she exhaled. Guess even angels had to use air to make a point. "The answer is obvious. Don't do it. Don't sell your soul. It's a reckless decision."

"Liam has always been reckless decisions, one after another. What difference does it make now?" I asked, my eyes never leaving his.

He frowned. "Ouch." He patted the spot where the arrow had hit him. "I don't think I will. Because if I do, and I live..." He stepped closer to me as my nose scrunched, eyebrows knitted together, and lips curled up. "I'd never get to see you again, would I?"

"This is the worst thing I've ever heard." I threw my head to the side.

He cast his eyes towards the floor. "I'd end up like Ayden, or worse."

Storming over, I slapped him. "Don't you dare speak about him! You do not get the privilege of uttering his name."

"Why not?" he asked, his voice penetrating.

"It's always been about what you want. Everything you do," I panted due to old habits that died hard. "How do you expect me to trust you now? I'm at my most vulnerable. No, what I am is easily enraged, and you need to steer very clear of what kind of wrath I fantasize of unleashing. You're the scum of the scum. What's happened has been solely your fault!" I screamed, shoving my finger in his face.

He threw his hands up—as if that would make me believe he was any less deceitful. "Elli, I know."

"Stop fucking calling me that," I seethed.

"But you have to believe this was not my doing. What Levi and Lucifer have done with Ayden, they planned all that without me!"

"And yet you're standing before me."

His eyes darted around the forest. Decadent. Wandering. Nauseating. "I still have no idea what's happening to me."

He flickered in and out much like the voltage of a light bulb dimming. The sooner he disappeared, the better off I would be. He could rot six feet under and I'd never waste another thought on him.

Shaking my head in disgust, I spat. Unfortunately for me, it went through his translucent form, further proving to us both that we truly didn't have a clue what was happening. According to Naeva, he was in a coma, stuck on life support essentially. Neither of them knew which way he'd end up.

"I want you gone. I don't want to see your face. You know what you did to him, and you can't take that back. You've ripped away the one man who's ever been able to love me. You ripped away my best friend when she promised to provide me with a safe place. You've made it abundantly clear, Liam, that you despise my guts. For whatever reason, you taunt me. You tease me. You play these games in hopes to watch me suffer. I won't give you the fucking satisfaction anymore." One stomp on the cloud and my wings unfolded behind me, flapping along with the wind as I soared down into the forest and far away from the most despicable man who had ever been conceived.

He'd lay in waiting. He had sat in that back seat because he knew what he was aiming for. He had planned the entire thing and he saw us coming that night. He couldn't pretend he was a victim in any of this, or some bystander, or even a man who seized an opportunity last minute.

Liam Brown was a serial killer. There was no coming back from that.

I'd be a fool to believe otherwise.

He was the moron who pinned blame elsewhere.

I'd also been the unfortunate soul whom Naeva followed.

When I landed, she planted herself beside me. "Eliana," she began.

"No." I cut her off with the slice of my arm. "Don't lecture me. He killed everyone I loved. He murdered me. He turned Christmas into a sour holiday. Now he's acting like he's in love with me and I despise it."

She rested her hand on my arm. "There's something I need to mention..."

"How will it make me feel?"

"Not particularly...good." Her brows dipped.

"Then keep it to yourself."

Her fingers tightened against me. "When I shoot an arrow..." My eyes shrunk to slits. "The other person feels love, yes, but what they feel can only be enhanced if it sprouts from *true* feelings."

I threw my head back, letting out a throaty, non-humorous laugh. "You're trying to tell me he loves me?"

"Maybe not love, but there's no denying he hasn't had feelings at one point, or that he's not attracted to you. Think about it. Why has he always followed you around? He's got a sick and twisted way of showing it. I'm not blind to human beliefs, and I know that many parents teach girls that if a boy likes them, he's mean to her. It's disturbing, of course. This is not me making excuses, justifying it, or telling you to date him. Now that I know what I know, it's difficult to look past such a traumatic event. Rightfully so. However, I figured you should know." Her arm returned to her side.

As I threw mine up, they dropped, hands slapping my thighs. "Why? Why should I know? What difference does it make? Whether he shows his feelings or not, he's made it clear he wants to destroy everything I have."

She didn't answer. *Rightfully so.*

"Screw this" tumbled out as I marched through the forest.

When I approached the city below, I scanned the residential streets. From here, most cars were returning home as the sun peeked just beyond the horizon. The last bit of day had been snuffed out as dusk crushed everyone in vacant promises.

"There." I pointed. "You see all the lights on, the cars lining up the streets and people pouring out onto the lawn."

Naeva stopped beside me. "What about it?"

Nostalgia settled in my bones as Ayden's familiar scent of alcohol and cologne washed over me. "It's a party. I'd once followed him to a Halloween party. He was so angry with me." I turned my head, my eyes searching hers. "But he was... That was a version of him so beaten and broken. He was begging to be saved. I couldn't leave him then, and I won't do it now, Naeva. He doesn't deserve to be punished and abandoned just because of Lucifer and his angels. If you have any humanity in you, *please* understand at least that."

"I can't have humanity in me if I was never human."

"Empathy! Understanding! Sympathy! Whatever you want to name it, just use it!"

Clenching my jaw, I faced the bit of night life that existed from seniors graduating. The laughter could almost be heard from here.

Doing something as reckless as Ayden would, I soared down to the party.

Had I bothered to change out of my flowy, white dress? No. Instead, I walked inside.

Not a face I recognized.

"I'm not sure why I still stick around in the city Ayden died in. He's being held hostage in Hell," I tossed back at Naeva as she lingered behind. Bold move for us to not hide ourselves at all. People around us had been too drunk to notice, alcohol dousing their sanity.

Music pumped in my ears, reminding me precisely what a heartbeat once felt like. Weed, sweat, and the concoction of perfumes and colognes saturated the air.

As hard as she fought to hide her expression, I didn't miss a wink of her disgust. "You met here?"

"No, I followed him here. I'd already become his guardian by then."

I shuffled my way through bodies. From the front yard to the living room. I found the kitchen in no time, before slipping out into the backyard. "Would you believe me if I told you I'd never been to a party before I was brutally murdered?" I'd added that last bit to remind her of the punch-to-the-gut Liam brought around with him.

My feet scuffed the pavement near the pool as my gaze fell on a couple arguing by the bushes.

The woman pointed her finger before shoving what I assumed to be his phone into his chest. He caught it with shock, attempting to run after her as she stormed off.

Long after they were gone, I was left replaying the ghosts of our past.

Dark clouds rolled in. Lightning struck first, making way for thunder to scare away all of the party-goers.

Naeva's hand rested on my arm. "Eliana, we should go."

"Why? It can't harm us."

"The party is over."

Rain began to pour, pity soaking the world around us.

"Eliana," she repeated.

"No!" I yelled, shaking her hand off. "Leave me."

I couldn't tear my eyes from the vibrant green euonymus. Leaves pitted in deep emerald with edges as bright and worn as faded book pages.

She didn't obey a word I said. But she didn't force me away, either.

Closing my eyes, that exact night wavered.

Ayden's cologne. The anger swirling in his irises as he said hurtful things to push my buttons.

The moment when he learned I wasn't going to go anywhere, and I'd be *everywhere* he went.

"He didn't want me there because he'd hated the way I could fit in with his people. That wasn't why I went, of course. But he could only see it one way. He hated that they all loved me, because *I'm not lovable.*" The very words he said to me then. My eyelids weighed heavy. "I know now he would take that back if he could, but it doesn't change that his feelings were valid. Something happened to Ayden to destroy his self-esteem. He doesn't see worth in his soul. I will never leave him, no matter how hard you force me to." I swallowed the lump in my throat. "Maybe I'm not lovable to Heaven. Maybe that's why every bad thing keeps happening to me even when this is meant to be paradise. But *Ayden* loves me. I'm inclined to gravitate towards the very man who refuses to love me any less. Much more than those who see me as just an angel to help them out.

"He sees me. He sees me for so much more," I choked out as a tear slipped. "He's the one person who has chosen to love me and I'll be damned if I ever make him feel less than a diamond. Don't you see that?" I spun to face Naeva. "He's mine. He's mine for eternity. Nothing will ever get in the way of that."

"You remind me of a rose" echoed in my mind.

He'd compared me to a rose, showing me the thorns I carried. The danger I could become if I'd been stripped of my pure intentions.

"If danger is what I'm to be to get the love of my life back, then so be it. You're either with me or against me, but make your choice carefully, Naeva, because I will let nothing and *nobody* stand in my way."

I pushed past her on my way out.

Something about unfinished business in my human life...

Whatever the fuck that meant.

My fingers itched to brush hair away from Angel's face, I desperate to taste her on my lips. But I forced those thoughts to the back of my mind, trying to shove them off a cliff. I needed to rid myself of them. I needed to rid myself of *her* to keep her safe from this destruction.

"What the fuck are we doing here?" I asked Levi.

He grinned, eyes wide and dancing. "You fit right in, don't you?"

"I was kidnapped and poisoned. I hardly call this fitting in. Answer the bloody question before I make you."

He let out the fakest sigh I'd ever laid ears on. "You're so stubborn, and not the good kind. Does Eliana like that?"

"Don't you dare say her name," I growled.

"Have you fucked? Oh, right." He coughed out a laugh. "She can't do that, can she? Died a virgin and now has to forever stay a virgin. That is, unless she breaks the laws." He *tsked* while shaking his head. "You're the enemy now. If you even so much as interact in a pleasant way, Heaven will be watching, waiting to scold and ostracise her. You think she'll cave and ruin her position, or find someone else? Best case scenario, she wallows and becomes a hollow shell of herself. Nothing left to love."

Screaming, I fisted his collar and slammed him against a tree. "You stupid fuck!"

Mischievous and sanguine flashed across his features, settling. "I touched a nerve, eh? Good. You're going to need it." He removed my hands, patting my shoulders as he stepped forward. "We've got plenty to do tonight."

"I'm not doing anything with you," I growled.

His eyebrows shot up as he elbowed me. "Not exactly your choice now, is it? Fallen angels work a little differently, Ayden boy. You won't be able to escape the urges. It'll call to you."

Sending a scowl, I backed away. Despite my attempts, he grasped my wrist, nails digging into my skin, then dragged me behind him.

He was wrong about those urges. I craved the kneading of dough, the sprinkle of flour, the beating of eggs. I'd give anything to be in a kitchen with the warm and sweet scent of sugar wafting through the room. Airy or dense. Soft or crispy. Whatever it was, I wanted more of *that* instead of *this*.

We arrived at a familiar business.

Too familiar.

Then it hit me like a bullet.

Blood splattered across the wall of clocks. A woman who refused to hand over the cash from the register, forcing the robber to pull the trigger.

No, that wasn't right. Why would I blame her?

Because she'd been foolish to go down with her shop.

"I can't be here," I sputtered. "I have to go. I can't *be* here."

Levi blocked the door, which then had me questioning if I even needed to use a human-made exit at all. "Don't try it."

"I can't be here! Don't you see?"

"See what?" His gaze waltzed along the walls.

He had no clue what tragedy rotted within the bones of this building.

He didn't know about the soul forever stolen. The stains from a woman's stubbornness. Why couldn't she just give him the bloody money? Why did I have to watch her brains paint the clocks?

I never even knew where she ended up after that night.

Gritting my teeth, my eyes found his. "I was in this very building five years ago. Eighteen, needed a job. My sisters and my parents wouldn't get off my arse about it. A robber came in here, and the woman wouldn't give him the money. He killed her. Cold blood, Levi. Took the money and ran. The cops came looking and they arrested me for the crime."

They'd held me in custody for almost two days before they cleared me. The money disappeared but I had not. It made zero sense for me to stay behind after murdering a woman and robbing her. Again, *without* the money.

Sure, I could have had a partner make a getaway. But they didn't find my prints on anything. Aside from that, my sister, Arabella, did come forward and say she'd been with me earlier that day looking at colleges. I really had been there looking for a job.

A street camera confirmed it, too.

With his lips pursed, his brows jumped up his forehead for a second before returning to their bones. "Don't make me envy you."

"Take it. I didn't ask to witness something brutal."

"Well, here we are now. And now that you mention it..." He cocked his head to the side. "You're going to rob them."

"What? No!" I shouted, backing into a wall of photos. Frames in all black, of people I'd never seen before. Colourless images, too.

Intentional. Someone bought it out, not bothered by the ghosts in the wallpaper. They'd taken advantage of the low price, of a woman's untimely demise. They'd flipped it into a photography business instead.

I said, "We don't need money."

"It's not about money. Sometimes predators kill for sport. Fallen angels committing crimes, like robbery for example, is for sport. It's not about the money. It's about the *principle.*" He pinched his two forefingers together with his thumb, flicking the wrist in front of his chest. "You're going to do it, and you won't say no, either. It's too tempting. When you finish, we'll go out and have a beer. A smoke. If you're lucky, you'll get laid."

Shooting him a glare, he only smirked in response. I could easily punch it off his face. "I'm not going to cheat on my girlfriend."

Girlfriend. What a foreign word. I'd never particularly used it, but I wasn't sure if I could now. I'd pushed her away to keep her safe from me.

"Is it cheating if you can't be together? You're a man, Ayden boy. You deserve to have a good time." He grabbed his crotch, and bloody hell, it made my stomach churn.

"Stop calling me boy then."

I despised the word more than I'd admit to him. I clenched my jaw, knowing Levi could effortlessly use boy and sex in the same sentence. Paedophilia was no laughing matter. It destroyed childhoods. Self-esteems. It took a healthy child and stripped them of all their security and left them with self-loathing. They blamed themselves even long after the trauma, long after moving on with their lives.

Some things were forever spoiled, tasting foul and sour at every turn.

But that was neither here nor there...

He smacked his lips together, eyes full of humour. "I don't know. It has a nice ring to it." Shrugging, he gestured to the counter. "Go on. Ring the bell."

"We're recognisable. With no weapons. I doubt '*give me your money*' is going to go over well when I look non-threatening."

What did I say that? I wasn't trying to rob a business to begin with. Cigarettes, alcohol, casual sex. *Those* were my things. Reckless driving, sure. People drove like shit. But robbing people? I'd never done more than steal a bloody stereo.

His eyes grazed the wall behind the register. "You're dead and I never existed. They'll have a blast trying to pin it on us. As for a weapon?" He slipped a gun from the back of his pants, handing it to me. "Make sure you cock it, then pull the trigger." He showed me. "I'm sure guns are foreign to you."

"What the fuck!" I stumbled back, dropping it. To my luck, he caught it before it hit the ground and possibly went off.

"Rule number one, Ayden boy. Always assume a gun is loaded." He shot me a warning. "And never point it at anyone you don't intend to shoot." A dark chuckle emptied out of him. "Unless you're me and intend to shoot everyone."

"I'm not intending to shoot anyone, you wanker!"

To my surprise, nobody emerged from the back due to the commotion. It must have been one of those angel things that...Angel could do. All angels could, I supposed.

Golden waves flitted through my mind.

Earlier that day, before I watched a murder, I'd visited a college with Arabella. A young girl ran by so excitedly, gushing about the campus. Her love for academics oozed out of her.

And her eyes...striking *blue*—bloody fucking hell.

I'd crossed paths with Angel long before her death, long before she became my guardian angel.

Did that mean something?

Something significant in the grand scheme of things?

Or did it simply remind me that we lived in a smaller world than I imagined?

She'd been fifteen. Young and full of life, unlike me at my withering age. Legally too young for me. Things did have a way of working out better in the end. I just had a hard time seeing that at this moment.

Angel hadn't been born in Utah. Neither of us, actually. But at one point, or multiple, we ended up in the same city. Alive. Then dead.

Maybe, no matter how hard I fought, I couldn't escape her.

Even if I shoved her into another corner to keep her protected from Hell and all I'd drag with it.

My fingers twitched as I stared at the register. Blood coating my skin, sticky and sweet with a hint of bitter.

I didn't want to admit that Levi had a point.

Deep down, I was fantasising about robbing a business.

But if I went through with it, would Angel forgive me? Did I want her to? Was I hoping we still had a chance even if I didn't want to corrupt her more than I had?

I yearned to see her smile again.

I'd be foolish not to admit that at the very least.

"Fine. We can go for a drink. Hang out in bars, and whatever it is you want, but I *won't* rob this business," I said in a firm tone.

Levi lifted his chin as his eyes roamed my features, searching for a tell, or any sign of weakness. "Is that so?"

"Did I stutter?" I hissed.

The corner of his lips tugged up to the sky as if that's where he belonged. Wings, yet forced to reside below the earth's crust. "We shall not keep anyone waiting then, Ayden boy."

Levi took us to a bar as I grumbled. He ordered whiskey. I stuck to my beer, having missed the bitterness and acquired taste a little too much.

When he nudged me, I grumbled again.

"Lighten up. Look around us. The entire world is at our feet now. You can sleep with all the women you want."

"I don't want any woman." Leaning my elbows on the edge of the counter, I wrapped one hand around my bottle as I scanned the crowd. "If she's not in my life, I'd rather not."

"Don't lie to me."

"Why would you say that?"

"I know you. You get off on casual sex. Otherwise, you would never seek it out. You lived for it. And having to abstain because your little *girlfriend* is a prude has to be torture. Those balls are only getting bluer." He swung his head back and downed the glass in one shot.

"She's not a prude," I seethed. "She's not ready."

"Same thing." He shrugged, slamming the shot glass on the countertop. "Is that really the case though? I mean, even good girls have fantasies. Unless she's asexual—which I highly doubt—she gets horny. She never fulfils the urge either. The woman has to be dying for a taste of it."

"She has self-control. What's so wrong with that?" I snickered. "Don't answer. I hate hearing you talk."

"All I'm saying is...she can't turn off the hormones. She can't hold out forever. And something tells me she's not the type to play with herself." He shot me a grin.

"You're abhorrent."

He chuckled, deep and rough. "I do my best." After clearing his throat, he nodded toward a woman. "You're a smart man, aren't you? Then you must know that the pleasure women feel is far greater than what men feel. We just enjoy ourselves. She'll explore her sexuality soon enough. And then some..." Another low laugh. "You can mope all night, but I've got a perfectly capable woman eyeing me." He slapped the back of his hand against my chest as he weaved between tables to meet up with a brunette by the windows.

Angel wouldn't move on.

As much as I begged her to do it, she wouldn't move on without me. Right?

Why were my emotions so conflicting? Why couldn't I just let her be happy without me around, dragging her down?

I needed her to do fine on her own. Even if that meant moving on and finding someone she could love. Smooth sailing with no storms made up of pouring rain and thunder, high seas that rocked the boat and made everyone fear for their lives.

She never should have fallen in love with me in the first place, and I'd been the villain for ever allowing her to do so.

I'd even done the unspeakable and craved her far more than she ever did me. She carved herself into my soul, slipping inside and laughing on her way in. I had let her, too. That made me worse than the Devil himself.

SANCTIFICATION

"Wait here," I told Naeva, shooting her a stern look.

Without knocking, I entered Matthew's office. He lifted his eyes and let out a disappointed sigh. "Eliana."

Good to see you, too.

"Your plan backfired. Naeva shot Liam and now he thinks he's in love with me." I stopped inches from the front of his desk, folding my arms across my chest. "If you have any heart, Matthew, you'll understand how that hurts more than it helps me."

The door closed behind me and Naeva stepped into my view.

With a scowl, I pointed to the door. "I told you to wait outside!"

"Listen, I know I don't come out of hiding often," she began, "but I hear you." She redirected her gaze to the Archangel. "I shot the wrong man. I've never been in love before, but Eliana has. And it's in my honest opinion that you should look into Ayden's situation and see if there's something we can do—any kind of loophole."

Shock crossed my features.

She wanted to help? She was on my side? What changed her mind?

Matthew's eyes darted between the both of us before he ran his thumb and forefinger down over his jaw and leaned back in his chair. "Alright. I'll look into it and see what I can do. It'll need to go through the Thrones, however. We'll have to drag the court into this."

I nodded over and over to drive my excitement home. "Of course. Whatever needs to happen."

Naeva flashed a soft smile. "Thanks, Matthew."

I turned to leave, pausing, then spinning back around. "Just the rundown of what happened: Liam hid in the back seat and killed Ayden in front of me. Ayden died, and then he came back as an angel. After that, Levi and the other fallen angels kidnapped him and did something to turn him into one of them. He rightfully earned his place and had it ripped away, and if Heaven is just at all..." I exhaled as I fixed the skirt of my white gown. "Thank you." Another second of hesitation and then I exited the room.

Naeva didn't leave. She probably stayed behind to help him figure out a plan to get Ayden back where he belonged.

Walking through City Creek Center, I inhaled blended perfumes and tuned in the babbling stream trickling down the center of the mall. An open skylight overlooked the store entrances, allowing sunshine to beat down on us. It hadn't been quite warm yet, but just enough to get a sweat in.

It normally didn't roast us alive this early in the summer.

Salt Lake had quite a lot to do, or so Selene told me. Before her death, she'd wanted to show me all the sorts of things you could do. The mall, snow sports, concerts. Whatever it was, she promised that

I'd enjoy it.

I'd never been to a concert. Now, I never would.

As I passed by a shop, I took a seat on a bench and lifted my eyes to the balcony above us. More stores stood above us, tempting me with bright colors and friendly faces.

I envied anyone who didn't get to experience a little piece of nature on their shopping spree.

"Eliana?" a familiar voice cracked.

I peered up to find Esme, Ayden's older sister. Well, both of his sisters were older than him. He was the baby of the bunch.

That brought a small smile to my lips.

"Esme," I muttered. "What are you doing here?"

She lifted her gaze towards the businesses. "Arabella and I were out shopping for a few things. Our parents are finishing what we need for..." A lump formed, tears threatening at the brim of her eyelids. "Ayden was murdered in his car. Did you know that?"

It had crossed my mind what his family was going through. To them, Ayden was gone. Well, to most of them. Esme knew though.

"I knew," I said in a hush. "I was there."

I expected the blows, the impending questions that blamed me for everything.

I received not even one.

"Last I heard, the man who did it was fighting for his life in the hospital. They found him stabbed in the back seat, but police say whoever did it is long gone. They confirmed a third person was present, given all the details. Case is still open." She planted herself beside me, resting her hands in her lap. "The way his throat was sliced made it clear the man in the back seat did that. They say that someone was there. Lost their temper. Stabbed him. Then fled the scene."

I allowed silence to hang in the air, amongst the chatter of passersby and the every-so-relaxing current of the creek.

"It was you, wasn't it?" She'd lowered her voice. "You were the one who was there. The one who stabbed Ayden's killer."

Patting down my skirt, I forced back whatever tears threatened to return. I'd been past this. I had to be—for his sister.

"I couldn't stop him. I got in the car and he had a knife to Ayden's throat. And when he killed him, I lost it. The only man I've ever loved. The one man who has ever taken care to love me in return." How did I explain to her the rest? How was I supposed to sit here and tell Esme that her brother was still alive in a sense, but he'd been kidnapped and turned into a bad guy?

How?

"Ayden's killer was the same man who murdered me." I refused to look her in the eye.

Cue the accusations.

Her tone reeked of offense. "I don't blame you for what happened. You were his guardian angel. He's still out there, right?" Hope flooded her irises.

My voice shrunk. "He is."

His genuine smile flashed in my mind, reminding me of who I fought for.

"Are we allowed to see him?"

I opened my mouth to say something. Anything. To tell her that she could possibly run across him, or that he was mostly tethered to Heaven and not given permission to freely interact with living people. Both had been lies, and she deserved more than that. I couldn't drag her down farther than she'd *fallen.* A scraped knee, a bloody lip. She deserved more than my pitiful decisions as of late.

"Nobody can tell me not to see you," that English accent echoed.

My heart soared at the mere sound of his voice.

Esme leaped to her feet, throwing her arms around him as he stumbled into a wall with a chuckle. He returned the favor, hugging her.

I tilted my chin away, ushering it up to privacy. But I knew it was jealousy. Knowing that I'd never get that kind of affection from him again because he'd pushed me away and told me it was for my own good.

"Mum and Dad are going to be so happy to see you!" She pulled away, inspecting every inch of his soul. No black wings on display—yet.

Placing his hands on her shoulders, he shook his head. "No, Esme. We can't tell them. You can't even tell Arabella. Things are different now."

My emotions began to simmer.

"We're planning your funeral and you're standing here before me. How can I keep that to myself?" She tilted her head, lower lip putting outwards.

"Please. Grant me this dying wish."

Dying.

Ayden Dyer was dying.

Or dead. Already dead to me. Dying to the only family he ever kept at arm's length.

"I don't understand." Shaking her head, she backed away from him.

"Ayden!" Arabella gasped as she dropped the bags she'd been carrying. Making a run for it, she jumped onto him—legs dangling like useless limbs—before he could protest or book it in the opposite direction.

Those small bubbles grew. Boiling.

"So much for Arabella not finding out," he mumbled. "Please, get down."

She set her feet back on the ground with a grin. "Sorry. I just..." Then her expression dropped faster than the balls of Matthew when

I gave him a piece of my mind. "Wait. We found your body. Blood was everywhere, Ayden. How are you alive without a scar?"

Esme placed a hand on her younger sister's arm. "We need to have a talk."

Ayden's eyes finally locked onto mine. "Let me explain everything, okay?" With a nod, he gestured for the two of them to follow him.

Fury bubbled over the edge of the pot.

I recalled the moments we shared. His laugh echoing, him profusely apologizing for what happened in Hell. His desperate, cracked voice as he prayed and pleaded for me to return to him.

Then I turned the burner off, letting my emotions cool.

When they disappeared into a store, I leaned back on the bench and pressed the back of my hand to my mouth. I wouldn't sob. Not here. Not now.

How much would it take for him to realize I wasn't going anywhere?

Ayden was so hellbent on keeping me at a distance, promising it was love. Was he expecting me to give up on him? To move on?

How far was he willing to take this?

Glancing at my dress, I hardened my expression before standing. It was time for me to break out a new wardrobe.

Fingers around the knob, I twisted it and used my shoulder to push open the door. "Hey, Mat—" I halted with a gasp. "Oh shit."

My bad.

He pulled away from Naeva (yeah, you heard that right), turning away and attempting to make himself right again. After clearing his throat, he faced me. "Eliana."

With a sly smile, I cocked an eyebrow. "Unless the next words out of your mouth are in favor of Ayden, I don't want to hear it. So tell me, how long has this been going on?" I wiggled my finger between the two of them.

Naeva sneakily—or not so much—slid off his desk and pulled her skirt down before fixing curls of her hair.

Matthew stepped around the furniture. "We should talk."

Lifting my head higher, a smirk settled in the cracks of my lips. "Indeed we should."

He fixed his collar again, as if he couldn't breathe. As if he needed air at all. "Naeva and I are..."

"Lovers?"

"We prefer the phrase *'seeing each other'*."

A shrug. Clasping my hands together, I said, "I prefer to have my boyfriend up here at my side, but we can't all get what we want right now, Matt." I shot him my best mocking smile. "Now I'm not the only one fraternizing with someone I'm not supposed to, am I? I'm going to go out on a limb here and say that a cupid and an archangel are not supposed to be making out, especially in his office. I don't want to have to blackmail you but..."

His eyes narrowed. "Eliana."

"No," I hissed. "Now you know how I feel. Now you've got *more* of a reason to help me and Ayden out. He did nothing wrong. He made it here, and then he was turned. You two can clearly understand how much you love someone. You can't shut it off, even if you're supposed to." I let my eyes roam her body. "I was gone for a few days. Damn, you two move quick."

"Language," Matthew scolded.

Throwing my hands up, a throaty laugh escaped. "Oh, please do tell me how damn is so terrible when *you're* having an affair."

Matthew opened his mouth to say something when Naeva chimed in, "She's right. We're not exactly great examples or in any position to be chastising her for a word."

Reeling my shoulders back and crossing my arms, I smirked. "So you'll help me with Ayden?"

Matthew shot back a warning which she brushed off.

"Yes," she confirmed. Brushing past his shoulder, she sent him her own cautious tale. "What? We dug our own graves, Matt. Now we must lie in them."

Twirling around in the new gown I'd picked, a scowl passed my lips. "I hate it."

Instead, I opted for a pair of black slacks, a white long-sleeve button-up, and a wool overcoat. I pieced the whole look together with black ankle boots and a fedora.

"He'll never see me coming," I told the mirror. "So let's make sure he never wakes up again."

Spinning on my heel, I exited the shop and headed to the hospital. The walk was the most brutal. The wait. The anticipation, knowing what I was about to do.

When I entered what was meant to be most people's safe haven, I asked for Liam Brown. They asked about my relation to the patient, and I told them I was an old friend who went to college with him. Naming a few details really did the job, or it could have been the confidence that threaded through me with my new outfit. I pretended to be someone else today.

But was it really pretending?

Walking into his room, I approached the large window. "You say you love me, Liam, but we both know that's a lie. You murdered me for a reason. You knew I was going to find out you killed Selene and I'd always take her side over yours. You were just the boyfriend. What importance did you hold to me?" I turned around to face his comatose form. "I know how these things work. The nurses are rarely checking in because you require the least amount of attention compared to their other patients. All I have to do is smother you." I stepped forwards, pressing my legs against the bedside. "I've never killed someone before, but you also ruined a lot for me. What difference would it make? This world doesn't need you." I bent down to his ear, knowing damn well he could hear me. "And here's the deal, *Liam*. I'm going to kill you here today, and you can't stop me." I ventured to the cabinet to grab an extra pillow.

"Sure, they know you were clearly in the car with someone else who ran. But what are they ever going to do about it? I'm already dead. They'll never catch me. *You* are the murderer here. I'm just finishing the job and guarding the world." I lifted the pillow over his head. "I'm taking my vengeance and you should fear me, Liam Brown. I'm your worst fucking nightmare." I laid the pillow over his face, watching his oxygen drop. I only needed a few more moments before the job was done.

As his oxygen lowered, his heart rate picked up.

When it flatlined, I stepped back, placing the pillow in the cabinet. They'd never find my prints because I had none left to leave behind. "You made me this monster."

Nurses came rushing in, and I stepped back, pretending to cry and scream. "Save him!"

I ran my fingers through my hair, tossing my hat behind me.

They dragged the crash cart in and shoved me out.

The PA system announced a *code blue*, repeating three times the floor and room number.

Time passed so slowly as everyone rushed in to bring back a murderer. I silently prayed he wouldn't survive this, and after an agonizing wait, they exited to announce he'd passed.

I said nothing, allowing fake tears to fall as my gaze fixed on his door.

A form flickered into view, and Liam watched me with pitiful eyes. "No," I whispered. "No!"

"You killed me."

I stumbled into the wall, shaking my head. "It's wrong. It's all wrong. This can't be happening right now. That's not fair! What about Ayden? How is he supposed to feel?" I yelled.

Nurses approached me. "Is there someone we can call? Maybe recommend counseling or something."

I sprinted out of the building, sure to take the stairs because who had the time for the elevator? There were so many, yet only ever one in use on all five floors.

I ended up in the parking lot. My piss-poor attempts to escape Liam failed as he followed. "Eliana!"

"Leave me the fuck alone!" I spun in circles as I threw my head back to face the sky. "How could You! How could You do this to me?" Pathetic sobs wracked my soul, tears streaming down my cheeks in protest. "He isn't supposed to be rewarded! Ayden deserves this and You refuse to come through for him!" I shoved my finger up to the clouds. "He *killed* us!"

He tried to approach with his hands out, steps slow and steady. "Eliana, please."

"No." I backed away, tripping over a curb. "Stay away from me!"

I fractured.

I screamed until my throat dried raw.

My vision was so blurred by the endless cries that I hadn't noticed when he sat beside me. "I loathe you," I wept.

"Let me help."

"What?" I clenched my jaw, wiping away the stains on my face.

He leaned too close for my liking. "If I can help you, maybe we have a better chance. I mean, you told me that Ayden was kidnapped and turned into one of them. I had nothing to do with that. I aided in his death, yes. I take full blame. But let me right my wrong now. I wish I could take it back, but I can't. Least I can do is make sure he returns where he rightfully belongs."

"And?"

"And?" His brows furrowed.

"And what if saving Ayden proves something wrong? What if a sacrifice is to be made, or a trade? Would you be willing to take his place? Would you sit in Hell for eternity to make sure he gets to spend it with me?" I forced down my emotions. "I need to see how far you're willing to go and if your words ring true at all." My eyebrows flashed.

After a moment of contemplating, he nodded. "Yes. I'll do whatever. Because—"

"Don't. Don't you dare say it."

"Because I care about you."

"You said it." I rolled my eyes so hard that a headache returned from my tomb. "You don't care about me. You killed me and my love. You think you do because Naeva shot you with her special arrows."

"Cupid?"

"Yes, Cupid."

"No, I'm pretty sure this is real."

"It's not!" I shot to my feet. "It never was. It was all a front. A front so you could murder me and my best friend."

"Selene," he uttered. "Is she here?"

"I haven't seen her."

"Do you think that means..."

I didn't entertain the idea.

I'd never ponder over the thought that my best friend was murdered and then rotting in Hell for it.

"Fine. If you help me rescue him, we need to establish rules. You do everything I say. You report everything you find to me. You are my bitch, Liam, and no less. You do not tell me you care me about or love me. No lies. I require total honesty from here on out." My eyes narrowed, shoulders reeling back. "Are we clear?"

He gave me a curt nod. "Crystal." His Adam's apple bobbed.

"Let's go, pet." I started walking, and he leaped up to follow.

I recalled that Matthew promised to look into it and help us. But Liam was going to do the things that Matthew refused to do.

"We need a plan," I stated. "Ayden's a fallen angel and as of right now, he keeps telling me to stay away for my safety. So I need to get into Hell and figure out exactly what they did to him. I need to know how they turned him into one of them. If we find the source, we should also be able to figure out if it's reversible." I glanced back. "Everyone tells me there isn't a way to, but they're all lying." I snickered. "They're too lazy to give a shit about a man I love."

Liam shoved his hands into the pockets of his white trousers. "We're breaking into Hell, okay. But how do I come into this? I'm an angel like you."

"You're *not* like me. Don't you dare compare us." I skidded, whipping around to face him. Even inches shorter, I still fought to intimidate him. "That's where you come in. You go to Levi and pretend you ended up in the wrong place. You become my spy, then you report back to me."

"But if I do that, they may do to me what they did to Ayden." He frowned.

"That's precisely not my concern. You'd be where you belong." I shrugged. "You agreed to help me whatever the cost came to you. Did you mean that or not?"

He wildly nodded, eyes growing. "I meant it!"

Whoever the hell stood before me wasn't the Liam Brown I knew. This was some game to him, and I intended to be the only player left standing.

"Then we have no time to waste." I spat on him.

Without another glance, I headed to the portal. He rightfully lingered behind, like a booger stuck inside your nose.

The mission only took us most of our day, and night had fallen by the time we arrived. We had an eternity, so time *wasn't* of the essence.

Stars twinkled and crickets chirped.

Must have been nice to relax and revel in the wonders of a summer dusk without a care in the world. I did not carry that same absentmindedness.

"You go in there and tell them what we agreed to. Fair? Then you come report back to me."

With a small nod, he chewed his cheek. "What are you doing in the meantime?"

I cleared my throat. "That's none of your business."

"Right." His eyes dropped to the underground cave. "I'll see you on the other side then."

I headed back into the trees and out of view as he shouted to them that he needed to talk.

Levi was the one to answer, eyeing Liam. "What the fuck do you want?"

"I ended up in the wrong place. I want to go with you."

"You refused to sell your soul to Lucifer. We're not idiots. You could have had it all."

He snorted. "How? Apparently Cupid is real and she shot me to fall for Eliana."

I cursed under my breath. He wasn't supposed to let that information slip.

Levi stepped forwards with purpose. "I see. So you're smitten for her. This wouldn't happen to have anything to do *with* her, would it?"

Liam's expression dropped.

I closed my eyes and pinched the bridge of my nose.

"Oh Angel! Come out, come out wherever you are," Levi shouted.

I could have stayed hidden but what use was it?

Jumping down, I entered the clearing. "I should have known Liam is a terrible liar now that he's an angel." A sigh escaped me. "But he's not wrong. He did end up in the wrong place, Levi. He doesn't belong with us. Take him."

"And give you your precious Ayden?" He tilted his head. "I don't think I like that trade. Liam is no use. You already hate him. But see, if we have Ayden, we can entice him to do terrible things. It's the maximum agony for you, and that's why he is so valuable to *us*."

"Heaven knows about you. They know what you did."

"Yeah?" He spun, hands out. "Where are they then?" His cackle bounced between trunks. "But..." He looked over Liam, gaze piqued. "We always prefer a little more company."

"Take him. I don't want him anyway." I shooed my hand.

"Get her," he said.

I widened my eyes as other fallen angels emerged from the branches and gripped my arms. "What the hell?"

"Well, you're right about that. It's where you're headed." They seized Liam all the same, dragging the two of us down into the portal.

I struggled against their grip, knowing I couldn't fight off two of them. It didn't stop me from trying though.

Levi led the pack, and to make matters worse, they rounded corners and tossed Liam and I into the *same* cell. He waved his fingers while wearing a grin. "Have fun."

They left us to burn against the scorching stone floor.

"This is all your fault," I told Liam. "You ruin everything. You can never be trusted." A growl. "I have to get us out of here." Nobody would come to save us this time. Nobody but myself.

Furnace

I'd peeled my jacket off minutes after we were thrown into this cell. I discarded my boots. Unbuttoned what I could. Rolled up my sleeves and my pants as high as both could go.

It wasn't enough.

The heat roasted me alive, forcing sweat to seep from my soul.

I fanned myself by clutching my collar and waving it away from my skin repeatedly. The air thickened and even as someone who didn't need to breathe, I wanted to.

Liam had discarded enough of his clothes that he wasn't dying as much as I was. He sat in just his boxers, and I made a mental note not to look at him. Although, I did take some pride when he hissed from the stones leaving burn marks on every inch of him that came into contact.

My feet made like potatoes and fried themselves to the floor.

I tried to use my coat as a barrier as much as I could, but down here, I grew tired. Exhaustion set in and I couldn't hold myself up. When I allowed my soul to rest, the coat hadn't been big enough to keep me protected.

"It's so hot," I croaked. My throat was parched. My tongue swelled.

Liam mumbled apologies and I shoved them away.

Sweat coated my forehead, drops slipping down into my eyes and blurring my vision.

I swore up and down, to Heaven and the earth, that this cell was growing hotter by the second.

If I wasn't careful, my soul would be fused into the rocks for eternity.

Scooting to the bars, I grabbed onto them. "There has to be a way out."

I swung my hair back from my face, hating that I'd never chopped it. Growing up, short hair had not been something I enjoyed sporting around. I kept my hair long so I could always throw it into a bun.

Well, now I didn't have a hair tie and I couldn't just sweep it from my neck. I had to grow *cold* and angry with the way it sat flush against my soul, allowing for a layer of sweat to bubble up from beneath.

"What do we have here?" Black boots halted before me, scuffing the pavement.

I lifted my eyes to meet that of a fallen angel.

When he saw Liam with his massive white wings dangling behind him like a flag, he smirked. "Oh? Angels are we?" He squatted down to my level and reached through the bars, grabbing hold of my chin. "Then what are we letting you rot here for?"

I scooted back, my black pants picking up any dirt along the way. He opened up the cage and stepped inside. "Stay away from me or I swear you are going to regret it."

"Will I?" His chuckle grated my ears. "I doubt that'll be possible when you have nobody to come save you."

Without another thought, I shot to my feet as his fingers caught in my hair and wrapped it around his fist, yanking me back. Another regret of never cutting it off.

I yelled out as Liam jumped to his feet. I'd be damned if I allowed him to come to *my* rescue.

"Let her go!" he pleaded.

The angel snorted. "And why would I do that?" He dragged his nose down the side of my neck. "I want to tear you apart from the inside out and leave you begging for mercy. You'll wish for death but receive none because you deserve much worse." A shiver scurried through him as he exhaled. "And trust me. There are much worse things than death."

I reached back, attempting to grab my hair to keep it from ripping at the roots. "Please," I begged. I'd never stooped so low, but I wasn't left with much of a choice when pain coursed through me. Throbbing. Aching. Sharp.

"You're one of them, too, aren't you?" He hooked his fingers at the top of my buttons and ripped through the rest, yanking the shirt off just to see my wings unfold. "You make me sick." He threw me to the floor. "Both of you."

With my hands covering my chest, I scooted back into the corner.

"Don't have too much fun without me. I've got plans for you two." Wagging his finger, he left us to our thoughts.

Liam rushed over but I shoved him away. "Don't touch me!"

He backed into his former spot and looked up at the bars as the angel returned.

When he entered the cell, something flashed at his side. I tried to bury myself in the corner with the stones, unable to get far enough away as he approached.

"Please, don't." It wouldn't help, but it'd been worth a try. Or maybe that'd been insanity pleading in my favor.

He kneeled down and grabbed onto my jaw, yanking me forwards. "You look familiar."

I shot a warning to Liam as he opened his mouth to reveal more information than the angel deserved to hear.

"Oh?" He dropped me, turning to face Liam before stalking over. "You have something to say?" Threading his fingers through his hair, he ripped his head back. "Well, don't be shy now." He pressed the blade to his throat. "Who is she?"

If he dared to say a word...

The angel pressed deep, drawing some blood. Blood only angels could draw in such a place so far below the surface.

I couldn't quite hide the satisfaction I got from watching my murderer finally receive a taste of his own medicine. And the terror in his eyes—that was just the *icing* on the cake.

"I can do my absolute worst, boy. Don't test me. *Who is she*?" He pressed deeper, forcing a cry out of Liam.

Liam fell forwards. "Okay, okay! She's a guardian angel. She's Ayden's guardian angel."

Was. I *was* his guardian angel until this bastard took him from me.

And now he'd caved and made things far worse.

"Ayden?" The angel tapped his chin. "As in the very one who we have just taken from Heaven and turned into a fallen angel?"

Liam coughed, rubbing his bloody throat as he nodded a little.

"You prick," I seethed.

The angel turned on me, primitive pupils swimming as a maniacal smile formed. He slowly approached, wrapping his fingers around my throat and yanking me forwards. "This just got so much better."

Gritting my teeth and narrowing my eyes, I commanded, "Tell me what you're doing to him."

"You don't get that privilege." He plunged the blade into my abdomen and I groaned, placing a hand over the wound as he slipped it out. Blood spilled between my fingers. "This is quite the adventure." He smeared some of the *crimson* onto my cheek—my inevitable flaws. “And now that I know exactly who you are, we can really amp up the excitement.”

When he let go of me, I stumbled into the wall, groaning louder as the hot rock seared away my morals.

He closed in on Liam, swinging and slicing his dagger across Liam’s exposed stomach. Blood splattered across my face, staining my feathers with our failure.

I never should have trusted this asshole in the first place. That one was on me.

Liam fell into the wall and attempted to patch up the injury, as if he could do something about it.

The angel returned, blocking all my escapes. I couldn’t go far, but being trapped in a corner with stone melting away at you had been less than ideal.

“Ayden’s little plaything.” He eyed the weapon, rubbing his thumb along the sharp edge.

I shook my head. “He loves me.”

“Do you think that?” He pressed himself into me, his hot, sewage breath fanning across my face, making me gag. “A man like that doesn’t love anyone.” His hands tugged at my pants and my instinct kicked in as I grabbed them to force him away. He slammed me back into the scorching stone. “Rumor has it you haven’t even opened your legs for him.” He ripped the button off. “That’s cruel punishment. Do you understand the kind of toll that would take? To be a man who goes from *all* the sex to none? The blue balls he suffers with. You’re the one putting him through that.“ He smothered me, his lips hovering near my ear as I swallowed my tears. “If you love him, why hold out?”

The sound of fabric causing friction echoed, and the angel screeched as he stumbled away from me. Liam held his balls, twisted in his hand. He let go as the angel crumpled to the floor, grabbing his crotch.

Liam glanced at me as if I were about to thank him or give him credit. He deserved none of that. It was the least he could do for destroying my life.

"Beautiful, ain't it?" Liam asked, clearing his throat.

I slid to the floor, pulling my jacket over me even if it'd been too warm. I couldn't live with the idea of this skank having access to me anymore than he did.

He finally stood and fixed his pants, buckling his belt. "You're going to pay for that. Just you wait." He hurried over and gathered up our discarded clothes, even yanking my jacket out of my grip. "You deserve to blister." He left the cell.

With nothing but my pants, I curled up and hugged myself as those third-degree burns formed. I attempted to wrap my wings around my body for a bit of cover, praying for someone to come.

I didn't have the energy to do this anymore.

The door opened, and I barely lifted my head as my hair created a wall between me and him. "Please, just leave me alone." If he wanted to torture Liam, he could. I wouldn't stop him.

A hand landed on the top of my wing, and I braced myself for the pain of him ripping it back to get a better look at me.

But it never came.

Lifting my head, I met the most beautiful green eyes I'd ever seen.

Ayden. *My* Ayden.

Letting a sob escape me, he bent down and grabbed my arms to pull me up. He wrapped his arms around my waist, lifting my bare feet off the stone to relieve some of the pain. "Angel, what are you doing here?" He nodded towards Liam.

I swallowed. "Our plan backfired. It was foolish of me to think Liam could do anything right."

"And you brought him?"

"I killed him." I pressed my cheek to his chest, savoring the last moments despite how much I ached to claw my skin off in hopes it'd cool me down.

Liam said, "She ended my coma."

Ayden proceeded to ignore him as he maneuvered to place an arm under my knees, his other around my back. "We need to get you out of here."

Liam stood to follow and Ayden scowled at him. "Not you."

"Right." He scratched his neck. "Here's the thing though. I'm not going to sit down here and burn my soul for eternity like this. Eliana needs help, so focus on her and less on what I'm doing. It's not exactly easy for me to leave her side anyway."

Ayden's eyes narrowed to slits. "What's he talking about?"

The asshole was the one to answer with, "Cupid shot me. I'm supposed to essentially replace you in her life."

He wanted to tear his throat out and watch him bleed. I couldn't miss the bloodthirst in his eyes even if I'd tried. It oozed from his pores, drilling into Liam. However, I had been more concerned with getting out of here.

He saw that, too, once he met my gaze.

He carried me back up to earth without alerting anyone nearby. Then he set me onto my feet, but I winced, so he placed me on the grass with the utmost care. Gentle like a *giant*. "You get yourself into so much trouble for me, don't you?" he mumbled. "You're a liability, Angel."

"You didn't even acknowledge me when you saw your sisters. You get *yourself* into trouble, but you seem to do just fine on your own." An ache throbbed in my heart. "Why would you do that to me?"

After pulling his shirt off, I tried to keep from staring at his chest, his tattoos on full display. Calling to me, begging me to run my fingertips across the black ink. Sharp points that curled around, dots lining the outer edges. It didn't mean anything at all, but it was part of him, and so it held meaning to me.

He ignored my question, slipping my arms into the sleeves and buttoning a few buttons. The bleeding in my abdomen had stopped by now, and I'd be fine when everything healed. It didn't subtract from the pain though.

"Ayden!" I grabbed his throat since I couldn't grasp a shirt collar, pulling him down just inches away. "Answer me, you stupid ass."

With a swallow, he wrapped fingers around my wrist to tug my hand away. "Careful, Angel. You don't know what turns me on." After a desolate sigh, he stroked a thumb over the red stain crusted to my cheek. "I thought it would keep you safe, but seeing as you're stubborn... Your intent to save me is our biggest enemy right now. They don't just want to hurt us. They want your soul to devour."

I didn't dare move from the rock, even after Ayden had returned to Hell.

I begged him not to go, but he wouldn't listen as my fingers slipped from his, reaching out for him once again. His forehead pressed against mine, promising it was for the best.

He'd decided that all on his own—without my input.

So I sat there with my arms crossed, studying every strand of grass that could exist in such a world. So many strands just living in a universe they had no idea was crumbling.

Oh to be a strand of grass.

Liam sat on the forest floor with his knees bent, his arms wrapped loosely around them. "I'm sorry about everything."

Sorry was never going to fix anything. It'd been far too late for apologies now.

He killed Selene. He took my life. He murdered Ayden. How many times did I have to repeat it—to relive it until everyone understood the damage? Here, he claimed to love me all under the guise of Naeva.

A twig snapped in the distance, and while Liam perked up at the noise, I stayed glued inside my own head. Wandering. Allowing myself to wallow.

A redhead stumbled through the trees and into the clearing with a yelp. "Oh?"

When I met her gaze, mine shrunk. "Sunny. What are you doing here?"

"Well, uh, some woman came to me and said Ayden really needed my help. I believe this was the right direction, but I can't be too sure." Her eyes darted from branch to branch.

"Some woman?"

"Yeah. I forgot her name, but she was Black. She also had a perfect face. Oh! She had wings, too. Not like you though. Hers were much smaller."

"Naeva?" My jaw dropped.

She gasped. "Yes! That's the name."

When I glanced over at Liam, I scowled. "What is she doing going to Sunny for help?"

He only shrugged.

Sunny stepped forwards, putting her hands up in defense. It did little to ease my frustrations. "I'm here to help. That's all."

"How? When I asked you to, you shut the door in the face." Essentially speaking. "Suddenly the prettiest woman comes knocking and you're more than eager to go to him. What did she promise you? What are you getting out of this?"

She opened her mouth before closing it. Picking at her nails, she swallowed. "She told me Ayden really needs help."

Shooting off the rock, I stomped over. "Tell me what she told you."

She cowered in my presence, eyes growing with terror. "She told me I could have Ayden if I did this."

"Have Ayden?" I whipped my head back at Liam who watched

with too much amusement. "Ayden is not some object to be bought or sold!" I growled. "When I get my hands on her..."

Sunny started to back away.

Throwing a glare in her direction, I grabbed her wrist to plant her where she stood. "Don't you dare move. I'm going to have a serious conversation with Naeva. She has some nerve promising my boyfriend to you when she damn well knows what it's like to love someone you shouldn't! She and Matthew are hooking up!"

Liam furrowed his brows. "Hooking up? Isn't that forbidden?"

"Exactly."

Wrapping all ten fingers around her two wrists, I dug my nails in. "It's bold of you to come to his rescue when you're promised his love in return. That's why you wouldn't help me. You're jealous and you'd rather not."

"It's not entirely like that, I promise!" she squeaked.

"Bullshit, Sunny! It's exactly like that or you wouldn't have come to risk your life for a man who no longer loves you." I watched the light flee her eyes. "I had to live in his apartment for so many months. I had to listen to you two giggle. I witnessed the kisses and the cuddles. I was the one who fell in love with him and I wasn't allowed to *say* anything. I had to bathe myself in jealousy and find some way to suppress it because that's just what good guardian angels do." A belly laugh slithered its way out of my throat and into the sky.

"No, no," I said with a shake of my head. "Good guardian angels don't fall in love with humans. I'm the smear. The one tainting our name. But if that's so true, why the hell did they tell me about it in the first place!" I screamed up to the clouds. "Why would You tell me and let me fall in love? Why would You even say You were okay with it after the fact, only to refuse to help when Ayden needs You most?"

I dropped my hands, a few beads of blood surfacing on her skin.

"I was in your place once, and you want to know what the worst part of it is?"

She rubbed her wrists, whispering, "Do I?"

My lungs deflated. "I died before I got to love anyone at all. This was supposed to be my second chance, and they've taken that from me, too. Someone is laughing—having so much fun—while I suffer an ill fate. Maybe I'm just cursed, or maybe I'm never meant to love at all."

Her eyes sank. "Hey, please don't say that."

"Why not? You know it's true." I cleared my throat. "Everyone knows. It's all some big joke. Naeva sent you here because even if she stands in my shoes, she refuses to help me out. Ayden's a fallen angel now. We can't be together. If I try, I risk everything. And it seems Heaven is not going to be of any help."

"When have they ever been helpful?" That English accent was the only sound keeping me stable for the moment.

Ayden stepped out of the portal and approached us. "Sunny."

"Ayden," she whispered. I could see it written all over her face—the dilated pupils, tint of her cheeks, and parting of her lips.

He didn't even want me anymore. He refused.

"Well." I leaned my head down into her view. "Ayden here is actually single now if you want to give it a go. I'm certain Heaven doesn't give a single shit if a human has an affair with a fallen angel, so be my guest."

"Angel," Ayden started.

"No! No, you're right." I squeezed past them. "You're absolutely right, Ayden, about the fact that we should not be hanging out anymore." It wouldn't stop me from trying to reverse whatever happened. "You and I are in the past. You're just lucky I truly love you because even if you're going to throw me to the curb, I'm still going to work my ass off to ensure you get to go back up to Heaven where you were in the first place. You're free to get it on with Sunny. I'm sure blue balls are very painful and you wouldn't want to wait for a prude like me anyway." I started again, turning to face him. "Oh, and my name's *Eliana*, not Angel."

Before they could say another word, I limped off into the forest, ignoring the searing flesh threatening to fall off my feet. Not that angels had flesh, but whatever it was that we had, it was dangling by a thread.

Liam eventually came running—to catch up.

The last person I wanted to follow me.

It could have been Ayden with his apologies and undying love. It could have been Sunny with her apologies and promise to stay out of our way, helping us just for our sake and not hers.

No, it was just Liam. The one man I didn't want to see was the only one who could stand to be around me anymore.

Fuck, what had my afterlife come to? Was this it? Was this all I was ever going to be?

"I don't understand what I did so wrong to make him not want me." I swallowed the lump, but despite that, tears still pushed at the brim of my eyelids. "Was his love always conditional? I fought so hard, Liam. I fought so hard to never fall in love, and then I left when it was right. He called me back. He kissed me first. Was it so wrong of me to believe his stupid lies? I feel like such a fool!" A few tears slipped as I sucked in air. "We were supposed to fight together, to be in this together. We were never supposed to let anything tear us apart, and now he's allowed that." Shaking my head, my vision clouded. "But that's just it. Maybe it was always going to end up this way. Maybe the fallen angels are right that he was only with me because it was wrong. I was another reckless thrill for him. He wanted to sleep with me and when I wouldn't...

"When I refused to have sex, he chalked it up to anxiety or fear.

He waited and hoped, and now? Now he's realizing I'm not worth keeping around, am I? I'm not worth a dime. He never loved me at all, and now that things have gotten too tough, he's backing out and trying to say he loves me—that he's *protecting* me," I mocked. "Whether he's with me or not, the fallen angels still want to hurt me! I don't understand why he has to be such a prick about it all. If something does happen to me, what then? If he loved me at all, then he'd have to live with knowing something still happened to me anyway and he never got to spend those last moments together because *he* shoved me when I needed him most. Am I in the wrong here?"

Liam sighed, breathless and hopeless. "I don't think it's foolish of you, Elli. I think you're just...hopeful. You've protected yourself for so long and when you finally see someone who could potentially make you feel safe, you let your guard down and allow them in. It's not your fault that you end up hurt in the end. You're trusting someone again, to create a connection that you never get to experience. They're the one who deserves to burn for ever breaking your heart."

Turning my chin, I locked eyes with him. "What?"

He rubbed the back of his neck, a nervous chuckle slipping between his lips. "Or so I assume."

I wanted to ask him more but he wasn't going to elaborate. Maybe I didn't really want him to. What had he meant when he said it wasn't my fault I'd end up hurt in the end? Was he referring to when he murdered me? Was he truly feeling remorse or was this all a front? If Ayden could end up a fallen angel without Heaven's support on his side, maybe Liam would have always ended up in Heaven when he didn't belong. He couldn't feel remorse. He couldn't feel guilt or shame for everything he's done. It'd been a character to him, and I'd not be that asinine to believe it.

I had to build those walls again, to protect my heart. If I didn't, who would? It sure as hell wasn't going to be Ayden and his toy, Sunny.

Liam blurted, "They poisoned him."

Eyebrows knitted together, I pursed my lips. "What?"

With a nod, he coughed up the subject. "Yeah, I figured out what happened. Ayden told me." When had they had time to talk? "The fallen angels, they poisoned him. He's not sure with what or how exactly, but he knows they injected something into him. That's what turned his wings black. He wasn't lying about the permanent part, but I do know that if we have this information, we can use it. If they poisoned him, we just need to figure out what with. Maybe there's some antidote. We could reverse it. He's just a little bleak at times." He turned red when he met my piercing gaze. "Sorry."

Poison? They'd poisoned him?

It checked out, in all honesty. You could infect a soul...

"Okay, so we just need to somehow get a hold of their poison and study it as if we're suddenly scientists, then figure out how to create an antidote and then inject him but somehow destroy the poison to begin with, right?" I cocked my head. "Yeah, so easy, Liam."

"I'm just trying to help."

"Well, if they poisoned him..." I clenched my jaw and rolled my eyes. "Going to Matt is no help. Naeva is still on the wrong side. We may need to find a few other reinforcements. I don't know who or where we'll find them, but that's our only bet for now. You're still willing to do whatever it takes for me to be happy, right?"

He frowned. "Why do you have to word it that way? Of course."

"That's why I worded it like that." I slapped his shoulder where flesh from his form had been seared. He winced, grabbing onto the wound. "First, we need to allow our souls to heal. We're absolutely useless walking around in pain."

He made no effort to disagree on that account.

Almighty

I stepped into my home. Portland, Oregon. Massive. Marble flooring throughout, hardwood upstairs. Intricate details along all the molding from the front door to the attic. Large open windows. Set far back from the road, of course, and further from the city itself.

Nothing had changed all that much.

Heading up the white steps decorated with an antique runner, I ran my hand along the chestnut railing. "We're rich, but damn these materials just clash, Mom." I snickered.

I wasn't all that surprised to find my parents hadn't left the house we grew up in. Well, a little. Maybe they should have just sold the home and bought a beach house to live out the rest of their days free of me.

Making my way to their room, I took in the dark curtains hanging from gold rods. Oak hardwood, kept up with a oil cleaner. A centered bed against the wall across from the bedroom door. Black pillows and gray bedding. Perfectly fluffed with not a wrinkle in sight.

Pictures hung from the walls with a few gilded sconces to show them off. Pictures of my parents, but not one of me.

I stalked over to the nightstand made of solid wood in a cherry stain. The top had been more organized than I'd seen. Clean as if the maid had just been through here.

Not the inside of the drawer so much though. Cluttered.

Maybe a sign of how they had fallen apart, or it'd always been that way. I wouldn't know entirely as I'd never been allowed into their bedroom.

Their sanctuary.

Away from me.

Opening the top drawer, my heart sunk in my chest. I pulled out the photo my mother had laying on top of everything, studying the way my parents laughed. Crinkles in their eyes, their fingers wrapped tightly in my small hands as they picked me up and swung me along the sand. The ocean stood in the background, the sun barely peeking out. Waves rolled across the shore.

My mother's feet were buried deep in the sand, wearing her favorite one-piece blue swimsuit, her head turned towards my father. She wore a straw hat to keep the sun from burning her face—a trait I unfortunately inherited from her. Little melanin in my skin, and no protection. That'd been a running theme in my life, no matter the context. I never had *protection* wherever I went.

Her blonde hair had cascaded in waves, stopping at her collarbone.

My father wore just a gray shirt with blue swim trunks. His eyes were lowered, focused on me as I'd been frozen in time in the middle of my own joy. My eyes squeezed shut, my blond hair up, knowing my parents had been reapplying sunscreen constantly to make sure I didn't end up miserable.

Wait.

No, they wouldn't do that. Would they?

I vaguely recalled this memory as it came in fleeting images.

Nothing concrete. All a blur, and even as hard as I tried to capture it, it slipped through my fingers and poofed into nothing.

My mind wasn't serving me well, so I returned the photo and stepped out.

I found my room at the end of the hall where I preferred my solitude.

When I entered, I found it exactly the same as the day I'd left for college.

Crimson splashed here and there, whether it was a decorative pillow or a throw blanket draped across a chair. Blacks and grays made up for the rest of it, reminding me that I'd never truly strayed that far from my expression.

My bookshelves were littered with mysteries and thrillers, a horror every now and again. I found my psychology books stashed in the cabinet of my black desk, but I made no move to touch them.

Sitting on my crisp comforter, I patted the spots beside my thighs. Not much happened in this room aside from studying and reading.

Not a boyfriend.

No late night kisses, or pebbles against my window. No sneaking a boy in.

I'd been nothing but a bore.

Ayden Dyer saw me as the good girl who refused to do anything. A woman who died a virgin due to her own vices.

A part of me had always been curious about sex, too. I'd always wondered what it would feel like to have hands run over every inch of my body, kisses making promises under the night sky. What it'd feel like to have someone between my legs.

I wasn't supposed to have these thoughts, yet I did.

How could I not picture something that could take a woman to cloud nine? Here I was on an actual cloud nine on a daily basis and yet I never came close to such a paradise.

Not once.

Because I had deprived myself of the experiences a woman my age could have had.

If Selene could hear my thoughts now, if she knew how much I regretted the choices I made...

Doing the right thing didn't turn out to be the *right thing* after all.

Ayden wanted nothing to do with me, yet I wanted everything to do with him. If I could, I'd go back to him and ask him to show me everything he knew. I'd tell him I was ready, regardless of whether we ever got married or not.

Why?

Because following this path didn't turn out well for me in the end. And it was selfish, sure, to think that if I had done good things, I would get a happy ending.

But was that not what humans were promised?

Why dangle a piece of candy in front of a baby only to eat it for yourself? That in itself *was* the selfish act. Manipulative. Cruel. Unusual punishment.

Yelling out in frustration, I made my way to my old bathroom. Nothing more than white tiles, a glass shower, and red towels hanging from the chrome fixtures.

I was sticky and grimy, so I peeled Ayden's shirt from my torso and dropped my pants, turning the shower knob to cold. I stepped in, hissing as it hit my wounds. Allowing it to cool the burns. For humans, cold on hot would prove to be worse. Well, how could it be worse for me in the long run when I was already dead? I simply needed instant relief, and I got that.

I washed myself, lathering shampoo in my hair despite not needing it. I scrubbed my body and cried out when soap trickled over my wounds. I brushed the conditioner through my strands with my old wide-tooth comb.

When every inch of my soul was clean, I leaned against the shower wall and closed my eyes.

"Ayden, I'm sorry. I'm sorry I couldn't be the woman you wanted. I'm sorry. I'm sorry," I repeated until tears poured down my cheeks.

I knew it was wrong to apologize for having my boundaries, but I still couldn't erase the pain that smeared my heart.

I was tired of being the angel getting screwed over.

The thought of that fallen angel wanting to get into my pants plagued my head, making me flinch. If Liam hadn't been there...

I despised that thought, but I couldn't run from it.

He would have been my first memory of a man, taking something I couldn't get back. He would have stolen a piece of my soul to claim for himself.

I hated that thought more than Liam *saving* me from him.

I didn't want men to continue to look at me as an object—a toy. They saw me and wanted nothing more than a piece until I'd be nothing.

Returned to the dirt I was made of.

I wanted control. Why should they have the chance to touch me before anyone else? Why should they have been allowed to touch me at all and strip me of my security? Make me feel unwanted and unsafe in my own skin? Why should they have the opportunity to taint what should be an intimate and special moment?

I just wanted to know what it felt like to be loved that way. In all the ways a woman *could* be loved.

Didn't I deserve that after all this time of waiting?

Or was that not how it really worked?

Turning off the shower, I stepped out and wrapped a towel around me. My hair had dried the second I went to soak up the water. My skin, too. Still, I felt a little bit better.

I pulled the black pants on, unrolling the ankles. I slipped Ayden's shirt over my shoulders and buttoned up what I could, knowing if I went higher, the buttons would end up taut.

I never enjoyed my boobs, despite how much everyone else around me did. Had I lived any longer, I would have gotten a reduction for the back pain, to live more comfortably.

Supposed it didn't matter now since I felt no pain at all.

Aside from the burns.

I sauntered over to my king size bed and laid back in the pillows, staring at the gray ceiling.

My parents wouldn't be home for days if I remembered the exact dates they'd leave for their usual business trips.

I had days here, alone.

Days.

Days to turn a few things around for myself.

Days to get a sample of what sex felt like.

Sliding my fingers to my pants, I unbuttoned them, questioning myself.

Why did it feel wrong? I'd been a grown woman for almost four years, dead for a year and a half.

I'd been brutally murdered before I had a chance to experience the best parts of being human.

It shouldn't have felt like I was committing a crime just by exploring my own body.

How did I shut it off—the shame?

My parents weren't here.

Ayden wasn't here *anymore*.

Yet, his laugh echoed inside my room. His emerald eyes sparkled just right in the moonlight. I ran my fingers through his soft, light brown hair, letting him whisper crude jokes to make me giggle. I'd playfully hit his chest, then let him steal me in a kiss.

Because even if he wanted nothing to do with me these days, I was still undeniably in love with the bastard.

I wanted to trace my fingers down his chest as we both ravaged one another.

Heaven had been the ones to tell me I was going to fall in love, and I couldn't stop it from happening anyway. They gave us the green light. Lucifer and his angels took him, and any chance I ever had at loving someone and getting the same in return. They flipped me the bird for simply being their guardian angel, and maybe I was being punished for letting Justin and Ayden die. For letting Ayden get kidnapped, even.

He'd still be alive had I never dragged him to Liam's to try and prove my murder.

His lips brushed my ear, his deep chuckle vibrating through me.

I wanted him here more than ever.

I needed him to come hold me, but he'd pushed me away and picked Sunny instead.

I could almost picture them now, kissing against a tree, hands getting far too restless as they fiddled with belts and buttons.

Forgetting all about me.

But *I* wouldn't forget about me. I could never do that to myself.

I deserved better than that.

Out of spite, I ripped the zipper down. Then, slipping my hand in, I let those betraying fingers graze my cheek. I discovered new places and feelings in myself that I'd never before. His warm breath fanned across my lips, and even as hard as I fought to shut him out of my mind as an act of revenge, I let him consume me whole.

BEHOLD

The morning my parents walked in the door, I rushed back up to my room, afraid to face whatever terrible things I'd hear fall from their lips.

I plopped onto my bed, freezing as the footsteps echoed up the stairwell.

"I swear I heard something up here."

I switched on my invisibility cloak, slipping off the bed to not leave any imprints, just as the door creaked open.

Mom poked her head in, eyes darting across the sunlit walls and empty bed. "It's nothing. I must be hearing things."

She closed the door, and I took that as my cue to slide through the wall in time to see my father step in front of her. "You okay, Di?"

Mom deflated. Like a weighted blanket, sorrow draped over her. "I miss her. Is it supposed to get easier? Whoever said that lied to us. Every day still hits just as hard as the first day that call came through. Every day I wake up and hope it's some bad dream, but it's not just a bad dream. Our baby is never coming home."

I hoped for tears.

Instead, she pressed her fingers to her eyes—sunken from all the sleepless nights. I wanted to shout and scream that she was supposed to love me. But a small part of me also saw a hint of exhaustion. She wasn't crying, and it hadn't been because she didn't have any to shed for her only child, but because she'd already released a whole storm. There was nothing left to lose.

My father's gentle fingers found her cheek. "I know. I miss her, too. We can only hope she's happy where she is now."

Mom pressed her palm over his hand, her eyes softening as they locked with my dad's. "Thank you."

They could have had another baby if they wanted that badly to see a kid again. Why didn't they? Was it because they knew they'd never really wanted a kid at all?

Most marriages fell apart after the loss of a child, too. My parents appeared closer than ever. Did that also confirm what I knew—that they never wanted *me* at all?

I lingered far too much around them.

And they haunted my room nearly every night. Why did they keep coming back?

And every time the hall light slipped through the crack in my bedroom door, I stopped. They couldn't see me, but I still sat there like yet another object that had frozen in time since my death.

I watched my parents filter through the room. They drank up as much detail as they could, then abandoned me again.

It became routine for us both.

And in some strange way...

It was also healing of all the pain they caused me.

I didn't spend a long time in Portland, but I spent most of the month there. When my burns became scars, I flew back to Salt Lake and made myself comfortable in the forest.

Liam was off doing whatever the hell Liam was doing.

I didn't care nor waste another second thinking about it.

I'd used a lot of being back home making up for lost time and doing the things I didn't get to do when I was alive.

Did I feel guilty about it?

Well, maybe a little, but I shouldn't have. It was my soul. If I wanted to touch it as I pleased, why couldn't I? I did the terrible thing by dying a virgin, then they went and took Ayden from me.

I wasn't the same woman they screwed with.

The soft padding of boots echoed behind me. I didn't dare turn around.

In fact, I kept my eyes glued to the trees and the colorful birds that chirped within them, a mom searching for food for her new chicks.

Pulling my knees up to my chest, I wrapped my arms around them. "If you're here to torture me in some way, go ahead. What's the use in fighting it anymore?"

They stepped closer, and I noted the lack of shadow that should have loomed over me. Angels didn't have such things.

My shoulders sagged. "I'm tired. I'm tired of giving so much only to receive torment in return. You're no different from the rest of them. Just take what you want. Even the only man I've ever loved decided I'm not enough."

A choke escaped them. "What? Is that what you think?"

His whiskey accent washed over me much like liquor poured over ice. Smooth, cool, crackling.

And it *burned* on the way down.

I twisted my head back to look up at him. "Am I wrong, Mr. Dyer?" A guardian angel was really all I ever was to him. He didn't think of me as a woman worth having. I was simply a means to an end—a body to conquer.

Only he gave up because I held back for too long.

"Absolutely!" He ran a hand down his face and released a sigh. "Look, Angel"—he shot me a glare—"and that's what I'm going to call you." He stepped around the side to stand in front of me. "I was trying to protect you."

"I didn't ask for your stupid fucking protection!" I leaped to my feet, refusing to let him tower over me like that. "Did you ever stop to ask me what I wanted? Did you consider? Ayden, I've been dead for a year and a half now. I know how things work! I know that the fallen angels are truly wicked, and I know that I'm not supposed to love you. But guess what, asshole? I do!" I slammed my hands to his chest as I choked on my next words. "You took yourself away from me and assumed that would be safer, but we both know that proved to be far worse. Now I've got a cupid following me around, and she shot Liam so now he's following me around, too. I hate you so much for doing this to me. I hate you!" I screamed as he grabbed my wrists before I could plunge them through his cold heart.

He wore a new shirt, one I had never seen. All black, extremely fitted and defining every inch of his soul.

"I hate you," I spat.

"That's too bad," he said with a frown. Then he crashed his lips to mine, ignoring every rule hanging above our heads. Showing me what it meant to be desired and loved—to be craved so deeply.

Before I had the chance to return the same passion, he pulled away. "I need to show you something."

I wasn't given a second to respond before he was wrapping me up in his wings and shooting off into the sky. Wind rushed towards me for a few minutes and when we finally landed, he grasped my shoulders and turned me towards a cabin.

"What's this" flowed softly from my tongue.

"This is ours."

"What?"

"Well, I found it. But it's abandoned, so don't fret. I didn't steal it."

At this point, I wouldn't have cared if he did.

"What do we do with it?" I chewed my bottom lip.

Lifting a finger, he hurried inside, bringing me in with him. "It's where we can meet. Clearly this whole staying away isn't doing us any good. And we need somewhere private."

"Heaven always knows."

"To be frank, I'm not fucking concerned with them anymore, just as they aren't me. I'm more concerned about the fallen angels like Levi who want to devour you."

A little pang bounced off my heart, and then it swelled. "Then we're on the same page."

He tilted his head.

"I'm not concerned, either. I'm done. If they've made it clear that they don't care about their own, or about anyone at all, then why the hell am I expected to?" Exhaling, I let my eyes drift up to the treetops. "I did something this past month." I dropped my arms to my side, taking in a gulp of air. "I did something that was wrong but... Ayden, I quite liked it."

His eyebrows jumped up in amusement as he took a large step

closer. "Oh?"

"I masturbated."

He choked, then coughed before fixing his expression. "Sorry, I did not expect to hear that come out of your mouth. You've never...?"

"No." I shook my head. "Never. Not once. It's always been wrong. Taboo. Something you just don't talk about, you know? I can't explain why anymore, but...it was. And now I feel...different. I'm liberated. And I want to explore things."

"Things?" The corner of his lips tugged upward.

Swallowing my nervousness, I nodded. "Those things..." The things Ayden wanted. Things I regretted not trying before I'd been murdered.

"We do have a whole cabin to ourselves," he said as he swung his arms around what I assumed would be a living room.

I couldn't deny the butterflies in the pit of my stomach at the mere thought of Ayden doing such things to me. Of us having sex.

"We do," I agreed.

In seconds, his lips were on mine, stealing my breath away—if I'd had one at all. He tasted me, his tongue running along my bottom lip until I parted them and allowed him to explore for himself.

I fisted his shirt, a specific warmth pooling south of my body.

It grew ever so slowly as he dragged his teeth across my bottom lip, leaving them swollen in his destruction. His fingers trailed down my hips, digging into the bit of skin that peeked just above my waistline.

My mind swam in all the possibilities and it never grasped onto just one. They replayed over and over all the ways Ayden would show me he was entirely mine.

He kissed me again, dipping into it further as I savored every last inch of chocolate. Dark chocolate and cherry. Tonight, he tasted forbidden.

I wanted to run my hands over all the secrets of his soul. I wanted to lick new places, and brand him to my lips.

His fingers glided up the shirt of his that I wore, starting to unbutton whatever was left.

He dragged his kisses down my neck, along my throat and collarbone. My skin burned under every inch he found.

I leaned my head back into the wall, eyes fluttering shut and mouth opening just enough for a moan to escape. He traveled down my stomach, and I couldn't quite explain the unbearable ache between my legs. It spread as he undid the button and pulled down the zipper of my black slacks.

My body screamed for him.

My mind had shut down.

And I—I forced the unease down my throat.

I attempted to bury the fear and anxiety with a hatchet. I wanted him to keep going, but emotionally, I disassociated. Nausea bubbled from the idea.

I wasn't ready.

As hard as I fought to open my mouth and say something, my tongue lodged in my throat.

If I said no now, when would I be ready? If I said no now, would I ever keep Ayden around? I wasn't ready to let him go, even if it proved he'd only stuck around for my body.

I wanted to be loved for once.

For once, I wanted to be someone's last thought at night as they drifted into a peaceful sleep.

Just for once.

My body was begging for him, but I couldn't shake the feeling of discomfort.

"—gel?" Words faded in. An English accent I adored, one I longed to hear every night. Everything sharpened around me, less fuzzy.

The dust floating around us. Birds chirping among the trees

outside the windows. The smell of dry, rotted wood.

I glanced down at him as he stood, cradling my face in his hands, a piece of his tattoo snaking down his wrist, over his hand. "Hey, talk to me."

Shivers scurried down my backside. "I'm not ready," I spilled. And with it, tears came. "I'm sorry. I'm so sorry."

Control flooded back into my system, filling me with enough composure but leaving me with guilt.

"I'm so sorry for leading you on and getting you all excited." I sobbed. "I thought I wanted this. I thought I was ready, that maybe if I can just force myself to be into it, I'll come out feeling better. I want you, Ayden. I do, I swear."

He shushed me, pulling my face into his shoulder and planting kisses to my hair. "Don't apologize. Please, don't you ever apologize for that."

Why didn't he hate me?

He allowed my cries to soak in his new shirt, knowing well it'd be dry when I pulled away.

I sobbed for a few minutes more as bugs crawled inside me and tore apart the butterflies that once flourished. Their thick, heavy wings beating against the inside of my stomach, their tiny legs hooking into the lining.

They faded, and with them, so did my cries.

I pressed myself further into his chest as if I could somehow meld myself to his soul. Fuse us together and never leave him again.

When I did eventually lift my head and pull back, Ayden's mesmerizing eyes searched mine for any signs of concern.

Like that, my tears and snot that once dirtied his nice shirt vanished with all traces of humanity. Angels could mimic all the things humans did, and when that angel had once been a human, it made it much easier. It became innate down here on earth.

It'd been all we really knew, a lifetime of habits that couldn't be snuffed out in just a year after death.

His fingers danced under my chin. "I know you're blaming yourself right now, but please know I'm not mad."

"I got you riled up."

"What, am I a kid? A dog?" He snorted. "Was I excited? Yeah, I was. But when you recoiled, when your moans stopped, my excitement disappeared. How do you expect me to enjoy it if you aren't? How can I keep going if the reason I don't tear the world apart is not into it? I once told you I like all my women to be willing, and I stand by that." Hurt, sincerity, and maybe even shame flashed across his face, neither one sticking but rather shuffling through like a deck of cards.

I was the reason he didn't tear the world apart, yet he was the reason I did.

My brows dropped inwards, but my gaze lifted to his. "Recoiled? I..." I leaned all my weight back into the wall, which hadn't been much considering. "I recoiled? And you felt that? I don't understand, my entire body was into it."

He shrugged. "Not entirely. There's always a little connection to every part of yourself, even if you don't see it. You might be into it, but not all the way, and that means you're not having fun. Body, mind, spirit. Whatever the fuck they say about it." He rested his forehead against mine. "And the deal is, Angel, that you should never gaslight yourself into believing you like it because your body shows signs. Whether you're warm in your pussy"—I gagged—"or fantasizing. Whether you use porn or touch yourself. It doesn't make what you did not consent to okay. It doesn't change that you weren't ready for something intimate with someone else, even if that someone else happens to be me." Such sweet, heartfelt words. "The greatest man you've ever had the pleasure of falling in love with." And there was the Ayden Dyer I knew.

Ignoring the joke, confusion flickered in my brows. "Is there something I should know about?"

The silence rolled over into something more deafening, weighing too heavy for me to shove it away.

Then he said, "No, nothing you need to know about, Love. It's just you and me against the world tonight. We'll take it slow. Anything to get that spark turning back into a burning flame."

"That's redundant," I muttered.

Placing a gentle kiss to my forehead, his hot breath fanned over my cheek, then my ear as he whispered, "At least tell me you pictured me when you masturbated."

A laugh burst out of me as I threw my head back and shoved him. "You wish."

He was on my mind. But that wasn't the dark secret I kept locked away for my own amusement.

Nothing was amusing about the people who had sifted through my mind when I brought my fingers to the softest spot on my body. It wreaked more havoc than anything else.

Because Ayden Dyer *was* on my mind when I did the unthinkable.

But so were Sunny, and Selene, and I dared to admit, Liam.

A lump sat in the back of my throat. My lip quivered a bit. Tears threatened at the brim of my eyelids, but they couldn't quite pick a direction.

Crying in my family's bakery wasn't a burden I wanted to carry with me.

But the customer...

They covered their child's ears, mouthing "s-e-x", then left the shop as if it meant nothing at all.

I grabbed the ingredients needed to make a vanilla cake. I mixed the dry, the wet, then combined them both. When the batter was ready, I coated the pan and placed it into the preheated oven.

Finally, the tears decided.

Bleak and sullen.

They poured down my cheeks no matter how hard I tried to hold them back. My eyes stung, face soaked as everything swelled. I wiped them away vigorously, but they didn't stop taunting me.

Humiliation. Shame.

They laughed as they turned me into a wreck, the very one I caused that brought Angel into my life in the first place.

No, I wasn't blaming her. I didn't regret falling in love.

I simply hated myself for being weak. I let the fallen angels take me. I allowed them to poison me with sin and urges I wasn't supposed to have but couldn't seem to turn away.

It was my own fault that I stood here, sobbing. I hated this side of me. I fought hard to keep him at bay.

My chest tightened, squeezing every pathetic cry out of me.

I hadn't realised how long it went on for until I heard the timer go off.

Pulling the cake out, I allowed it to cool while I hurried to the bathroom and washed my face in the sink. My eyes were bloodshot, my heart far too vulnerable for my liking. I needed to shove it back into my rib cage and lock it away.

Until Angel asked for it back. She was the one who was careful with it. Gentle. She cradled it in her hands like it was the most precious object in the world, and maybe it was. She took care not to ruin me.

She did though. She crushed me in the best way.

Her fingers merciful, peeling away the layers with so much forgiveness. Tender. Understanding. She stitched up the tears in my soul and pressed a kiss for good measure and let her love do the rest.

"You're such a dick, Ayden," I seethed. "You're a dick to yourself, to Angel, to everyone around you."

Why was it too easy for me to fall into the same patterns?

I fought to shove the memory into the back of my mind.

But I couldn't quite ignore the realisation.

When the customer had spelled out sex in front of their child, I kept thinking *'Well that's useless, all kids eventually know what it is anyway. Spelling it out sounds like saying it.'* Because at eight years old, I knew what a condom was. I knew what sex was. I thought that was normal. I wore my pyjamas, locked my door, then climbed into the bottom bunk with blankets hanging over the sides to hide me away. I would touch myself. And I thought it was normal for an eight-year-old boy to know about, normal for an eight-year-old boy to do at that age.

I *never* questioned it until now.

It wasn't normal. I wasn't supposed to know. I wasn't supposed to know any of that stuff, yet I did because he introduced me when I was barely able to talk. I couldn't have told a soul for two reasons: I had no voice, and I had no understanding of what he did.

I wiped away the final remnants of my tears. The lump in my throat sat low, too big to swallow.

Fuck him. "I hate you so much. I was a child. I was supposed to trust you with my life and instead you used me. You tore me apart." I sucked in sharp breaths to try and keep it to myself. I didn't wanna drag anyone into this. I was supposed to have healed, to be over it.

How did one truly heal and get over trauma like this though?

More understanding washed through me.

When I was twelve, I'd become majorly depressed. For a year. It was a constant battle, one I fought endlessly against. Even as I fantasised about suicide every day, and still I couldn't gain enough courage to follow through.

Something always held me back from jumping out a high window or stabbing myself to death. Violent acts. A promise to end a distraught memory.

Those horrid scenes started to seep back into my soul at the age I hit puberty. I couldn't rid myself of the rot and decay. I began to believe that was all I was, too, and the world would have been better off without me in it. This had been the time I discovered porn, which had been the key that unlocked such memories. That led to all the destruction and war in my own head.

It began with the addiction, then the flood gates opened. Then trickled in depression and violent ideas of ways to end my life. I had no idea how I was supposed to cope with such heavy burdens, or how to confide in anyone else.

So I never did. I kept his dirty little secret to myself, because much like it would bring him so much disgrace, it would have drenched me in the same.

After a good twenty minutes or so, I slathered icing over the top and sealed up the pan. Not my best work, but *something*. Something to bring me some peace.

Then I left it on the counter while I sauntered out of the bakery and strolled down to the bar.

It was wrong to give into the desires. It was even worse to walk all that way, to sit down on a stool and order a beer.

I wanted to turn it around.

But how could I?

How could I stop the voices from persuading me?

It'd been wrong to be sitting here. Maybe I was supposed to prove to Heaven I could still be good even when I'd been poisoned. This could have been a test, really, and I was failing miserably.

Could I be entirely to blame? No. They proved that I didn't matter in the grand scheme of things, so should I have cared at all?

"Hi, Ayden," a brittle voice said behind me.

"Sunny." I glanced back at her, not bothering to hide the shock.

She took her cue to drop down on the stool beside me. "I know about what happened to you. I'm sorry." Yeah, I was there. And so was she. Did she forget?

I shrugged, eyes falling back on my bottle of beer.

"You and...Eliana are still friends? Or..." She blushed. "More."

Taking a swig, I dropped the bottle onto the counter. "We make out and love each other if that's what you're implying. Why are you here, Sunny?" I hadn't intended it to come off so harshly but I wasn't about to correct myself.

Her red hair fell into her face as she lowered it. "I guess I don't really know anymore." She slammed her palm onto the bar. "Actually, I just need to say a few things. When we dated, I thought maybe it was going somewhere. You and me. I mean, we never ended up having sex, which is fine, but come to find out you're not even a virgin, huh?" She snorted with the roll of her eyes. "No, you're a fraud. You go out and get drunk and fuck whoever you see."

I lifted my finger. "To be fair, I do not get drunk. Well, I have a few times, but I've never got drunk *and* screwed a woman. If I wouldn't do it to a drunk woman, why would I allow it for myself? It's not consent, now is it?"

"That's not my point and you know it. You strung me along, and then you shut me out. For what reason?" She leaned forward. "To date your therapist, who's not even your therapist by the way."

"What—was I supposed to come out and tell you the woman following me around was my guardian angel? You'd have laughed in my face."

"Maybe. But it'd be honest from the start." A laugh escaped, lacking all bit of humour. "You're such an asshole. I can't believe I ever let you in, and something must be wrong with me for still being attracted to you."

Closing my eyes, I scooted my elbows forward on the counter. "Sunny..."

"What? Am I wrong? You led me on for some stupid bet, which I do know about by the way. People talk."

"And did they tell you about the part where if I won the bet, I'd kiss Angel?" I popped an eye open to see her shrink. "Yeah. That was the goal. She even begged me to do it, but I refused. Even after I won, I never claimed my prize, because you and I were dating and I wasn't going to do that to you. I'm an arse, alright, but at least say it for the right reasons."

"You didn't kiss her because of me?" His wrinkles vanished.

"I didn't do a lot of things because of you. I stopped having sex. I also didn't cheat. Even if Angel was living in my closet, nothing ever happened while we were together." I had even managed to fall in love, but I never did anything about it.

Silence grew between us, stretching much like a piece of gum more stubborn than a married woman with a point to prove.

Why couldn't anyone see that I made my decisions intentionally?

Nothing I did was accidental. It hadn't been because I was hurt or otherwise. I was a terrible man for the choices I did make, and I owned up to that. How I'd got to Heaven was beyond me. I didn't belong there. I belonged here, with feathers as black as a raven's.

How was I supposed to tell Angel that?

She knew, in a sense. I'd told her before.

What she did not take the time to consider was that the feeling had never gone away for me.

"But everything I did because of you, Sunny, was also because of Angel."

"Dare I ask, are you trying to say you care about us both?" She placed her hand on my bicep. I glanced at it before meeting her blue eyes.

I supposed I could see how she took my words that way.

"No." I peeled her fingers from my sleeve. "I built a relationship with her. She saw the real me and loved me anyway. She saw all the ugliest parts, yet she continues to fight. When I found her dragging herself along because I'd made her feel less than, it broke me. It also made me realise how deeply rooted her love is. I'm a stem, maybe even just a leaf. But she—she's the whole bloody rose. Thorns, petals, bud. She has no idea she holds us together, and I'm the dickhead who screws it up. She puts in this effort for us that I can't even fathom."

How could I be worth her love?

"If you don't think you do enough, then *do* enough." She crossed her arms, putting distance between us. "I'm serious. Moping around like a sad sack of potatoes is pathetic of you, and it won't make me take your side."

"I never asked you to."

A hearty laugh escaped her. "Good, 'cause I won't." She blew out a string of air. "How do you plan to do it?"

"Do what?" I furrowed my brows.

She let out an exasperated sigh. "How do you plan to up your game?"

I sat back. "I guess I could maybe...become more of eye candy. What does she like, besides just me? I mean, her style. Maybe I could put in the effort to look like a slice of cake all the time."

She actually laughed at that. "A slice of cake? Sure, if you say so. Honestly, I'd say be yourself first and foremost. Don't do anything that isn't you. Don't go out of your own way just to make her happy, because then she's only attracted to a different version of you that isn't *really* you. I know your style isn't wearing cardigans, for example, so don't try to. Are men who wear cardigans over dress shirts with glasses hot? Abso-fucking-lutely. But you, Ayden, are never going to get away with it because it's not your personality."

I finished off my beer and folded my arms across my chest. "Fine, then, who am I? Since you seem to know so well."

She tilted her head as her eyes roamed my body. Bloody hell, I gave her permission to check me out. "If you come with me and allow me a little bit of freedom, I can help. I'll have to ask questions along the way though."

Did I trust her?

Well, if I didn't, what other choice did I have? I still wouldn't measure up to Angel. The worst that could happen would be that

Sunny was dressing me up for herself and Angel would hate it.

Or Sunny would kiss me, and I'd have to shove her off.

But the payoff was worth it. If she was on my side, I'd be able to make Angel trip over her own feet.

"Let's get going then." I hopped off the stool and followed her out the front door.

I waited just outside her bedroom door, in the hallway, as she rummaged through some things. When she exited, she carried men's clothes. Did she sleep around a lot?

She must have seen the confusion written on my face as she said, "Mason's stuff."

Mason. Mason...

Right. Her brother.

I forgot he *existed.*

"Mason won't mind too much, and he gets a lot more women than people assume. He's just good at hiding it because he's gay." She shot me a look. "You didn't hear me say that."

A curt nod. "I wouldn't care if he was. It's not my business." I'd make note to ask Angel later about the whole sexuality topic. It never bothered me personally, but I knew it had bothered many, and given that I'd landed myself in Heaven...

The million-dollar question simply hung over my head: could they, too, get into Heaven?

I didn't see why not.

But again, not everyone saw that reasoning.

"What do you have for me?" I asked, pointing toward her arms.

She laid out a few things. "Okay, well. We can't pierce you, unfortunately. That's out of the question."

"Pierce me?" I scanned my own form. "Where was I gonna be poked and prodded?"

"Well...it was between your ears or your nose. Men with piercings are pretty damn hot, Ayden. Anyway, the next best thing is jewellry of other sorts." Her gaze landed on my chest. "Not necklaces, but...something most men end up wearing in their lifetime." She laid out silver and black rings. "Rings, of course. Men who wear rings are—" She closed her eyes. "Something hits so right when a man wears a bunch of rings."

Cocking an eyebrow, I slipped one on. "Really?"

"Yes! I don't mean just one, either. Wear a few. Easy adjustment, plus it feels very much like your style. I'm not changing anything about you. I'm merely enhancing you, and what *she* already loves." She laid out some more clothes.

"Why?"

"Because you want to impress her, don't you? You said so yourself." When she lifted her face, a pout sat on it.

Shaking my head, I slipped another ring on, both on varying fingers. Index and pinky. "Why are you helping me woo Angel? Earlier you made it clear you still want me. Wouldn't you be vying for my love and all that shit?"

She exhaled, goosebumps immediately raiding every inch of her flesh. "She helped me when I needed it most. Even when she had feelings for you, she never tried to steal you away or compete with me. She let me have you when you still wanted me around. It's only fair that I do the same. I'm not the type of girl to fight over a man like that. Jealousy isn't a good look."

Nodding a little, I rubbed my thumb over the small silver ring, twisting it. "Thank you." I wanted to marry her someday, as crazy as that sounded.

Was it ludicrous?

I couldn't look at another woman the same. I didn't want to go screw the next prettiest thing.

I was certain of what—*who*—I wanted.

Eliana Wilson. A woman I had never intended to fall for yet couldn't imagine a life without. Her laugh was infectious. Her do-good attitude. Her persistence regardless of what she was trying to achieve. The little crease between her eyebrows when she worried about something miniscule.

I wanted to be able to call myself her husband and start each new day with her at my side.

Maybe I was broken but so be it. If broken was what I had to be to choose one person forever, I'd wear it with pride.

"And here we have suspenders." She pulled out straps.

My eyes widened. "I'm not wearing fucking suspenders. What am I—Grandpa from the 1980s?"

I almost gagged at the thought.

Her cheeks reddened. "I was thinking more about her having to...slide them off your shoulders in a moment of passion. But you're right, they're far from your look. Leather jacket is too cliche."

I snatched it from her. "I'll wear it. I love leather. It's what I always wore before. Why stray from a good thing?"

"If you do, you should wear a white shirt beneath it. To contrast."

I wet my lips with my tongue before slipping on the jacket. "Not a chance." With a groan, then a sigh of relief, I relaxed. "It feels right, Sunny. This is me. This is who I've always been."

"Which is?"

"The bad boy."

When I met her eyes again, she dropped her head. "What does that make her then?"

"Like I'd tell you." I scoffed as I roughed up my hair. "Anything I'm missing?"

"Wear black boots with it. Trust me. Sneakers just give off this immature, douchebag vibe. Oh!" She ran back to the room, emerging with sunglasses. "Obviously." She put them on me. "She's totally going to do a double-take."

Popping the collar, I smirked. "Good. That's what we're going for here. She won't be able to take her eyes, lips, *or* hands off me."

Was it cliche of me to run and impress the good girl?

I was only falling deeper, and I couldn't help that.

And I didn't want to dig myself out.

Before I could even burst into Matthew's office, Liam went to open it himself.

"Locked."

"Lock—" I went to open it, and it caught immediately. "What the hell?"

Liam knocked. "Matthew, come on, man."

A small noise sounded from the other side, a mechanical movement, as if the lock had come undone.

When he pushed open the door and stepped inside, Matthew looked up from his desk. "I figured since everyone doesn't respect knocking, a lock would do. What do you want from me today, Eliana?"

"Actually," Liam started as he closed in on Matthew's desk. "I want to ask you."

Matthew's eyes shrunk into slits as he rested his chin atop his knuckles. "Go on."

"I know that Naeva shot me and I'm all head over heels for Eliana, and yes there are these feelings I cannot fight against. I look at her and see this pure aura. The world around her dulls in comparison. She—"

I cleared my throat while Matthew said, "Get to the point, please."

"Even if I love her, she deserves someone else. Someone better, Matt. Ayden is better for her, and what happened to him isn't *fair*. It wasn't his fault. Shouldn't someone be looking into that? If the fallen angels can steal us away and poison us and Heaven won't do anything about it, what does that tell humans? That doing good is pointless? That having faith isn't worth having because you could be taken and ruined even after passing the Great Test? Aren't we to set an example, to follow through on our word? God's Word?"

I hadn't even asked him to say that. I hadn't asked him to come in here and speak on my behalf at all. I'd never stoop so low.

But he did...impress me.

It meant nothing in the long run though.

Matthew leaned back and brought his fingertips together, tapping them as if playing a piano. Maybe he would have played if he'd ever gotten the chance to be a human.

Was it terrible of me to wish he could have experienced that?

The man who stood between us and God on legality (or spirituality) matters had no way to relate to any of us. Ironic.

Matthew stood, gathering a few papers as if he needed to take notes. He resembled a child playing office to feel important in this world. "I wanted to actually bring that up." He straightened them, then flipped through a few. "There seems to be a...mishap."

"A mishap?" I furrowed my brows and pulled my face back a little, unnerved. "What do you mean?"

His eyes darted to my murderer. It did me good to remember that every now and then. "Liam was never supposed to be here. Something got messed up, and I believe it has something to do with Ayden. I've been writing out possible theories but my best guess is that when Ayden was kidnapped and poisoned as you say, it disrupted the balance. Tipped the scales if you will."

I crinkled my nose towards my left eye, curling my lip up.

"When Heaven lost an angel so quickly after gaining one, it somehow had to make up for it and Liam slipped through the cracks."

On cue, Liam lowered his head in shame. "I see."

"I'm bringing it up and we'll get this sorted."

"Thank you," I said in a quieter voice.

We turned to leave, Liam exiting first. "Eliana?"

I stopped and turned my head towards him. "Yeah?"

"Please tell me you haven't said anything about me and Naeva," he pleaded.

Whoa.

Matthew was *actually* my bitch.

"I haven't said a word, at least as long as the two of you act like good Samaritans and right what was wronged." I pressed my forefinger and thumb together, yanking them across my lips and twisting them. "Safe with me, Matt. I'm counting on you."

He didn't say much, so I left his office.

I ached to go to the cabin and see Ayden, but that wasn't about to happen. The only other ways I could see him were fateful run-ins on earth. I never wanted to leave his side, yet I was stuck with Liam Brown of all people. Liam Brown—who should have been sent to Hell yet made it to Heaven because of what the fallen angels did to *Ayden.*

Walking by his side, I sighed. "Why?"

"Why what?"

"Why'd you do it? Why'd you kill us?"

He glanced at me, face sinking. "When I was young, my mother got cancer. I begged God to save her so I wouldn't lose my only family. She died anyway. I've blamed Him for so long, vowed that I'd do everything in my power to hurt Him."

"And me?"

"Well..." He swallowed. "There's something you should know, Elli. About *me*. Something you seem to have forgotten."

"Oh fish sticks, you're going to say you loved me." I didn't know if that was worse than him claiming I was attracted to him once.

"No." His chuckle vibrated through my soul. "Now I do, because of Cupid. But no. What exactly do you remember?"

"I was figuring you out, so you came into my dorm. You slit my throat to keep yourself hidden."

"Not quite."

"What do you mean?"

"I came to you pretending to miss Selene. And you were there, so easy... You kissed me, but the mistletoe I had, I used that to poison you when you did."

"You liar."

"It's not a lie. And when you died..." He squeezed his eyes shut. "I tried to steal your soul. I was close to it, too, but you escaped my grasp. That's why I killed Selene, why I killed you. Ayden was more just to spite you. But I discovered a power where I could rip souls from vessels and take them for myself."

I exhaled, jaw hanging as I shook my head. "You're lying! I would never do that!"

"You liked me for some time, Elli. I just thought you deserved to know."

"I deserved to know? Is that supposed to be some great sacrifice you made for me? Some great thing you did? You're the one filled with a cupid's love potion and now you're trying to tell me that I once was attracted to *you*? That I kissed you?"

"Well, I was actually trying to just let you know that I ripped your soul from you, and not that I killed you for any *other* reason. But on the kiss thing, what makes you think I'm lying?"

"For starters, you want me because of Naeva. It'd make sense as to why you'd try to say that's the reason you want me." I marched in front of him, dying to leave him behind. I'd give nothing more than to escape the clutches of a manipulative and poor-excuse-for-a-man who now walked with the angels and bathed where animals drank.

"When this is all said and done, I'm the one getting sent to Hell," he seethed. "I'm not trying to woo you, especially by telling you how I really killed you and admitting you were simply an experiment for me. That hardly counts as romantic. I'm helping you get Ayden back, knowing where I'm going to end up. You *kissed* me. Your undeniable hatred for me didn't stem from nothing. You're the one who hates me far more than anyone, more than Selene and Ayden—even combined!"

I halted, whipping to face him. "For good reason, Liam! You murdered my best friend! You dated the one person who had loved me! You took her away from me and left me with nothing! How would that lead to me kissing you? I'd never stoop that low—and never do so to hurt Selene. Fuck you for implying otherwise."

"You didn't know I had killed her. You had no idea until I poisoned you with that mistletoe."

"It doesn't matter what I did or didn't know! I wouldn't hit on my best friend's boyfriend!"

"Because little Eliana Wilson is just so perfect she could never make a mistake," he mocked in a high-pitched voice. Was he attempting to mimic me?

What the absolute fuck?

I screamed in his face, slapping him before he could reach out and shut me up. "You ripped my entire life out from under me. You took the love of my life from me. We wouldn't be in this damn mess if you hadn't killed Ayden, and you know damn well it's your fault. You killed Selene. You are a villain and nothing will ever change that." He softened, as if he hadn't just accused me of claiming to be sinless. "Even Matthew confirmed you don't belong here. You didn't change. You feel no remorse. All these emotions of yours, the changing, it's all false. You're a character, and nothing more. Selene was my best friend. She was the one person who made me feel like I mattered, and you stole her from me."

"Even before I killed her," he spoke quietly.

"Even before," I confirmed.

His eyes studied every detail of my face before he released a small puff of air. "I see. I didn't realize..."

"Well you should have. I was the lonely girl that everyone avoided. I just wanted a friend—and she loved me. She made me feel special. I'd never felt that much before."

"You loved her."

"Of course I loved her, asshat."

His tongue darted out to wet his lips. "You were *in love* with Selene."

"Of cou—" I froze. My chest pounded against what once was a ribcage, puzzlement crossing my features. My brows dipped inwards. "What? No I wasn't."

"I don't think you ever realized it, but I see it written all over you. It's hidden between every word you utter about her. There's a certain kind of passion attached to her name."

"I'm not gay, Liam."

"No, no. You kissed me and you love Ayden. But you also loved Selene. Or love, depending on if you believe that kind of thing ends or not."

I scowled. "Shut up. I did not love her like that."

"Why are you so sure? What would be so wrong with it? Because you're an angel? Because others believe it's wrong?" He tilted his head, amusement flitting between every wrinkle, every hair, and every inch of humanity. "Why, though? You're already willing to risk everything for a fallen angel. Even when you were his guardian, you loved him when you weren't supposed to, didn't you, Elli? You want love, and you want it in the ways you never thought someone could give it to you. With anyone you could. Men and women are very attractive, no? I won't tell."

I eyed him, glaring. "I'm straight."

"But you wouldn't truly know that, would you? You didn't have the opportunity to figure it out for yourself." He released a sigh. "I said I won't tell. And I *won't*, Elli."

"Stop calling me that."

He threw his hands up in defense. "Fine. Eliana. Matt is gonna help us, and at least we're starting to get answers. Right?"

I grumbled, proceeding to ignore him the rest of the way.

I didn't entertain his claim much more, but I did begin to ponder Selene and the way I'd thought of her.

She had crossed my mind when I was in Portland, doing unspeakable things to myself...

No, she was a friend. I loved her like a *friend.*

I always had. It was never romantic.

I could prove it, too. I'd find her and show everyone that I wasn't into women. I'd simply been nothing more than a human once, and one who'd lost her only best friend too soon.

I wandered the forest. No sign of Ayden.

No sign of Naeva, or Matt.

Liam was leaving me alone per request, or maybe it was because he thought if I spent enough time by myself, I'd realize he was right.

He wasn't. He couldn't be more wrong.

I ventured into the city, daring to linger near the college.

Maybe I could find her here. I hadn't seen her since Liam stole her from this world, and I couldn't quite explain why. I could, however, explain that I was never in love with my best friend.

I hadn't *kissed* Liam, either.

That bastard could go rot in a ditch for all I cared.

Planting my feet into the sharp, dry grass, I lifted my gaze up at the gray building the size of a hospital. Summer had now begun, with dorms emptied and students home for the season.

I'd never had a home to return to, however. I always stayed at the dorms and spared myself the heartache that came with my life.

"I thought you moved on," a familiar voice sounded.

My heart squeezed, and I held my breath in anticipation.

If I didn't look, maybe it'd be real. I didn't want this to be some cruel trick.

"Elli," she said.

I closed my eyes, then spun around to face her, exhaling. "Selene."

Her eyes flicked to my wings before sorrow flooded every crevice. "Was it Liam?" Her voice was soft, much like a feather drifting through the wind, afraid to wake the birds.

Slowly nodding, I balled my hands into fists to keep from twiddling my thumbs. "A week after you. I was trying to figure him out, so he *had to* kill me." I studied every inch of her soul, from her black tank top, straight brown hair, dark eyes, down to her black skinny jeans. She'd never deviated from the style, and I admired her for always sticking to the look.

"I'm sorry for that. On the other hand, it's good to see you again."

I stepped closer while choking on a sob, asking permission to hug her. As soon as she agreed, I threw my arms around her.

Burying my face in her shoulder, I allowed the scent of citrus and cinnamon to slither around my soul and engulf me in the comforting familiar. "I missed you so much" came out muffled against her skin.

A nostalgic laugh erupted as she pulled away. "Well here I am."

When I took her all in, ensuring to myself she was real and not in my imagination, tension fled every nook it once made home. "Where were you? I've been dead so long and I've never seen you." I wiped away the few stray tears with the back of my hand.

"I've been here and there. Exploring, really. Now that I'm just an angel, I've been doing a lot of traveling. I can visit all the places I never got to see, like Paris and London. Cheesy, I know. But your perspective shifts when you learn how other people live, and I want that. I hated being cooped up in my own little bubble." My eyes lingered as she put some more distance between us.

"Have you visited Portland?"

She scoffed. "I visited Oregon alright. It's an absolute dump in Portland though. The further out you go, the prettier it gets. There's nothing in Portland worth seeing. And the people there are assholes. Oh, sorry." Did she realize...?

She covered her mouth. "My language."

No. No, she didn't.

A certain kind of nausea blended with chills fell over me like a curtain. "Oh. Yeah, not much to see there. Stupid Portland."

"So! Now that you've found me, what should I know? What have you been up to?"

Forcing a small smile, I fixed my gaze on a strand of grass dipped lower than the others. "Just became a guardian angel for a bit. I've been taking a little break, considering I'm not very good at it. The last two guardees of mine both died under my watch."

"And?"

"And neither of them made it to Heaven." Sure, Sunny could have counted as one of my guardees. But she'd come back only to try and persuade Ayden to choose her instead. Did that count as succeeding, even if she didn't die like Justin, her father, and Ayden?

Ayden was one hundred percent my fault though. Nobody could ever deny that given where he currently was. I'd led him right to my killer.

We had run into Liam once, and he'd memorized Ayden's face just enough to spot him in his own car in the parking lot. To sneak into his car and take his life from his body.

For what purpose? To rip a soul from its vessel?

No, I didn't believe that.

Nor did I believe it was to make me tremble and beg for mercy.

Selene huffed. "Sounds like you blame yourself."

"Hard not to when the reason they're dead is because of you. I couldn't change them in time." Well, not entirely true. I'd changed Ayden but look how that panned out.

Did I tell her?

"What? What is it?" She dipped her head into my view until my eyes landed on her. I noted how full her lashes were. Was it natural, or had she asked for that in Heaven?

I started to chew my bottom lip before messing with the buttons of Ayden's shirt. "I met someone."

"Someone?" Her eyes grew wide. "As in a romantic partner? Elli, that's amazing! Who is it?" She pulled back, expression falling flat. "Wait, you met someone after you *died*?"

"That's the thing. It was...my guardee." How poetic of me.

"One of the ones who died?" Both eyebrows shot up. "Elli," she said as if scolding me. Her voice had been too soothing to ever mean such things, a voice made of water flowing over small pebbles down a stream in the middle of the forest, grass spilling over the sides to drink up.

Ironing out the shirt, I reeled my shoulders back. "His name is Ayden. He's so real, Selene. Everything he does. I love him, truly. But...he's a fallen angel."

"Oh, sh—itake mushrooms." She cocked a brow.

"It's not what you think!" I threw my hands out in front of me, palms facing her. "He did end up in Heaven. He did, but...things went askew. The fallen angels took him and poisoned him, but Matthew said he's going to help us with it."

"Ohhh, yes. Matthew. Great guy." I studied her expression, the way her eyes flickered to the corner as if she'd been ready to roll her eyes. But she held back for *my* sake. Maybe Matthew annoyed her at times, too. Valid, I supposed. "Do you still see this Ayden then?"

I'd begun to fiddle with my fingers. "On occasion."

She took a massive step closer, forcing me to swallow on instinct.

"Have you had sex?"

My eyes grew. "Selene!"

Leaning into my space, a sly smile flittered on her lips. "What? I'm curious. Come on, we would have talked about this anyway." Why was she so interested in *that?*

Shaking my head, I showed her my hand. "No ring."

"Right." She slipped her hands into her back pockets and teetered her weight from one foot to the other. "Well, Liam and I had sex. I still ended up here." I hated when she said things like that—when she talked about Liam. The man who betrayed us all. How would she react if she knew I was working with him? I was such a hypocrite.

I scratched my arm, recalling the way Ayden's lips moved with confidence down my front. Then, it made me feel out of place. Thinking on it now, it sent signals to my brain that then shot down my body, warmth swirling right where he had *almost* touched.

Had he really intended to do *that*? Ayden? A man of self-gratification?

Bringing forth memories from his casual days, I didn't catch any glimpses of him showing women what he could do with a tongue. It didn't mean he didn't know though.

Suddenly, his green eyes shifted into a dark brown. Shaking my head, I blinked away the thoughts, only to be met with the same brown gaze before me. "Elli?"

"Hm?"

"You good? You look dazed, and your face is flushed." I would never bring up that fluke to anyone else. It didn't mean anything, right?

I blurted, "We almost had sex once."

Her eyebrows flashed, pupils dilating. "Is that so? When?"

"Last week."

After a gasp, a grin formed as she swatted my arm. "Eliana Wilson.

Kudos to you." Why? Why say those things?

Digging my toe into the pavement, I sighed. "I backed out. I wasn't ready. Ayden is a fine specimen of a man, and he's so good to me." I frowned. "He stopped having sex, and now he waits for my sake. Did you know that? Yeah, the bastard *waits* for me." I pressed my lips inwards. "No, that's not fair. He's not a bastard. He has a dad and knows who he is, and his parents are married. Pretty sure they married before having Ayden, since he's the youngest of three."

"I see."

"I hate it." I dropped my head, dread washing over me. "I hate feeling like I'm holding him back. He's very experienced, and I don't understand why he loves me at all. Did you know that most men don't want virgins, simply because we're clingy and they don't wanna be responsible for our first time? I mean, we have this unattainable idea of how it should go and they can't meet it. Why does he love me? Why doesn't it bother him? What if when we do finally take that step, he decides I'm not good enough anymore?"

"That's not gonna happen." She snickered.

She didn't know him like I did. She had too much faith, and yet I had none after knowing everything from the moon to the sun.

"But it could." Flattening the collar, I met her eyes. "What makes me so special?" I had intended the question to reflect what I liked about myself.

But deep down, I wanted to hear it from Selene's lips, too.

"You're questioning that?" She grimaced, stepping closer, placing her hands on my shoulders. Heat flared, fanning up my neck. "What doesn't make you special?" She'd taken my bait. "When we were roommates, you were...different. You didn't want to go party with everyone else. You stayed to yourself. You'd push your glasses up and cast your eyes to the ground, tugging your book close to you."

I found myself tilting my head and attempting to see myself from her perspective. Did it mean something...? Why did it matter to me if it did or not?

"And then when I got you to open up, you'd start to ramble on about the things you loved, like the mystery of social butterflies vs. homebodies. You wanted to know why some people craved their friends and others preferred their own company. Sure, we're born that way, but you wanted to know *why*. You wanted to test if you could change that through environmental exposure. You let me be your friend, and then I learned how much you really needed someone to just have your back." She held onto all these memories even after our violent departure.

A flutter surprised me in my belly.

"Oh." Clarity slammed into me, and I stumbled away from her. "This has been lovely, Selene, but I must go. I've got a meeting with Matthew I forgot about." I shot off the ground before she could stop me, although she did yell out my name.

Still, she didn't follow.

Landing on a cloud, I approached the edge and slid down, pressing one knee to my chest while the other foot dangled thousands of feet above the earth.

When a presence lingered behind, I patted the spot beside me. "Just sit."

Liam plopped right down. "What happened?"

As I turned to look at him, pure worry fell over me. "I found her. I found Selene after all this time."

"How did it go, seeing her again?" Head turned my way, he tilted his chin to his left.

A shiver racked my soul. "I think you're right." I almost heaved just saying it, and I'd be damned to ever say it again. "I think I was..." Backtracking, I started again, "I think I'm in love with my best friend."

And how in the hell was I ever supposed to tell Ayden?

I never said a word to him, and I didn't plan to.

There was nothing to say. It'd simply drag him down, and I'd never want to do that.

Admitting to Ayden that I loved Selene in a different kind of way—coming to terms aloud with my sexuality—was never going to happen.

The front lawn of this random house had already been littered with beer, red cups, and adults dancing or making out by the time we arrived.

It'd only been a glimpse of the inside because when I stepped foot in the front door, alcohol and weed slapped me in the face, music pumping in my ears.

A few people clogged up the seating arrangements, tongues down throats and hands up shirts. Everyone else danced to the beat with a cup in hand and joint in the other.

I passed by a few of them hiding in the corner with bongs.

"Let's see if the backyard is any better," Liam yelled into my ear.

Oh, and he came with me this time.

"It's not, but sure!" I ventured out back as people launched themselves into the pool. "Whoa, that's quite a lot." Nipples slipped from bras and the men flaunted their bulges as they climbed out and shook their hair in nothing but briefs. "We're in Utah, aren't we? Mormon capital," I mumbled.

"I guess I should blend in," Liam joked. When he caught my disgust, his expression fell. "Or not."

Shaking my head, I chewed my lip. "You're right. We should blend in actually. What difference would it make? You're going to Hell and I'm living in it." I shrugged.

His jaw dropped a little as I began to unbutton *my* shirt some more—the black button-up Ayden had given me. It was all mine now.

I didn't unbutton all the way, but enough to show off cleavage and maybe a bit of my stomach. I rolled up the sleeves and then squatted to roll my slacks up to my knees, as far as they'd go.

"Would you believe me if I said I've never actually tried beer?"

"No. Well, maybe, but also no. Knowing your parents, they would have only allowed you to drink something like wine or champagne." He shoved his hands into his pockets and squeezed through bodies.

Knitting my eyebrows together, I asked, "I talked about my parents with you?"

His chuckle was cut short by the crowd. "Oh yeah. You were always telling me and Selene they practically spoiled you and it may not have always done you good. But you also didn't complain about having a house to live in and food to eat. Plus your trips to the beach made it all worth it."

Grabbing his wrist, I pulled him back. "My parents barely acknowledged me."

"Not from what you told us."

"But… Liam, where was I from?"

"Portland, Oregon. You enjoyed going to college away from home but you missed the pacific northwest too much to want to live in Utah forever. You planned to move back someday."

Locking my gaze on his, I dropped my hand. "I told you about all that. Which means if I told you, I told Selene."

Nodding, he tilted his head. "Why?"

Selene *knew* I'd been from Portland. She wouldn't forget, would she? A friend wouldn't forget... But she hated it there, which was fair. Still, it had been a punch to the gut the way she'd spat out the name as if Portland itself were a curse, and so was everyone who'd ever had ties to it.

I lowered my head, palms face up as I studied every crease.

"Eliana?" Liam's voice echoed, gravel scraping across my ears.

My eyes darted back and forth as I racked my brain for answers, heart squeezing so tight I almost couldn't feel it anymore.

A knuckle slipped under my chin, lifting until I came face to face with my killer. Now I could feel *everything*.

He widened his eyes a bit as his hand dropped. "Sorry, I didn't know how else to get your attention. Something is bothering you."

"It's nothing. Really." I stepped away, trying to shove every fleeting feeling down into a void they could never escape from. Selene was my best friend. Liam had murdered us all, and it'd do me well to remember that.

Sliding between sweat-riddled partiers, I hurried into the house again and made my way up the stairs. There'd been a few less people but still, they lined the halls as if waiting for the bathroom.

I snuck into a bedroom, and without thinking, hid myself in the closet to think. "What the hell is going on? You can never let that happen again. Everything is wrong. All wrong." I pounded my fist against my temple. "Why can't I remember? Liam has to be lying about everything."

Something tugged in my chest.

"Angel?"

I froze, chills seizing me.

Then I turned to face Ayden.

"Why are you at a party?" His face softened.

Simple. It was the only place I felt sane these days. It connected me to him when I couldn't make sense of anything else.

"I want to be."

Those nagging and antagonizing thoughts swirled in my head.

Selene said those things about Portland just by coincidence, right? Nonsense. I didn't believe in such things. Was it truly intentional? Would she want to tear me apart from the inside out? Why?

He stepped closer, forcing my heart into my stomach, heat beginning to build in my core. "I thought I saw you in the hall, and I told myself I was going crazy, so I followed you and here you are."

But Ayden wanted me. He loved me. He saw all the things she wouldn't.

"Here I am," I whispered, begging him to kiss me.

This whole *seeing him less* deal was making me crave him like the ocean waves crashing against the shore when all you got was a car horn blaring in your ear. The coast brought peace. It was home.

Lifting his hand, he brushed it across my cheek to scoop some strands behind my ear.

Whether intentional or not, she tore my heart out and stomped on it in front of me. Ayden cradled it. Between my conflicted feelings for Selene and the memories I struggled to pull from the trenches, I needed to just feel *something*. Something real, and raw.

"Ayden," I breathed, "for fuck's sake, just kiss me."

And he did.

Like his entire soul was staked on me. Like the world was crashing and we didn't know where we'd end up—with or without each other.

Like he'd suddenly craved...

Wait. Something cold pressed against my cheek, and I pulled away from his desperate kiss to see a couple of rings. "What is this?"

"Trying something new." He shrugged it off, stealing the next words out of my mouth.

I ran my fingers over the leather jacket, sliding them underneath and bunching up his cotton shirt. Slamming him back into the wall, I dragged my lips down his neck, planting kisses along his throat for a little taste, to ensure every inch of him tasted the same.

I concluded he did not.

His lips had been fresh from the oven, a crème brûlée. A caramelized shell that once you cracked into, spilled the sweetest custard.

His throat was a sun ray beating down on you. The dry summer air with a faint smell of a storm in the distance. Dark clouds rolled in and rain poured as the earth drank up every inch of hydration.

"Angel," he panted. "You know you don't have to do this." He grabbed my fingers as they fiddled with his belt.

Frustrated, I grabbed his wrists and pinned them into the wall beside his hips, knowing it wouldn't hurt him. "I know. And I want to."

"Bloody hell, she was right about the rings," he muttered.

I brushed it off, getting his belt undone and pulling away for a second of clarity.

If I followed through, I'd answer questions.

If I didn't, I'd be left with far more. I'd be left with regret and a world that didn't notice my existence.

Did I choose shame, or did I choose regret?

"Eliana," he said in a low tone that set off every signal in my body.

Shame I could live with. It'd eventually wear off. But regret, that was something I wanted to part with *tonight*.

"I'm sure," I repeated.

He grabbed my cheeks, forcing me to look at him. "Listen, I love you but I don't think our first time should be in a closet at a party."

"Maybe not. But we can still have *some* kind of fun. I was never a party girl before you came along, and I'd like to do a little bit of something to enjoy them in the same way everyone else does." I released a sigh. "Everyone always judges me, and I'm not trying to say I'm doing this because of that. But that's the truth, Ayden. Everyone looks at me and sees a prude or a good girl, and I never felt ashamed of that. I stuck to it. And now that I've met you and I've fallen in love, I'm certain."

"Certain?"

"Certain that this is the memory I want to create. Allow me to do that." I swallowed. "If *you want.* Don't feel pressured. Crap, I don't want you to feel like I'm forcing you. You should consent at least."

A deep chuckle vibrated through his throat as he leaned closer. "With you, I always consent." As my lips landed on his neck, a small moan escaped him. "If it's any help at all, I want to marry you. Now of that *I'm* certain."

His words struck a chord, and I peered up at him. "What?"

"Hm?"

"Say that again."

He wrapped an arm around my waist. "I want to marry you?"

"You're not just bullshitting?" I exhaled, my breath shaky.

His fingers dug into the little bit of skin on my hip. "I would never joke like that with you." I shot him a look, and he chuckled. "Okay, maybe a little. But this time, I swear to you I'm not."

"In that case..." I traced a finger under his shirt, across his stomach. "It's technically only wrong for the moment, but it'll be justified when we do get married. I think I'm well overdue for a rebellious phase." I unzipped his pants. "Just you and me, Mr. Dyer." Slipping my hand in, my world broke away from me. It didn't seem real, getting this close to a man. Yet I was, and Ayden had said he wanted to *marry* me. Sure, they could be words.

He could even go back on them.

However, I trusted him. Was that not what love was? I believed he would never do anything to hurt me, and so I allowed myself to give in.

The day I stopped trusting in him would be the day I knew something was wrong and our relationship would need to be evaluated. But that day wouldn't come.

Not for us.

In a strange way, with my hand down his briefs, I saw the world differently. I saw it for what it was. It'd never been about black vs. white. It has always been black, white, gray, and all the in-between.

And if doing everything right led to heartache, I deserved to live a little. After all, I'd been murdered at twenty years old.

His head fell back, fingernails embedded into my skin. Moans unfurled.

Something small sprouted in the pit of my stomach, stemming upward to bloom into something much more mature.

When he finished, a sense of calm washed over me. As if I had fully accepted what transpired. No regret. No shame.

Just...content.

Ayden ran a hand through his hair. "That wasn't what I had in mind coming to this party, but I'm not complaining at all."

"The evidence of that is inside your pants." I grinned, patting his chest. "Now we should head back out before Liam comes looking and finds us stashed away in here."

"Why can't he find us?"

"I still don't trust him. Matthew confirmed that Liam was never supposed to get to Heaven and he knows the second we sort this out, he goes downstairs."

Ayden zipped up, then buckled his belt. "Right." He opened the door and let me out first. I led us down to the main floor, grabbing a few snacks from the kitchen. Sure, we didn't need to eat, but I could still enjoy delectable food.

Somewhere in the back of my head, I recalled the simple fact that my boyfriend was walking around with briefs sticky to the brim. Because of me. Because I had satisfied him. The aftermath of pleasure could stick around for angels on earth, as it was intended for humans from the beginning. It'd only been the aftermath of pain that would disappear.

Or maybe that said something about Ayden that we didn't know about...

Now that I knew I could, insecurity could bury itself in the cemetery.

After I found a small corner unoccupied, I turned around with a gasp as Ayden placed his hand against the wall beside my cheek, leaning over me. A faint ghost of my heart raced, pounding in my ears—above the rhythm of the music pumping through these walls. "Do you ever think we'd date if we hadn't died?"

A shiver scurried down my spine as I parted my lips. "Maybe."

"Maybe?"

"Maybe not."

He frowned. "Why not?"

"Because the truth is, I... We never would have had reason to hang out or fall in love."

"If Liam had not killed any of us, including Selene, you don't think we wouldn't have crossed paths? We lived in the same state, same city." He brushed some hair from my face. "Think about it. Selene would want you to socialize so you'd agree to go to a party to shut her up. I'd spot you in a crowd by yourself after she left you. I'd approach."

Or in my case, I would have let jealousy devour me until I discovered my feelings for her and later questioned if I liked men at all. Maybe I would have assumed I did, or maybe I would have never gotten to claim that because men didn't normally treat women like me as human beings.

It'd be so easy to tell Ayden the truth, but what could I do about it now?

I wasn't going to admit my feelings.

"Why would you approach me?"

"Because you're hot. And I definitely talk to hot women."

If Liam never killed any of us, what could have happened? Would I have ended up with Selene? Would I have ever loved Ayden at all?

The question sent anxiety full force into my system, my mind beginning to spiral.

I needed to quickly refocus before I lost my sanity in front of everyone—including the man I called my boyfriend.

"Me?" I snorted. "Hot? You mean the version of me who wore cardigans and glasses and threw her hair into a bun? I was a walking bookworm."

"Yes, but..." His hand slithered down my hip before he grabbed my butt.

He hadn't been saying *but* as in *however.* He had actually said *ass.* "I'm just saying, Angel. You wore skirts everywhere and showed off your legs. I would have looked. Besides, I might be a creature of habit but I also happen to be a man of mystery. This man would want to know why a bookworm went to a party." He leaned closer, but I placed a hand against his chest to push him back. "What?"

My eyes darted into the crowd. "Everyone can see. I'm not risking it." I slipped away from between him and the wall just as he dropped his arm, and our hands brushed one another. Fingers reaching out just an inch further, like a sunflower drinking the sunshine, to the soul it died for.

When I shifted my gaze to the people, I spotted Liam in the dead center, watching me, not a word sliding off his tongue or a readable expression sitting on his face.

VOW

Thumping my leg, I fingered the hem of the button-up I wore.

"You don't look so good," Naeva commented.

I shot her a glare. "What do you want?"

Maybe I could talk to Naeva about the feelings I harbored for my best friend. I had to do something to shove them back into a box because I was tired of staring them dead in the face.

She sat beside me, placing her hand over mine. "You went to a party the other night, and you told me it was one of the things you and Ayden did. Now I'm here, curious and wondering what else it is that has you so smitten."

My shoulders sagged as I dropped my gaze. "What doesn't have me smitten?"

Then rubbing my eye, I started, "I saw a man who needed help. A man who was hurting and believed he didn't deserve better so he wouldn't do better. Everyone else saw him as a menace to society. He tried to get rid of me, but I knew it was a front. He wanted someone around. He wanted someone to help. He needed someone who wasn't going to turn and run when things got hard—at the first sign of conflict. That was me. He was ruthless and stubborn, but I was far more persistent.

"I promised to stick around. He didn't want me to, but I did it anyway." A gentle smile graced my lips. "He despised my presence, but I think he grew to enjoy it. I gave him the chance to work on his wit and comebacks. He was lonely, though he'd never admit it. He liked having company around. And I didn't entirely realize that until I left him. After we had been tortured in Hell, I told him I had to move on if he wasn't going to make any real change. And back then, Sunny needed me more. So I left.

"But that's when things became clear to me. The moment I heard him praying. He was begging me to come back because he needed me. I'd already fallen in love and confessed to him, of course. But he admitted to needing me, and I went *back*. He was changing, Naeva. I can't tell you when he fell in love, but I can say for certain that he changed for himself and not just for me. He genuinely wanted me around."

Something unrecognizable flickered across her expression. Understanding, maybe? Empathy?

"I get it," she whispered. "You fell in love with someone for who they are." At the mention of *someone*, a memory came rushing back to me. Did Naeva possibly know about the puzzling feelings for Selene? She couldn't. But why say *someone* instead of *man*?

Turning her head towards me, she rested her hands over her smooth thighs. "I can't fault you for that. Besides, attraction and love are separate things, but I do believe you can learn to be attracted to someone you fall in love with first. I also believe love isn't something we control." She gulped down some extra words she'd hoped to say but couldn't gain the courage to. "Truly. You love him."

"I've made my vows, Naeva," I said quietly. "By loving Ayden whole, I've vowed to always fight for him even when he won't. I can't give up on him, and I won't leave him just because."

A visible chill took over her as she stood. "We're still sorting it with the Thrones. I'm doing my best."

"Thank you."

She started towards the door of the cottage, pausing to look back. "I'm sorry nobody was on your side. Nobody deserves to feel that way, regardless of who they are or what they've done." Then the door softly shut behind her.

Slowly rising to my feet, I left the cute little home for a visit back down memory lane. College.

It'd been empty so it was easier for me to explore the campus and dorms.

Specifically my old dorm.

Running my fingers along the stale furniture, I studied every nook of the barren room. Two beds, two desks, two dressers. Nothing more than that.

A foundation for a friendship to form, or something more.

"A lot has changed, hasn't it?" Selene asked from the doorway.

"Too much," I muttered.

Plopping onto the perfectly made mattress, I glanced at her. She didn't know, did she?

If Liam saw it...

Smoothing my hand over the bare mattress, I exhaled. "I thought I was supposed to grow here. I wanted to get my bachelor's, then my PhD. I wanted to do big things, Selly. It was taken away. Maybe I'm glad I had a chance to meet Ayden, but what about all the other things in life I missed out on? What about the experiences ripped from my grasp? What about kids? Do I want kids? I don't know, but I never got that choice." I swallowed the lump in my throat. "We were supposed to be best friends. We were supposed to grow old together.

You were the first person to ever make me feel like I mattered in this world." Tears began rolling down my cheeks as I choked on a sob, attempting to hold it back.

She closed the distance between us, dropping beside me. "Hey, I'm here now." She rested her hand on my leg, hoping to comfort me somehow.

I couldn't be sure if it did. Scare me—yes. I supposed it was because she openly insulted the city I'd grown up in, or it could have been feelings bubbling in my chest.

"Everything's different!" I yelled as my cries broke the dam. "It's not the same. We could have had so much more than this."

In a hushed tone, she said, "I know." She reached for my hand, wrapping her fingers in mine. "*We* could have had so much more than this. You and me against the world. And fucking Liam," she spat. "He's the one who did all of this to us. I never should have trusted him. I thought he cared about me. But when we went on that date..."

I lifted my eyes, watching her search for clues in the low carpet.

"I should have seen it coming. He wanted my soul. Nothing more than that."

Sniffling, I squeezed her hand. "He wanted your soul?"

Spinning her head towards me, her hair whipped around her face. "Of course. One minute we're laughing, and the next he's saying he's sorry and trying to tear my soul from my body."

Something cold, something slimy and empty seized me by the throat.

Selene and Liam would never have talked. Not now.

If she was speaking the truth, it meant Liam had been right about everything.

He ripped my soul from me. He poisoned me. I *kissed* him.

Why the hell couldn't I remember any of it?

"You look as if you've seen a ghost," she said with a small laugh.

Forcing a smile, I shook my head. "It's nothing. I'm just sorry you went through that fear all alone. I can imagine how it must have felt to be betrayed by someone you loved."

"I didn't love Liam." She sighed. "I cheated on him, and I didn't love him. Sure, he got me pregnant, and I had almost got an abortion. But I used him to feel something, and to keep someone familiar around. It was stupid, Elli. Not that it excuses him murdering us, but I'm not entirely innocent."

I hung on to the fact that she'd been *pregnant*. What? And she never told me? Had she not trusted me?

My thoughts swam, but the ocean crashed at the base of the cliff and drowned me in turmoil.

Getting up from the bed, I crossed the room. "Why?"

"Because I was stupid. Because I was afraid to lose him and break it off. There's no justifiable reason. I just did it."

"But you regret it—the cheating?" I turned on my heel to face her.

She nodded. "Of course."

"What do you think would have happened if you had ended things with Liam?" Tension dissipated from my soul.

She shrugged a little, leaning back onto her hands. "I mean, maybe we would have stayed alive? I don't know. Sometimes it's fun to imagine what could have been but then you spiral into this rabbit hole of depression because you realize it'll never happen."

I released a sigh. "I like to think we would have lived. Finished college. Been best friends for life. I'd be your maid of honor in your wedding. Maybe the best aunt to your kids if you had any." Those words alone sent the pierce of the knife right into my heart. A pang of panic settled. I'd always have come second in her life.

"Maybe you would've helped me out of my shell more. I'd tag along with you to parties and social events to make some friends. Maybe I would have crossed paths with Ayden at a party, meeting him all over again. Maybe he would have spotted me and struck up a conversation because I didn't fit in. We could have been the cliche couple." I shoved my clammy hands behind my back, eyes cast to the ground.

"You think?"

I looked at her, brows knitting together. "Why couldn't it happen?"

"I didn't say that." She laughed. "Do you believe in fate? Do you believe that no matter what we do, we'll cross paths with the same people and end up in the same general vicinity?"

Hugging myself, I began rubbing my arms. "I don't know. Possibly. Sometimes. Ayden believes it. I believe we have a few paths to choose from, and sometimes we might veer from one for a bit before steering back in the right direction, but we get there eventually. I think that despite the paths, we always end up taking the one that...God knew we would. We always end up in the same place, because while we have free will, our future is still known well in advance."

"Profound," she joked. She shot up from the bed. "You and Ayden do anything yet?"

"Huh?"

"Figured I'd check in with you now." With a shrug, she started to pace around the room.

I turned my head to follow her, feet firmly planted. "I touched him."

"Touched as in, felt his chest, or as in, you grabbed his dick?"

"Selene!" My eyes grew wide.

She laughed again, leaning both shoulders back against the wall with one ankle crossed over the other. "This is the conversation we missed out on because our lives got cut short."

Heat flooded my cheeks. "I may have...grabbed that."

"Are we talking a little warm-up or full head?"

"I'm not sure what that means."

"Hand or oral?"

Flames seared my soul. "Just hand. Um, can we talk about something else?"

She rolled to her side. "Sure. That's it though?"

"Yeah, that's it, Selene."

"Oh, full name. Okay, I get it." She crossed her arms. "I'm surprised to see Eliana Wilson wearing black. And pants. You were always more of a skirt kind of woman. What's that about?"

Picking at the invisible lint on the shirt, I started to button it up some more. "It's Ayden's shirt. The fallen angels stole mine. I wanted to try something different so I opted for pants. I have worn pants, you know."

"Sure." Another infectious laugh. "We'll pretend that's it. Nevermind having your boobs practically on display."

"It was for a party!" I sucked in air. "I had to blend in. My boobs are all I have."

"You think that's all you have to offer? Nevermind the pretty blue eyes and blonde hair that never has a bad hair day?" My pulse quickened as warmth rose to my cheeks.

She lifted one perfectly shaped eyebrow. "Girl, please."

"Oh yes, because being Hitler's ideal human is so marketable these days." I shook my legs to let the pants unroll themselves. "Maybe I'll see you at the next party."

She shoved herself off the wall and passed me, flipping to face me. "Maybe you will." Opening the door, she glanced back and winked. "I expect more cleavage there." She shut the door behind her just in time to miss the crimson that seeped from my cheeks to my earlobes.

One minute I was walking the forest grounds, waiting by the cabin for Ayden.

The next, a bag was thrown over my head as hands restrained my arms. I fought back, kicking as they dragged me. A scream erupted, but it made no difference.

After minutes of darkness, I landed on hard things. They clacked as I threw myself away, only to fall onto more. I ripped the bag from my head and found myself swimming in a sea of bones. Skulls, femurs, spines, ribcages. "I'm gonna be sick," I pressed the back of my hand to my mouth.

Even if I tried to climb my way out, I couldn't do that. My wings flapped, but the lid came down as I crouched, trapping me inside the pit.

I fought against the bones and attempted to lift the bars. Nothing budged.

"Angel?" an English accent drifted my way.

I glanced up to find Ayden's green eyes peering down. "What's going on?" I yelled up.

"I don't know, hold on!" He started to pull up the metal, but a shadow loomed over him as I shouted for him to watch out. They yanked him.

Quiet fell as my chest squeezed with uncertainty and terror, pounding until I couldn't recall anything else.

"Ayden!" I yelled.

Who knew how much time passed. At one point, my feet grew tired and I dropped into the skeletal remains. Actual sweat formed in my pores, coating my skin. I leaned my head back against the wall with an exhale. I despised the heat, and having grown up by the ocean solidified that. There hadn't been time for me to adjust to warmer temperatures either.

Moans stretched through the walls.

And just when I thought everything was going *so* dandy, someone slid the metal grate away. I expected Ayden—hoped for his face to appear. To my *luck*, someone else had.

"Levi," I spat.

"Hello, *Love*," he mocked. "What a nice surprise."

"What, you mean you didn't throw me down here yourself? I have a hard time believing you wouldn't take the credit." I snickered and jeered my chin down at the wall.

With a rough chuckle, he jumped down, somehow managing to land on his feet when nothing but bones rumbled beneath us. "Your afterlife must be so hard. I'd hate to be you. Come." He reached out his hand.

"I'm not going anywhere with you." I attempted to blend myself in with the stone, begging it to swallow me so I could escape his wretched breath.

"I think you'll beg to differ. Unless you have made yourself such wonderful company down here in the remains of others. *Come.* You'll want to see what we have to show you."

"Show me?" I narrowed my eyes.

He wiggled his fingers. "Trust me on this, if you choose to trust me in anything at all."

"And if I don't?"

"If you don't, we'll drag you there. But if you really don't want to see your precious Ayden..."

Forcing my pride down my throat, I slowly grabbed his hand. "Fine. Take me to him."

"Atta girl," he said with a grin. I sent my foot into his ankle, but it hadn't made any impact. Still, the thought was enough for me.

He flew back up to the ledge, holding me by the bicep and shoving me forwards. As we wound through hallways, I thought maybe he'd throw me in another cell. But we kept going. And as we kept going, the hallways dimmed. No lakes of fire. No torches on the walls. In fact, the heat even shrunk away.

He opened a large metal door and sent me inside, and I had to hold back from gasping at the sight.

Was it terrible to admit this room was pleasing to look at?

Black leather couches and chairs circled around a table made of glass. Candlesticks, sconces, candelabras decorated the walls. In every corner stood a statue carved from the finest marble, and the cement flooring had been polished to shine.

Gothic architecture had been the only thing on their mind when building this. Details molded so perfectly into the corners, and not an inch had been left abandoned. A few skulls sat atop black tabletops that stood beside the lounges. Pressed and dried spiders, centipedes, and other creepy crawlies had been framed in glass along the walls.

Even the finest crystal chandeliers hung from the ceiling.

"I didn't realize you guys lived in luxury," I said with a little too much admiration. I'd been going for judgment initially.

Levi's cunning smile flashed my way. "Glad you like the view." He guided me to what I assumed was the chair, but he dropped into it and snapped his fingers, pointing to the floor in front of him. "You can sit there."

"I'm not a dog," I hissed.

Leaning back, he stretched his arms, shirt riding up his stomach. The sight of him physically made me nauseous. "You'll want to sit for this."

Crossing my arms, I folded my wings back. "Where's Ayden?"

He opened his mouth to answer, but wheels rolling across the floor bounced between walls. Both our gazes shifted to the source, another angel pushing a chair with Ayden in it. "Speak of the devil and he doth appear."

I tried to rush over, but Levi slid his foot out a little too far, and I kissed the floor. So well that my nose began to bleed.

Reminding me I was still in Hell, even if the vibe of the room was dark and soothing. Only down here could an angel still bleed, still beg for mercy... *Lucky me.*

A groan echoed, and when I pushed myself up into a sitting position, Ayden lifted his head. "Bloody hell, I've been hit by a bus." As his vision cleared, he saw me and immediately lurched forwards, catching on the rope tied around his bare chest. I hadn't seen him shirtless in a while, but my eyes fell to the chest hair and black ink splayed in tribal patterns. It was wrong of me to be ogling over him at a time like this, I knew that.

And I also was aware that chest hair wasn't most women's weakness.

But something about seeing it...

It'd been no different to seeing him with a beard compared to without. I preferred *with*, too.

"Ayden, please, I'm fine," I assured him, voice as soft as the feathers that grew from his wings. "It's just blood."

"It's just blood," Levi repeated. "So, Ayden boy, would you like to show your little girlfriend here what you discovered?"

My eyes grew bigger as my eyebrows dipped inwards. "What?"

Ayden growled, pushing against the rope. "Let her go. You have me. Why do you need to keep doing this?"

Levi chuckled, and then he was on his feet, approaching Ayden fast. "Because where's the fun otherwise? Besides, she deserves to see what beauty we've created." He swept his arm back my way.

He spat in response. "You created fucking nothing."

Wiggling his finger, Levi tsked. "You can do what you can do because we turned you into something greater. What was your other option? Become a fucking guardian angel?"

My *boyfriend* glared.

Levi reeled back. "Fine. We'll bring it out of you." He spun on his heel and came for me. I scooted back onto my hands, scrambling for an escape. He swiped up a handful of hair and dragged me to a desk cluttered in papers as I yelled in pain. Ayden shouted at him to let me go.

"We're gonna do this the right way." Levi pulled out a cleaver, holding it up just enough to inspect it, allowing it to glint in the low lighting. "This will do." He hauled me back to the center of the floor, the other angel grasping Ayden's jaw to force his eyes on me.

When he pushed me down onto my stomach, hair fanning around my head, I thought maybe he was planning to chop it off and leave me feeling out of place.

What he did was far worse.

Pressing the bottom of his heavy black boot to my neck, he wrapped his arms around the edge of my wing, smoothing over the feathers.

"No, please," I begged. "Please don't do this."

Ayden jerked some more, starting to shout at them. But Levi wasn't taking the bait.

As his grip tightened on my radius, I pleaded.

And then he brought the cleaver swinging against the bone fused to my soul.

My screams pierced the lair, my wailing following suit.

I couldn't hear whatever Ayden was yelling over my own.

Another sharp pain jolted through my back, seizing every limb and leaving me with a dull ache.

Just when I thought it'd been over, that it'd been enough... Levi rounded to the other wing, boot pressed so deep into my neck that I'd exhaled out of fear.

He took that one with him, too. Away from me.

Left me a bloody mess.

The love of my life panted, tears streaming down his face as he fought the restraint, but to no avail.

Levi sighed, grabbing hold of my arm and yanking me to my feet. "You really are useless. Oh well."

I couldn't decide if he was talking to me or Ayden.

Regardless, he returned me to the pit of human remains, tossing me back in. My blood stained far too many, and the truth dawned on me.

These weren't human remains after all.

The bones belonged to *angels*.

Angels couldn't ultimately die, but we could cease to exist if there'd been enough torture. If they stripped us of all we were, we'd be nothing. We'd bleed dry, rot until we couldn't fight back anymore.

We couldn't call for help.

Eventually, I'd be nothing more than a speck of dust floating, making an example for angels everywhere.

Curling into a ball, my wounds began to fester and ache amongst the smokey air. My wailing became cries which eventually dried up altogether.

The dim glow that illuminated the death around me vanished. I glanced up to see a wisp of a shadow slithering down towards me.

Eyes the size of saucers, I scooted back into the wall, attempting to escape its grip. I bit back the shriek pressing against my throat when my fresh lacerations seared against the stone. The shadow wrapped around my ankle, cold as ice and as smooth as silk, then pulled me right from the pit.

When it dropped me onto the floor, I lifted my head to watch as a tendril returned to its owner.

And I gasped.

"Ayden?"

He stood, exposed and shrouded in darkness, a solemn look plastered to his face. "Angel..."

"Ayden," I reached for him, my hand falling back at my side. Everything weighed two tons, and I faltered.

Boots scraped across the cement. Hands grabbed my face, cradling me before sliding around my body and hoisting me up.

"Stop them, for fuck's sake!" Levi yelled.

An arrow zipped through the air, barely missing me.

Ayden cursed under his breath, tucking me safely into his chest and turning away from them. He groaned—winced—and stumbled forwards. But he never lost his grip on my soul.

They were firing arrows, and he was taking all the blows.

But why?

How?

He was a fallen angel now. Wasn't he supposed to feel no pain down here?

Screaming out, he pushed on, leading us away from the stench of death and forgotten souls.

Peering down at his fingers wrapped around my thigh, I inched my hand towards his, taking in the difference in size. I slid my palm over the top.

A small hiccup emerged.

Throwing my head back to look up at him, I studied the growth in his face. His lips, his green eyes, his jawline. His throat.

Dropping my gaze again, I noted the way his hand wrapped around three-quarters of my thigh. My *upper* thigh.

When sunlight washed over us, he collapsed to his knees and returned to the same Ayden I fell in love with. Stubble on his chin, brown hair, light skin.

"Were you just..." I choked on my words.

He tightened his embrace, resting his jaw on my hair. "Shhh. You're safe, Angel."

For now.

But I couldn't stop replaying what I'd seen in my head. What I'd seen with my own two eyes.

Ayden Dyer had looked exactly like Nephilim.

ECCLESIASTES

"Walk with me," Matthew said.

Liam and I both obliged.

I never uttered to anyone what happened with Ayden. But when Liam found us, he questioned a lot. And it wasn't exactly easy to hide the gaping wounds on my back, or the crimson-soaked shirt.

It was because of Liam I got back up to Heaven.

I didn't want to sit around, either. I asked them to patch me up, to which they helped my wounds scar over to spare me the extensive recovery.

"The Thrones are always busy, believe it or not. The more people, the more angels, the more work. But we've got the case officially submitted. Now we must wait."

If I told them about what I discovered with Ayden, they'd never let him back in.

A small part of me gnawed at the realization that maybe they already knew.

Regardless, I tucked the information to myself, hoping we could reverse it somehow before it was too late.

"Wait," I muttered. "My favorite pastime."

"So, Matt," Liam began, "now that you're dating Naeva, how's that going? How did that begin exactly?"

Matthew shot us a stern look. "That's not your business."

Liam shrugged. "Then make it our business. You know every detail of our lives. It's only fair. If we are to trust you, that is." He weighed his hands before shoving them into his pockets. "This trust thing is a two-way street. It's earned, not just given."

I scolded myself for even entertaining the thought that Liam reminded me of Ayden at this moment.

"I never asked you to trust me." He opened a door to a bowling alley. "In fact, I don't need it. I'll do my job either way."

The murderer lifted an eyebrow. "Why are we here?"

From the doorway, blue and pink lights flashed from inside.

Matthew turned down his nose. "I'm here for myself because I happen to enjoy bowling."

I snorted. "Easy to enjoy bowling when you're perfect at it."

The Archangel's brows knitted together, a crease forming. "Who says I'm perfect at it?"

"You're an angel, and an archangel. It's kind of just...implied that everything comes easy and naturally." I gestured.

A real laugh escaped him. I hadn't known Matthew *could* laugh. I didn't think he even knew what the word meant.

"Bowling doesn't come easy just cause. I mean, I suppose if you want to be perfect right away, it could. I didn't want that. I wanted the chance to learn and get better, so it took me years and years. And now it's my favorite nightly activity."

Liam poked his head inside, turning it left, then right. "Can we join you?"

And the resemblance between him and Ayden stopped there. The

English bad boy would never have asked Matthew for permission.

Matthew shrugged. "I suppose if you wanna get smoked, be my guests."

We piled inside. Many of the lanes were occupied, and many weren't. And seeing as it wasn't the kind of bowling alley on the ground, hundreds of lanes swept across both sides. No counter to trade in for shoes. As we pulled up to an empty lane, they appeared on our feet, socks and all.

When I glanced back, I noted the bar of fried foods. Nothing beat the bowling alley food. The one we'd gone to when I was a kid had the best fries around, and I'd beg my parents just to go for the food alone, as if it was a restaurant and nothing more.

To ten-year-old Eliana Wilson, it had been.

"I'm not much into bowling," I stated. "I'm actually not much into anything these days. I wasn't the active type of kid."

"Nonsense," Liam said. "You are now. Come on. Matthew needs two of us to take him down."

"I won't be taking anyone down," I mumbled.

Matthew picked his ball—black with sparkly green swirls—then he took large steps, swinging his arm back, then forwards, letting it fly down the lane. It went for a straight shot.

And knocked all ten pins in one go.

"Strike! Impressive," Liam said with a grin. "But I can do better."

"Better than a strike?" Matthew let out a lighthearted chuckle.

With a glare, Liam grabbed a red ball, rushed forwards, and swung. The ball rolled most of the way before hitting the gutter right before the pins.

A genuine laugh erupted from me.

Liam grumbled as his ball reappeared. Then he went one more time, managing to knock a few pins. "I'm warming up. The ball didn't weigh right."

I refrained from correcting him and telling him that he could make it weigh right by wanting it to be perfect. But it wouldn't be a victory if he cheated by supernatural forces.

"Eliana, you gonna go?" Matthew asked.

I glanced between them, but then I stepped forwards. "I guess I don't see why not." I went for a sky-blue ball, a color made of metallic. I slipped my thumb and middle fingers into the three holes, using a minute to feel the weight in my arm. As the bowling shoes appeared on my bare feet, I turned on my heel and faced the lane. I brought the ball up to my face, blowing on it as I'd seen done in the movies. Then I jogged over and swung back before bringing my arm forwards and letting go of the ball.

It rolled.

The ball continued down the center before veering a little to the right and managing to knock half the pins. "Not terrible." I faced the guys. "Let's see how I do though."

As the ball returned, I swung again.

It rolled more to the left this time, hitting a few more pins except one. "Not terrible at all!" I clapped.

Matthew threw his hand out to Liam and let out a short laugh. "Better than this one. And I thought you said you were going to do better than me?"

Liam rolled his eyes. "I told you I'm warming up. I still have a chance to come back for vengeance. And I will." He pointed his fingers at Matthew's eyes.

The Archangel chuckled some more, but the world around me melted as my smile faded. His words echoed in my mind. Maybe he'd meant it as a joke, but knowing the kind of man he was in life, I couldn't take them for anything *but* serious. What had he meant? Was he going to sabotage Ayden?

He'd never stand a chance.

A man who claimed to rip souls going against a man who was... Well, I hadn't been entirely sure what Ayden was. Nephilim? He'd resembled one, but knowing that they were generally the offspring of a fallen angel and a human woman, there was no way. His parents had always been human, always been...

A familiar voice I couldn't place whispered in my ear, *"It's not always so black and white, Eliana."*

Unless his dad had never been human and had simply been a fallen angel who fell in love with one.

Maybe that had been why they targeted him. They knew, and maybe Ayden had, or hadn't. But no way could Lucifer or the fallen angels or Hell not know who their own were. Making Ayden's father one of them, and to punish him for his crimes against their achievements, they took his son.

Or it all could be one big theory that was way off course.

I couldn't say for sure, but that didn't stop curiosity from killing me in the first place.

I'd have to find his sisters and ask them now that they knew what happened to Ayden. Someone could confirm or deny it.

But if they knew, why hide it? If they knew, wouldn't that mean God and Heaven knew? Yeah, Ayden made it here. The white wings weren't a hallucination. Why accept him in the first place?

What if that'd been it? What if I was assigned to Ayden because of who his father was, because they wanted to see if they could save a soul?

Were Nephilim considered souls? I wasn't entirely sure, nor did I recall that part of the Bible.

If I was right, this case could expose the truth of it all.

I couldn't quite wait that long, however.

"Eliana," someone said, a hand waving in front of me.

"Hm?" I snapped back to reality and found Liam standing there, pointing at my ball. "Is it my turn?"

"Has been for a few minutes now. Where'd you go?"

"Nowhere. Just hoping Ayden's okay." I grabbed my ball.

"How did you escape Hell again?" he asked a little too wary.

"I told you." I started towards the lane, throwing the ball forwards. "Ayden found me and ran."

I needed him to buy it, but I doubted he would. No matter what his feelings, he said nothing more, and neither did I.

"What's this?" A soft voice asked.

Matthew turned to find Naeva watching us in awe, head tilted. I noticed the way his cheeks tinted pink and his eyes lit up. "This is bowling. I'm very obviously crushing them."

"Oh? May I watch?"

"Of course!"

Liam and I shot each other a glance.

Matthew did win, but surprisingly not by a mile. Liam had started to catch up. He wasn't lying about warming up at least. He managed a few strikes, but more splits than anything.

I didn't do too bad myself.

When the game concluded, I asked Liam to drop me off on earth. I had some business to tend to, and I could have jumped from a cloud and landed just fine, but I figured my chances were better floating from the sky.

So we said our goodbyes to Matthew and Naeva.

On our way down to the city, Liam threw his gaze back up. "So, Matthew is good at bowling. It was a little strange seeing him act so...casual."

"He is very business-like and formal all the time, isn't he?" I scooted my feet across the pavement, not at all bothered by the texture. "Well, this is it. I can find my way."

"What is it that you're going to do?" He shoved those blood-soaked hands of his into his damned pockets.

I crossed my arms. "That's not really your business, and I'm not obligated to relay every detail of my plans to you. You came to me, telling me you could help us. That's as far as it goes."

He opened his mouth to argue, then closed it. "Nevermind."

"Tell me. Since you're so daring and bold, say it, Liam. I'm a big girl."

He shrugged a little, eyes skipping from cloud to cloud. "I was just going to say yeah, you're right, but I am giving up my soul for this. I'm the one who's gonna end up rotting in a cell. The least I could have is some details, to calculate how long I have before my eternity is spent wasting away."

"Ah, the pity route." I shook my head with a snicker. "I don't pity you a bit. You dug your grave, now you lie in it. If I need you, I'll call. You're my bitch. It'd do you well not to forget that." Before he could sneak another word in, I spun on my heel and ventured down the city street, towards Ayden's parents' bakery.

I expected Arabella, but Esme exited the back first. "Eliana."

I gave her a small wave before fixing my shirt. As if I could do that… "May I talk to you?"

"Oh! Yes, yes." She waved me over to a chair. There was no other place for us to hide ourselves from the eyes of Heaven or Hell.

I planted myself on a small wooden chair and glanced around the shop. "This is about your family."

"Is Ayden okay?" Concern laced her eyebrows.

Resting my hands on the table, I tapped my fingers. No, it felt wrong. I tucked them back into my lap beneath the tabletop. "Ayden is… This…" I met her gaze. "How do I say this, Esme? I'm not sure he would want me to say something at all but I don't see how I couldn't. I have questions and…" I dropped my chin. "I need to know what you know about your parents."

"Excuse me?" A snotty tone.

I could see how it came off that way. "No, Esme, not like that. I promise. There is something that happened with Ayden and I simply need to know if my theory is way off or if I'm on the nail's head."

Still wary, she leaned back, waving her arm for me to continue.

A shiver racked my soul. "How much do you know about the supernatural world?"

She shrugged. "Enough."

"Have you always known?"

"I suppose I always suspected."

"Ayden told you what happened to him. Does that mean anything to you?"

"Is it supposed to?" Her eyebrows shot up, the corner of her lips tugging to the side.

Esme was the oldest. If she didn't know...

Maybe I'd been way off after all.

"Nevermind." I shook my head and sunk back into the chair.

Even as I fiddled my fingers, her eyes pinned me to my spot.

"Wait here," she said as she scooted from her chair and disappeared into the back. She emerged again with something. When she placed the plate in front of me, a piece of cake with raspberry filling made my mouth water. "On the house. Now tell me." She dropped back into the seat, crossing her arms.

"I'm dead. You don't have to bribe me with sweets."

She said nothing, her stare narrow. Locked on me.

I saw how it was gonna be.

Releasing a sigh, I ran a hand down my face. "Your dad, is there any chance he wasn't born on earth?"

Her expression loosened. "What?"

"Something happened, and I just want to know if it happened because your dad is...a fallen angel." I picked a crumb from the cake, twisting my hip into the bottom of the chair as I tried to shield myself away from the scrutiny.

"Are you saying my dad's a fallen angel because Ayden is? Come on. He told me what happened, and it's a pretty sound story. He made it to Heaven, Eliana."

"I know!" I ate the crumb, dropping my arm because I didn't deserve any more sweets. "He did. But I keep asking myself: *why are they targeting us?* And then I come up with theories. Even before Liam killed us. Before Liam contemplated selling his soul to Lucifer, before he knew who Ayden was. The second I was assigned to Ayden, the fallen angels targeted us. It never made much sense to me as to why they picked me out of all the guardians. Why as soon as I was assigned Ayden? And then...even after he died and got to Heaven, it wasn't enough. They kidnapped him and poisoned him. And now that he's them..." I couldn't admit what happened down there. I couldn't admit I was no longer one of them.

An angel without her wings. Fitting for a failure.

I deserved nothing more than the two pieces of clothing on my body.

"When I was in Hell, something happened to him. Ayden just...lost it. It wasn't entirely him, either." I met her eyes. "Esme, I saw a man who wasn't a man at all. He wasn't a fallen angel, either. He was..."

Swallowing my fear, I whispered, "He was both."

"Both?"

"In the Bible, there are mentions of Nephilim. They're children born to a fallen angel man and a human woman. They're different because they're...like giants. Well, they *are* giants. I saw these shadows around Ayden and he controlled them, and then he grew. He wasn't just your average man. He was the size of a giant, or a giant in human standards. And it kind of clicked. Now I just want to know if maybe I was assigned to him for a reason and if they're targeting us for that same one." I turned my body to face her.

The silence spoke more volumes than I ever could. I'd always been a naturally quiet person. People constantly asked me to speak up in my lifetime, and I hated the idea of feeling like I was a passing thought.

Arabella emerged. "Eliana! I didn't know you were here!" She hurried over. "You didn't touch your cake. Is it wrong? Did Esme put too much sugar again?" She frowned, glaring at her older sister.

Esme rolled her eyes.

I snorted. "No. Trust me."

Esme turned her head, studying the busy streets. "I suppose we're due for a talk with our parents, aren't we?"

I kept my lips pressed together.

Arabella swung her head back and forth, eyes darting between us. "Why?"

"I'll fill you in later," Esme answered.

Nodding a bit, I stood.

"Whoa, whoa." Esme pointed to the plate. "Eat your bloody cake."

"Esme."

"No, I mean it."

I slowly slid back into my seat and used my fingers to eat. The vanilla breading exploded on my tongue, then the raspberry filling coated the roof of my mouth. The buttercream frosting really sent me back to Heaven, even without my wings.

"You do make delicious cake," I said between chews. When the last of the delicious dessert slid down my throat, my fingers came away clean, and I looked up at them. "Thank you." I got up and said my goodbyes, heading for the door. As I opened it, the bell rang, and Esme's voice stopped me.

"Where are your wings?"

With my eyes glued to the pavement, I said, "Levi chopped them off."

I let the glass door close behind me.

"We ready?" I asked, glanced at Liam, then Matthew.

"Ready," they both said at the same time.

We entered the courtroom.

Grand walls, pews lined on both sides, a judge bench at the head.

I couldn't see any other doors aside from the one we'd entered.

The furniture has been made of wood with gilded details, marble flooring beneath our feet.

Matthew gestured for us to move towards the front and we took our spots.

As Thrones filled in and a judge dropped into his seat, I fixed my skirt.

I changed my attire to a white dress to hopefully try and look presentable. My scars were on full display as I shoved down the memory.

Levi had taken a piece of me, the piece of me I had left through all this hell we'd been through. Murdered too young. Lost two charges. My own boyfriend kidnapped. Wings removed.

He stole my dignity along with them, and I couldn't seem to bury the hatchet no matter how hard I tried. Horror branded itself to my skin when my wings were taken. I was now closer to a weapon than my own soul.

And somehow, everyone expected me to move on as if it'd never happened at all.

Matthew stayed standing.

The gavel sounded off the block.

The Archangel opened his mouth, but the judge opened his first.

"We have decided this case is a waste of our time and there's nothing we can do about this. Ayden Dyer is a fallen angel and that cannot be reversed."

Matthew stepped forwards. "Sir, Liam wasn't supposed to even be here." He threw his arm back at the killer himself. The soul that slipped through the cracks, the blemish to Heaven's name.

"Yet he is, and we don't believe in mistakes." He hit the sound block again. "Court is dismissed."

I shot up from my chair, shaking my head. "That's not fair! You didn't even give us a chance!"

"I made my decision." He nodded.

I choked on a laugh. "So the fallen angels took my wings for nothing? This is absurd!" I splayed my palms out on the surface of the tabletop. "We're not saying Ayden is a mistake. We're saying he was kidnapped and poisoned. How is any of that just?"

He shot me a stern look. "Miss Wilson, you will not speak to us that way. You've made your decisions; we made ours. Court *dismissed*," he spat.

A slap to the face. I stumbled back, energy fleeing my form.

As they piled out of the courtroom and eventually kicked us out, I stomped on a cloud. "They can't do that!" The tears started to pour down my cheeks. "Is it my fault? Did I lose my wings because of this? I never wanted Ayden Dyer! I didn't want to fall in love with him! Is this my punishment?" Another sob ripped through me. "He rightfully ended up here, and they're telling me that none of us are safe. The fallen angels can take everything from us and we can't advocate for ourselves. How is this paradise? How can that be fair?" I pressed the back of my hand to my mouth, stifling more cries. "What's the point of doing good and getting into Heaven if this is what can happen and nobody cares to correct it? Nobody will do anything. Do we matter at all in the grand scheme of things? Does

Ayden not matter to anyone but me and his family?"

Matthew's hand landed on my shoulder. "Eliana."

"I don't want to hear it." I dropped my arms.

Liam stayed silent on the whole matter, and *good* he did. Part of me wanted to shake him for not speaking up, but the other part of me knew if he had, I'd punch him.

"Eliana," he started again, "please. What they did in there today was...unethical." I glanced at him, noting the way he avoided *unbiblical.* Nobody knew if it was or not. "I've heard your case. I've seen the evidence, gotten to know you all as people, and the way they tossed you out as if you were a bug under their shoe was abhorrent. That's not right. I'm on your side, okay? I know it won't help much, but I'll do my best."

I went to wipe my eyes only to realize they were already dry. "Why? You suddenly understand because you like Naeva?"

"No," he sputtered. "I understand because no soul deserves to be treated this way. Nobody should feel like they don't mean anything in Heaven. This is paradise, or was supposed to be, for *everyone.* I wholeheartedly believe in that, and if someone doesn't feel that way, it's my mission to make it right. That's my purpose. I'm not going to abandon you."

Chills tingled from my stomach down to my shins.

Hearing those words uttered from Matthew rocked my morality in a way I didn't know I needed. After my parents... After Liam. After losing Ayden. I needed someone to be on my side, and it was silly, but it gave me an ounce of light.

"Well..." I nodded a bit, closing my eyes. "Thank you."

"I take this seriously." He removed his palm. "No angel should lose their wings and then be made some spectacle in front of the Thrones. You're not an example for them, okay? And it was never your fault. To blame that on you is disgusting behavior."

My shoulders sagged. “I suppose...”

“I now see what you see.” He grumbled. “I see the unfairness and the lack of empathy around here. I will never associate with that again. You can count on me.”

“What if you get into trouble?” I opened my eyes to peer up at him.

He shrugged off their insults and judgment. “Then be it. Even if it puts my position in jeopardy, I’m going to fight for what I believe in, for what we were always supposed to stand for. Souls.”

I waited a good week, just in case.

But last night was not what I expected. Maybe it had been a theory. However, hearing the words said aloud only made it more surreal.

"You were right. Our father is a fallen angel, and Ayden's the victim of it all."

Now I knew why they targeted us, why this had been such a complicated mess in the first place.

And I had to be the one to tell him what I knew.

I checked the windows every few seconds, assuming he'd show up just in time. But Ayden didn't make an appearance like he promised.

Had he stood me up?

No, he would never.

What if finding out what he was, what he could do, had been the factor in him realizing he was too good—or not good enough for me? Maybe out of my league, or a hazard.

I hated when he decided shit like that.

The sun set behind the trees, rays spilling between the trunks. Dusk came too early, and I was left comforted in the darkness of the cabin itself.

"I hoped for more of us," I whispered to anyone willing to listen. "You and me, Ayden. We were meant to be in this together."

I slid down the wall and pulled my knees to my chest, allowing the cold to seep into my soul and sing me lullabies. At one point, they must have worked, because when I opened my eyes to the pitch black of the living room, I screamed as a knock echoed.

Something tugged at my heart once again.

Turning my head, I slowly climbed to my feet and approached the door, pulling it open. "Ayden." I cleared my throat. "I didn't think you were coming."

"Yet you stayed," he joked as he entered.

The moonlight bounced off bloody cuts slashed over every inch of his back.

With a gasp, I pulled him further inside, slamming the door. "What the hell happened?"

He let out a snicker, dropping onto the torn couch. "You don't want to know." He rubbed his eyes with his forefinger and his thumb.

Ripping pieces of my white shirt, I sat beside him. "Then let me at least clean you up." I'd changed from that stupid white gown to my black slacks, and a new white shirt. One that fit my chest better and didn't remind me of how much I had lost in a short time.

His hand landed on mine. "You do too much for me and I never do enough."

"Don't start with that nonsense." I dabbed the blood from the cuts I *could* see. Just how many did they carve into his soul? "You've done plenty. Besides, that's not how love works. You don't keep a record of wrongs or mark down every time you do them a favor just to match it. You just...love them as they are and do your best to take care of them. Whatever that looks like." The crimson stained the eggshell silk. "You did enough, Ayden. You saved me. You've always been enough. Please know that." I dabbed blood from the cut on his lip. "Your family loves you. I love you. No matter what happens. We've always decided that, because love isn't conditional. I can't switch it off. Even if you're poisoned. Even if..." I traced my fingers down his chest. "Even if you're more than they say."

He wrapped his fingers around my wrist, careful not to press too hard. "You saved *me*, Angel."

"I'm not an angel anymore," I mumbled. "No use calling me that. I lost my wings."

I'd been nothing more than a disgrace to angels everywhere.

He reached out, grabbing my jaw and pulling me closer. "No. You saved me, *Angel.* I was nothing before you. I was out there wreaking havoc on the world, leaving my mark in the worst ways. You showed me that I mattered regardless. You helped me learn to love myself again."

"You saved yourself. I merely guided you in the right direction." I shrugged, tearing another strip off my shirt.

His voice softened, his green eyes never wavering from mine. "Exactly. You saved me from myself. You were called my guardian angel for a reason, and nobody can take that away from you." He traced his knuckle down my cheek.

I rooted myself where I sat on the couch as I twirled my finger. "Turn around so I can get your back."

He groaned as he flipped himself around so I could tend to the wounds he couldn't reach. They were much larger, running down him in all directions, oozing blood.

As if an artist had used crosshatching, his soul the canvas.

"Ayden Dyer, you're going to tell me right now what happened out there."

He released a sigh, not out of resistance but rather exhaustion. "You saw. I just had to get you out of there, and when I returned to Hell, I lost it. What Levi did to you was unfair and I couldn't hold it together anymore. What you saw didn't happen this time, and they overpowered me. Decided to show me what happens when I disobey. They tortured me for days."

I soaked up as much blood as I could. "I don't get it, Ayden. You're a fallen angel. You shouldn't *be able* to bleed in Hell."

He winced, hissing. "Well, I do. Maybe it's because I'm not like them entirely. They kidnapped me. I didn't go willingly. I didn't choose that fate."

As I cleaned up the last of the blood, I frowned. "And here? Why is it hurting you on earth? You shouldn't feel a thing."

He had no answer to that.

"I'm done. Not sure I can do much about the bandage. I mean, I could run to a store and steal some. Getting some from Heaven could take a little longer."

"Shh," he hushed as he turned to face me, grabbing my face. "I'll be okay. I'm already dead. This is nothing."

"It still breaks my heart to see it." I grabbed his hands, peeling them from my cheeks and lowering them into my lap. "Don't downplay your pain."

He lifted my fingers to his lips, pressing a soft kiss to my knuckles. "You help distract me."

I debated telling him the court threw out the case. It'd make him feel worse. Matthew was going to help us, anyway.

But...

"Ayden, there's something you should know."

He furrowed his brows. "What is that?"

I squeezed his palms. "Your father isn't human." I wet my lips. "Your father is a fallen angel, and Esme confirmed it for me. Which makes you...Nephilim. This is why they've been targeting us from the start."

More of her words rung in my head. *"But if they had never poisoned him, they would have found other ways to destroy his happiness, and yours, for simply loving him at all."*

I shook my head, eyes stuck on the floorboards. "I don't know what it means for the future but I know it means Heaven won't be on our side. You're an abomination. And what I assume is that they assigned you to me to see if you could be saved. You were, but the fallen angels poisoned you, and to them that means you're no different from the rest. They're not going to want to help you anymore."

Ayden's throat bobbed. "Oh."

I slid my fingers between his. "But I'll never leave you. Ever. I promise you that. Neither with your family, and..." I shivered, not sure if I should tell Matthew what I found out. Would he leave or continue to fight?

"We'll get through this together, however we have to," I finished.

Something swirled around in his eyes as they darkened. Animosity? Hurt? Maybe both?

I lowered my tone. "Ayden?"

"I've been cursed since I was conceived is what you're saying," he mumbled.

"No." I grabbed his cheeks, forcing him to look at me. Resting my forehead against his, I kissed him sweetly. "Not cursed. Never cursed. You were just dealt a horrible hand. You have your family, and me. And we'll never abandon you. I know it doesn't count for much but—"

He cut me off with a rushed kiss.

We pulled away for a second, before he closed the distance again.

I tasted the emotions that made him up as the cake reminded me of who I fell in love with.

I had no regrets.

As I deepened it, he leaned into me more, his hands dipping into the rough cushions on either side of my hips. Without sparing a thought, I laid back, taking every second of him in. The scent of cigarettes, which hadn't bothered me all that much. The taste of raspberries. Our kiss filling the room, a small groan escaping him as I attempted to grab his back.

I ripped away with wide eyes. "Oh my gosh, Ayden. I'm so sorry. I forgot and—" I swallowed. "I'm sorry." His skin was dry, with prominent ridges beneath my fingers. Scorching, even, as heat stayed trapped under the surface.

I longed to see his smile instead of his scars.

His crude jokes never bothered me to the fullest extent, and that'd been because they made him laugh. His laughter cured the cracks in my heart.

"I'll be fine. Really." He grabbed my hands, rubbing his thumbs along my palm. "I think you should opt for this anyway." He lifted them to his hair.

With a snort, I threaded them through. "Okay, Mr. Dyer," I teased.

An eyebrow lifted as he lowered himself, planting kisses to my jaw. He trailed up to my ear, whispering, "It's not for me, Angel."

Unsure of what he meant, I let him return to leaving a trail of hot promises along my throat.

His fingers grazed my wrists as he began to unbutton my shirt. He left me ample time to say no if I needed to. Or if I couldn't do that, my body could say it for me. Because somehow, Ayden knew me too well.

Or maybe he was just that experienced with women.

I much preferred the former reasoning.

A strange sensation tingled in my lower abdomen as he pulled the button free. That same feeling grew into something more. Warm, painful, desperate. Moving further south with Ayden's touch.

He'd managed to pull down the zipper before he paused, lifting his eyes. "Angel."

I didn't know where to look, or to put my hands—and thank Ayden for figuring that part out for me. "Hm?"

"I won't do anything you don't want."

My lips parted, as if I was able to say something. But it lodged in my throat.

After another minute of hovering, he shook his head. "We won't do this. Okay? Not until you're comfortable."

Before he could pull away, I blurted, "I am!" I exhaled. "I'm comfortable, Ayden, with you."

I wanted to say so much more.

How surreal it was to be laying here with Ayden Dyer. To be exposed. To lay bare all my emotions and my love. To promise him that he'd always have me and hope he felt that same way in return. That he wouldn't break my heart into a million pieces.

Raw.

It had been the most vulnerable I'd ever been with someone.

He nodded slightly. "Okay. I'll ease you into it. And you can always stop anytime."

Those words hugged me, tightening around my middle. I believed him, too. He made me feel safe, and I knew I could trust him.

Because even if we'd been through Hell and back, he was always careful with me when I needed it most.

Hooking his fingers on the hem of my slacks, he pulled them down my legs, and I closed my eyes to avoid seeing his reaction.

He kept his word.

The one person I could count on to have my back and support me kept his promise. He proved to me that he was there when the rest of the world crumbled. He took it slow, showing me feelings I couldn't comprehend on my own.

And I indeed needed that hold on his hair.

But more importantly, I needed that grasp on his heart.

I feared I wouldn't survive this afterlife without it.

HYPOCRITE

I loathed this part, but it was only fair to tell him the truth.

And so I said the words we all dreaded to hear.

The Heavenly Court dismissed our case.

"Nonsense," Ayden spat with the shake of his head. "I don't think it's that big of a deal. He must know they kidnapped me. They turned me into this monster. I rightfully made Heaven. I did my part, didn't I? Why can't the Thrones do theirs?"

My chest tightened. My heart began to ache. Why was life so utterly unfair? Why were we the laughingstock of the afterlife?

"I don't know. I wish I had answers," I said in a quieter tone.

"You'd think I'm no more than a flyspeck for such troubles they face. They'd accept the case, confirm it, and judge in our favor. Instead, they threw it out. Is that it? Do I not matter at all because I'm just one soul? This shouldn't even be allowed."

It shouldn't have been.

But again, I recalled the way events played out. A mark prevented souls from entering Heaven. Black wings were only one of those.

Regardless, it hadn't been his fault. They forced him into this fate. I was going to rip them to shreds. I would take pride as they begged me for mercy before I crushed them into nothing but ash. A warning against everyone else, and I was not going to sit idly.

"Maybe it's wrong of me, but if Heaven won't have our backs, why should I have theirs? Why should I continue to fight for what's right? What's right is giving people free will, and you had that. You proved your place, and they took everything from you. They laughed in your face and spat on it. What's right is protecting those you call yours, and we were *supposed to be* part of Heaven." I twisted away, knees tucked into my chest as I chewed the insides of my cheeks. "I want them all to fucking understand. I want karma to bite. I want them to get a taste of their own medicine."

Arms wrapped around me, he rested his cheek to my shoulder. "Don't jeopardize your soul for me. I couldn't bear it. Even if this side of you is hot."

"It's about to be very hot, then." And I meant that in the sense of temperature, because I'd been to Hell countless times. They didn't care about us from the start.

A knock echoed, and both our heads snapped up. I glanced back at Ayden with my brows furrowed, and he shrugged. "Nobody is supposed to know about this cabin." He climbed up from the couch and approached, slowly opening it. "What are you doing here?"

"I stumbled upon a woman who said you might be here!" *Sunny Smith.*

Did Naeva tell her? What the *hell*?

Ayden grumbled. "And you came because?"

"Because I want to help."

Help?

Words I also dreaded to hear.

Everything that filled my ears these days was more bad news after the other.

"Sunny, I'm fine. I don't need it. Really. You don't need to drag yourself into this." I regretted ever telling her in the first place.

"Well, didn't it work? My advice?" she practically chirped.

Advice?

"Mhm," he replied.

She pushed her way into the cabin with a smile, pausing when she saw me sitting on the couch with no pants on. "Oh." Her cheeks tinted. "Hello."

I quickly scrambled for my pants, pulling them up and fixing them before I fixed the buttons on my shirt. "Sunny," I said as I cleared my throat, trying to shove down the jealousy bubbling inside.

"I didn't realize..."

"Elli!" another familiar voice shouted.

Anxiety seized my limbs, weighing me down.

I turned to find Selene popping her head in, and my world tilted on its axis. "What are you doing here?" A laugh slipped out with a shaky breath. Ayden and Selene in the same room?

What if things went awry?

What if they figured out what Liam did?

Sunny pointed. "She told me you'd be here. Well, Ayden would be. I didn't realize he...had company." She let out a nervous giggle.

Why had my dead *friend*—and nothing else—told Sunny that my boyfriend would be here? Why send her in at all? Was I missing something?

Selene's eyes darted between Ayden and I, a smirk beginning to form. "Oh? What did we stumble upon here?"

Now it'd been *my* turn to blush. "Uh, it was just... Nothing."

Ayden snorted, then muttered, "I wouldn't call that nothing, Love."

Selene wiggled her brows. "Did you finally have sex?"

My eyes widened as I shook my head. "No, no, it wasn't like that." Did Selene feel some type of way about it? She showed no envy, and that sent a jab to my heart. Why had I wanted her to be jealous?

Sunny dropped her head, averting her gaze.

Chewing my cheeks some more, I cleared my throat. "We...uh. We simply just..." How did I say the words?

Ayden closed the gap between us, grasping my chin and pressing a possessive kiss onto my lips. Maybe it'd been for show, but I didn't mind at all. "Angel finally learned what a tongue feels like." He chuckled as he crossed his arms.

Sunny leaned into Selene, whispering, "I found her without any pants on."

And seeing as I didn't need to wear underwear, it'd all been out there. Laid out bare.

"I'm very impressed, Elli," my best friend exclaimed. "Impressed and proud."

"Can we change the subject" tumbled out of my mouth like a bag of rocks. Anything but this topic. "Ayden's a pervert, we get that. But he's an angel now, or should be, and he's a different man."

He snorted. "Angel, I've always been one. That's inevitable."

"Oh! The whole gang's here." Liam waved. "Okay, so who's gonna be Scooby, exactly?"

I ran a hand down my face with a groan. "Liam."

Ayden scowled. "Why's he here?"

Selene inched herself towards the corner, away from our murderer.

Pressing my lips together, I frowned. "Did I forget to mention that Naeva shot Liam and now he's in love with me?"

"Naeva?" His eyes narrowed. "Is this what he meant when I found the two of you in Hell?"

Liam dropped onto the couch. "Yeah. Cupid. I mean, I don't know the gritty details. Besides, it'll all be dandy when it gets sorted out.

You'll get back into Heaven and I'll go rot in Hell where I belong. Although I can't say for sure when. The court threw out our case, and Matt is actually pretty upset about it, but he's warming up to me." He flashed a smile.

Ayden growled. "Is that true?" He peered up at me.

I clasped my hands in front of myself. "Yeah. And this dumbass actually believes that I could reciprocate!" I threw my arm towards the killer. "Can you believe that? He says I'm remembering my death wrong, that I was actually poisoned. That's absurd."

"That wasn't— Nevermind," he grumbled. "Did you ever see your body? After your death?" the *oh-so-wonderful love of my life* asked.

"Well, no. I went to the funeral and my mother went on and on about how much they loved me and I couldn't bear it anymore." I squeezed my hands into fists, pressing them into my thighs. "He says I kissed him. Before he killed me. I'd never betray Selene like that. I didn't have feelings for him."

Liam's eyes darted back and forth.

The room fell silent.

"Someone say something," I demanded.

"What are we supposed to say, Angel?" His green eyes bore into mine. "None of us were there. We can't confirm or deny anything."

A laugh escaped my throat, dry and tasting of dirt. "In what world would I forget such details?"

He shrugged. "I'm not saying you would. Just keep an open mind, alright?"

"What the fuck does that mean?" I crossed my arms.

He threw his hands up. "I'm just saying things have been a little strange lately, given what information is beginning to surface. About me, about you. I'm starting to believe anything is possible. Bloody hell, I don't know what to believe anymore."

"You're wrong, Ayden. You're a damn liar, and I'm not going to take this kind of talk from you of all people." I narrowed my eyes on Sunny. "You. You mentioned earlier you gave him advice. What was that about?"

She scratched her head. "Ah, yes. That. I just told him to...enhance his attractiveness."

My blood began to sizzle.

"Ayden was at the bar, and I found him there. He made it clear to me that what we had was over." A desolate smile passed her lips. "Yeah, I'm very much in love with Ayden, but he loves you now, and I decided to help him figure out how to keep you on your toes. He has a duty to be your eye candy, right?"

Ice dropped into my hot veins, sending my body into some kind of frenzy.

Sunny had helped my boyfriend look good for *me*.

I'd been a horrible person for trying to go to war over a man.

Loosening my fists and wiggling my fingers, I whispered, "Thank you."

I glanced over at Selene leaning against the wall with an unrecognizable look in her eye. Confusion? No. Curiosity, maybe? Gears were turning, and someone was home. What looked like an ounce of rage flickered in the depth of her walnut irises, but I must have been mistaken.

"Hey," Ayden said. When he captured my full attention, he waved me over.

I slowly walked over, and when I was within reach, he leaned forwards, wrapped his hands around the back of my thighs, and yanked me into his lap. He bit back the pain in his shoulders. "You and me, okay? If you're going to promise that I won't get rid of you that easily, then I make that same promise tenfold." His thumb grazed my bottom lip.

When his other hand squeezed my hip, I shook my head. "Please, everyone's around."

"So. They invaded *our* private space." As his fingers brushed the skin under my shirt, chills slithered over every inch of me.

I closed my eyes to attempt to refocus my mind. "You want them to watch?"

With a low chuckle, he pressed his lips to my collarbone. "I really don't care. I'm not too concerned with that."

"You should care; you should be concerned." I grabbed his face, pulling it away from me. "Because I'm not so sure you want Liam to see any part of that."

Liam. The murderer, the criminal, the serial killer. I hadn't really been that concerned with him, or Sunny—even as much as I didn't want to be jealous of her, I still was.

Selene was the one on my mind. And for once, I hadn't meant it like that.

No fleeting thoughts of two roommates, two best friends tumbling home late from a party, one sober and the other drunk. I wasn't sure which one was which either. The drunk one of us collapsed into the bed, the sober one helping the other get changed into comfortable clothes only to fall asleep, keeping water and medicine on standby. A trash can, too.

An early morning. A hangover. A thank you. An accidental kiss. A friendship forever ruined by the feelings of one.

Thank God I never made that mistake.

No, it wasn't like that.

What crossed my mind was the way Selene studied us, the way she leaned against the wall as if she owned us. I didn't like that theory.

Something had been off tonight.

Because why had she sent Sunny here, to Ayden, thinking he was the only one home?

I needed to confront her. I was tired. I was done waiting, done being a doormat.

I was a woman on fire and ready to burn whoever got in my way.

"I'm sorry," Dad said. As if it'd be enough.

"We had a right to know," I replied, glancing at my older sisters. "It affects us. I understand wanting to protect us, but we had a *right* to know. Heaven knew. Lucifer knew."

"I didn't think you were going to die so early. I thought I had time."

"That's just it! Nobody knows. We all think we have time. We don't expect to die so early unless doctors tell you otherwise and you have time to prepare. I was caught in a crossfire that I know Angel blames herself for." I waved him off. "It doesn't matter anymore."

Mum rested her hand on his shoulder. "You're right. We were wrong. It affected your soul just as much as ours."

"What does this mean?" Esme asked. "For us?"

I shrugged. "They're trying to sort it out. But according to my girlfriend, they wanted to see if they could save us from damnation. It worked, until it didn't. I still have urges. I want to steal, drink. Cause riots. I want to fuck Angel senseless and it doesn't help that she wants the same." I rubbed my hands.

"Okay, that was a little too much information," Esme said with a snicker.

"Things are different. If they do reverse it, what then? I'm Nephilim. They all know now. I have these shadows, and I'm a giant when things get out of control. Does it go away? Is it always there?"

Mum glanced down at Dad while he returned her gaze. "It's hard to say."

He stated, "Not sure they can reverse it." *Father of the year, everyone.*

"Dad!" Arabella gasped. "Way to be optimistic."

He stood, pulling his shirt off. Large black wings unfolded before us, fanning out. They extended a few feet beyond the couch. And I had to keep myself contained for the massive span they were.

It had just occurred to me I'd never seen my dad shirtless before.

"This is what we are. It's in your DNA. Maybe you did make it to Heaven. Maybe there is a chance your sisters can be saved, but they can't remove the poison. They can't remove who you really are. It's fused itself to you, Ayden."

One looked at Esme and Arabella, and I knew. They were admiring the sight of our father's origins, while also battling the negative emotions that came with reality.

We'd been cursed since we were a thought.

"That's very reassuring. Thanks, Dad," I said with sarcasm.

"I didn't see any point in lying to you anymore. You and your sisters are going to pay for what we did, and for that, we will always bear the shame of what we've put you through."

"Didn't stop you two from shagging like crazy." I leaned back against the couch. "Did you ever stop to think about how we'd be affected?"

"Of course we did!" Mum stepped forward. "We couldn't stop

relaying the consequences. But Ayden, you've seen it. Haven't you? You've experienced that kind of love." Love didn't have to mean creating new life to fill the holes in your own relationship. It didn't have to mean being selfish and dragging your own children down with you.

Angel's laugh echoed in my mind. Her blue eyes sparkled in the sunlight, golden halo cascading down her back, whipping around her face as she spun to look at me and scold me for making such jokes.

Her soft touch.

Her hesitation to break rules.

She'd had such a knack for reminding me that I had a duty to do right by myself, and others.

The way my name rolled off her tongue like melted butter ready to be added to a fresh bake mix.

She smelled of the salty air when you travelled to the coast. Summer promises. The plans you'd make and ponder on for months until they finally came around and passed by. Even the second they did, you'd still be reminiscing and doing everything to relive that moment again, no matter what it took.

Every little thing reminded you of that vacation.

"Ayden?" Mum interrupted.

Lifting my arms to the back of the couch, I exhaled. "Yeah. I know what that's like. You can't keep yourself away no matter what you do. You can't get them out of your head. You can't help but love them anyway, even if it tears you apart. You allow yourself to be ruined, to be consumed by their soul. You become theirs and don't care what it costs you. All you care about is what it costs them."

Arabella had scooted closer to me. "But you and Eliana still see each other, right?"

"Of course. Every time I stop her, she weaves her way back in. I can't keep her at arm's length." I shook my head. "She's stubborn, just as stubborn as when I first met her."

"She's a keeper," Dad added.

Esme reached forward. "I'm going to suggest something, and you have to hear me out. When this is over and you come out together, you have to marry her. Okay? No more waiting. You're so in love it's not even funny."

"She's irritating." I laughed. "But she's irritating in the sense that you miss her presence every time she's not around, because you know she's the only one around who talks sense." I met Esme's eyes. "That's what I'm afraid of."

"That she'll say no? Or that you're going to settle for one woman?" She cocked her head.

"That she'll say *yes*," I answered. "What if she realises she made a mistake? What if there's someone better, like that book nerd in the library?"

A frown disgraced her. "What makes you think he's better? Because he looks like a nice guy? Nice guys are not always the best for someone. Do you love her?"

"Of course."

"Do you promise to always love her?"

"Yeah."

"Do you want to protect her?"

"Always."

"You treat her like a queen and think someone else is going to come along and do better than that? You dickhead, stop putting yourself down! You constantly pull that shit. You always try to make yourself worthless, and you're not. She loves you. Isn't that enough proof? Or is she wrong? Are you trying to imply that the woman you love is both wrong and stupid for loving someone like you?"

I grumbled. "I see your point."

"Good." She slapped my leg. "You're a twat, you know that?"

That I did know.

"But only I can call you that. Not you, not anyone else. Just me. And Arabella. Because we gotta keep you humble while your girlfriend lifts your ego. Healthy balance."

Arabella nodded with a grin. "She's right about that. Esme is always right."

I folded my arms across my chest.

I sat next to her, looking over every few seconds to check if she was still there. To ensure she wasn't about to leave again. I doubt she could, given all the pain. It didn't make me feel much better. She was stuck in my presence because of me.

She rested with her knees to her chest, expression blank. She was impossible to read, and I wanted her to say something. Anything. Anything about how much she hated me.

I finally asked, "Are you alright?"

"Define alright. Am I still here? I suppose I am." That'd been code for not alright.

"We should talk about...everything that conspired the past week." I resisted the urge to grab her hand.

She lowered her knees and slipped a blanket over them. "What is there to talk about? You made it clear I'm nothing to you, and that's fine. I could never expect you to feel the same. It was wrong of me to run away and let them torture you."

Those words stung to the core.

I was an absolute dick.

"Me? Angel, I wasn't the only one tortured. I'd seen you cry, but seeing you weak and vulnerable, that was the worst. *You have scars from that." I waved my hands over the wounds. I couldn't stop replaying the scenes in my head. When they ripped her dress off, when they whipped her, when she couldn't take it anymore but she chose to anyway to protect me. Why would she go and do something so*

reckless and stupid? I wasn't worth that much agony.

The noticeable wince from her sent shame spiralling down from head to toe. I was forever bathing in it.

"It's fine. *I deserve it for giving you over to them. I'm not a very good guardian angel," she said.*

Rubbing my neck, I replied, "I'm the one who sent you running. Nobody deserves to be tortured to the point of breaking. All you did was confess your feelings and I responded with insults. You were targeted and tortured because I failed you."

She folded her hands between her thighs, fidgeting slightly. "Ayden, being hurt doesn't excuse getting you into that situation. If I were hurt after my friend betrayed me, would it be okay if I left her behind to drive herself home while drunk? No. Feelings get us into a lot of trouble, and mine happened to do just that."

She was trying to wear the blame all by herself. I'd fucking kill to make sure that didn't happen again.

"Were you lying? You told them I can't change. I don't think that's a lie." I wanted to believe it wasn't, but a childhood of trauma proved otherwise.

My sister came out with our tea, setting the cups down on the table next to us. "I wish I could help speed up this healing process. You both look brutal." She shot me a look as if this was all my fault.

That was fair.

I slapped my thighs and practically jumped from the couch. "You can't do anything. Nobody can save me."

I hated saying the words, but I needed to redirect all responsibility onto me. I needed to own up to my mistakes.

The agony she'd gone through for my sake was unfair. The misery I witnessed her fight off when we returned with countless cuts all over us, hurting us both the same.

"Angel, look at me." That didn't work. "Eliana, look at me." She

turned her head my way.

As much as I loved calling her Angel, her real name slipped from my tongue too easily. I savoured the taste of it.

"You'll never believe it wasn't your fault, will you? Why don't we agree it was both of us? I said bad things; you let your pain control your words. We both could have handled it differently than we did."

She said nothing.

I leaned closer. "What you did was stupid. Taking the torture for me like that—that was stupid."

"I did it because I love you. You may not like it, but I can't control how I feel. When you love someone, you take the pain away from them, upon yourself."

She loved me. She loved me; she loved me. Why did she have to go and tell me that? Why did she want to break her own heart all over again? I wasn't worthy of her love.

I placed my palm on her arm, pulling her closer. I could kiss her. I could end both of our pain, but what would it achieve? I was still dating Sunny. I'd become a cheater. I'd be leading her on for no reason.

I leaned in, resting my chin over her hair. I wrapped her in my arms like a present. Mine. My guardian angel, and nobody else's. Forever.

Why couldn't I keep her? Why couldn't we stay this way? Why did she have to go and admit her feelings when we had such a good thing going?

Why did I open my stupid fucking mouth?

But she didn't fight it or fight me.

"You're a fighter, are you not? How did fallen angels manage to control you?" I whispered against her soft waves.

She sucked in air before releasing it, those bright blue eyes peering up at me. "I didn't fight back all that much. There was no use in it. I tried to..." She closed them. "I told them to go after you since you were the one they really wanted."

I attempted to clear my throat. "And I tried to stop them, but when they told me that you gave my soul to them, I had no strength then. I was in shock that the Angel I knew would do that," I paused. "It was true. You did."

She twisted her head, hiding it in my chest. My skin absorbed her tears, her suffering becoming my own. I began stroking her hair.

The subtle scent of salty waves and damp earth swarmed me. I revelled in it.

Lowering my voice, I said, "But I deserved it for the things I said to you. Telling you that you're nothing isn't right. I'm sorry for that and sorry for getting you into that situation to begin with. My mum taught me better."

She pulled herself away from me and wiped her cheeks. "I'm sorry, too." One glance at the clock. She got up, leaving me aching for more. "It's time to change our bandages. It's not as if I need it but I want it to soothe the pain. I did not miss this part of being human."

I had a duty to make it up to her, even if she didn't agree. I'd never redeemed myself after the trouble I got her into with Hell. To think that now they'd taken her wings, and that I couldn't stop reminding her how much I ached to keep her soul tethered to mine for eternity. I craved the taste of her every morning—and every night. Every waking hour.

She dropped beside me with the first aid kit in hand. "We can't allow the gauze to get all gross. I was never a doctor, but I knew enough about first aid to know the importance of taking care of wounds." Why had that been necessary to explain? Was she covering for something?

Giving her my back, I rubbed the tiredness from my eyes. "Why are you doing this?"

Her touch was gentle, peeling away my bandages. There'd been some stinging, but it was bearable. "Why am I helping you? Because that's what you do when you love someone."

There it was again.

Love.

I winced as she dabbed the wounds, biting back the pain. Whatever power I still had, I used that to hide the agony I was in just to keep her from riddling herself with more guilt.

To keep her from noticing the way my muscles flexed under her touch.

When she laid the bandages to protect every fresh injury from infection, I held my breath. I waited for burning. But I focused on the brush of her fingers, their softness, and the proximity in which she was.

"I'm done."

I heard footsteps and immediately turned to find her heading back to the bathroom. "Where are you going?"

She spun on her heel to face me, looking as naive as ever. "To get my bandages changed."

I owed her that.

"Why don't I just do it myself? Since we're here. It'll be part of my apology." I patted the spot beside me.

She closed the gap and plopped back down.

Slowly pulling the straps of her white gown from her shoulders, she crossed her arms over her chest to hold the front together.

"Do these leave scars?" I asked, pulling back bloody gauze.

"They will. Hell is the one place that can physically hurt angels, so it'll leave scars."

I took my time to ensure I didn't make things worse. I gently pulled her wings away to make sure every inch of her back had been cleaned and on the journey to recovery. One last bandage and... "All done."

She pulled her dress back up as I gave her some privacy.

Her voice came out small, fragile. "Why are you being so nice to me? You're claiming you haven't changed but you're playing the good guy."

Something about her penetrated all the walls I'd built. She had managed to knock each one down as she climbed through and held her hands up to show she was harmless. Was she, though?

She was too easy to trust, and that made her far more dangerous.

However, I was tempted to give her my heart and ask her to keep it safe.

Instead, I flashed her my smirk. "That's what friends do, Angel."

"You're both right," I mumbled. "I can be the man she deserves."

"Don't forget it!" Esme exclaimed from the kitchen. "That we're always right, I mean."

"I didn't say that."

"That's what I heard." She wiggled her brows.

I dismissed her.

"I may as well bake," I muttered as I entered the kitchen. Not that my parents or my sisters would turn me away. A family of bakers. The perfect picture. The American Dream. Or however that shit worked.

Esme and Arabella helped me get the ingredients, from fruits to flour. I wasn't entirely sure what I wanted to bake, but when I glanced at them, I asked, "Can you guess what Angel's favorite dessert is?"

Esme took a stab at it with a guess of banana split, but it wasn't even close. I tried to give her a hint that it was Angel's favourite colour, but I couldn't recall if she knew what that was. "Favourite colour," she said in a low voice, tapping her chin. "Red! She told me when you went on your first date. Wait. Red." She tilted her head a bit, eyebrows flashing. "Red velvet."

Arabella snorted. "That's not—"

"You're right. Red velvet," I answered.

Arabella shot me a look of surprise. "Really? That's so simple.

And red velvet isn't even really red! It's just vanilla mixed with cocoa powder and food colouring."

I cocked an eyebrow. "I'm a baker just like you. Even if I am dead." And Nephilim.

I started mixing the ingredients. Flour, sugar, chocolate mix, eggs, butter. A dark, blood-coloured food dye. "But I won't give her less."

Esme leaned over the counter. "Oh my, is Ayden baking red velvet just for his girlfriend?"

The corner of my lips tilted upward.

As I stirred the batter, tension eased up in my body. Everything loosened, contentment spilling out of the bones and seeping into all the cracks to soften the blow.

Everything was going to be okay, right? It had to be.

I had Angel at my side.

And this cake.

Now blended together, I poured the batter into the non-stick pan, greased of course. After I slid it into the oven, the muted red mixture stared me in the face. "It'd be wrong not to lick the bowl, right?" I glanced up at Esme. Arabella practically had the whisk down her throat when she froze, our eyes locking together.

A good laugh left Esme as she jabbed her thumb at our sister. "Arabella might beat you to it."

Before she could grab it from me, I swiped it off the counter. "Too late!"

I took a spoon and scooped what little batter was left, licking it. Sure, raw egg was technically a risky situation. But I was already *dead*, and I clearly never worried much about the risks anyway.

My sisters were the butt of the joke though. That thought kept me sane.

Getting to dabble in the smell of cake, icing it, and knowing how happy it would make Angel was enough to keep me grounded.

I promised to return the container, eventually leaving them behind.

The closer I got, the more warmth spread in my chest.

When I entered the cabin, I found Angel lying on the couch. As soon as she spotted me, her eyes lit up and she sat up. "Hey."

"Hey," I said as I dropped beside her. "I brought you red velvet cake."

The sugar nearly melted into her bright blue eyes. "Really?" she squeaked. "Ayden, you shouldn't have!" But she dug into the delectable treat, moaning. That did something to me, but I shoved it down for another day.

I adjusted my pants, clearing my throat.

She managed to only eat three pieces before I put it on the kitchen counter.

Then she burrowed into my arms the second I laid back. "How did it go with your family?"

I wiped a bit of frosting from her lip, licking it from my finger. I perfected the dessert. There was no argument against that, and I knew she'd agree with me. My guardian angel. My muse. *My heart.*

"Same as usual. You know." I found my eyes wandering the ceiling, fingers stroking her hair. "You should know, Angel, that I'll do anything that means keeping you safe and promising you a better outcome."

"What's this about?" She peered up at me.

"Nothing." I scooped hair behind her ear. "I love you."

Her expression softened, tension fleeing every tight and twisted muscle. She rested her head against my chest. "I love you, too. But if you ever leave again, I'll march down to Hell and drag you back myself."

I let out a small laugh, closing my eyes. "I don't doubt you for a second."

Reporting to Hell, black wings, an urge to go drink in the bars—whatever it was—it weighed on me.

The heaviness of being nothing more than Nephilim. Son to a fallen angel who had disobeyed laws to fall in love with a human woman.

Yet I had been a human who fell in love with my own guardian angel, all the same...

I truly didn't understand how Angel still chose me time and time again. But I wanted to find out.

After she and Liam left, I followed them. At first they flew back up to Heaven, and I had to wait around for nearly a day. But when they did return to earth, I was there, watching them go to...another party.

Why?

Staying close behind without getting caught was a lot easier than it looked. The hard part rested solely on hearing the topic of conversation. I couldn't hear a bloody word.

Angel sipped on something in a red cup, knowing it was probably alcohol. As if the way Heaven was handling our situation had destroyed her faith in them.

Liam didn't drink anything. Instead, he shoved his hands into his pockets. Then the two of them headed outside into the backyard. They headed to a quieter spot, as quiet as it could be with music thumping in our ears, laughter ringing, and frat boys yelling about women or beer.

I still couldn't make out what they were saying.

Out of the corner of my eye, some drunk hit on a woman who attempted to reject his advances. He leaned too far into her bubble when she shoved him off. He stumbled back into some other women who shot him a nasty look as he laughed and called her a bitch.

She immediately disappeared into the house.

It was another woman who caught my attention though. The quiet one standing by herself, cup in hand. She scanned the area before retreating where more people grinded on one another.

From across the yard, another frat boy smacked his friend's arm, pointing and nodding toward the woman who just left, then he went inside, his friend scanning the area before following them both.

Something deep in my gut clawed its way up, growling. I had to trust it, too, and so I followed my instinct and trailed behind the guys who went wherever the woman went. As she sauntered up the steps, we all did. Them first. Then me.

The bedroom door closed behind them, locking.

My stomach twisted, a dull ache forming.

Without hesitation, I stepped through the door. The woman ripped her arm away from one, yelling at them to stop, to get off her. They took it as some sick joke, some game. Bile rose up in my throat when they shoved her onto the bed, the other guy already going for his belt.

The madness in me exploded. I became visible, yanking the one that'd been forcing his way on top and tossing him into a wall. He groaned as his other friend shouted.

Shooting them daggers, I scowled. "You two are going to run like pussies, you got it? I'll happily rip your dicks off if you try it again."

The alpha scrambled to his feet, debating on coming for me. When I lifted my black wings, his eyes widened. "Shit!" They booked it out of the room.

I hadn't realised I'd grown in size, too, until I glanced at the girl in the corner of the bed whose eyes had filled with terror.

Closing mine, I exhaled, allowing myself to return to whatever *normal* form I could. "I'm sorry to scare you. Do you have anyone to come get you?"

She slowly shook her head.

I cursed under my breath, not wanting to scare her further than I had. "Hold on, we'll find someone who can take you home safely." I headed for the door, pausing when she didn't jump off the bed to follow. "Come on. I may know someone who can take you."

She hurried to my side, chewing her chipped nails. As we headed down the stairs, she halted, grabbing my arm. I turned to catch the fear in her eyes. I followed her line of sight to see the men who'd attacked moments earlier.

When she met my gaze, she shook her head. "Can't you just take me home?"

I let out a sigh and grumbled. "If you're sure about that."

She nodded anyway.

I searched for a new route, nodding her toward the back door. We headed in that direction when another voice rang in my ears. A young man begged for them to leave him alone.

Nausea and something sinister clawed from my stomach up my throat, lodging itself until I choked.

"Stay here." I swung my head back toward the woman. "I mean it, don't move." I moved quickly toward the guy, shoving the two who'd been harassing him. A woman stood there, not saying much, with a cunning smile on her face.

Another culprit.

Crossing my arms, I faced the three of them. "Feel free to leave now."

Their amusement fell away as they turned to go. One wanker took a second, pointing at me. "Ayden? Is that you?"

Fuck. I forgot how recognisable I was around this city.

"I was never here." I grabbed the innocent one by the arm and hurried over to the woman. "Okay, you two. I'm walking you so you can get home safely, okay? This party is filled with a bunch of dickheads anyway."

As we exited, the smell of booze and sex faded into the musk of the dry summer air.

"What were they upset about?" I glanced at the man. He wore a light blue jean jacket with black jeans and a graphic tee underneath. His shaggy brown hair swept over his forehead, dangling in his eyes just the slightest.

He shrugged a bit. "If I tell you, you have to promise not to laugh."

I *wanted* to make that promise.

When I shot him another look, he rubbed his neck. "They found out I've never slept with a woman before and they were trying to..."

"They wanted to force you to sleep with one, huh?" the woman to my left asked, tilting her head to see from around me.

His face reddened as he nodded. "And you?"

Hugging herself, she rubbed her arms. Her dark blue dress did little to keep the cool air at bay. Although, here in Salt Lake, temperatures didn't drop all that much during the night. Back home, the heat would be gone before the sun finished setting, if the heat ever came at all that was.

"Two boys thought I'd make for a fun time...even though I didn't want that."

He frowned. "They're pieces of shits." He took his jacket off, handing it to her.

She looked at him as if he'd lost an eyeball just now. "I'm okay, really. I don't need your jacket."

"Just take it. You need it more than I do."

After a minute, she grabbed it and put it on. I held back a snort as she tried to subtly sniff it.

"Jake," he said.

"What?" Her brows furrowed.

"My name is Jake, by the way." He nodded.

"Oh." She smiled a little. "I'm Brittney."

Jake nudged me. "And I suppose you're Ayden?"

I shrugged a little. "I suppose I am."

I used to associate myself with these kinds of people. I'd party with them. Get drunk. Make excuses for the type of guys who would hit on women and take it hard when she said no. I'd justify the way they talked to these girls after being rejected by them.

I never once spoke my mind, never had her back. I silently watched, making my own bed full of rapists and pieces of shits. I had been no better. I'd been just as culpable.

Knowing who I was and the people I surrounded myself with, it made me sick to my stomach. Women deserved better. Guys like Jake deserved better. Angel deserved better than a man who'd been defined by sins. I still hadn't figured out why she loved me even after all the countless reasons she listed off.

"Okay, this is me," Brittney said as we stopped at the end of the pathway that led up to her door.

Jake waved a bit. "You sleep well."

She smiled right back at him. "Goodnight."

The two of us stood there, watching as she walked up to her door and disappeared inside.

Her safe haven.

"Okay, your turn." I grabbed Jake by the shoulder, patting it as I turned us around to go back toward his house.

The party had mostly died down when I returned. But I did find Liam and Angel still sitting in the backyard.

I leaned against a tree nearby, tuning in to the conversation. For once, I could make sense of it.

"I know, I know," she started. "It's silly. Something just wasn't right. Anyway, that's enough of that. The alcohol here is cheap." She smacked her lips together, peeking into her cup.

He laughed. "You know cheap alcohol?"

"Of course. I'm not uncultured, Liam. I tasted wine. Champagne. Vodka, tequila. Quite a bit, actually. My parents weren't around and I tried a few things, quickly figuring out that I hate alcohol in general." She swished her cup.

"It's an acquired taste."

She snorted. "Everyone says that, but I don't understand why you'd want to acquire it. It's not like it's greens. It's alcohol. It screws with you in the worst ways, and it's also a bitter taste. Not just a little, but a lot. And I know it's not because I hate bitter tastes. I love broccoli, and my coffee black. That's not it."

As he stared, another laugh echoed. "Try telling that to Ayden." He bumped her shoulder.

This time, she snickered. "He'd never listen." She tossed the remaining liquid into the grass. "I just wish he'd listen to me some of the time, like when I tell him he matters and that he's worthy. He's always downplaying himself. He tries hard to say he deserves the bottom of the barrel, and it hurts. He deserves to love himself. I see the way he wants to, but something is holding him back from getting there. This kidnapping has backtracked on all the progress we made."

Liam rested his arms on his knees, forearms forming an *X*. "I guarantee someone made him feel that way. You don't start believing that on your own."

"Someone? But his family..." She frowned. "His parents, and his sisters."

"Family extends beyond that. And sometimes it's someone else. My point is, somewhere along the way, someone important made him feel less than, and he was probably so impressionable that he believed that lie over time. It's not so easy to reverse that. All the terrible things he's done, those are excuses. They're covering for something far deeper."

Something too deep to tell anyone.

"Well, regardless, I'm still going to remind him. Every day if I have to. It's what I would have wanted. Besides, I don't think beating yourself up constantly is healthy or a means to do better. People won't strive to do better when they don't think they *deserve* better."

"Possibly," he said in a quiet tone. "Maybe sometimes they just want to prove otherwise, to shut that voice up for good."

"Did you mean that?" I asked Liam after he'd dropped Angel off in Heaven. The stars twinkled above us, the moon barely glowing.

"When you told her the other day that she was poisoned..."

He shrugged, sitting back against a trunk. "Why wouldn't I?" His eyes met mine. "Okay, don't answer that. Yeah, I meant it. I didn't slash her throat, Ayden. I poisoned her. It's easy to clean up. Blood is messy and easier to trace back, but by using mistletoe during Christmas and allowing her to make the move on me, nobody would ever suspect. What she doesn't know is how unnoticed she went. Nobody knew her name, and they especially had no idea she was crushing on someone, let alone me. It was easy." His sigh filled the gap between us, sitting stale. "I wanted to rip her soul. But she won't believe me anyway." His brows knitted together, nose pinching. "I'm not so sure why she forgot in the first place. Her details are scattered. And it's not even that. There are other things." He shook his head. "She talks about her parents in a negative light, which doesn't make any sense because she used to talk about how great they were. So what changed between then and now?"

Her death.

Eliana Wilson was murdered, and somewhere along the way, her memories shifted. Could they do that?

Hadn't she once mentioned something about...souls? Fragments?

No, no. That was absurd. It couldn't be.

But something was wrong, and for some sick reason, I believed Liam.

"I don't know," I muttered. "I wish I did though."

OBSTINATE

"Ayden," I exclaimed as I stumbled upon him. "What are you doing here?"

Liam and I had been walking through, taking a moment to stop and smell the roses. Or in our case, stop and dip our toes in the cool water. The heat didn't affect us all that much, but it didn't take away the refreshing feeling of a cold lake on a hot day.

"I could ask you the same thing," my boyfriend said.

I snickered. "I asked you first. Besides, I don't have wings. It gets boring and I need to expand my horizons." I glanced out at Utah Lake. Green waters and a backdrop of mountains, or canyons? I couldn't be sure and while I'd been smart once, I was not experienced enough to know the difference.

"To be honest, I was spying on you." He shrugged so nonchalantly that I almost dismissed his excuse as a normal thing to do.

"What?" I chewed my lip. "Why would you do that?"

Crossing his arms, he shrugged again. Okay, that would get annoying quickly.

"Ayden," I said with a little more irritation.

He threw his hands up. "I simply wanted to see why you were so in love with me after everything."

"Really?" My brows knitted together as betrayal flashed across my features.

"Really." He started to pace, taking big steps. "And yes, I got my answer. It was harmless. I'm more intrigued by the idea that you go to parties and drink alcohol all on your own. Also yes, Angel, alcohol is bitter but you do acquire it. There's a reason to, when your life has spiraled so far out of your control. In my case, it has."

Why would he spy on me? Did Ayden not trust me? What was the real reason?

Warmth fled from the crevices of my soul. Rot sat on my tongue, but I couldn't conjure up the right words to scold him for the breach of faith.

Liam nodded towards him. "Told you someone hurt him."

With a scowl, Ayden marched forwards and shoved him. "And you have no right to be getting into my business like that."

The murderer snickered. "It's hardly poking around when it doesn't take a rocket scientist to figure out that you hurt people because you were hurt once."

"Not once," Ayden mumbled.

Sludge almost spilled from my lips. Accusations. Assumptions. But I couldn't do that now.

Not here.

I couldn't allow bad faith to allow me to say something I'd regret.

"Who hurt you?" I asked with more sincerity.

He turned away. "I seem to recall a conversation the other night where you told me what you think of Angel."

My eyes snapped to Liam as he clenched his jaw. "What? What did he say?"

"That's not entirely important." Ayden shook his head, swinging his whole body around as he threw his arms up and slapped his legs as they fell down to his sides. "But don't be so quick to trust him either."

"Trust?" I gritted my teeth. "Is that what you think this is? *Trust*?"

"Looked pretty cozy to me last night!" He laughed, humorless and full of disloyalty. "Sitting down in the grass with beer in your hand, drinking with the man who murdered you and chatting away about how cheap the alcohol was. Talking about me and digging into stuff you know nothing about."

"I worry about you, Ayden!" I screamed. "Is that so damn wrong of me to do? I love you! Heaven forbid I do that!" I choked on a tight laugh of my own. "In fact, they have! And I still fucking do it anyway!"

Shaking his head, he pointed at Liam. "This is about him. Not you. He's the murderer."

Liam narrowed his eyes. "Hey man, I know my fate. That doesn't stop me from trying to do the right thing now. I want Heaven to reverse this!"

"But they won't, will they?" Ayden stumbled as if he were drunk, but I didn't think he was. If he had been, I'd chalk it up to pure rage that clouded his better judgment. "Because you see, Liam, they hate me. Heaven looks at me in disgust. Do you know why? Because my father is a fallen angel! Because I'm the product of something so wrong, and they dangled that hope in my face by giving me white wings. Now that they've been taken from me, Heaven couldn't give a fuck less." He threw his arm out, dismissing us.

"Do you know what we talked about last night?" Liam glanced at me. "What I think, Eliana, of you?"

My teeth tore at the insides of my cheeks. "Tell me."

Was I ready to hear it?

He threw his head back, pinching the bridge of his nose. "He asked, so I told him that something is wrong with you." He paused to watch my eyes sink. "The way you forget how I killed you, how you forgot that you were attracted to me, and how you forgot how much you love your parents."

"What the fuck are you talking about?" I spat, tears welling up.

Liam laughed. "And here's the kicker, Elli! Ayden believes me!" He tossed his head towards my boyfriend.

When I glanced at Ayden, he shot a glare towards Liam. "You fucking wanker. I could kill you right now."

"Then do it! What's stopping you, huh?" Liam antagonized him.

With a yell, Ayden lunged for him and I stumbled back with wide eyes.

I wanted to pull them apart, but how could I?

How did you tear your eyes away from something like that? A bad dream you didn't want to continue, but a good story waiting to be published.

He tackled Liam to the ground, beginning to pound his face in.

Liam took the beating for a moment, getting us all to believe he had changed and accepted his fate.

Only for a minute though.

Then he threw Ayden to the rocks, at which point I wanted to step in. But like double Dutch, how did you?

Ayden groaned before climbing to his feet to meet our killer's gaze. "Now you want to defend yourself?"

Liam spat blood on the rocks. "Try me."

Why the hell was Liam beginning to bleed from the inside out? Nothing was making sense anymore.

My boyfriend went for him again just to get himself thrown into the water. He splashed in the shallow end, scraping himself on a few rocks, shaking his hair. "You've been holding out on us, haven't you?" He stood, facing Liam.

All hell broke loose.

Clouds rolled in, skies darkening as lightning struck the water and thunder boomed. Shadows crawled out of Ayden's form from every angle, like arms, reaching for Liam.

"That's cheating!" he yelled back.

Ayden laughed. "Oh? I wasn't aware we established rules!" He stepped forwards, his soul growing in size. He himself had been swirling in shadows, every color of him swathed in darkness until I could only tell him apart by the shape of his face.

As he stepped towards him, he grabbed Liam by the neck, attempting to crack it. It hadn't done much damage as Liam collapsed and spat up more blood, rubbing his throat.

So Ayden lifted his foot, towering over him, and smashed it into his head. Blood splattered across the rocks.

"Stop," I shouted.

Dropping down to straddle Liam, he began to swing his fists at his face, his neck, his chest. He beat him until he physically wore himself out. And as Ayden fell away from Liam who'd been covered in crimson, still moving, my Nephilim boyfriend returned to his form.

Terror crossed my face.

Then, my boyfriend stood, covered from head to toe in the blood of our murderer. "That's for killing me, and for killing Angel. Regardless of our chat, you still ripped her life away. You were due for a reminder." He spat on his face.

I couldn't be entirely sure if that rage had been Ayden's or the darkness that resided in him. I wanted to say the latter, but it'd most likely been the former.

He lifted his head to meet my eyes, a cunning smile dancing on his lips.

And something stirred.

Something deep down in the pit of my soul awakened with a sudden jolt from bed, rubbing its eyes. Blinking several times.

Something dark, something feral, something absolutely terrifying.

"Fuck me," I muttered.

And some horrid, lingering thought—I wanted him to *do exactly that.*

After minutes of staring, I whispered, "You should get cleaned up. Both of you. Now that you got that out of your system."

Ayden stepped over Liam and approached me. "If you say so, Love." Before I could turn away, he grasped my jaw and pressed a bloody kiss to my lips. "Let's go."

Liam rolled onto his side and climbed to his feet, dragging behind us.

Daylight dripped away. Night draped over us, making promises the light never could. Nobody would find us. We were safe.

Liam stayed outside while Ayden and I went into the cabin to clean him up. There wasn't running water, but after a few minutes of wishful thinking upon a star, he was as good as new.

"Like what you see?" he asked with a small smirk, eyeing me as he fixed his hair with his fingers.

Pink tinted my cheeks. "Whatever do you mean?"

He chuckled. "Out there, on the lake. When you looked at me, I'd never seen that before. You wanted to tear me to shreds, in the good kind of way."

Was there a *good kind of way*?

"You just looked...protective was all." I shrugged a little.

"I looked protective? Covered in our killer's blood? All three of us dead?"

"Maybe."

He dropped his arms and grabbed my face, kissing me. Within seconds, he slid his hands into my hair, pressing more into it. I reciprocated every feeling.

His tongue made very friendly acquaintances with mine, and as I went for his jeans, his fingers wrapped around my wrist. "Don't."

I furrowed my brows. "Don't touch you?"

He nodded, loosening his grip when I pulled my hand away. "Please, just not tonight."

I wanted to peek inside his head and see what had him on edge. I wanted to comfort him and hear him out. I got none of that. Not the raw side of Ayden Dyer, or his feelings. Just a simple no.

"Okay," I whispered. "I won't."

I hoped he'd tell me when he felt comfortable enough to pour out his heart to me.

Our kiss slowed. Tender moments and thoughtful touches. Ones that made promises neither of us were going anywhere anytime soon. A hug under the starry sky, or cuddling on the hood of a car with a blanket at a drive-in movie. All things I'd never once experienced, but maybe someday hoped to.

Because of Ayden.

Because he loved me so immensely I couldn't fathom what made me special, what made me different from all the other women he'd kissed before. Why had I been the one to make the bad boy fall in love for the first time?

I wasn't that remarkable.

Eliana was the type of woman that went unnoticed. She walked through the halls and slipped between bodies, daring to excuse herself each time only to be met with ignorance. She struggled to speak up or break a rule. She wished for love, but knew it'd be impossible. So she settled with her own company just fine and accepted her fate.

Until one day, she'd been murdered.

And then she'd be assigned a man so reckless she couldn't understand why the fallen angels wanted him.

She'd fall in love.

So, I made it my vow to love him back, as hard as I could with not a single apology.

FLOOD

Stepping into the large foyer decorated with intricate molding and pictures of us, I glanced at Liam. "It doesn't make sense. How can my parents have loved me yet I don't remember? I wouldn't just forget something so significant like that. I *wouldn't* have."

Yet the frames filled with me didn't make any sense...

"Okay, okay." He nodded, throwing his hands up in defense.

Still, I started to scour the house for more evidence. I needed proof.

The picture of us at the beach in their nightstand. Our pictures *framed.* My bedroom kept pristine, instead of them ripping it apart to turn it into a gym or a movie theater.

As I sifted through my mother's drawers, my fingers brushed over something. I pulled out a folded piece of paper, then slid down the wall as I began to read.

The letter itself had been addressed to me, from my mother. However, the date was off.

August 18th, 1996.

I hadn't been born yet. Not conceived. Not a thought.

Just...nonexistent.

Swallowing my pride, my eyes swept over the lines again and again. The emotion and longing bled through the page, ink smudged where she'd been writing. Mom had been left-handed growing up, and it was a trait about her I never dared to forget, even if she didn't claim to care.

But it didn't make sense.

In this letter, she mentioned she had made mistakes in her youth that she hoped her daughter someday could learn better from. She had hopes for me, and she knew whoever I'd end up as, she'd be proud. She dared to mention she'd always be at my side regardless of what happened.

As I lowered it, a sniffle came. Then tears rolled down my cheeks as torment shook me to my core.

Liam's shadow cast over me.

"She wrote a letter to me before I was born. She wrote about how much she loved me and I didn't even exist yet. How can that be? How could I have forgotten my own parents' love?"

He sat beside me. "I'm sorry, Eliana. I truly am. I just didn't want you to go on living in this bubble that they hated you. You spoke so highly of them. You adored them and aspired to be like them. Your parents were your introduction to love and a healthy marriage. And it was because of them that you told us you were entirely happy never having siblings. They made sure you never felt alone. Whatever it was that happened..." He gulped. "Maybe it's my fault? I ripped your soul out. It wasn't your time. And sure, you went to Heaven just fine. But maybe it was because of me that you couldn't keep some memories."

Wiping away the stains on my cheeks, I closed my eyes. "I'm not even sure it is your fault this time." There was no stinging or my puffy mess left behind. As if I'd never cried at all. "You seem to know everything I don't. Selene is...different now. But the version of her when we were alive, I loved her. How could I? Isn't that supposed to be...wrong? Growing up, I always asked how people could question who they loved. I didn't understand it. Wouldn't you know you wanted to kiss them? Why deny it?" I exhaled. "Now here I am. Sometimes that love shows up differently, and you're blinded. You don't want to believe it because you've grown up thinking that's not right." I shook my head. "This isn't my coming-out story, Liam. It's just... How could I sleep two feet away every night and not know?"

"You answered your own question." He let out a light chuckle. "But hey, proof is in the pudding. You're bi and you still made it here. No use dwelling on it."

A small part of me swelled. A *thank you* lingered on my tongue, never fully sailing off. Even in all his anger, he'd never told Ayden my secret. I wasn't quite ready to reveal it. I wasn't so sure I'd come to terms with it myself, and when that day came, I'd tell my boyfriend. Hoping he wouldn't make jokes or tell me I was making it up...

Ayden wouldn't do that.

"The hardest part is how much it makes sense." I peered up at him. "Not liking girls, but more about loving Selene. I think deep down, some part of me had always been jealous, but not of her. It was you. Because you had all her attention. I just told myself it was friendly jealousy. And now here you are, telling me I liked you, too. Maybe I liked both of you because you made me feel loved. You were my introduction to the romantic side. And if I had remembered that kissing you would lead to my death, I would have been far more terrified to love Ayden. Especially given his nature." I gestured.

"But you do love him." No recognizable emotion flitted about on his face.

A calm washed over me. "I do." I rubbed my arms, eyes falling to my lap. "One day I was on my own, dead and guarding humans. Suddenly here I was, guarding this man who couldn't keep himself straight. He irked me in many ways, but I couldn't show it. I was good at that, Liam. The whole pretending thing. I learned how to mask all my emotions and keep a level head. He started dating Sunny. We made a bet to kiss if he won it. But then he never kissed me." I rubbed my thumb over the top of my wrist. "Until one day, later, he *did* kiss me. And I had believed at that point I'd never kiss someone, but it was so damn good. He knows how to kiss a woman and make her weak in the knees." A heavy sadness hugged me from behind as a thought grew louder. If Liam was right, my first kiss was my demise. Maybe there had been good reason I forgot that part. I got a second chance to relive it with Ayden. A kiss worth remembering.

"Even after I left because I thought he couldn't love me, he came begging. Praying. He's truly the first person to ever love me like that, and it feels warm, and fuzzy, and addicting. Like I want more all the time. I need more of him to drink, to bathe in. And then I question if it's just this honeymoon phase and if it'll fade eventually. What if this forbidden romance between us is keeping it alive? What if we won't want to be together a decade from now? What if the excitement fades and it's just us pushing through because we have history at that point? I'm worried that all these feelings we have are the kind that only last a year before they vanish. Even a new relationship becomes old."

Anguish flashed in his eyes. "Have I ever told you about the time Selene cheated on me?"

"Excuse me?"

"No, just hear me out." He put his hand up, replacing the torment with more sorrow. "This is going somewhere, I promise. One night, Selene and I went to a party. She drank too much and she kissed this guy. After that, he was following her around and wanting more, but she told him to keep quiet. It didn't make a difference. I knew. So I killed her." He squeezed his eyes shut. "I took her life because she wronged me. I wanted to rip a soul, but she gave me reason to. I loved her and she tore my heart out first. But that's just it, Elli. If I loved her, why did I want to hurt her?" His face sank. "You and Ayden have something deeper. You've seen all his darkness and the worst parts of him. He's seen you at your lowest, the version of you that gives up on Heaven and says, '*fuck it.*' I don't think your love will fade over time, because you've made it through the hardest parts. You love him as he is. I could never do that with Selene. I was simply looking for excuses to practice my ability. I used it on you, too, and I'm so sorry," his voice cracked.

"What if our relationship is so full of drama—I say for lack of a better term—that when it's finally normal, I don't want him?" came out in a whisper.

He dipped his head into my view as I turned away. "What are you getting at?"

"Everything is so fucked up, Liam!" I swallowed, more tears threatening to spill. "Selene is fucked up, and I'm fucked up, and Ayden is struggling. You're not you; you're some version of you that pretends to care." I threw my head back into the wall. "You think you're in love with me."

His eyes shifted to the bed. "And?"

Tightening my arms around my knees, I said, "And I can't make sense of anything anymore. What if my love for Ayden is exactly like that?"

His jaw clenched. "Quite frankly, your love for him is the one thing you *can* make sense of. You've stayed persistent and stubborn, making sure he knows you're always at his side. It's fair to say it'll stay tried and true." A bead of sweat rolled down his temple from memory—when he had a body once.

"Liam," I whispered once more. "I'm so tired. I'm physically exhausted, and I simply want to be happy. Don't I deserve that?"

Genuine remorse crossed his features. Haunted. A sharp inhale of a breath. His shoulders slumped, head lolling forwards. "You do. You deserve that and more. I'm sorry that I stole your future from you."

Turning my head to meet his eyes, I asked, "What if I'm just a means to an end? I was in the wrong place at the wrong time. I knew the wrong people. And I wanted to live and experience so much out of life. But then I think, what if I lived and never fell for Ayden? Would living a full life be worth never loving him at all? I'm not sure I can answer that. Yet now I'm here and Heaven treats me like an afterthought. After everything I've done to earn my place, after becoming a guardian angel. I passed the test, too."

"I wish I could take it all back. I would, I swear it." He swallowed to rid himself of shame. "Shit, Eliana, I deserve to rot in Hell for what I've done. You had everything going for you. I'm sorry."

As hard as I tried to cry again, the tears no longer held power over me.

Exhaustion did though. Mental exhaustion that manifested by weighing on my soul.

I didn't have the energy to hit him, or to scream in his face. I grew tired of the same games. I no longer wanted to dance in our insanity.

So I chose to step out of this chaotic waltz of ours and let it all go. Maybe for now. Maybe for good. I supposed only time would tell.

Resting my head on his shoulder, I deflated. "We were friends once, weren't we? Was that a lie, too?"

"No, no, not a lie. Even after Selene cheated, I didn't blame you. I just allowed my sickness to control me. But our friendship, it was real. And even if you liked me, a part of me had wondered if I could be someone worth having around. You were so smart, and so cute, and I definitely wasn't good enough. You deserved better." He reached for my hand before pulling back.

"You really think you were a piece of scum *before* you killed us? And why is that?"

"Because of men like Sam."

At the mention of his name, I went frigid.

He must have felt me tense up, because he continued, "He was a friend of mine, and I knew what you did. And at the time, I was just angry at you. Even knowing the kind of person he was. He had it coming. But I blamed you and that was wrong of me. I should have spoken up and disowned him after shit like that."

Chills rushed down my entire back.

"We should head back," he said in a low tone. "Or maybe I should at least."

He moved to stand, but I grabbed his arm, appalled at myself for saying, "Please stay."

Liam hesitated, wavering on my words for too long. Then he settled. "Okay. Okay, Elli. I'll stay only because *you asked me to.*"

"Do you think it's possible to run a library?" I asked.

Liam scanned the area, brows knitted together. "You mean you? Down here? On earth?"

"Yeah."

"Uh, I don't know how you'd plan that when it'd need funding just to stay open. Plus you'd need documentation and all that at least, to run it, and you're no longer alive."

I frowned. "Yeah, but I'm sure Heaven could make it possible for me. Nothing big and fancy. Just a small library of used books. I need a purpose because I won't go back to being a guardian angel. I'm nothing right now. Useless, unable to help my own boyfriend. But...you're right. It's Salt Lake City. There are plenty of libraries around and there's no need for mine. It was a nice thought though." I shrugged a bit, turning back towards the trees.

Liam and I entered Lagoon, sticking to the amusement park. He attempted to talk me out of stealing wristbands, but I figured it was the least I was owed after losing my wings for eternity.

I could never shake the vacancy in my soul no matter how hard I tried. I was lesser than all the other angels, and they knew it. The staring, the whispers. Without knowing *my story*. With knowing *every* detail. They labeled me as reckless and ruined. They put me in a box.

Liam did his best to shield me from the brutal reality, but he could only hide so much.

I felt their gazes burning holes in me everywhere I went.

I was no longer considered one of them.

So I spent far more time on earth than I did in Heaven.

When we put the wristbands on, we allowed our invisibility cloak to slip off so we fit in with everyone else. The one perk of being dead was the chance to get in everywhere for free.

And I'd never been here before.

Without wings, it gave me a whole new perspective.

The only silver lining to all of this.

"I say we leave Wicked for last," he said, leaning into my bubble. "It's the best one. Shorter, but pretty good. Colossus is also a favorite. Oh! You're going to love Samurai. It spins in three directions at once."

"We didn't go to parks like this often."

"No? Were there any nearby?"

I shrugged, scanning the rides as a coaster of people flew by, screams fading away with them. "Oaks Amusement Park. But we went once. It was fun, but it was probably more the size of a state fair. This"—I gestured wildly around us—"is massive compared to that."

His laugh bounced in the air around us, between bodies, blending with the fun, fast-paced music. "You're gonna love it. If you don't, I did something wrong. Come on!" He grabbed my wrist and dragged me over to Tidal Wave. When I glanced up at the large ship, it swung back and forth as screams and laughter floated into the sky.

It looked like a blast.

I changed my mind the second I got on though. Liam talked me into sitting in the back row, furthest from the middle. And when the ride started, I widened my eyes. "We're barely strapped in! What if we fall out?"

He shot me a look. "You'll be fine!"

I was in fact *not* fine.

The higher we swung, the tighter my hands gripped the bar. "Liam, I hate this!" I closed my eyes, leaning back against the seat, shoving my feet to the bottom to try and brace my body to keep from moving around.

A hand grabbed mine. It eased my fear only a bit, but the second the ride stopped, I climbed off and dropped to the ground. "I'm never doing that again! I did not feel safe whatsoever!"

"I'm sorry. Lesson learned." He put his hands up. "But at least you're already dead."

"Nobody else knows that! What if they questioned why I didn't break my neck?"

He simply shrugged it off. "Extra protection. Noted."

We went for a less intense ride. Well, in the sense of being lifted so far off the ground, sure. But the Tilt-A-Whirl still threw me around. The pod we sat in had a lap bar very similar to the one on Tidal Wave. However, when it started to whip around from one side to the other as the platform spun, I yelled out the second I flew into Liam. The shape of the floor had been wavy, almost like a wiggling worm, circular plates that dipped down underneath each pod for us to fly around in as if our life depended on it.

By the time we got off, I grabbed onto him. "I'm so glad I'm dead. Can you imagine the amount of nausea and dizziness I'd have right now if I were human? Despicable."

"Not too bad, right?" He chuckled.

With a small smile, I shook my head. "No. Not too bad."

Lifting my eyes, I caught a glimpse of a familiar face.

Ayden Dyer, the one and only. My love. My boyfriend.

It'd been *weeks.*

A few people passed by in front of him, and then he was gone. I was left wondering if I'd imagined the whole thing.

But the ease in my chest told me otherwise.

"Come on, we have to go to the next one!" He patted my arm and ran off.

I sprinted after him, slowing to a stop in front of a drop tower. "Oh...shit."

"I promise you'll feel safe." He stepped into the line.

It'd been made up of three beams that formed a triangle, each with their own row of seats. Riders stepped up, climbed in, pulled a bar over their chest, then slowly rose to the top before dropping.

Tapping my fingers against my thighs, I tried not to think about it. Sure, I could fly once. But dropping was a whole other ballpark. I hadn't realized I was thumping my foot until Liam pointed it out, asking if I was okay.

Sure. Okay. I was fine. I was *great.*

When our turn came, I climbed into the seat, reminding myself I was dead. Nothing could hurt me now. I pulled the bar down, pushing against it to ensure it was locked. Only when they circled to check, mine came loose, and I started yelling at them to fix it. Maybe I was being a little dramatic.

They came back around and pushed it down, locking it again.

And sure, it was stuck this time. But I wasn't convinced.

The moment the ride started, I kicked my legs, trying not to dwell on the fact that my bar had come undone earlier. Anxiety tickled my soul.

When we reached the top, I glanced at Liam. "Did I mention I'm actually quite terrified of heights?"

He snorted. "You're an angel."

Sure, I was. But being here, like this and with no wings anymore, my human senses kicked into full gear. I couldn't keep the fear at bay. Maybe it wasn't a terrible thing either. I could at the very least enjoy the rides to the fullest extent.

The thrill. Adrenaline.

Blood was pumping through my veins once again.

We dropped about a foot and I yelped, closing my eyes. "I hate this, I hate this, I hate this."

"Hold my hand." Liam held his palm out.

"That does not make me feel any better!" I grabbed it, squeezing.

And then we dropped.

I screamed, tightening my grip and struggling to catch the breath I didn't need.

The entire ride was spent like that. Every time we bounced up and fell down, I squeezed my eyes along with his fingers. I wanted the whole thing to be over.

When it was, I dropped to the ground and ran out of the gate. "Never again!"

"You don't like thrill, eh?"

I swallowed, shaking my head. "Not like that."

I spun around, ready to ask if we could just stop for food.

My gaze crossed Ayden again, the racing in my chest beginning.

"I'll be right back," I told him as I pushed through the crowd of people.

I quickened my pace, spotting a building. Then, I wrapped my fingers around his wrist and yanked him behind it, shoving him into the wall. He didn't get to finish asking "*what the hell*" before I crashed my lips onto his.

His lips molded to mine, a perfect puzzle piece fit. Colors bled together and the world around us fell mute. I could stay like this forever, my fingers tangled in the black cotton of his shirt with the taste of bourbon on my tongue. Ayden rarely drank it, but it must have coursed somewhere through his veins.

He broke away first. "Angel."

"Mmm?" My eyes fell to his lips.

"Didn't expect to find you at an amusement park."

"Talk less." I took his kiss captive again, begging for far more than we could have here.

It didn't stop Ayden from trying though.

His hands slithered down my waist, resting on my hips. His thumbs slipped under the hem of my shirt, rubbing along my hipbones—or the memory of them.

I let out a small laugh, my lips parted and still very much tethered to his.

I'd let him have all of me if I could give him that much.

Pulling myself away, I released a sigh of content. "Sometimes death is just work and stress, and today I wanted to feel alive again." Oh, I felt very alive alright. Impossible not to when I worried about my soul even after my murder. "I suppose I should get back before Liam starts asking questions I don't want to answer."

I didn't miss the subtle falter in his smile. "Of course." His hands fell away from me, a cool breeze coming in to envelop my soul. Not the kind of cool breeze I craved, either. It nipped at me, icy within seconds.

Pulling out the folded note I wrote to him last week, I slipped it into his front pocket. "So you don't forget how much I love you," I whispered.

I stepped back, turning to go when he said, "I'll see you in a few."

That squeezed my metaphorical heart, and I returned to Liam with more excitement than I'd left with.

"Okay, so you don't like drops. You don't like lap bars, and you tolerate spinning. What can I take you on?" He pointed to a map with furrowed brows and a tilted head.

"All of it," I said. "Take me on all of it. You only live once."

He opened his mouth to say something, promptly choosing to stay silent.

He led me to the next ride.

We tried a smaller coaster called Spider, which I'd enjoyed far more than the previous. No major drops, no loops. Just a fast slope.

We'd circled back by Tidal Wave, trying out Turn of the Century. It'd been made of individual swings that circled around a tilting top, which I definitely loved. That would have been the ride to eradicate my fear of flying, if I hadn't done so by dying.

We hopped on Musik Express, which was a string of bobsleds that moved like another wiggling worm in a circle, around a center point. The tunes blasted so loud you could barely hear yourself think, but I'd laughed my heart out and savored every second I could.

Screamer had been a whole different ball game. There were these carts lined up in a giant circle, and when the ride began, the wheel spun. The base lifted the wheel upright like a Ferris Wheel as we went around and around, flying upside down for half of the duration.

When Liam took me on Samurai, I hadn't prepared myself. The ride itself was made up of one giant arm that was attached to a center where five branches of seats hung off. The arm spun. The center turned. The branches flipped. I couldn't keep my head, my eyesight, nor my morals straight.

That checked out these days.

The Roller Coaster, or what Liam called the Old Wooden Roller Coaster, had been one of the oldest rides here. It'd been taller, placed in front of the parking lot, and when we went up, we dropped down and rode around the tracks. My hair flew in every direction as I laughed, throwing my arms up from time to time.

It was over too soon.

"That's actually my favorite. Always has been since I was a kid," Liam said with a smile.

"I can see why. Okay, okay. What's next?"

"Cliffhanger!" He patted my arm with both hands, running to the ride.

The riders were lined in rows connected to a *Y* shape, like a sling, flipped upside down.

Liam made me close my eyes and plug my ears because of reasons. So, when we eventually got our turn, the rows flipped around while the poles spun us up in the air.

Then water shot up at us from below, multiple geysers lined up, hitting us in the face as we rolled by.

I screamed and laughed all at once, not even bothering to give a second thought to the people who stared at us in shock when we exited the ride as the only two riders who were completely dry.

We rode Colossus next, which Liam had been right about. Something about the two loops made it a favorite.

Then we approached the final ride of the night as the sun set beyond the parking lot. Wicked. The one he specifically told us to save for last.

"May I?" that English accent asked behind us. When we turned to face Ayden, he gestured to me. "May I have this last ride with my girlfriend?"

Liam wanted to say no; it was written all over his face. But he couldn't, and so he said yes because it'd been the right move.

The line for Wicked had been one of the longest ones. I thanked *someone* for my death because at least I wasn't feeling the unbearable ache in my legs and feet.

When we finally got to the ride, we loaded in, the three of us in front with a single rider. The coaster had been made up of two rows of four. As a lap bar lifted up to our stomachs from between our legs, I grabbed onto it. We weren't given even a second to prepare before we shot into a tunnel, exiting only to immediately fly up a rise. I cheered, fingers wrapped tightly around the bar. We rounded the top, dropping straight down before leveling out and soaring around the tracks. I threw my arms up as we swung and twisted, upside down for few seconds.

As we came to a semi-abrupt stop, I laughed, my hair flinging into my face. "What a thrill!"

"Told you it was the best for last," Liam said with a proud grin.

As we exited the coaster, Ayden's arm slid around my waist, tugging me into his side. "Definitely best for last," he mumbled into my ear, pressing a kiss to my temple.

Our love—our relationship—resembled exactly this night. An amusement park. Thrills. Never knowing if I was safe to ride, but always ready for more after.

Ayden had utterly corrupted me in all the best ways. He'd shown me what it meant to love and be cared for, and how to break a few rules. He showed me how to dive deeper into my own soul.

I was never coming down from a high like this, and I knew he'd never ask me to.

PROVERB

"Trust me. Please." Liam waved me over, grabbing something from under a rock.

When he placed it in my palm, a small bronze key stared back at me. "What's this?"

"A key."

"Yes, dipshit, but what for?" I held it up.

He chuckled, stepped away from a glass door. "Open it up and see."

Eyeing him, I approached the handle, fit the key into the lock, and turned. When it clicked, I pulled it open—and a small bell dinged.

Walking inside, books lined every shelf from top to bottom. A wide counter stood to my right, by the door, with a slot marked:

RETURNS

Dusty, old books lingered in the air, taking me back to a time when I was young and begging my parents to take me to the library.

Library.

"Liam, what is this?" my voice nearly caught on my tongue.

That damned man shoved his hands into his pockets. "It's your library, Elli. You deserved something after everything you've been through. With Matthew and Naeva's help, it was easy to convince them to allow it. And it's yours. Paid for. You just work when you please. Or I can. Or whoever. And people will come and check out books."

The emotions squeezed my chest so tight I thanked God I couldn't choke on the pain.

The feeling of being heard threatened the brim of my eyelids, spilling over my cheeks immediately. "Liam, this is too much."

He rushed forwards, hands landing on my shoulders. "No, no, please. Don't think that. It's the least I can do for ruining your life."

The words lodged themselves perfectly in the thick of my throat. I wasn't so sure anymore that he had ruined it. In a way, yes.

But as pieces started falling together, I grew to realize that I was better having met Ayden like this. Loving him wasn't a regret, and Heaven always knew he didn't have long left. That had been why they let me date him when he was still a human, because he had been destined to die at Liam's hand anyway.

Turning to face the counter, I placed my palms flat against it. Solid oak. Properly built, sanded, stained. None of that pressed sawdust. I circled behind it and brushed my fingers over the register, popping it open.

"It only opens with your say so, essentially. Or anyone you'd give permission to." He pointed. "No key. But I figured you'd want one for the store at least, to feel a little connected to earth. I know I cut it short, and I can't do enough to apologize, but I can try. I've got limited time, and I'll do my best with what's left of it."

"It's a *library*. I don't need money."

He leaned his elbows onto the surface, leaning over. "Look, it's not for money. You can make copies of library receipts. Like those stamp cards. One in the book, one in your drawer."

Pressing the key to my heart, tension fled as warmth flooded in and hugged me like a mother consoling her sick child. I was safe. I was okay. "I love book cards. The stamps. Something about them tickles the right spot in my brain. Of course that doesn't exist anymore, but the thought counts."

"Good!" He slapped the counter. "Then you can have this, if not an answer from Heaven about Ayden. We will get there!"

When I met his gaze, my eyes softened. "Thank you," I said in a quiet voice. "Thank you for this."

I couldn't wait to show Ayden.

A shiver passed from my neck to my knees.

"Well, then that's it." I faced the door. "We're open now."

These days, I wallowed too much. I'd relied too heavily on the pity and sorrow of my afterlife. Between Ayden's situation and me losing my wings, I wandered too deep into the ocean. Farther than I could touch. Past the waves that swallowed me whole. I sunk, drowning in my own emotions. Down, down, down. The twilight zone. The midnight. Abyss.

The trenches.

Rock bottom.

As far as one could go.

And as hard as I tried most days to gulp for air or kick my feet and swim up, the current pushed against me.

On the days I did surface, I washed up on the shore, sand clinging. I tried to brush it away, but it stuck to me the way dark thoughts did—stubborn. The trees laughed at me. The world closed in, making it hard to breathe.

Liam found me crying, kicking, screaming every time.

Letting my mind idle was the Devil's playground. Quite literally.

So, I found bits of peace in the moments I could. I occupied my mind and never allowed myself to fall into that rut for long.

This library would be a big help in my healing. I'd be allowed to move on, and maybe even start anew.

"Welcome," I said with a smile as the first person stepped in.

A tall man with shaggy brown hair and glasses.

He headed towards some shelves after nodding at me, sifting through books.

I glanced at Liam with a grin. "My very first customer. Look at that. I'd be what—twenty-two, and I'm running a library? Granted, I'm dead. But that's not important. It's still mine. I still get to interact with people in some way and keep my mind off of the horrid things that nobody tells you about in the afterlife. Because nobody else is as unlucky as *I am* in paradise."

Liam turned his back to the counter, elbows resting on it, back pressed against the edge. "We're fighting it. We'll change it. Even if I have to scream to get some kind of attention finally, I will. I just simply want to right my wrongs."

"You think this change is because Naeva shot you with the love juice?" I tapped my fingers on the wood.

He chuckled. "Love juice?"

I shrugged. "Wasn't sure what else to call it. But you think that's what all of this stems from? Because you were so hellbent on ruining my life, and even more pissed when you found out what happened after you killed me. Why?"

His expression dropped. "I've been angry with God for a very long time."

"I mean, I could deduct that much."

He exhaled on habit. "He took someone special from me. When I was young, He took someone I cared about, my mother, to cancer. Remember?" I recalled when he shared that with me. "And I figured at that point, I vowed to destroy everything He cared about in return. And then when you appeared that day, looking alive, it didn't sit right. I was confused and angry as to how you survived. But then I saw your wings. At my apartment. And I knew. God was real. Heaven was real. So every time I begged Him to help me, He *ignored* me." His eyes darkened.

My tapping slowed. What did I say to that?

He was pouring his heart out onto the counter.

"I didn't understand why the only person I had left was ripped from my life. I was just a boy. I was expected to grow up alone, to raise myself. And then I discovered, by accident, my ability. I could rip souls." Pride was it?—flashed across his features.

I kept my opinions to myself, far too curious to hear more.

It'd be easy to argue and say God didn't take people away. He simply refused to save them from death in the first place. But I was at least aware that he didn't want to hear that. Nobody ever did. And I wasn't about to start some conflict when he was crumbling deep down.

And I couldn't console him, nor explain God's reasoning for not saving his mother when he needed her around to watch him grow up.

"It happened after I lost her, but I was still young. Maybe eighteen. I had a best friend. Things were still rocky, my grief. It consumed me. They wanted no part of it, and so I freaked. I grabbed their hand when they tried to walk away, only it didn't work. Instead, I somehow grabbed their soul and ripped it free. They dropped dead, and I took up running. I couldn't quite explain it to anyone. But I wanted to practice. I kept trying, Elli. I became desperate, curious, with nothing left to lose. So I lost every bit of who I was and silenced my conscience. It was easy to do after my mom's death." He dipped his head, turning away.

The guy approached the counter with a book, *The Great Gatsby*.

It was a common read when I'd been in school, but they focused more on *Of Mice and Men*, as well as *To Kill A Mocking Bird*.

My favorite had been *The Outsiders*, however.

I grabbed a stamp, dating it on the book card and letting him sign his name. When he left, a copy magically appeared in my drawer.

I knew I was going to love this job, even if my dream had been psychology.

But psychology was constantly changing with society, and I was not a fan of such things, and so I couldn't handle having to keep up with it.

At least books never changed. The classics would always be there, even if humans were not. Stories always existed, even if our bodies decomposed in the dirt.

I'd always carry them, too, regardless of bans or censorship.

It was nice to know something would be around long after us.

"I'm sorry," I said. "I'm truly sorry that you dealt with that. I know it doesn't excuse what you've done, but... I like to think I can still sympathize, still understand how horrible it must be. When you have nothing left to fight for, why try?"

"Hurt people hurt people," he repeated to himself. "I acknowledge my transgressions. I take responsibility for them. Because even after losing everything, I still knew better and I chose worse. I was a grown adult." The sincerity never quite reached his gaze.

I wanted to laugh, to tell him his frontal lobe was not fully developed at that age, but it was the wrong time to make such remarks.

He glanced outside, eyes moving along the busy streets and cars that drove by. People passed us. The sun rose high in the sky—peak day.

Buildings towered over ours.

But even if we were tucked away in a little library placed in downtown Salt Lake, I still smiled to myself. It was going to be okay.

I was going to be okay.

"Selene, what a surprise," I exclaimed, stepping out of my new little business. As I locked the door, her eyes lingered on the sign. "Liam got it for me. His way of apologizing."

"Liam," she repeated. "Good ole Liam, huh?"

"Hm?"

"Nothing."

I glanced at her, frowning. "Sorry, it's a soft topic, I know. Anyway, what's on your mind?"

"You and everyone else." She shifted her weight to the other leg. Me?

My heart skipped a beat.

I laughed a little. "Everyone else? Who might that be?"

"Apparently fucking Liam," she spat.

I stiffened. "I didn't mean to bring him up, Selly. I'm sorry. It won't happen again."

She dug the toe of her brown combat boot into the cement. "Doesn't stop you from being friends, does it?" When my eyes flickered to the rage in her foot, I didn't miss the way the earth physically caved in under her power.

I tried to pick out delicate words. "He's helping me with Ayden. He's going to rot in Hell when this is sorted. And he's the one person who has been able to fly me up to Heaven. I'm not justifying what he did at all."

She clasped her hands behind her back, pacing. "I don't get it. I die, and it's whatever. You die, and suddenly Liam is obsessed with you. You manage to make a bad boy change for you. Somehow, Heaven is okay with you dating a human. You're the center of all the attention."

"I'm sorry?" I furrowed my brows. Was she jealous? I'd always been jealous of her, but not in the sense I didn't want her to have it. I just wanted to experience the same and apparently *be* with her.

"I said what I said, *Elli*," she forced a smile—conniving.

My chest tightened, a weight heavy where my heart should have been. "Did you miss the part where I was murdered? Where Ayden was killed in front of me? Where they took Ayden and now I'm expected to move on as if I never fell in love? What about the part where they chopped off my wings? Or where I was tortured multiple times in Hell just because I happen to know Ayden, yet he was picked *for* me? Did you miss all of that, *Selene*?" I added bite to her name.

Something dangerous, and terrifying, flashed in her eyes. "Not a beat."

Crossing my arms, I narrowed my gaze. "What is this about?"

Halting in her tracks, she shrugged in the slightest, and if you hadn't been watching her, you'd have missed it. "Do you know why I hate Portland?"

My confidence faltered. Fear seeped deep into the softness of my soul.

She continued, "It's humid. Too close to the ocean, and I hate the ocean. It's too busy, full of idiots. It's clogged. It's full of rich snobs in their big homes—far too massive for a family of three, who take up the housing when there are so many homeless people struggling to get by each day. Snobs who pretend to be humble as they move to another state, take up space, and walk the halls oblivious to how daddy's money is the only reason they got into the school."

Among the weight, a blade pierced my chest, making it hard to breathe at all, and I badly wanted to.

"The rest of us were drowning in student loans, in so much debt we couldn't keep our heads straight. They parade around with their big boobs and tiny skirts and heels, pretending to be a prude."

The *knife* twisted, and I choked on the crimson.

Why would she say these things about me?

"They pretend that they're not looking to get laid when that's all that's on their mind. So they tease men. They give them something to look at, then turn around and tell them no. They pretend to play the victim when they murder a man. Portland has a knack for producing ignorant little cunts."

I swallowed, every inch of me sinking into the ground. "Is that how you think of me...? I thought we were best friends." *I've been in love with you.*

"We were best friends before you took everything from me. I could have had so much." Her upper lip curled. "I was a Throne, Eliana. I had so much going for me."

Throne? I— I had been under the impression that Thrones were angels who'd never been human, that they didn't know what it was like to live and die, to be tormented and tempted and love the imperfections of someone. I believed they threw our case out because they had no humanity in them. To find out that empathy was a trait they refused to visit after their death...

"What do I have to do with it?"

She lunged forwards, fingers wrapping around my throat, as if it'd do anything. Her nails dug in, drawing nothing but air. "Everything. You and your stupid fucking Ayden."

"Ayden?" I squeaked.

"I got my revenge, and hearing the events unfold the way I've wanted them to is the cherry on top. Turns out you can have your cake *and* eat it, too." She let go of me, her forefinger trailing down my cheek.

Grabbing her wrist, my insides began to boil. "What the fuck are you talking about?"

She tilted her head, bringing a finger to her chin in one swift move. "Oh? You don't know? Ayden's a fallen angel because I told them to do it."

Everything that I'd ever felt, every ache, every smile, every dream I shared—it all dissipated.

And a fire burst from the pit of hell I carried with me.

Screaming out, I tackled her to the ground, punching her countless times, hoping it would do anything. She felt nothing. She watched me mockingly, a stupid smirk plastered to her damned lips.

I wanted her to pay. I wanted vengeance, and now I knew exactly who I was supposed to take it out on.

I wanted to rip out her throat and feed it to her just for sport.

Straddling her hips, I pulled back.

"Are you done?" She propped herself up on her elbows.

"You fucked up my entire afterlife simply because you were jealous. I will never be done, Selene."

She threw her head back and laughed. "You've got it all wrong, pumpkin. I fucked it up because you fucked up mine first. Karma's a real bitch."

"What the hell did I ever do to you?" I gritted my teeth.

Her eyes fell to my legs. "Get your ass off me and I'll tell you. Or do you quite like this position? You seem to have a thing for villains these days..."

Growling, I got off of her without offering a hand. Just for fun, I sent a kick to her stomach as she climbed to her feet.

Before she began, wings unfolded behind her, and my feet rooted themselves. I had to keep from showing any kind of shock. Selene, once my best friend, was a *fallen angel.*

How? When? Why?

She leaned back against the brick wall of my library, and it took everything in me not to march over and uppercut her. "Let me preface this by saying I lost my Throne position, so I went after someone you loved most. Ayden." When I didn't respond, she went on. "The reason your relationship was never punished was because I fought for you. Heaven wanted to punish you, but I found evidence that Ayden was about to die anyway. I stated that you were murdered simply because of me, and you were owed a chance at love. It took a hell of a lot of convincing to let that happen.

"And then one day I showed up to the court and they informed me I was no longer a Throne. I was simply just an angel. But after I did some more digging, it wasn't about just being fired because I saved your relationship. It was about so much more." She checked her nails. "Ayden's Nephilim. Nobody told me, of course. I had no idea, but that didn't seem to matter when I pleaded my case. They were so sure I knew. All they saw was that I had supported an angel dating Nephilim. And that very day, I had intended to talk about it, to talk to you finally. See, being a Throne forbid me from really conversing with you, a guardian angel. But I was fired so why wait anymore?

"I was on my way, but you had other plans. Catch Liam. Put him away. And the second I saw Liam slip into Ayden's car, I knew how it was going to end. Ayden would die. And I wanted my spot back as a Throne, no matter the cost. You owed me that for falling in love with the enemy. So, I told the fallen angels to promise me they'd help me however they could. And the second he was murdered, I cursed at the sight of his white wings. It wasn't right, nor fair. They took him. They poisoned him. Ayden's where he's always belonged."

"Your position, you didn't get it back I see," I seethed.

She released a sigh. "No, I did not. When I told them what I did, they claimed my deal with fallen angels was more proof I wasn't fit for it. I went down to Hell and asked them to make me like them, to do to me what they did to Ayden. I never wanted back into Heaven. I've sealed my fate because I don't want to associate with you any longer."

"I never asked you to defend me!" I shouted.

Shaking her head, she placed the sole of her boot against the bricks behind her. "No, but that's just what friends do. You worked hard to solve my murder and it cost you your life. I returned the favor. But Heaven isn't fair, I've discovered. And if not that, why should I be?"

I stepped forwards. "You destroyed my future because of a choice *you* made that went awry. That cannot be pinned on me. What a stupid fucking excuse, too. You gave up everything because you couldn't be a Throne anymore? How pitiful."

"And what about you, Elli? You've put your entire soul on the line for some dick. I've had sex. It's never that good."

"What a sad way to live," I started, "to have so many options and never be satisfied with any."

She scowled. "Watch your tone."

"Or what? You'll drag me to Hell? Cut off my wings? Murder my boyfriend and turn him into a fallen angel? Been there. Seen that. And to think I ever called you a friend at all." I spat at her feet as I closed in. "I pity you."

"Take your pity. I never wanted it."

"Careful now. Your envy is showing." I began walking backwards, swinging my arms up, slapping my thighs as they came back down. "Be sure to tell Ayden I say hi. And when this is over, I'm going to ensure you are tortured every second for all of eternity. I've got nothing left to lose, Selene." I spun on my heel, and with my head held high, I let her fade into the background. "Watch your fucking back."

LAMENTATION

"She admitted it. She fucking admitted this is all her doing," I told them as I held back tears.

Ayden sat beside me while Liam leaned against the wall.

My boyfriend rested his hand on my thigh. "I'm sorry, Angel. You deserve better. You deserve to be happy." A stupid, cliche line.

Scraping my bottom lip with my teeth, I shook my head. "All those times I stood up for her. I loved her so much that I spent my whole Christmas break trying to solve her murder until it killed me." Liam dropped his gaze, guilt flashing across his features. "And now that she's gone and done this as if it's my fault, I take it back. She deserved to die. Who knows who else she could have snapped on. What she could have done. If she ruins a man's life to get back at her best friend over a job she lost... How is that my fault? How is any of that *my* fault?" I screamed.

"It's not," Liam said. "It's not your fault that she lost it. How were you to know what Ayden was? You were assigned to him and you said so yourself that you didn't want to be."

Ayden frowned. "Why?"

I was faced with reality, the damage in his eyes. "Because I knew I was going to fall in love, and that was wrong. I wanted to prevent it. I tried so hard to stop it, but Heaven said yes. I didn't know it was because of her. She blames me for everything as if I never tried to do right in the first place. She burned everything we had in our friendship just because she couldn't be a Throne. I've lost my job as guardian angel because of all this. I already passed the test once but there's no way I will again."

Ayden angled his body forwards. "You mentioned that all guardian angels take a test, right?"

"Yeah." I leaned against him, resting my cheek against the back of his shoulder. "Why?"

"I'm just curious about something. That's all."

My eyes flicked to Liam who was giving Ayden certain looks, ones of knowing.

"What are you hiding?" I squinted.

His fingers tightened on my leg, as if what he was about to say could set me off. "It's just interesting to us. Yeah, Selene is the bad guy here and nobody is refuting that. Yes, Liam killed us, and nobody is minimizing that pain. But the fact that both of them remember things about you that you swear are wrong, that has me concerned and thinking."

I pulled back, the bite of his tone tearing my ears off. "Excuse me?"

Liam took a step closer in an attempt to take the heat off my boyfriend. "All we're suggesting is that maybe we should talk to Matthew."

"About what?" I snapped.

"About you! About souls and fragments and this test you took." He let out a low groan. "It's not personal, Elli. It's not personal. We promise. Just allow us to clarify a few things, okay?"

"This is piss-poor timing." I jumped to my feet, shoving my finger in his face. "Even for you, Liam."

I began to storm out of the cabin, but Ayden's fingers wrapped around my bicep as he whipped me around to face him. "Please, Angel. Don't go. We just got here."

"You think something's wrong with me. You're taking Liam's side. In what world do I want to be around that any longer?" I ripped my arm from his grasp.

Ayden glanced back at our killer, shaking his head.

Now what the hell did *that* mean?

When his eyes met mine, they softened. "Can you please trust me? The same way I trusted you when you told me that my dad's a fallen angel and what that makes me. You told me a hard truth about myself and I had to listen. I listened because I trusted you weren't doing it to hurt me but you wanted to make sense of things for us, for *me*. You also made it clear you love me no matter what. Can you do that?"

Swallowing whatever hateful words I dredged up, I threw my gaze to the side. "Fine."

Liam cleared his throat simply to get our attention. "Should I go talk to Matthew now then?"

"If you go, how can I believe whatever he says to you is you repeating the truth to me?" I asked. "But if we invite him here, he'll know about our hiding spot and even if he is on our side, I'm not ready for that to happen yet."

"What solution do you propose?" Ayden brushed a thumb over my cheek.

A chill seized my soul. "We meet him on the ground somewhere. I need to hear what he has to say to make sure *nobody* is lying." I glanced at Ayden. "I'm only doing this for you, okay?"

I elbowed Ayden as Matthew emerged from the clouds. "No fraternizing in front of him."

Liam snorted. "He's making out with Naeva behind closed doors."

"So."

Matthew landed on the grass, crossing his arms. *Way to close us off.*

Liam stepped closer to him. "Matthew, always a pleasure."

Ayden let out the deepest belly laugh.

"What's this about?" the Archangel asked.

Our killer replied, "Eliana. There's been some events that have us questioning a few things and you might know the answers to them. She's forgotten some of her memories, like how much she loved her parents, and how I killed her. But Ayden mentioned something about souls and fragments, and some *test.*"

Matthew shifted his weight. Did this make him uncomfortable? Did he know something?

I shot to my feet, approaching him in such a hurry. As if he couldn't hear me properly from where I was. "Tell them they're lying. I'm perfectly whole."

"I don't deal in that department, actually. Thrones do." Selene. "But we can get another case up—"

"It's a waste of our time." I dismissed him with the wave of my hand.

Ayden approached. "What about that test? Do all guardian angels have to take it?"

My soul locked up.

Then he answered, "No."

"Then why did Eliana take it?" His eyes narrowed.

Matthew's eyes darted to me. "Because Eliana is not a whole soul."

A scream tore through me as I lunged for him. Liam wrapped his arms around me, pulling me back as I kicked, yelling, "You fucking lied! You said you don't deal with that!"

Matthew's eyes flashed with pity. "I actually said I don't deal with souls. I never confirmed nor denied that you're whole. I figured my answer made it clear you are not, but if you have any more questions, you'd need to take it up with the Thrones to find that missing piece."

Liam set me down when I had enough control.

I dropped to the forest floor anyway. "Is that why this is a mess? Is this entire shitstorm happening because I'm *broken*?" The last word spilled from the crack in my heart.

The Archangel lifted a finger. "We prefer to say fragmented. Broken is an offensive and heavy term to use, implying you're not yourself. It gives a different kind of visual than fragmented would. We simply find that piece and stitch you together. You'll be good as new."

"I still need to be fixed," I spat. "I've been broken this entire time."

"You passed that test, Eliana. We concluded that the missing *fragment* had no impact on your soul. You were cleared to be a guardian."

Tears poured down my cheeks as I shouted, "It impacted me! I've been living in this despicable lie that my own parents neglected me! You didn't seem to think that could affect my job? The jealousy I'd feel over my guardees' parents loving them? The pain in my chest?"

He said nothing.

"Nobody thought to tell me!"

Matthew finally lowered his voice, squatting to my level. "We thought you knew, Eliana. All honesty, I swear it. We were certain you knew."

I wanted to ask how he could've figured that, but I didn't have it in me. The energy fled every aching ghost of my bones. I was left hollow, yet a mushy body without a shell. Emotions bled before seeping into the dirt, leaving me numb to the touch.

I—a fragmented soul. Ayden—Nephilim.

It all made sense now. Everything that had once started to fall into place had since been scrambled until they found better-fitting pieces. I'd fallen in love with a man so reckless and bad for my soul simply because I had been bad for myself from the beginning.

Since my death.

Since Liam Brown ripped me from my vessel after he poisoned me, after he let me *kiss* him.

Selene had lost her job, then sent the fallen angels after my Ayden to poison him. To undo all the work we'd done. And she joined their side, pretending to be someone I could trust for a short while.

Had this all been a giant test? I couldn't say.

I could say that we'd been pawns. Between Heaven and Hell, we were the pieces they moved when they chose to do so, and we didn't have any real control over that.

That had been why no matter how hard I tried to do good, or how hard Ayden tried, or how much we were promised a perfect paradise in Heaven, it meant nothing. It backfired.

We were the two left to scour the grass in hopes of finding the pieces of glass that went flying in the aftermath of the war.

Casualties were all we were to them.

"We've never mattered at all, have we?" I met Matthew's glassy eyes. The answer had been clear as day.

Ayden and I were just a means to an end.

PLEASURE

"Angel, I absolutely worship you," Ayden started as I fiddled with his belt, "and don't let anyone else hear me say that." It was meant to be a joke, but it didn't land. "I don't want our first time to be revenge sex. Sex that sticks it to the man. Or God in this case."

I dropped my hands. "Why? Isn't that your whole persona?"

He snickered. "Really? No. If you knew me at all, you'd see that it's more than that. I'm whipped now. I've changed, and with that change is a man who wants to have sex with the woman he loves and have it mean something. I want to experience it in a way I've never had the opportunity to experience before. Is that really so wrong?"

"And what about me? What if I want to experience it just *once*?"

He leaned closer. "Don't go all hard on me now. I know you did not just suggest my consent doesn't matter."

Guilt rippled through me. "Ayden."

"We will." He grabbed my fingers, giving them a gentle squeeze. "We will, someday. But today is not that day. I'm not a rebound or revenge, or whatever this is. You're fragile and vulnerable and full of so many emotions after this morning with Matthew. You're essentially drunk on rage, and drunk is never a time to shag someone." He shook his head. "I want us both to fully be in it when we do. Okay?"

I hated how much I loved him.

"We're just a game to them, Ayden," I choked out. "We were never important. We've always been this game to them."

His arms slid around me, caging me in his body to protect me from the big bad world. His wings, black as the night itself, wrapped around us both, a few tendrils of shadow filling in the gaps so no light could slip through. *Just me and him.*

Us against the world.

The world that revolved around us.

It hadn't entirely been about revenge. There were feelings in places I wanted to satisfy. But Ayden was right, again, about how it should happen. He was right about us, and him, and consent.

He did everything *right*, and I wanted to go feral for him. But another time. Hoping we got another chance.

He pressed his lips to my temple. "Then let them play us. If I've learned anything, it's that karma's a bitch."

The words Selene relayed to me.

I hated them, too.

"And what of it if the karma we're hoping will bite them in the ass is the same kind they invented? They're immune to it. You must know that."

"Then we'll create our own," he whispered against the surface of my soul.

It'd been intended as a threat towards them, but I saw it for what it had been. Not vengeance, but moreso about protection for us.

The way his tone slithered out a cool, smooth, thick promise had clung to me. Warmth settled in, pooling and setting a fire in the pit of my essence.

But I said nothing.

I allowed Ayden to seep into the cracks and crevices, making me whole again. He'd fill those missing pieces until I could search them out myself.

His bright green eyes, his smile.

A man who prayed when he had no other way to get me back. And while he didn't admit it, he loved his family. His older sisters, and his parents, despite the lie his father kept from him for so long.

The way he got so lost in baking, like it could pull out all negative energy and fill him with something genuine, softening his sharp edges.

Despite the terror and chill I should have felt due to his nature compared to mine, I felt safer. Content. I'd been loved in ways nobody else had bothered to love me.

Unconditionally.

At some point, I returned. I woke up from the dream that nothing could hurt us.

Ayden's thumb gently rubbed the skin beneath my shirt, where my hip was. My cheek had been pressed to his bare chest, listening for a heartbeat that no longer existed. His feathers brushed the tips of my toes, soft as silk fresh after being woven together.

Sitting up too quickly, I scooted off him and got up from his lap as his wings folded away. "You should go check in. I'm sure they're missing you."

"Angel," he said.

"No. Please. Selene wants us both to suffer, and she knows what you are as well as where this cabin is, and who knows how the hell that happened. I'd rather them not find us here and make matters worse."

He reached forwards, brushing a strand behind my ear. "Okay. But

I'm coming right back." If they'd let him.

I nodded anyway, to get him to leave sooner.

With his hand to my cheek, he leaned in and pressed a kiss to my lips. Goodbye for now, but not forever. Sweet like cake, but not like a strawberry. Tempting, even.

And then he slipped out the front door and disappeared beyond the forest.

I explored the cabin a little more.

A run-down bathroom. Bedroom withering away.

A foundation beginning to rot.

But it couldn't be us, right?

No.

Never us.

Stepping into the bedroom, my gaze swept over torn curtains as thin as a sheet you'd find in an old farmhouse off the coast. Memories haunted the space as dancing ghosts. Dust floated in the dim sunlight attempting to slip in from the curtains, soaking up what little was left. The dead of winter when birth had crumbled into the dirt. Barren. Harsh. Yet an ounce of charm to salvage traditions before spring breathed new life into the world again.

I fell onto the bed, hair creating a halo that I no longer carried.

To drive that point home, I closed my eyes and conjured up a world I'd rather be in.

One where I'd been loved, alive, and sane.

Sure, that was probably a bit dramatic on that last part. But I felt I had fallen so far away from everything I once knew just because of the happiness I was promised yet never given. They dangled the candy in front of me, leading me into the white van. Only the van on the outside appeared as home, a place where I could go and feel safe.

I'd give anything to feel *safe* in my own soul.

I pictured those green eyes, the strong arms around my middle.

That English accent whispering the worst jokes in my ears to make me laugh. His messy brown waves, the beard that made him look far more masculine. The chest hair peeking from a half-buttoned shirt.

His tattoos swirling alongside his shadow tendrils.

I used my imagination to fuel my hand as it slipped beneath the fabric of my pants and did things I would have been scolded for if caught.

The floorboards creaked, but when I opened my eyes, nobody was there. I listened for any sign of life, or afterlife for that matter. Nothing.

Maybe my mind had been too powerful.

Regardless, I finished my work. I'd finally got some sort of release after the array of hormones from hours earlier.

As I sat up in one swift movement with my hands placed on the bed behind me, my gaze moved across the splintered wall.

I eventually left the sanctuary of the room and paused when I found Ayden on the couch. "When did you get back?"

He leaned into the dusty cushion and wrapped an arm behind his head, looking up at me. "Oh, you mean you didn't intend for me to find you masturbating?"

Crimson flooded my cheeks. "Ayden." Humiliation seeped in there, too. "You weren't supposed to be back this early."

"If I had known you were going to send me out so you could touch yourself." He shrugged, a genuine laugh spilling into the air between us.

I rubbed my face, groaning. "I didn't do it on purpose! I swear it. I mean, I did but I didn't plan for it. I just had some leftover feelings. That was all. Please. I've caught you before. Don't make a big deal out of this. It's all new to me and it's embarrassing as it is."

"Why? You have needs. Being a woman doesn't negate that."

I let out a sigh. "I'm not comfortable with my sexuality. And I know I'm a grown woman, or I was. I know that it's part of life. Or the afterlife, whatever. It's natural. I get that. But that doesn't change that it's all *new to me.* I've just never been all that comfortable in it and I can't make it happen overnight. Maybe that makes me strange. Maybe I'm abnormal for not being comfortable about it right away."

"Hey, hey." He waved me over. I hesitated before closing the gap. His fingers wrapped around my wrist and he pulled me down onto his lap, my legs straddling his. "Don't be ashamed or embarrassed. Okay. I'm not going to tell anyone. And I'm not going to make fun of you, either." With his forefinger and his thumb, he grabbed my chin. "I'm only comfortable in my sexuality because it was forced on me, and I would never wish that on you. You do what you need to for your body and your sake. I'm not here to make you feel bad."

I'd been tempted to poke and prod, to ask him what he meant by it being forced on him. Had something happened that I never knew about? Just the thought of Ayden having to deal with that made me ill.

"I know," I whispered. "You were right earlier. I don't want it to be out of spite—our first time together. But I was...a little excited. I just wanted to relieve myself of that without pushing anything on you."

"You can say horny, Love. I won't mind. You were horny for me."

I playfully hit his chest. "I'm being serious."

A deep chuckle passed his lips. "What word do you prefer? You want to fuck me? You're feral for me? Horny? Take your pick."

I opened my mouth to get onto him again, only to close it when his thumb rubbed circles on my bare hip. "You're foul."

"I'm foul?" His laugh brought me back to life. Vibrated through me. Started my heart and swept air into my lungs.

I forgot what it was like to cower under the scrutiny of being the only angel without her wings.

"Yes. You. Foul." I narrowed my eyes, attempting to climb off him only to be pulled back, his grip tight. "What, I'm captive now? Wasn't there a day when you wanted me to leave?"

His hand tangled in the back of my hair as he pulled me closer, his lips dragging across my throat. "Me? Want you to leave? Never." He closed on my neck, tugging angel skin between his teeth.

"Why do you love me?" came out in a whisper. "I'm supposed to be your annoying guardian angel. I'm the prude, the good girl. Why would you ever love *me*?"

Ayden pulled away, his eyes swimming with offense. "What? Angel. How could I *not* love you?"

A shiver ripped through me.

Threading a hand through my hair, he frowned. "You're a breath of fresh air. You bring me back to life. You have always loved me regardless of my darkness. You believed I could do better. You've showed me that I can mean the world to someone who has no attachment to me at all." The emerald in his eyes swirled into a sage shade. "You have a heart of gold. You have restored my faith in people when those closest to me tore it from my heart. It was impossible not to fall in love with you," he mumbled the last words against my cheek.

My heart swelled. A spark ignited in the pit of my abdomen before roaring to life in an abundance of heat.

He had been the one person who didn't quit on me regardless of what happened or who stood in our way. His wings had been stolen, and yet he stayed and trusted me to love him whole.

If I'd wanted to say something, it had long floated down the river.

His hands made their way to my hips, yanking them back towards his when I made an attempt to move. The friction awakened something buried deep in me, something entirely electrifying.

This hadn't been anything like what happened at the party, or that night on this couch.

This was damp. Moonless. Rotted tree roots deep in midnight soil. Something that tasted sweet, decadent, yet earthy. Something that should have been forbidden. Something parents warned about. Dangerous. Tempting. And I was far too curious not to continue to explore that.

"That," I breathed. "Do that again."

As his gaze darkened, amusement flitted across his irises. "What exactly about *that* is it you like?"

Maybe he was messing with me or getting me to admit it. Or it could have just been Ayden unsure of what it was that got me going.

But without a second thought to stop me, I hooked my fingers onto his belt, repeating the movement that sent a whirlwind of flames up my body.

Understanding set in. Ayden offered to try something, and I gave in as if he'd just asked if I wanted him to go to the store and buy me chocolate.

Who'd turn it down?

Not I.

I gave him control. I relinquished my trust.

He undid his belt, pushing his pants down his thighs, helping me remove mine entirely. He pulled through in the same way a world of colors exploded before me, his hands on my hips, fingers hooked deep into my soul. I grinded against his briefs, the *hard proof* in them that his attraction to me ran in every direction.

Bright reds. Hot pinks. Passionate purples.

Letting him lead had been a good choice on my part.

Pleasure was everywhere, and everywhere each touch hit differently. Like musical chords coming together in harmony. Fire burned through my body while my mind twirled in a frenzy. I was on my knees whenever he asked, at his every whim. He begged, I obliged.

It was more than suggestion. It was more than want.

It was a need.

The two of us planting our own roses and creating a garden after they'd yelled that we'd never be able to grow one.

They doomed us to fail.

We would rise to victory.

Ayden was right yet again. I was *feral.*

And tonight, everything about sexuality stopped appearing in black and white.

A familiar angel came into view. The same one we'd seen just yesterday. Apparently I *hadn't* been ready to face the truth all over again.

"You," I spat, stomping up to Matthew.

"Me?" He frowned, eyes scanning the area.

"Yes, you!" I jabbed my finger into his chest. "I can't believe I've been broken this entire time and you said nothing. You can't truly believe that any angel would want to go around *fragmented*," I mocked. "You can't truly believe we would ever feel comfortable that way! Do you understand that kind of feeling? To lose yourself, to lose who you are and your memories and the most important parts that made you, you? Of course not. If you did, you'd have cared. You'd have said something so I could find it long ago, before this stupid mess. Now I'm *here*." I began to pace, unable to keep my mind from being sucked out into the waves, down to the midnight zone. "You let me wander around without a piece of myself. I believed my parents neglected me. If you had known, you'd have done something. If you experience it, you suddenly understand. You finally find yourself caring. Empathy is important, Matthew, but you can't always use it! Sometimes you need sympathy or something like it. Humanity."

"Eliana."

"No! Do you understand the kind of fucking pain I've been through? I was doing fine. I was hurt when I lost Justin, but I was doing *fine*. When you guys gave me Ayden, you told me I was going to fall in love. I didn't want to break the rules. I wanted anyone but him, but you insisted I'd be fine. Was I? Was I fine? No! Because guess what had actually happened then? I fought my feelings in every way possible, still falling in love. Love is not something one can control. And then I thought: *shit, this is wrong*. No, you guys decided it was okay!"

"Yes."

"Selene fought for me. That's why it was okay."

"She did," he repeated solemnly.

"But then the news came out about Ayden's true nature. Liam murdered him in front of me. He made it to Heaven, only to be ripped from my arms moments later. When I saw him again, guess what happened then? Can you guess?"

His expression sank. "I can."

"He was poisoned. A fallen angel. I figured: *oh, the courts will understand. He was taken against his will.*" I snickered. "Wrong! They threw it out. And nobody ever told me the truth as to why they threw it out. We thought it was simple. That everything was just wrong for wrong's sake. Things got jumbled. Liam ended up here while Ayden fell below. Oh, oh! And then Selene, of course. Turns out she got revenge because it's somehow my fault she lost her job. She was the one who told them to take Ayden. And when they did, she became one of them." I swallowed. "Did you know that, too?"

He sighed. "I knew."

"Of course! You know everything, don't you? So all this time I've been fighting and nobody thought to tell me my soul was broken. Nobody thought to tell me I was also in love with the very person who took everything from me when it inconvenienced her. Nobody told me that the man I've fallen for is Nephilim." I stopped in front of him, fists tight at my thighs. "You've always known what he was, didn't you? And you continued to let me love him, trying to make this out to be my fault. I had to find out when Levi chopped my wings off. Turns out *those* aren't replaceable."

Too much pity in his eyes.

"It's not fair, Matthew. Heaven was supposed to be fair. That was the promise." I gritted my teeth. "It was promised to me and everyone else. So why now? Why now are we paying for crimes we didn't actually commit? I should never have had to suffer anything that I have. I was supposed to be protected! The fallen angels have stolen from me time and time again. If you don't step in now, what's next? There may not be a chance for me. They're coming for my soul."

Matthew ran a hand down his face. "I wish I could make it better. I'm sorry. Truly." Was he though? Did I believe him even an ounce?

"What about me? Can you save me? Can you save Ayden? Or is this all just for show?"

"It's not for show, Eliana. We promise."

"How can I trust that?" I swallowed. "How can I truly trust that you mean that when I've been treated worse in Heaven than I was alive?"

He sat on a rock. "It's true. We knew. We didn't always know about Ayden, of course. Well, that's a lie."

I scoffed. "More lies."

"Hear me out!" he shouted back. It threw me off guard, so I pressed my lips together.

"God knew, of course. But *we* didn't know. None of us were kept in the loop because it wasn't our business to be in the loop. He assigned you to Ayden for the purpose of seeing if we could salvage a soul. Maybe we could set things right again despite what his dad was. We hate the idea of children paying for the sins of their father. Ayden was no different. We knew you'd be right for the job because of who you were. You'd grown up so persistent. Always headstrong, never allowing anyone to influence you no matter what. We knew you could resist his charm. We knew you were the one who'd be able to tell him no. He'd get on your nerves, but you could handle that because you were the woman who had been resilient your whole life. You always stood your ground even if most people hated you for it.

"Even if it meant you fell in love, we wanted to see if it was possible. Ayden is not the only soul born from a fallen angel and a human. He was just..."

"He was an experiment for you."

Shame washed over him. "Yes. We assigned you to Ayden in hopes you could be the one to prove him wrong. We thought you knew about your missing piece. We did. And we figured you'd be perfect for Ayden because of the fact that you believed your parents never loved you. You'd be able to make sense to him, that his parents had always been great, even if they committed such a terrible sin. He needed someone the opposite of him. He was weak, begging to be loved as he was so that he'd choose to change. And maybe that's the wrong way of looking at it, but it was important to us."

"You used him; you used me. That's gross. My missing piece is not some trait for you to say that I'm your best pawn. And you can't use Ayden like that and tell him he's wrong about feeling the way he does about his parents! He has his own battles, his own demons in his life he never got a chance to defeat. I was never going to be able to heal that."

"No, of course not. You weren't there to heal him. Your job was to just plant seeds and help him see the light again."

I crossed my arms, swallowing all my emotions. "But it backfired because I ruined it by falling in love. And to make matters worse, he fell in love with me, too. Nobody told me that was going to happen!"

Matthew let out a nervous chuckle. "Well, yeah, we chose to keep that a secret. We figured if you knew about that, you'd definitely never agree to be his guardian. You have self-control. We thought maybe it was enough to keep you and Ayden apart, but I suppose God knew that wouldn't work, huh?" He shook his head. "He went along with it anyway. Again, we're always out of these loops."

I grinded my teeth. "So everyone knew."

"As I said before, not everyone. God knew what he was. Yes, He used it all to see if Nephilim could be redeemable. But the plan went sideways. Ayden made it to Heaven, which was a win. A success, a victory, and proof that we could. Until the fallen angels took him back and claimed them as their own. Of course they had no idea what he was. Lucifer knew, because he memorizes all of his own. He knew Ayden's father, knew Ayden's secret and his potential for darkness."

"I was forced to find out when they stole my wings, when the man who carried me from the flames was bathing in shadows, three sizes too big."

"Nobody ever faulted you for falling in love with Nephilim."

"No? Because Selene seems to think that's exactly why you faulted her. You fired her because you thought she knew. If God knew but said nothing, and still allowed it, why was she fired?"

"Selene was fired because she'd already been poisoned." He slid into the grass, back pressed against the boulder. "She didn't know, but they had already caught her and poisoned her. She was showing signs. When she came to us about your love, we saw something change. Her skin was festering. Subtle, but noticeable. Like bugs hiding under the surface. Her irises were no longer a warm brown, but rather burning.

Turning to ash. We had to give her some excuse, but that was it. It wasn't you or Ayden."

"So Ayden was poisoned because you *lied* to Selene about why she was really fired, somehow making it sound like it was my fault to the point she'd want to get back at me?" I tilted my head, laughing as if I'd heard the funniest joke. "Tell me you're not serious."

He groaned. "That is definitely on us. Okay? Definitely our fault. And that's why we've been trying so hard to make it right, but the courts keep throwing it out when I submit a case, even with all the evidence and every bit of truth I've left out before." He stood, arms swinging at his sides. "Just listen to me for one moment, please." He approached slowly. Cautious. "Something is wrong."

"What?"

"Something is *wrong* in Heaven, too, and I don't know how to explain it. For a while, we've suspected it but now we know for sure. It never should have gone this far. I submit a case and they immediately close it. I'm an archangel. I should be able to get through to Thrones. I'm ranked fairly high." He technically wasn't but I wouldn't correct him now.

He circled around me, nearing a tree and glancing up to the sky. "Every time I go to the Hall, nobody answers. God has never *not* answered. He's never shut us out and refused to talk to us for this long, either."

I scratched my arms, gaze faltering. "What are you saying?"

He glanced at me. "I'm saying that we have a lot bigger fish to fry than just you and Ayden. If we can get that sorted, maybe we can actually get his situation fixed, too. But you have to help me. You have to trust me."

I narrowed my eyes. "Trust you?"

He shrugged. "Sure, I wasn't human. Sure, I've never had parents or a family, nor have I ever been a boy who grew up. I was created as a man, Eliana. But I'm not any less alive than the rest of you. I have a purpose, too. This is it. I love bowling, I'm in love with Naeva, and I see that sometimes we have to do things a little differently to make sure things stay right in Heaven. You're correct about being promised fairness and happiness. You are *correct.* You were promised an eternity of joy. And something has been off balance for a while, and it's since gotten worse. God is the closest father I've got. I can't let Him down. I need to figure out what went wrong."

My eyes scanned the trees some more. "Okay. We'll help. Liam and I will help at least set it right, but I do expect the same in return. Maybe I should be selfless, but those days are behind me. I expect an eye for an eye. Fair?" I cocked an eyebrow.

"Fair." Disagreement flashed in his eyes, but he said nothing more.

I turned to head down to the city when his voice stopped me, "We didn't fault you for it because we knew you didn't know. We didn't tell you because it would've ruined everything we were trying to prove. I promise when this is set straight, you will not have this sin smeared against you. This one falls on us."

This one falls on us.

I hoped he believed that like a mantra.

WOE

"And who was there when you always needed her?" Naeva asked. It had to be her, because her honeyed voice slipped so freely through the dim lighting.

"Angel," Ayden repeated.

"No, no, no. Sunny. Try again." She lifted her fingers to his head, wiggling them.

No, sprinkling something on—in his mind.

"What the fuck is this?" I asked as I rounded the corner, drinking up every detail I could in this piss-poor darkness.

Naeva stood in front of my boyfriend who sat in a chair. She wore her usual outfit, Ayden his. Sunny waited in the back as if she were a theater kid ready for her cue.

Dressed in dark blue shorts, a white shirt, black sneakers. Her red hair fell down her back in curls today, and if my calculations were correct, she was dressed to impress my boyfriend after promising me she wasn't going after him anymore.

"Angel," Ayden said as he jumped from the chair.

Naeva clasped her hands behind her back, shaking her head.

"Eliana."

As Ayden headed for me, I dodged him, marching over to the Cupid. "Answer me."

Her eyes darted to Sunny as if she could have stepped in and saved her. "Listen, it's not what it looks like."

"It's exactly what it looks like," I seethed. Hence why I studied every detail. I knew she'd pull this bullshit line. "Don't you dare try to pin this narrative that I'm inept."

"Apparently they want to try and replace my memories," my boyfriend said. "Of you."

My head whipped around so fast I almost lost it. "Excuse me?" I screamed. "What the fuck for? What do you need to replace me for?" I pointed to Sunny. "Is that why she's here?"

Naeva hurried over to me to try and calm my nerves. Rookie mistake. "This whole idea of you dating Nephilim is terrible."

"And Sunny makes more sense?"

"You're a guardian angel! Your soul was already saved." As I studied her eyes, something seemed off. Her eyes weren't normally this burnt shade of brown.

"So your solution is to say: *fuck Sunny's soul*?" I snorted. "Be fucking for real right now, Naeva! Do I look saved to you? No, you know what, don't answer that."

Sunny frowned. "Is that really it? You were going to throw me under the bus because you care about Eliana more?" Still, she slipped in, "I came here because she promised she knew how to fix him. I didn't know she was erasing his memories of you."

Anything to save herself.

I scowled. "She does not care about me. This isn't what it even remotely looks like. She's in it to save her own skin. And what are you doing here? You aren't trying to stop her. I thought we had established that Ayden and I are together? We made it clear!"

A tear slipped. "You did! I'm not lying!"

When they really said it wasn't black and white, they weren't kidding. Everyone here was a piece of shit in some form or another.

"Forbidden romance is bad, Eliana," Naeva interjected. "I have a duty."

"Says the bitch who is breaking laws to play twiddle-thumbs with Matthew's dick." It was maybe a bit harsh, but I couldn't see beyond the red hues.

Shock crossed Naeva's face, her lip twisting upward. "Oh?"

Sunny's eyebrows jumped up and she backed away. Better if she did.

Ayden stayed silent on the whole matter.

"You think you can just replace me." I pointed to Ayden. "You think it's that easy to replace his memories of me with Sunny instead. Are you trying to say I'm forgettable?"

"That's the issue. You're not."

I choked. "The issue? Oh, I'm sorry! I'm sorry I'm not a fucking nobody that you can dump on the side of the road when you don't need me! Heaven forbid I matter to anyone!"

She sighed. "That wasn't what I meant."

"Oh. What did you mean?" I furrowed my brows, crossing my arms, sweeping one arm. "Please, do explain." My jaw clenched.

She shook her head. "Nevermind."

"Did you know something is happening in Heaven?" I cleared my throat before I punched her into next week. I desperately wanted to.

She snapped her eyes to me. "What?"

With a nod, I said, "Yeah. Or did your boyfriend keep you out of the loop because you can't be trusted? Well, that's the sitch. Matthew came to me telling me something was wrong."

Ayden crossed his arms. I didn't dare ask him why he wasn't fighting back against the magic of having me erased.

That'd be for later.

"What's wrong?" he asked.

"He said the Thrones won't even look at his cases. That everything is changing and God won't answer. Nobody has seen Him in a while, and we can't seem to get into the Hall where He's usually around. He said if we can figure out what's going on in Heaven, it could help us, too."

Naeva shifted her weight, casting her gaze away from us.

He grabbed my hand, fingers slipping between mine as if he could lace us back together. "Let's go then. What are we waiting for?"

Naeva and Sunny both stepped forwards, but he shot them a glare. "Don't even think about it."

It was probably wrong to leave them, but we did it anyway.

I explained to Ayden what Matthew told me, to help clear up confusion and misplaced emotions, as well as ease his fear that he was being punished.

"And what can we do right now?" he questioned a little too roughly.

"Matthew is looking into it. He'll let me know when he needs my help. Or yours. But keep an eye on everyone down there, including Lucifer."

"Will do."

People walked by and entered shops, bars, and restaurants. Cars honked at each other. A construction zone blocked off one area of the sidewalk.

Construction was nothing new to me, being from Portland. We'd always had it. Everywhere you drove, those damned orange cones stood out. You may as well have named them a new species, part of nature's finest. Coneopius or something like that, spotted in the wild, more common in some cities than others. You couldn't get around them no matter which way you went. They were as invasive as English ivy. Traffic was *always* backed up. Here it had been a breeze compared to that.

The locals didn't agree, but I didn't blame them, either. Nobody liked traffic, or construction. Whether it was everywhere or in select spots. I wouldn't fault them for that.

"Let's go on a date," Ayden interrupted my thoughts.

"Date?"

"A real date. You and me. We never get to go. I mean, we have our cabin. But I should take you out on a real date, like the movies."

"The movies where people yelled at us to shut up because of your jokes."

"Exactly."

"I'm not really interested in a movie," I stated. "What about swimming?"

"And where should we go?" He smirked a bit. I knew where his head wandered.

"Somewhere private."

He snorted. "Private? In the blazing summer of Utah? Yeah, right."

Damn, he was right. "Okay, okay. We can go elsewhere."

"What?"

"We're dead. You can fly anywhere. Go to some other country."

Something flashed in his eyes, something of knowing. Childlike. "Yes. Let's go." He wrapped his arms around me, tugging me against his body before jumping up into the sky and soaring over the town.

The flight had been shorter than a plane or a car ride, but I experienced places I never thought of.

Day turned to night. Dawn to dusk. Sky blue became rippled with stars, a moon, and the darkest blues a color wheel could find. Thousands upon thousands of city lights beamed up at me as we flew over what I assumed to be London. At least I recognized Big Ben from up here. I'd never taken the time to visit Ayden's home. I wondered if he missed it. Surely he did, right? At least now he could come back whenever. No money, no stress.

Just a flight away.

"This must have been what Wendy felt like," I said.

"Hm?"

"Wendy. Peter Pan. When he took her and her brothers for a ride to Neverland, this must have been it. It's magical. It's absolutely beautiful. How do you top this?"

And of course, I'd been proven wrong.

We flew into a few countries I didn't recognize. Where the sun hid beyond the horizon, moon bright in the night.

Then we landed.

"What's this?" I asked as his grip loosened.

"It's a swimming spot. I once visited as a kid, but I remembered it when you said private. Not many people come." When he saw my confusion, he chuckled. "Blue Lagoon. We're in Iceland, Love. We can find a spot toward the back. It's still summer, so you probably won't find as many people here. It's a spa. It's better to come during winter when it's colder and steamier, but it's not as if it makes a difference to us. Besides, people here aren't going to stare or care about us."

The water had been crystal blue, a few stone pathways cutting through. So many different watering holes and a beautiful view of the cemented bottom. Man-made, sure. But gorgeous, nonetheless.

He dressed down to his briefs. "Let's go."

I glanced at my clothes. "I would have to change first." That was fairly easy. I swapped it out for a simple swimsuit. I opted for black high-waisted bottoms and a bright red top that fit my boobs, only because it'd been made different from human clothes.

Ayden pulled me down into the water, wading backwards, fingers wrapped around my wrists. "We'll relax here." He yanked me closer.

"You and me. Nobody can bother us." His fingers brushed up my backside, over the ridges of my scars. "Sorry," he whispered when he noticed me wince.

Shaking my head, I lowered down to my neck. "It's not you. It doesn't hurt. It's just a painful reminder." I swam over to the edge, resting my chin on my arms as I laid them on the corner. "A reminder of what I once had but no longer do."

His hands slid up, fingers moving deeper into my shoulders. "You deserved better than all of this." His thumbs worked out the knots I didn't know had managed to form.

I shrugged a little. "I did. But it's not your fault. I always wonder what would have happened if you hadn't been poisoned. Would I have lost my wings? Would the fallen angels still be after us? I suppose we'll never really know, will we?"

"We can't focus on the past, or what could have been." He pressed a soft kiss to my shoulder. "It'll only make us feel worse."

He was right, again. We couldn't control it anyway.

"Then tell me, Ayden," I began, "why you didn't fight Naeva's attempts to erase me."

His fingertips danced up my soul, leaving traces of shivers. "She promised to fix it. Us. Everything. I assumed she could remove the poison. I swear it. It was stupid of me to trust her at all." He pushed my hair to one side. "The way she worded it made it sound like she had found a solution for us. She was going to find my memories. The poison had infected my mind, but I see now she thinks *you're* the disease."

That word shook my core.

Disease.

I spun around to face him. "Why? Matthew said it was never my fault. How can he love her when she despises me that much?"

"Because we can't help who we love. You said that." He placed his knuckles under my chin. "But that doesn't mean when he finds out what she's doing behind his back that he won't take action. I just hope he chooses our side."

"I hope so," I said in a quieter tone. Wrapping my arms around his neck, I did the same with my legs around his waist. I needed to soak in every bit of him before it was too late. If things didn't turn out well, I couldn't forget the way he felt, tasted, smelled, touched, or loved me in return.

His arms slid around me as I rested my forehead to his. I squashed all the rotten words climbing in my mind, trying to break through the solid earth. Ayden Dyer was at least mine. We fit together perfectly, and he was made to love me as much as I was him.

I wouldn't forget him even if they erased him from my mind.

"Oh how fast the time passes," I said to Liam. "Well you heard the night. It's Halloween."

"Which we don't exactly celebrate anymore, do we?" He cocked an eyebrow.

My laugh carried with the wind. "Nonsense. I do. Because of Ayden. It's party time." I grabbed his wrist and dragged him over to the edge of the cloud. "Let's go." I pointed to a house with lights and tons of people hanging out on the lawn in one of the nicer neighborhoods. Cars wrapped around the block. "That one."

We jumped down, landing.

"Wait!" I covered my mouth with both hands. "I need a costume. Last time I used my wings but... Well, you know." My lips twitched. "I know it's late but we're also angels. We can make something work."

"Scary or sexy?"

"What?"

"Those are usually your options." He chuckled.

Wiggling and twisting my wrists at my side, my brows knitted together. “How about both?” I twirled a strand of hair. “You think I’d look good as a redhead?”

He furrowed his brows. “What do you have in mind?”

“Close your eyes.”

He followed orders, hands shoved in his pockets.

I switched out my clothes for a costume. A brightly striped turtleneck with long sleeves in the colors red, blue, green, and yellow, with a skirt of blue jean overalls and a front pocket. Knee high white socks with 3 stripes at the top in the same colors, yellow converse pumps, and bloody scars across my face and one around the right eye. I changed my hair color to a vibrant, natural red. “Done!”

When he opened his eyes, they widened. “Wow.”

“You recognize me, right?”

“Well, I mean...”

“Liam! He’s literally just like you, for crying out loud.”

“I’m sorry!”

Rolling my eyes, I turned away. “I’m supposed to be Chucky. Ever seen *Child’s Play*? You know, the guy who plays with voodoo so he can keep killing as a doll and escape the detective? He’s a classic. Dare I say the best killer around, and I can say that as someone who’s been murdered. Might as well embrace what I cannot change.”

We entered the house and I glanced back to find Liam staring. I scoffed before pushing my way through the crowd. “Let’s have some fun.”

I grabbed a red cup from the kitchen and took it with me, sipping from time to time. I definitely got compliments and pleased looks from men and women, and it didn’t bother me.

I had a few conversations about the afterlife, both in character and for fun. Liam didn’t say much, and it was at that moment I realized the roles had reversed. In the last two years since my death, I was coming out of my shell and attending all the events I never got to just to make up for my short life. Liam was folding in on himself as if this was never his scene at all, when we both knew otherwise.

An hour later, I was dancing amongst the college kids who convinced me to shotgun my alcohol. People cheered as I downed another red cup and slammed it on the counter.

"How good is your aim?" One guy nudged me.

"Better than yours," I shouted back, eyes flicking down to his crotch.

He threw his head back, a laugh floating in the air soaked in sweat and sex. "Then let's test that!" He pointed at two other party-goers with his middle and forefinger, waving them over. "You and me against the two of them! Beer pong. You up for it?"

Throwing a smirk, I set up empty red cups as they poured alcohol into every single one. "Bring it on!"

Liam stood off in the corner, hiding away from the world.

Now he knew how I felt.

Leaning forwards, I grabbed the ping pong ball. I stepped back, aiming for the ten cups forming a triangle. I tossed it and it landed in a middle cup. "And that's how it's done!" I threw an arm up. "Drink," I twirled my forefinger.

The guy grumbled, fixing his glasses. "Do I have to?"

The woman shot me a glare. "Don't be a pussy."

I folded my arms while a smirk danced in the corner of my lips. "Go on."

He grabbed the cup and threw his head back, swallowing it in one gulp. He threw an elbow over his mouth, coughing into it. "Shit. That went down strong. What the hell is this?"

I leaned in, resting my hands on the table. "Vodka."

"Isn't it supposed to be beer pong? Kinda in the name." The guy gestured.

I shrugged. "The guys already took it and left us with vodka. Don't hate the player, hate the game. Or whatever the fuck they say."

My partner grabbed the ball. "My turn." He stepped back, throwing it. It bounced between the cups and he groaned. "I swear I'm going to come back from that."

"Uh-huh," I said.

The woman grabbed the ball and it bounced before landing in the first cup. "Time to drink your sorrows away."

I removed the ball, handing it over and shooting the alcohol back. "Done."

"Ah, ah." She pointed to another cup. "You know the rules. It bounced off the table so you have to drink another."

Reaching forwards, I grabbed another cup and took the shot. "Happy?" I slammed the cup against the wall.

"Very." Her eyes sparkled as she handed the ball to her partner.

He tossed it over and we both watched as he hit me straight in the chin. "Sorry!"

I snorted as I swiped it from my boobs. "Yeah, or so he says." I leaned inwards, making direct eye contact with the woman as I tossed it.

"Daaaamn," my partner exclaimed. "Where did you learn to play beer pong so well?"

I flashed my eyebrows at her as she downed the cup, humming. "I was an only child."

Was.

I needed to be more careful, not that these tipsy partiers noticed.

"That makes zero sense." He grabbed the ball and tossed it, landing in a cup. "Score!"

The opposing woman cursed as she grabbed the cup and downed it again.

I leaned against the table with one hand, the other palm out as she tossed the ball into it. "When you're an only child in a big house, you get bored and find things to do." I flashed my sly smile before tossing again and landing in another cup. "It's my secret power."

"Angel?" That name froze me in my spot.

And the simmering promise squeezed my heart, thawing me again.

I turned, nonchalantly, to find Ayden standing there. Of course he'd be at a Halloween party. It was too fitting for us both.

"And now we know your weakness," the woman said as her partner drank the cup.

Ayden's eyes roamed down my body, taking in the costume. His pupils were practically blown, and I couldn't quite tell if that was a good or a bad thing. "I didn't think I'd find you here, like this." His tongue slid over his bottom lip. Maybe he had a thing for killer dolls, given our track record and all.

I winked. "Did you think you'd find me here?"

"What else should I know?" He stepped so close I could smell the bourbon on his breath. "Sneaking into parties, dressing as murderous toys. You're a master at beer pong."

"I look good as a redhead." I twirled my hair.

"That you do," he said in a deep, low accent.

"Excuse me!" my opponent yelled. "Look at me so I can make my shot."

I spun on my heel and faced her. "Don't miss."

She scowled. "Don't plan on it."

Ayden's hands slid on my waist as he pressed himself behind me.

When she aimed and let it fly, it bounced off the edge and to the floor.

"Aw, no. You really could have had that." I shot her a grin.

She flipped me the bird.

The game went on for only another twenty minutes. My partner came through, and between the two of us, we really pulled ahead and took home the victory.

They wanted another game, but Ayden grabbed my hand, telling them I was his for the rest of the night, and then he pulled me through the crowd. I wasn't sure where we were headed, but I let my mind wander.

We ventured down into the basement, my eyes scanning the light gray walls. The music was still thumping down here through the speakers built into the house so I could barely hear myself think. I forgot Liam had been here somewhere, but I didn't care either.

When Ayden closed the door behind us, he pressed me against it. I had a split second to note the rows of bookshelves behind him before his lips crashed to mine. Another split second and his tongue was sliding along until I gave him permission.

I wrapped my arms around his neck as he lifted my thighs to his hips.

His tongue played well with mine, a low moan vibrating through him. When he pulled away, he dragged his lips down my jaw, igniting a fire in my core.

Deep down I knew we weren't going to go too far, but if he'd asked me to, I would have said yes in a heartbeat.

"You know, when we were at that first Halloween party, I despised your guts so much. But I entertained the thought of kissing you. Just for the night. How I kept self-control is beyond me." He planted kisses along my throat, pulling the fabric down my neck.

Without even thinking, he slipped a crumpled piece of paper into my front pocket. *A note.*

For me.

"So you know I still love you," he mumbled against my skin.

I leaned my head back into the wood of the door, threading my fingers through his brown locks. "Kiss me all you like, Ayden Dyer. The night is yours."

I left room for the idea of sex, knowing full well it wasn't going to go there.

I'd been ready to give into him wherever, whenever. Ayden had gone soft on me, but I wasn't going to admit to him that it turned me on even more. He was the best kind of addiction—bittersweet—and a little poisonous. The taste of sugar on his tongue made it far too easy to allow him to infect me all the same.

He nestled himself between my thighs, head buried against my throat as he picked a spot and sucked. I arched into him, my moan seeping into the pages of books.

A knock sounded behind me, and they attempted to turn the knob and push us forwards. Ayden slammed his hand against the door, shutting it a little too hard.

They must have gotten the hint because they didn't try it again.

"Ayden," I breathed. Heat burned from his kisses, a trail leading back up my jaw, and then the fire exploded on my lips when his landed. Demanding, tempting, inviting.

Slipping my hands down his chest, I panted between kisses. "We should head up." For a second, I thought he was going to take my advice. However, he carried me from the door to a lounge chair, setting me in it. The monster I'd unleashed in us both clawed through the logic, all thoughts bleeding. The only thing left intact was my heart telling me it was right, that we were where we were meant to be.

His rough hands slithered under my skirt, up my thighs. A whine escaped him. "Bloody hell, Angel. You didn't wear underwear?"

"I didn't find a need to," I said quietly with hooded eyes.

He pressed another kiss on my lips. One to my neck. He lowered himself onto his knees in front of the chair.

My gaze followed as I gripped the arms to pull myself upright. "Oh, there's no need for that."

"Is it because you don't want to, or because you just feel guilty? I assure you, Love, you do not need to feel ashamed." His green irises were no longer visible, eyes entirely black. Maybe I was supposed to be afraid, or wary, but I simply wanted more. Giving him a slight nod, his fingers wrapped under my thighs, pulling me closer to the edge of the seat. Claws dug into my soul, my eyes darting to his hands. They'd grown in size, and when I met Ayden's gaze, so had he.

Again, I should have feared him. I should have screamed or ran. But I wanted to do those things for different reasons. To be chased, to be caught. To scream his name.

Someday, I told myself.

His head disappeared under my skirt, my eyes finding the ceiling, nails digging into the sage fabric. Just before I closed my eyes, wisps of shadow floated above me. The air dropped a few degrees as heat pooled in my core, spreading outwards.

My gasp was swallowed up by the darkness, a tell that nobody could find us or hear the very things we were committing. I gave myself the right to be as loud as I wanted. Tension faded as I melted into him, our souls in tune.

The way his mouth moved was enough evidence that he enjoyed himself just as much if not more than I did, and hell, I had relished the glory.

I couldn't forget how he praised me even if I tried. I quite savored the view of him from here.

He never failed to finish the job, either.

A keeper.

Swiping my thumb across my lip, we made our way back upstairs to the party.

The extra pip in Angel's step had been obvious, and the knowing look on Liam's face confirmed it. Telling by the way people could sense these things, I didn't bother trying to hide it, and I didn't think she cared either.

Lifting my chin some more, I followed her through the crowd, her fingers wrapped around my wrist to keep us together.

My eyes drifted down as she swayed her hips to the beat of the music. The lyrics were easy to make out, only because they'd been popular songs in the early 2000s. They were ingrained in our heads already. Otherwise, the music vibrated through the walls and floor, forcing most people to move their bodies in some form or another. It was impossible not to nod your head even a little.

She twirled on her toes, facing me as she moved backward into the crowd of people. Clapping her hands, rhythm started from her head down to her toes.

A laugh cracked me open as I watched her bop her head, hair flying side to side.

People loved her, too.

She shook her fist, clicking her heels together, her grin shining bright.

At some point she forgot I was even there.

She swooped from one side to the other, getting lower as the music did, knees pressed together. If she wasn't careful, she'd flash someone.

She mouthed the words, and somewhere along the way, sound came out. It had been at that moment I realised I'd never heard her sing before. And I wasn't sure if you could count rapping as singing, but whatever she was doing, she killed it.

She lost herself to the atmosphere in the best way.

Leaning against the wall, I allowed her to be my event of the night.

The music cut out for a second, switching gears. I didn't recognise it. It'd been more of an alternative sound compared to the pop and rap before.

"Dance with me!" Angel grasped my hands, dragging me in the midst of the crowd. She swayed, twisting some more. I didn't complain about being this close to her, and I said not a word when she put her hands on my chest because some strangers squeezed by.

Leaning into her ear, I shouted, "Do you like when I call you Angel?"

Something must have slipped because she looked taken back. "What? What kind of question is that?"

I shrugged. "Figured I'd ask!"

She shoved me through the crowd, my back hitting a wall. Her eyes narrowed. "If you stop calling me Angel, that's the day I know you've moved on."

A smirk flashed. "That would never happen. You're entwined in my soul." I swiped her wrist just in time to spin her into me, yanking her back against my chest. I tightened my arms around her stomach, burying my face in her neck. "You keep me sane. I'm asking you to stay, for me."

She craned her head toward me. "What makes you think I'm ever going to leave? I think if I let you eat me out, you're mine for life."

A laugh burst from me. "Angel!"

She shrugged. "What? Am I wrong? I don't allow just anyone to do that."

Pressing my nose against her skin, I inhaled the scent of roses in full bloom during a rainstorm. "And you taste of the sweetest candies."

If I'd lifted my eyes, I knew I'd find her flushed.

"You're the snowflakes that shimmer under the winter sun. Sharp. Unique. You're the petals that float from the trees when spring comes around. You're everywhere, and beautiful, and you make the world a prettier place to be." I pressed my lips to her cheek. "Summer daisies. Bright and as bold as the sun. You're stubborn, and you get me so angry for good reasons." I allowed my eyes to fall shut. "The colourful leaves that change, promising that even if death is near, you'll return on the other side. You don't give up. You make people feel something again."

She twisted herself in my arms, cradling my face between her hands. "Don't lie to me, Ayden. I swear if you lie to me."

Lowering my voice to a whisper, I leaned in, "I'd never lie to you."

She kissed me. At first, I'd felt the want—the need. But buried in there had been a woman who'd been splintered.

That was us. Cracked.

Working on a repair.

This kiss had been only a stitch, but it was enough to give us more hope than the last one.

Her lips were soft. Tender. There was something so raw and vulnerable just beneath the surface of her heart, and she peeled back that layer to allow me inside, to hold her together when she was no longer strong enough to do so.

She'd saved my soul, and I'd forever be indebted, making it up to her in every way possible.

Pulling away just a bit, she took a deep breath as our foreheads pressed together. Her hands slipped from my jaw, and I caught them in mine, creating a promise in the way I encased hers.

"You should sing again," I broke the silence with a chuckle. "Is there anything you suck at?"

Her cheeks tinted pink. "Well, of course."

"Mm, what's that?" My eyebrows danced.

"You."

The answer didn't register until her eyes cast south.

A laugh ripped through me. "Clever, Love. Very clever."

With my fingers wrapped around the back of her hands, I rubbed my thumbs in the centre of her palms. "I do like it when you sing."

She kissed my fingers. "Then I'll sing just for you."

"Well we're at a party. Don't hold back." I gestured.

She laughed, and that had been the real music to my ears tonight. That and her singing, of course. "I don't know the words to these songs. Now if it's Soulja Boy singing about how she should kiss him through the phone, then yeah, I memorised that by heart."

I leaned back against the wall, pulling her closer to me, as if that was possible. "Little did I know seeing you dressed up as a killer doll would get me going tonight."

She shrugged. "Liam did ask if I wanted sexy or scary and I opted for both. I think I pulled it off. But!" She lifted a finger. "I may not be able to sing. However, I can still dance." Her shoulders sank a bit. "I never got this back then. These Halloween parties in some strange way make me feel alive and like I belong somewhere, like I'm not just the murdered college student who then got tossed out of Heaven's clique because she lost her wings for loving a man."

I opened my mouth to tell her but she backed away, letting go of me as she disappeared into the crowd. She'd show up every other second when her red hair flashed, and I'd find her swaying to the music with the biggest grin on her face.

I meant to tell her she did belong. They adored her here. I recalled the moments last Halloween when she showed up. I didn't want her to, but she had always gone against my wishes. For good reason.

Besides, she deserved to feel like she had a place in the world again. How could I take that from her?

I spotted that familiar golden halo and white wings taking up the bloody space around my *party. What the fuck? "You followed me again! And you say you're not a stalker?" I shouted, refraining from grabbing her shoulder and making her face me.*

I could kiss her. I wanted to. No. A fleeing thought.

I'd never stoop so low.

She tilted her head my way. "I can't let you out of my sight. You should know by now I'll follow you. I have to make sure you don't get yourself almost killed again." Again? Was that all she saw in me? Was I simply a victim?

I yelled, running my hands through my muted hair. I then shook my head, crossed my arms, and spat, "You have no idea how much I despise you. Can you just bloody leave me alone?"

I spun on my heel and hurried to the kitchen as I chugged the last of my beer. Bloody fucking Angel. Always ruining everything. Ruining my life.

Taking what didn't belong to her.

Fucking hell, I despised her so much.

Just as I chugged down another beer, she was already strolling over. Red clouded my better judgment, or maybe it'd been the alcohol. Maybe both. But as she approached, I shoved past her. "Don't fucking follow me."

"Ayden," she called out, grabbing my arm. I whipped around, slapping her. Shock crossed her features as she held her hand to her cheek, not fazed by the pain. No red mark, either.

Still, I knew it was wrong.

I'd hit *her.*

No, that couldn't be right. Could it? I was tempted to ask her, but I couldn't get the words to form. They weighed heavy on my tongue, jumbled.

What a fitting song though. *Psycho Killer*, by a woman artist I couldn't name.

Given Angel's costume.

"Jake! Brittney!" I yelled as I spotted them in the mash of people. They emerged to greet me all the same.

Angel approached us. "Who are they?"

"Ayden here saved our asses last time," Jake said, pointing at me. "At another party."

The very one I'd spied on her at. She didn't need to know that was the night I followed her. I'd been to countless parties over the summer.

At least before I would mentally age out and the world would go on without me.

Brittney dragged Jake over to a game, waving bye.

Angel leaned back into me. "Now she's got some nice boobs." I furrowed my brows at the comment, wanting to ask, but not sure how to pry into that one. "Jake's cute, too." She shrugged. "I wonder if they'd be Frens or Wisps."

"Friends or what now?"

"No, no." She faced me, grabbing my chin. "Frens," she pronounced. "Or Wisps. Brain or heart, essentially." She laughed at my confusion. "They're terms that guardian angels mostly use to figure how best to approach a charge. Oh, and that's what you were. Guardee, or a charge. We called anyone who needed a guardian a charge. Also the Rising. Charges are a forever growing group of humans because you tend to use either your emotions or your logic a little too much."

"And me?"

A cunning smile appeared. "Definitely emotional, my love." Emotional? Me? What made her look at me as emotional?

That felt like a jab to the chest.

"Frens, or Wisps. Frens tend to focus more on the logical aspect. They think about the outcome and everything else in between. Wisps use their heart more, so they think about how it will make them feel. They go with their gut," she threw in before I took offense. "It's not always a bad thing. But sometimes people take it too far."

I nodded a bit, pecking her cheek. "Fair."

"Oooh, I know this song!" She gasped as her fingers slipped from mine and she vanished back into the bodies.

With a content sigh, I let her singing and dancing be the end of my night. I didn't ponder any longer about the faltering and unforgiving memories in my mind.

I slipped between the gates, the squeal piercing the sky as I pushed them back together. I could have walked through if I really wanted, but I didn't think anyone would stop me from sneaking into a cemetery on Halloween night.

Walking towards my own headstone, hushed voices floated nearby, and I redirected my steps. When I came around a large tree, I crossed my arms. "What the hell are you three doing here?"

Ayden, Sunny, and Liam all turned to face me. Ayden was standing near another grave, Sunny on her knees, and Liam wavering with his hands in his pockets.

His eyes went wide and he stepped back. "It wasn't me."

"We figured we'd try a seance," Sunny answered casually.

"A seance? Are we serious?"

She glanced between the guys. "I am. They might see it as a joke. Anyway, I figured it couldn't hurt. If y'all are real, I'm curious to see what a seance can do on Halloween night. In a cemetery."

"We're summoning good ole dad," Liam chipped in.

Justin Smith? Sunny's father?

I wasn't ready for that can of worms to be ripped open.

"Mason, you made it!" Sunny squeaked as her brother brought a few more things. "Ooh, you brought the candles." She laid it out. "The Ouija board!"

Liam grumbled, and Ayden snickered.

I rubbed my arms as if it could warm me up at all, or keep the chills away. "Is that a good idea? That shit is dangerous."

"Ouija boards?" She furrowed her brows. "I figured you guys were here so it wasn't too stupid of an idea."

"There's a reason we didn't invite you, Angel," Ayden responded, stepping closer to me and slipping an arm around my waist. "We knew you wouldn't approve, even as naughty as you've become."

"I am not naughty!" I gasped as he slipped a hand under my red skirt.

His laugh woke the dead. "Says the woman not wearing underwear."

I grabbed his wrist. "I told you I don't like wearing it. I'm not naughty. I'm filled with rage after all the shit we've dealt with. Fair?"

"Mm, fair." He pressed a kiss to my lips. "But in all seriousness, you should go. Things might get ugly."

"A seance, without me." I frowned, fingers fiddling the hem of his black button-up.

"And a game!" Sunny exclaimed. "Never Have I Ever."

I shot Ayden a look. "And what, you assumed I wouldn't want to play that, too?"

"You've never done much. You'd win by a mile."

"Or you don't know that much about me and maybe it's time you learn." I brushed past him, dropping down and tucking my legs under me. "I'm staying."

Mason pointed. "Aren't you his therapist?"

"Guardian angel, Mason," Sunny corrected. "She was mine, too, when I went to the hospital. The therapist thing was just a front. Now they're fucking."

I choked. "We are not!"

Ayden sat beside me, yanking me into his lap. "Not yet we aren't. But we're doing many other things."

"We're not just friends with benefits. We're actually dating in case you forgot, and she makes it sound like there are no strings attached to this. There *are*." I shot Ayden my best heated gaze.

"Okay!" Sunny lit the candles while Liam mumbled about fire in a dry field. "So, whoever is partaking, put your fingers on the planchette."

"The what now?" Ayden leaned forwards.

I elbowed him. "It's the heart-shaped piece. If you're gonna summon demons, learn what the hell it is you're using."

He put his fingers on it with Sunny and Mason. Liam stuck his arm in, too. I supposed if you were destined to go to Hell anyway, why bother being careful? Why not play games with evil? Or the Devil in this case.

I kept myself out of it, burrowing a little too deep in Ayden's lap. His presence made me feel a little better, and knowing what he could do.

They opened up that conversation, the planchette moving around letters and spelling out words. I didn't pay much attention. I wanted to tune it out as much as I could.

What I couldn't shy away from were the flickering flames, the low tone in which Sunny asked questions, and the gasps she let out when the entity answered back. Long story short, it wanted to kill us and take Ayden.

Definitely not Justin Smith, and I knew so. You couldn't summon souls rotting in Hell cells through Ouija boards. What people summoned were far more sinister...

They should have taken it seriously. They didn't though.

And it must have sensed their stupidity and hopefully it gave up, because when they said goodbye, nothing else came of it.

"Well that was boring as fuck," Ayden said, arm tightening around my middle.

I shook my head. "Boring is good. Trust me. The last thing we need is Lucifer or his Legion coming to terrorize us more than they have."

"Maybe they're just extra busy tonight," Sunny added. "Whatever. We tried. Happy Halloween, everyone." She set the board aside, humming. "Let's play, shall we? Everyone know the rules?"

A chorus of *yeahs* and *uh-huhs* echoed.

We lifted ten fingers, each of us. Everyone was in it this time.

A game wasn't about to summon the darkness. That was fine by me. I did that enough on my own without even trying.

"Never have I ever died a virgin." Ayden shot me a smirk.

I lowered a finger, glaring. "That was personal."

"Maybe. Have to keep it fair, right?"

Of course everyone else around me was alive or had sex once upon a time.

Clearing my throat, I came back swinging. "Never have I ever had sex."

Everyone else groaned, lowering a finger and cursing Ayden for setting them all up for that one.

We went around a few times, too, lowering fingers from silly things like going to the ocean, being born in another country, and having siblings.

It came as no surprise to me that Liam and I were the only ones who grew up without a brother or a sister.

I was still in the lead though, and Ayden took that as his challenge.

Liam, did, too, I supposed. "Never have I ever dated a redhead."

"Does that count if you are the redhead?" Sunny asked.

"Suppose if you think you can date yourself."

Sunny frowned, dropping her second to last finger. "I've spent quite a lot of time with myself. And I assume using toys definitely counts as dating yourself."

Her brother groaned. "I didn't want to hear that. That's disgusting. What the hell is wrong with you?"

"I'm a woman with needs, Mason. You couldn't have been that oblivious. Besides, when Ayden and I were dating, I had to keep up with my own fantasies."

When her turn came, she sent a sly eye towards her brother. "Never have I ever been attracted to the same sex."

"Okay that was personal, and that was cold." He tucked another finger into his palm.

I wanted to ask him if he liked women, too, or what it meant. But it wasn't my place. Even if it'd make me feel a little better.

Regardless, I had to lower a finger. Most of them missed it, except Liam and Ayden. Liam said nothing. Ayden wanted to say *something*, but my tongue swelled, and I wanted to get this night over with.

"We all know Ayden does have a thing for redheads though," Liam said with a laugh. "Last night, Eliana was dressed up as a famous one, too. Charles Lee Ray." So he *did know* who Chucky was.

"Who?" Sunny's brows knitted together.

"Chucky, you dumbfuck," Mason piped in. "He literally looks just like you."

"One minute she's crushing it in beer pong, then the next minute you can't find her or Ayden," the *real* killer finished.

A shiver violently shook through me as memories rolled back into my head.

"I thought you said you weren't having sex," she shot me a look.

"We didn't, and we aren't."

Ayden leaned back. “There’s a whole lot more to sex than vaginal sex, Sunny. If you were ever introduced, you’d know. A good man knows his way around.”

“A good man is willing to learn what she likes and implement that,” she replied.

“And women?” Liam wiggled his brows.

“All women know what women want.” She smirked.

“That’s you assuming your kinks are universal,” Ayden said with a snort.

“There’s no competition.” While glaring, she crossed her arms. “Unfortunately for me, I only like men. Pros and cons, sure. But here I am, wasting away,” she said nonchalantly, then pouted.

Liam jumped to his feet, starting to pace around the gravestones.

I scooted back against a tree, allowing my head and shoulders to rest against the bark. It wasn’t all that uncomfortable for me since I was already beyond my expiration date. I went to put my knees up only for Ayden to grab my ankles and pull them into his lap. “Why don’t we massage your aching feet?” He removed my heels and started massaging. We both knew my feet didn’t ache.

No, he’d pulled my legs down because I wasn’t wearing underwear. Everyone would’ve gotten a lovely view of my personal belongings.

“Feet don’t bother you?” I asked him.

“Definitely not. Feet are feet.” He shrugged, massaging knots from the ball and then the heel. “There’s not much that bothers me.”

Sunny and Mason were over by the Ouija board arguing about something.

“Aye, what does this mean?” Liam yelled.

“What’s what mean?” I shouted back, wherever he was. I couldn’t see him from this angle.

“This weird looking symbol!”

Symbol?

I rolled over and got up, trotting down to where he was. He was squatting down in front of a tombstone, pointing to a funky looking mark.

"They're symbols for the supernatural," a familiar, navel voice said.

Liam glanced back at Matthew, eyebrows raised high. "Didn't expect to see you show up here. Isn't Halloween a scary night?"

Matthew scoffed. "Scary? Who am I meant to be scared of?" He brushed his fingers over the symbol that'd been engraved in the corner. "They only show up to those who believe in the supernatural. In this case, usually not humans."

"What does this mean?" he asked the Archangel.

It'd been a circle with a line straight down the middle and a large dot in the upper corner just outside the circle.

"It's a sin." He glanced at the sky. "Every grave has a mark. Sin, or virtue. It tells you, or those who believe, where someone ended up. Now, humans don't recognize these symbols. But if they were to do their extensive research and crack the code, they'd know that if they found one, it explicitly states if that person ended up in Heaven or in Hell. There are five for each. Five sins. Five virtues." He held up his hand, fingers spread out.

Smoothing my skirt, I rooted my feet in the grass to keep from finding which symbol was on my own. I wouldn't have known what it meant anyway.

"The five sins are sexual impurity, murder, wrath, greed, and vainglorious. Murder needs no explanation. Wrath, greed speak for themselves. Sexual impurities encapsulate all the things such as adultery and assault." He clasped his hands behind his back. "The five virtues are as follows: chastity, generosity, humility, patience, and salvation. People who stay faithful, people who wait for consent, people who—dare I say—wait for marriage." His gaze darted to me and Ayden. I wanted to shout that we hadn't technically had sex yet.

"All self-explanatory I hope."

Liam stood, wiping his hands on his jeans. "That answers that. Thanks, Matt."

Ayden tilted his jaw down towards me, brows furrowed, mumbling, "Matt? We friends now?"

Matthew crossed his arms. "Angel could learn a thing or two from a pair of underwear. But as angels, we don't concern ourselves with that, do we? With as much contact as you have with the living..." His eyes were more forgiving than suggestive or demeaning.

Mine grew wide.

Something croaked in the distance, and we all turned.

Matthew dropped his arms, peering down at the candles and board. "What were you doing out here? Are you out of your minds?"

"I didn't do anything!" I jabbed my thumb at the others. "I stayed out of it."

"Who did you talk to?" his tone dropped an octave as he growled.

Sunny swallowed. "We don't know. We said goodbye!"

"As if they follow those ridiculous rules that humans made up." Our big brother, Matthew, stepped forwards. "Show yourself!"

Claws wrapped around a tomb, scratching down the stone and leaving marks. The darkness stepped out into a ten-foot-tall silhouette, wings unfurled behind it.

"What in the fuck?" Ayden screamed.

Matthew cursed under his breath, to which I almost lost my balance.

"Use words!" Ayden yelled at him.

Matthew grabbed Ayden by the collar, dragging him and pointing. "You summoned more Nephilim, you ill-fated fingernail!" He let go as my boyfriend stumbled back, fixing his shirt. "To make matters worse, you used a Ouija board to call him here." Then, mocking us, Matthew said, *"Happy Halloween."*

"Okay so he's like me. What does that mean?" Ayden hit Matthew.

Liam threw his hands up as he stepped out of their way. I didn't miss the hint of fear in his eyes as he turned the other direction either.

Matthew shot him a glare. "It means he's dangerous!"

"Oh, thanks!" Ayden said sarcastically. "Why can't we just ask him to show his other form, the fallen angel looking one?" He threw his arm up.

Matthew gritted his teeth. "Because, Ayden, you summoned him using a Ouija board. You've called specifically to the Nephilim side of him, the side of him that he has no control over. He's stuck like this. This is why Ouija boards are stupid. You better hope nobody ever uses one to summon your Nephilim side. Now run!" He threw up his hands, waving us all to sprint in the opposite direction. Sunny and Mason were flying past us first, feet hitting the ground as they pushed forwards.

We hadn't anticipated Matthew not scolding us and leaving us to *burn*, but we didn't abuse it either. We ran like hell.

As shadow tendrils shot out, circling, Ayden wrapped his arms around me and dove into the mud. He rolled onto his back to keep me from hitting the ground first.

But they didn't come for me.

They slithered around Ayden's ankles and yanked him from under me.

He let go of me before I could grab his hands.

"Ayden!" I screamed.

Why would he attack his own? Or was he trying to snag Ayden to give himself an ally?

As if it'd work.

I scrambled to my feet and made a run for him, cursing myself for not having wings anymore.

"Liam, help me!" I screamed. "Matthew!"

Matthew pulled out a dagger made of gold, lunging for the creature. He jumped out of the way, wings flapping fast as he hovered above Matthew and sent his foot to his face.

The Archangel rubbed his jaw. "That doesn't work down here." He wrapped his fingers around his ankle, yanking him forwards.

Ayden was fighting off the wispy arms wrapped tightly around his throat.

Liam bounced off the grass and tackled the creature to the ground, both rolling around in the mud.

My eyes widened as the Nephilim grew another few feet, swallowing Liam in his darkness. "No!"

Matthew lunged for him, dagger stabbing the mud as the pool of darkness absorbed into the grass.

I scanned the pitch-black sky. "Ayden? Liam?" my voice cracked.

But they were here. I knew they were because Utah didn't have starless skies out this far.

The darkness in the sky wasn't from lack of sun. It was a black cloud, the Nephilim spreading its shadows out to hide our view and trapped us on earth.

"What's going on now?" Sunny asked.

I whipped around. "What the hell are you doing here? Run! We told you to go!"

Mason scowled. "I tried to tell her but she won't listen!"

"I can't leave Ayden!"

I wanted to scream that she could, that Ayden was my boyfriend, that he didn't need her. But it wasn't the time to argue.

It was *her* funeral.

"Matthew," I grabbed his arm. "What do we do?"

"I need to find the origin of the shadows, his form. I need to stab him. Nephilim are powerful, yes, with abilities others don't have. But they still cannot withstand a weapon forged in Heaven." He lifted the blade, searching for a glint. You'd find none down here—smothered in hopelessness.

A flesh-colored dot appeared in the smoke. I jumped up, reaching for it, grasping a hand and yanking him back down. Liam slid out of the shadows and hit the ground with a thud.

"Where's Ayden?" I shook his shoulders.

"I don't know! I couldn't breathe in there!"

Could Ayden? Angels didn't need to breathe. But did the weight of the darkness make them feel suffocated, like they thought breathing was crucial to their survival?

Throwing my head back, I jumped again, reaching my hand into the darkness. But instead of finding Ayden, something slithered around my wrist and sucked me up.

I couldn't inhale. I couldn't smell a thing. The shadows hung so heavy that I swore I had my eyes open but there was no way to know for sure.

I was floating, spinning, flying directionless. I reached out to grab anything, but I couldn't find anything concrete to grasp onto.

Twisting, or what I hoped was twisting, I tried to swim up or down, or whichever way would work in my favor.

I screamed when fingers wrapped around my wrist and yanked me.

The moonlight almost blinded me when I dropped to the grass before throwing myself onto my back. Liam stood over me, pulling me to my feet. "Did you find Ayden?"

As I shook my head, the wind whistled.

Matthew attempted to get higher, close enough to grab the thick tendrils dancing in the smoke. He shoved his blade in, ripping it back out and cutting himself with it.

Then Matthew collapsed, sucking the blood from his palm as the darkness swallowed itself up and stars appeared above us.

I spun in every direction, eyes peeled for Ayden. No sign of him.

"Where is he?" I screamed. "I can't find him!"

Liam grabbed my shoulders. "We'll find him, Elli! Okay? We'll find him and we won't stop looking until we do."

Trying not to hyperventilate, I rubbed my face. "He's in Hell, isn't he? That's where they took him."

Matthew clenched his jaw as he brushed past us.

"Where are you going?" Liam asked.

Matthew spat, "To save Ayden. I know that Nephilim didn't take him to Hell. He's hiding him, like a dog does a bone. If we don't get to him fast, Ayden is in deep shit, and I fear there will be no saving him then." He marched out of the cemetery, and I slapped Liam's arm before jogging to catch up.

I hadn't heard Matthew curse before, and quite frankly, I didn't know he could.

The five of us began our hunt.

"I can't go on any longer. My feet ache." Sunny fell to the grass.

Mason grumbled, stopping and giving her his back as he squatted. "Hop on."

She climbed to her feet and wrapped her arms around her brother's neck, letting him carry her. "I'm so tired."

"Then take a nap," he shot back. "You agreed to this journey."

"I didn't know it would take all night!"

She was right.

The sun began to peek above the horizon, splashing the sky in oranges and blues.

"You four stay here." Matthew held his hand up. "I'll be right back." He stopped before a cave, stepping inside to investigate.

I supposed it was easier to worry about yourself than four others who couldn't keep quiet to save their lives.

Mason set Sunny down to go pee behind a bush in the meantime.

I leaned against the rock wall, glancing at Mason, opening my mouth to ask a question. But I couldn't get the words to leave my tongue.

"What?" he asked, not bothering to look my way. "I can tell you want to say something."

After fiddling my fingers, I began to scratch my arm. "How did you... When did you..." The questions were wrong. If I could just word it the right way... When his gaze locked on me, my cheeks tinted. "I just wanted to ask how you accepted that you like men," I said in a quieter voice.

Liam's attention snapped towards us, but he kept quiet.

Mason laughed a little as he crossed his arms. "Don't you love Ayden?"

I knew asking would tip him off. There wasn't an exact science to this sort of thing.

"Of course I do." I frowned. "I suppose it's silly to ask. I'm certain Ayden and I will be together forever, regardless of how things pan out. I never knew you could love someone this much that it physically hurts. It's like being so excited that you forget to breathe."

He shrugged. "But?"

I swung my head towards him, ready to ask what he meant. I knew, though. "I'm with Ayden. That I'm sure of." I pinched my brows together, pursing my lips. "But it's in the back of my mind and I can't keep it quiet. It's like things make sense for me now."

In high school, I'd pass a girl in the hall. She never knew I existed, but I always wanted to befriend her. Her laughter would sooth any bad day, and her curls were perfect from roots to ends.

Back in Portland, during the summer before college, I'd gone to the beach multiple times a day to get my fix of the calming waves against the shore. The smell of salt filled my nostrils.

And then I'd hear her running up the beach with her friends, in shorts and a bikini top. Watching her play volleyball with them was always the fun part, like a habit or ritual I'd repeat just because it made my day better. I never knew why then, but now I supposed I did.

Especially when her girlfriend went jogging up to her side, kissing her cheek.

"I just simply want to understand, and I want to love myself, and I mean all of me. I don't want to shy away from it. Is that so wrong?"

"Is it supposed to be?"

Liam shook his hair. "Well, you made it to Heaven. And I guarantee it's not some secret here. Up there?" He tilted his head, squinting. He sure loved to hear himself talk, pretending he could offer any help at all, knowing damn well nobody asked for his *expert* opinion. "Love yourself, Elli. Just be yourself like you've always been. You're no different than you were. You're bi, so what? Whether it be boobs or a dick, what's not to like?"

Of course all he saw were body parts, but it had been so much more than just that.

And with a roll of my eyes, I almost cut him off. *Almost.*

Pausing to take in my stony expression, he said, "Right, you didn't ask me." He threw his head back into the wall. "Mason, just take the reins."

Mason snickered. "He's right about that first part though. Just be who you've always been. Now you're just more aware that you also find women attractive. Don't be ashamed of it. Plus, I knew Ayden for a short time when he was alive and he was very much a dick, but that man loves you. He's gonna accept you regardless. You should, too."

"At what point am I supposed to admit that to him?"

"When you're comfortable. Don't push it. He'll understand, if he's worth anything." He closed his eyes. "What the hell is he doing in there—taking a shit?"

I choked on a laugh just as Matthew poked his head out. "All clear."

"Clear from Nephilim? Doesn't that defeat the purpose? We're supposed to be finding him," Liam threw Matthew a look. "Or have you been leading us the wrong way this whole time, Matt?"

Matthew rolled his eyes. "You don't want to be trapped in a dark cave with Nephilim. Trust me, even as an angel. They're more powerful than just a fallen angel, remember? Don't test them. You got that?"

"Got it," he mumbled back.

"Good. Your boyfriend's not here, Eliana, but I know where we can find him." His eyes landed on me.

"Really? Where?" I pushed away from the wall, hurrying over.

He lifted something as it glinted in the moonlight. A small silver ring.

Ayden had been wearing it. I memorized both rings every time he ran his fingers over my skin, and it'd been too many times to count.

"Wait, isn't that mine?" Mason squinted. "How did Ayden get my ring?"

Crimson rose to Sunny's cheeks as her gaze darted away.

Matthew continued, "They were here, but he's toying with us. Unfortunately for the Nephilim, we have one thing on our side that keeps us one step ahead."

"What's that?" Mason asked.

He grabbed my shoulders. "Eliana. She knows him better than anyone else. That Nephilim took him somewhere only she would know to find Ayden."

What? I was supposed to answer this kind of question?

"Matt—"

"Where is he?" he questioned with more authority.

But what if I truly didn't know? Did I know Ayden at all? Would he be okay? Why couldn't I just answer the question?

What if we couldn't get to Ayden in time?

What then?

SOUL

"The bakery. The apartment where we met. But there's not some secret hideout he told me about." Aside from the cabin.

I racked my brain for a sign, or anything I could give them. Matthew tapped his foot while the other three stared. They expected a solid answer.

I had to let them down. "I'm sorry. I don't know."

Matthew shook his head. "Well, then we should get going. We have a lot of searching to do. We'll search high and low. Dark corners. Places that Nephilim like to hide. What do you know about them?"

"I mean, other than what they are? Not much. Other than the darkness. Ayden likes bars and places where people harm themselves, if you word it that way. Maybe we'll check there!"

I was certain they only agreed just to start somewhere and make me feel better. We checked every bar, every strip club, every adult shop—which I did stop and find myself wading through some lingerie for future ideas—and his old apartment. Liam checked the bakery for my sake, then his own place.

Technically it was the first of November. *Technically* all students were likely at home after a night of drugs, sex, and alcohol. Or just a late night of eating candy with a scary movie in the background.

Something gnawed at me, tugging the second I even pondered the idea of the campus. A place Ayden's never been, surely.

But something...

"We need to go to the campus where Liam killed me."

Nobody questioned me, as if they knew I had a good reason. As if they knew this was going to lead us somewhere worth looking.

When we arrived, an icy breeze nipped at my skin.

The main building loomed over us, students filing in and out of the doors.

If you asked me, Halloween should have been observed as a national holiday at this point, given how huge it was.

"Sunny, Mason, you two will have to stay here. Liam, Matthew, and I will be quick."

Mason rubbed at the bags under his eyes. "Okay."

I led the two of them through the giant circular field, sidewalks paved through in triangle formations. Considering they called themselves a Mormon capital, the view from the sky was certainly a choice.

The football field was massive, off the side of many smaller buildings, all detached and forming one campus. The main building resembled a capital in itself. That was the one we passed by. The dorms were further out, closer to the parking lots.

When we entered the red building, I wound around corners and down hallways until I stopped in front of my old room. The second I passed through the door, my eyes went wide and a gasp escaped me.

Liam rubbed his neck, and Matthew placed a hand on my shoulder.

"My missing piece. It's here." Without bothering to hesitate, I reached for it. I needed to know. I had to know if Liam had lied to me all along, or if he was telling the truth.

The light flashed, filling me with warmth and knowing.

A knock came through my door and I opened it up to reveal him. Letting him in, a sigh escaped me. "I was just getting ready for bed."

Liam shut the door, throwing me a sorrow-filled smile. He wore leather gloves with a jacket as if getting ready to head back out into the wintery night. "Times are getting tough. It's Christmas and it doesn't at all feel like it." He leaned his back against the wall, burying his hands in his pockets. "She would have made it all better."

Something fluttered inside me. "She would have."

He fiddled with something in his pocket. "I was saving this for her. It was supposed to be romantic." He pulled out a piece of mistletoe. "It's not very romantic when she's no longer here."

For some strange reason unbeknownst to me, my heart began to race. Why was I feeling this way?

"Christmas was her favorite. It was the one holiday where she could be wholly herself." He twirled it between his fingers. Hurt—pain—settled where it shouldn't have. Like it'd been locked in a box, waiting for someone with the key to open it.

My heart began to beat louder, and my mind moved at the speed of light. Maybe it was grief, acceptance, or even just having a shoulder—but whatever it was, it was forcing its way into my skin like a demon possessing a body.

I wish I could have blamed my desires on a demon.

Liam continued to twist it between his fingers, mesmerized by its vibrant colors. He was well unaware of my presence now. He was unaware of the look in my eyes.

I reached out and grabbed hold of his collar, pulling him against me. Our lips millimeters apart. I wanted to feel shame for wanting Selene's boyfriend, but I didn't. I couldn't muster up enough.

With our hot breaths coinciding as one, I brought our lips together until we were no longer hesitating. My hunger grew stronger, my breaths shallower. A need spread through my body, aching and screaming for more.

Liam reached down, grabbing my thigh and pulling it up towards his waist. "Eliana, you and I both know this is wrong on so many levels," he spit out. Yet, he never pulled away.

Selene had always gotten the first pick of the barrel, and I was left out to dry. Liam was always around, always there to have my back and this past week, we grew closer over our shared trauma. He never had a clue, and maybe I never had either... But I was falling for Liam, and I wanted him in ways I had never craved another man before.

He brought his hand up to my lips, parting them with his thumb. "I always knew you felt some sort of way about me."

I closed my lips around his thumb, using my teeth to pull the glove off. "And you never said anything?" I paused. "How could you? Selene was your girlfriend, and my roommate." My best friend.

Liam leaned down to kiss me again, but my throat began to close, squeezing shut, and then it had cut off all airflow. I began to wheeze. He snaked his arm around my waist, grabbing hold of my wrist. "I'm sorry it has to end this way." He tugged, and a sharp pain shot up through my arm until my entire body was screaming in agony. As he tugged again, I stumbled away and choked while clawing my throat. My lungs wouldn't inflate. My throat wouldn't cooperate.

He released a small, disappointed sigh as he tossed the mistletoe. "I suppose you should be careful of what you allow into your mouth. You made it too perfect, Eliana." He grabbed my wrist before I collapsed, pulling on my fingers. Before I had the chance to question what he was doing, my entire body became as light as a feather and the burning sensation in my lungs dissipated.

Something thumped against the floor, and when I looked back, my body lay on the carpet, as lifeless as Selene's.

I faced Liam once more, yelling out as he stared me in the eye. "You're coming with me." He yanked, but my hand slipped from his and I began to drift higher and higher. "Damnit! One day I'll get this right." He hurried and pulled his glove off the ground. "And one day I'll be running the show."

"You didn't lie," I whispered. "You actually told me the truth."

Liam's eyes sunk, eyebrows dipping inwards. "Of course. I told you I wasn't going to lie anymore. I had to take responsibility for my actions." I wasn't sure why he'd changed his mind so obtusely since he died. He'd made it clear then that he wanted to destroy my world and master his power. To run the show, as he put it.

I had once had feelings for my own killer, which made me an easier target.

And then there was a matter of finding Ayden.

What I knew now was that I'd already found him.

"Come with me," I said.

We hurried back to Mason and Sunny, and when they asked what happened, I ignored them entirely.

The two siblings stayed behind since the flight to Portland was quite a distance. They needed sleep anyway.

When Matthew and Liam lowered me back onto my feet, I stared up at my old childhood home.

The one I remembered properly. The parents who had raised me and loved me so deeply that I kicked myself for forgetting.

Were Ayden and I both doomed to fail because we came from loving families?

"That makes no sense," Liam mumbled.

"What?" My eyes snapped to his.

"You both had healthy childhoods and you think you're not going to love each other forever? Even though you watched your parents do just that?"

I furrowed my brows. "I didn't realize I said that aloud." I shook my head, gaze returning to the house. "He's gotta be here. You said the Nephilim wants darkness. What's darker than the childhood home I couldn't return to? But the Nephilim doesn't know that I've already faced my fears."

I simply feared whatever I was about to walk into.

Yet my heart tugged, a low heat beginning to bloom.

The door creaked as I pushed it open, peering up the dark stairs. I was the one who led the way. Up the steps. Down the hallway. Into my bedroom. Then I threw open the closet door, utter disbelief visible on my face. "He's not here." I turned around to face Liam whose eyes were the size of saucers, his finger shaking as it pointed up at the ceiling above me.

No, not the ceiling. The corner behind me.

When I turned around to lift my head, I found tendrils of shadows wiggling in all directions, a pool of darkness just hanging out.

Without thinking, I backed away, feeling for the light switch. I flipped it on and Ayden was trapped with a snake of black shoved in his mouth.

Ripping the gold dagger from Matthew's hand, I grabbed a chair and placed it below him, jumping onto it and swinging the blade. The arms hissed as I sliced into them, retreating into the corner. Deeper. Further.

Until Ayden dropped on me, the two of us tumbling off the chair.

"Matt!" I screamed.

He rushed over and pulled him off, cursing at the sight.

My hands shook as I scooted back, shaking my head vigorously. Blood seeped from the fresh wound in his stomach—the one I'd created when he fell *onto* the dagger.

If he hadn't been Nephilim, it wouldn't have mattered.

But now...

"Matt," I sobbed. "Please, save him. Make sure he's okay!"

He tore the weapon out and applied pressure, shooting me a look. "You didn't see me do this." I was about to ask what that meant when he covered the injury with his palm, blood spilling between his fingers. Rays of light seeped out before vanishing. When he peeled back his hand, the wound was gone, too.

Ayden groaned, and I crawled over to him, pulling his head into my lap. "Hey, hey. I'm here. You're going to be okay." I kissed him. Desperate. With longing. With an: *I told you so.*

He curled into my chest as I tightened my grip on him, pressing more kisses on his head. His fingers dug into my arms, but I didn't truly mind. "I'm a mess, Angel. I'm dangerous. You see that now?"

"Ayden, please," I started.

"What? Am I wrong? Is loving me really worth all the agony you suffer?" He choked on a cry, and my heart cracked. A lump formed in the base of my throat.

I lowered my lips, shushing him, whispering into his ear, "My rose is worth my thorn."

Maybe it had been my fault. If I had been honest with my family, or if I had stopped what happened—just maybe I could have prevented this trickle-down effect.

It had begun subtly. Things that never made me question him. I went to his house all the time because back then he had internet. We couldn't afford that luxury.

He knew that, too.

On one occasion, he decided to take a piss with the door wide open. I could only have been maybe four or five at the time, but I went to find him. I had seen everything, and I remembered the anger he had when I saw him. I was the one in the wrong for snooping, and not him despite leaving the door open. And as punishment, he spanked me. But a detail stuck with me somehow. He took *pleasure* in spanking me. At the time, it made no sense. Now I understood why.

It escalated from that point on.

I'd be playing games on the computer and he'd come in needing to use it, and then we'd be watching porn. A small part of me felt uncomfortable but because it had been anime at the time, it looked like a cartoon. It couldn't be wrong then, right?

From there, it turned into real people. I didn't question it. I couldn't. To cover his tracks, we'd occasionally watch a legitimate action scene—women or men fighting. I enjoyed those, and I made sure he knew. When I asked to watch them again, he used that as leverage to sit down and watch porn that appeared to start out from a fight. It wasn't just any kind of normal porn, either. No, it was lesbian porn and it stuck with me to this day. The horrid feeling of being touched.

No matter how hard I tried to erase the memories, they fused themselves into my head.

Angel would say it was tragic that a young boy had no real memories during that time of his life other than abuse. Reality was cruel that way, wasn't it?

I never questioned my own grandpa or what he did.

At least not until I'd became a teenager and unlocked the porn addiction.

I tried to quit, but every time I relapsed, it grew stronger, its claws sinking deeper into my soul. I stopped fighting. Then Angel strolled in, and I could no longer bury the guilt that came with it.

The shame weighing on my shoulders was something I'd never allow Angel to bear. This would stay my dirty little secret for eternities to come. She would never have to suffer my burdens.

I owed her that much.

Standing before the shop, I eyed the sign:

ANGEL'S LITTLE LIBRARY

Classic. Simple. Cute.

Very Angel.

I stepped inside, a bell dinging behind me. The ring sent a wave of dreams through my head, but a specific one stood out. Owning my own bakery and listening to the sound of customers enter, specifically for my own sweets.

It was silly to dream of at this point, being dead and all.

But if Angel could have a library, why couldn't I have a bakery?

"Welcome!" came from behind the counter. When she popped up from crouching low, her smile faded into curled lips. "Ayden?"

My eyes danced between shelves and shelves of old books. "You've got yourself quite the allure here."

She shrugged as she said, "Liam got it for me." She tried to pass that statement off as if it didn't mean anything. He had feelings for her, and nobody could deny that. We saw right past the walls he built. He didn't want to go rot in Hell when this was over. He wanted to stay by her side in hopes she might lose me, we'd break up, or she'd choose him instead.

It was the same look Angel gave me when I was dating Sunny.

I recognised it too well.

"You've got so many books." I cleared my throat, forcing the subject to another topic. "How many does this *little* library carry?" I asked with a stout laugh.

"Well, to be technical, a library has to be over a thousand books. They might be harder to find but that's the fun in it, even if they're stashed in odd places and cramped on shelves. People spend more time here. I also happen to know where every book is. To answer your question, at least three thousand." Her smile lit up the dim room.

I took a stroll through the shelves, tempted to count but far too lazy for that—even if I did have an eternity. Three aisles made up the back of the store, books shoved into tight spaces to make room for more, as if more would ever be able to fit.

More shelves lined the walls around to the front where the windows were. I supposed if you were a reader, part of the fun was sifting through spines you could barely recognise. Not that I'd know.

Or ever attempt that. Instead, I rounded the corner and headed back to the register.

"And which one do you recommend?" I leaned my elbow on the counter, wiggling my brows.

A cute little laugh escaped her. "You? Ayden Dyer wants to read a book?"

"I do." I nodded, scanning the shelves. I wanted to pick it up and learn more. Not about life, no. But they said that you could learn things about someone by their favourite books, and I wanted to be able to do just that. There were things about her that maybe she never meant to show, and I wanted to pick up on them. I wanted to know what it was about the story made her love it so much.

She stepped away and disappeared behind some shelves before returning minutes later with another novel. "It's not always classic, I know. But I managed to get my hands on it when I was a teen and it resonated with me. You have to have an open mind. Also it's the third book in a series, so you should read the first two." She laid all three out on the counter. "The first book is okay, but not my favourite. Books two and three, however, *are* classics to me. If you hate them, please don't tell me." Her eyes sparkled when they met mine.

I rested my hand over the top of hers, a bolt of electricity shocking my heart back to life. "I doubt I'll hate them. What are they about?"

"Zombies."

"Zombies?" I chuckled. "I never picked you for a zombie girl."

She scratched her arm out of habit. "Back in middle school I went through an entire zombie phase. It was a thing. You had to be there. The funny thing is I can't stand them now, and they're semi-plausible but also not. Anyway."

I grabbed the books. "Then I'll take them. I have plenty of time to read."

As she began to ring me up, which was as simple as a library card log—or whatever they were called—appearing in her drawer, I tapped the counter. "Do I need to return these?"

Her eyes drifted from my fingers up to my face. "It's a library, Ayden." She pointed to the cards I'd just signed with a notable date.

"I know, but what if I wanted to keep them? What if I love them so much I don't want to return them?" She parted those kissable lips, but I beat her to it, "Forget it. I'll bring them back, okay? I promise." I waved the books in my face.

She gave me a slight nod.

"Remember the last time we were in a library?" It was a library in someone's basement, sure. But... The corner of my lips tilted upward to one side. "You found a new way to say my name."

Her eyes grew a bit as her face flushed. "Ayden, that's not appropriate here."

"There's nobody in the store. Sorry, the *library*," I corrected myself, waving my arm around.

"But anyone can walk in!"

"Not if we put the *closed* sign up."

She reached forward. "No."

I frowned, eyes grazing her embarrassment. "I tried." I stacked the books and straightened them. "Can I at least get a kiss goodbye?"

"You're leaving?"

"I have to go read these books." I snapped my fingers, pointing at the stack.

More heat flooded her cheeks. "Right, of course." She circled the counter, reaching for them, but before she could grasp any, I grabbed her wrist and yanked her against me, sliding my arms around her waist. She almost said my name again, but I replaced it with something better—her lips tangled in mine. A nibble here and there. The sweet ecstasy of her presence that I'd never be able to get enough of.

To all the men who had passed over her for any reason before, they truly missed out. I was the lucky winner.

Her fingers scrunched up my shirt as a giggle left her throat. "Okay, okay."

"One more, one more," I whispered.

She fit so perfectly right in my arms. Nobody could ever deny that.

I kissed the soft spot right under her ear. Her grip on me loosened as she let out a small sigh. I pressed one last promise to her lips before letting her go. Not for good, though. No, it'd never be for good. They'd have to burn my soul into nothing before I'd ever let her slip through my fingers again.

With one arm, I swiped the books off the counter and caught them with both hands. "Okay, I'm off to go read your favourite series, Love. You better behave yourself now."

"I always do." She smoothed out her white blouse. "Okay, maybe not these days. But I promise. As long as you don't try to summon Nephilim again."

I grinned. "Nah, they can't get rid of me that easily."

I exited the building and returned to the cabin. It was the only place I could safely read the books without Hell trying to burn them just to spite me, or Angel.

As I leaned back into the couch, I opened up the first book.

It wasn't bad, of course. But I could see why Angel wouldn't have liked it too much. What a tragic ending, for a girl to love a man only to lose him.

The second book had been far more enjoyable, easier to get through. Still, to love a man only to lose him? Sure, she had found someone more perfectly suited for her, but what did it really mean?

But the third book, that was when everything changed.

She'd won me over, and I began to understand parts of her I couldn't before. She unravelled like a bow coming undone. Ink bleeding out onto pages. I needed to take my sister's advice and give her my soul to keep forever, or I feared I could lose her for eternity.

BABYLON

Gold and crystal chandeliers hung from the ceiling, lighting up every inch of this event in the most elegant manner. Silk black banners curved across the crown molding along the corners where the ceiling met every wall. They opted for a classical music vibe, including the tunes themselves.

A few Christmas lights had been strung across the beams and around pillars in a warm white.

It didn't extend much beyond that and a seven-foot tree standing to the left of the grand staircase. Decorated in gold. Bulbs, tinsel, unique ornaments such as deer and a ballerina. A white skirt lay around the base, and an angel stood on the top with a trumpet in hand.

Everyone had been dressed in their finest fabrics, flitting across the ballroom floor in pairs.

Liam expected me to dance with him, but I wasn't so sure I could. Not after seeing that he'd been right all along about my memories.

It never would have been an issue if he hadn't murdered me.

Yet he had.

The city had decided to host a Christmas event in hopes of raising money for sick children. Much like a toy or food drive. A ball, or gala to raise funds. They did it every year, and this year, I chose to attend in hopes these kids would get to live much longer and fuller lives than I had.

A chance to remind myself of who I fought for.

But this holiday... It lodged a stake in my heart.

Tonight was the two-year death anniversary.

A knot formed in the base of my throat as I inhaled sharply.

Liam dressed in a sharp white tux, perfectly fitted to every muscle in his body. His hair had been slicked back to show off his square jawline and sculpted cheekbones.

It hadn't been any surprise as to why Selene and I found ourselves attracted to him at some point.

But it had been a disappointing revelation.

Seeing as he showed up in white, I wanted to make a bold statement by showing up in black. I had lost my wings after all.

I left my hair down in loose waves, not all that concerned about putting it up. Instead, I put all my attention into the gown that complemented my body.

A sweetheart neckline that didn't allow for my boobs to nearly squeeze themselves out, with lace detailing from the neckline down to the skirt, dripping into layers of tulle that fanned out behind me. One-inch lace straps looped over the tops of my shoulders. Half sleeves started from my biceps and flowed down to my wrists in the same tulle material that had been intricately sewn into the embroidery detailing, cuffed around the ends.

As for my shoes, I opted for bare feet. I didn't want to wear heels, and I couldn't pick up pain or dirt on earth anyway.

The back of the gown dipped low enough to show off my scars, something that Liam convinced me to do. Hiding them wouldn't make them disappear. And if I was ever going to heal emotionally from the turmoil, I needed to listen to him. He'd been right. I admitted that.

Railings that climbed up the grand stairs and lined the balcony were painted black. The walls were molded with many details, decorated in black and gold. Sconces hung on the walls every few feet, a bright light in each and every one. Except the one in the back corner, *I noted.*

People from all over had come to dance and mingle. Single people looking for a partner, or a good time—whether that had been in another person or their own company. Married couples with each other, or I dared say those who came to cheat on their spouses.

I couldn't tell any of them apart, aside from the wedding bands.

A yearning sat in the pit of my abdomen, aching, clawing. I wanted what they had.

It was silly of me to dream of marriage now that I'd been dead, and I couldn't escape that truth no matter how hard I tried. I couldn't even be sure Ayden wanted that these days, although he said he did.

The thought was nice. I just couldn't be so sure it'd ever happen to me. I didn't want Ayden to marry me because we'd been through Hell and back together. I needed him to be genuine about spending forever with just me, and only me.

At one point, I assumed he only agreed to wait until marriage to get in my pants. To up and leave once he did. It was silly of me...

But did I know the difference?

I was supposed to.

I knew Ayden well enough to know he'd never hurt me like that, but there were moments when I questioned if it was all too good to be true. I'd never been so lucky, and given the way things played out lately, I rested my case.

I didn't want to question his intentions. I fought my own mind on it. But some days I still wondered if he would have been happier with a woman who could give him all the sex he asked for.

Was it on his mind every time he *saw* me?

"Elli," Liam said as he tapped my shoulder. "You and me. Let's dance."

I'd never be here with him if he hadn't blatantly taken my life. Or maybe I would have been.

"Do you realize how dangerous that is?" I spun to face him. "You're hyped up on Naeva's love potion and now I remember how you made me feel once, and not just the bad parts." With a scowl, I lowered my gaze to his hand. "I'm dating Ayden."

"I swear to you it's just a dance. I won't try anything." He moved his finger over his heart, drawing an *X* to cross it.

Why was it so easy to believe that he was telling the truth? Shouldn't I have suspected a lie? After all the times he lied *before* he killed me?

Besides, I needed to forget the weight sitting on my chest.

He held his palm out again, and so I reluctantly set my hand in it. He whipped me away to the center, hand still in mine, sliding his other one down to my waist. There it stayed, not straying far north or far south. I gently set my other hand on his shoulder, following his lead.

Curse us both.

"I love Ayden."

"I know."

"I'm always going to love Ayden."

"I'm not asking you to stop."

"I want to marry him, Liam. I fantasize of giving him all of me. He won't go that far yet. He wants it to mean more to us this time than it did in all his past relationships—if you call them that. I'm looking forwards to that day."

"I know that, too." His brown eyes dropped into mine, filled with insult, and a hint of longing. "I'm not here to try and whisk you away from him, as much as I'd love to have you to myself." His sigh permeated the air between us. "That's the issue though, isn't it? I did have feelings for you before I killed you. I just let my need for power and vengeance cloud my better judgment. I used you because you let me in. I'm not asking you to forgive me or to look past that and choose me. I'd never choose me, either. I'll still continue to make it up to you though." His gaze lifted to the balcony, something unrecognizable flashing in them.

When I turned my head, I found Ayden leaning against the rail, snarling at us.

"Ayden," I breathed, letting go of Liam and rushing up the stairs with my gown bunched up in my fists.

When I halted, staring at the spot he'd been in, I frowned.

I lost him.

"Damn you, Liam." I wanted more than anything to shove him down a hole and listen to him cry and scream for help.

Of course nobody would come. Lucifer wouldn't fit down there for his sake.

Maybe I'd scared Ayden off by choosing to dance with him. It was my own fault for saying yes. I should have stood firm. Stomped my foot like a child, threw a tantrum. Ayden would have approved of that long before he approved of me cozying up with the enemy.

I wanted to drown myself in alcohol, and now I understood why Ayden did all those years.

But Liam once told me he resorted to such things because someone had hurt him. Someone had broken his trust once and corrupted him for a lifetime in ways I'd never fathom.

If only I could have helped. I'd promised to never let him hurt like that again.

A hot breath fanned my neck.

I turned around to find air behind me. A vast hallway smothered in dim lighting.

I headed back down the stairs and returned to Liam, no longer in any mood to dance.

The ball dragged on with no sign of the man I'd seen before. Did I hurt him?

Of course I did. What kind of stupid question was that?

Liam nudged me. "Hey. They're hosting a small dinner if you want to come."

What was my other option, to stay here and hope Ayden would come back?

"I could eat." I shrugged, glancing back at the balcony as we disappeared into glossy black double doors beneath it.

I thought maybe I spotted a snake of shadow slithering down, swaying. But no, I'd lost my mind then.

I dropped into a chair beside Liam just as the waiters brought out appetizers and drinks. Champagne, which hadn't been as good as people made it out to be. Unless you mixed it with orange juice or something.

There'd been a set of plates at every spot. One larger and one smaller, and a bowl settled on top of the stack. Cutlery and utensils were splayed out on a napkin to the right of every plate, and a wine glass had been placed at the upper left corner.

As the waiter strolled by, I handed him my glass as he poured the alcohol. I didn't want it, but I'd sip it for looks. For the vibe, I supposed.

To blend in.

My eyes grazed over a small piece of paper tented on my plate. Scanning the others, I noted it'd just been mine. Was this seat saved?

I opened it up to read the note: *'So you don't forget I love you.*

Enjoy me, Angel.'

Written in a bold, black marker.

As food was dished up, something brushed my ankle. I lifted my toe to scratch at it.

Liam waved the smell of the fresh chicken, pasta, and bread into his nose. "It smells divine."

Cold, yet soft touched my thigh. Then fingertips stepped their way along my skin, closer to my center.

I gasped a bit, grabbing the edge of the table.

No. He wouldn't, would he?

When Liam faced me and found me with wide eyes, his brows dipped, forehead wrinkling. "What's wrong?"

"I have to use the bathroom." I pushed my chair out, standing. "Excuse me."

Before he could argue that I didn't need to use a bathroom, I slipped out of the dinner hall and found myself a restroom anyway. Thankfully, here they had been for the rich, meaning they didn't use stalls. They were singular rooms.

I locked the door, lifting my skirts to inspect my skin. I shook them, too, just in case bugs were hiding. Sure, they couldn't harm me. But I didn't like the idea of a spider just crawling up my thigh.

Exhaling, I glanced in the mirror, smoothing out my skirts and scooping my hair behind my shoulders.

"You're officially losing your sanity, aren't you, Eliana?" I asked the girl in the mirror. She didn't need to respond. I knew the answer.

Again, something chilly and as gentle as a feather brushed the skin on the inside of my thigh, right above my knee.

It didn't tickle like a bug.

Maybe it'd been fabric.

However, my gown didn't touch that area of my leg.

Whatever it was, it slid higher.

The touch felt *familiar.*

Like Halloween night familiar, and then I recalled the note left on my plate. I concluded: *he would.*

"Ayden?" I whispered.

My grip on the sink tightened as a breeze wrapped itself around my thighs, sliding up my hips, dipping between my legs. Encasing me in the sensation of cool silk sheets on a hot summer day.

I succumbed to the fingers that formed and found their way around, exploring under my gown. Over my stomach, my navel, then low again. The way they danced, moved, and worshipped me.

Whatever he did, I couldn't explain. But this was Ayden.

Leaning forwards, my gasps echoed around me. He brought that uproar inside, easing whatever fear or guilt I carried earlier. I slowly lowered myself to the floor, skirt pooling around me as I folded my legs underneath.

To think there were people who expected me to replace him without someone else, or perhaps loneliness. My hand couldn't work wonders like this though.

As my sweet little dream—nightmare?—came to an end, I tucked myself into my gown.

"Hey," that beloved accent whispered against my hair. "I'm not mad at you, Angel. I could never be mad at you." His cold hands slid over my throat, my shoulders, into my hair, tugging me into his lap. "You can't scare me off. You're *my* girlfriend."

How could I ever forget? He looked fine as hell in his black dress shirt, a few buttons undone for the chest hair and black ink to greet me. His hair had been left a mess, just how I liked him. I reached up, cupping his cheek, feeling the stubble under my palm as I rubbed my thumb over the cheekbone. "But you scared me. I wanted to talk about it, and you disappeared. I wanted to dance. Nothing was ever meant to happen with Liam."

His hand moved to my waist. "Then let me fill in."

I squinted as he hoisted us both up off the tile floor.

He slid his hand into mine, leading me back to the ballroom for one final dance of the night.

When he yanked me against his chest, he started out slow. Both hands on my waist, mine on his shoulders, breaths mingled together. We moved in small steps, swaying to the tune.

Accelerando described the atmosphere, and with it, Ayden moved quicker. In circles, to the side, and back again. I might have even described it as allegro.

We began to spin around other couples as Ayden gripped my hips, lifting me a foot off the ground as I soared. When my feet touched again, he moved with the tempo as if he'd done this before. Had he?

Grabbing my hand and lifting my arms above my head, he twirled me and pulled me back into his chest, taking my breath right from my mouth.

"Ayden," I uttered in surprise.

But he wasn't done.

It'd been a mixture of several different styles, the waltz much slower than this.

We swept the room, people moving with us before stumbling away as we stole the floor. I didn't pay any attention after that. I was dead and I deserved one final dance, and that was what he gave me.

Like that, he dipped me upon the music coming to a halt, my chest rising and falling from habit.

"Merry Christmas, Love," he mumbled as he pulled me back up, pressing a kiss on my lips. It said all the things we needed to. He wasn't angry with me, that he loved me regardless. That no matter how long we waited, he was in it for the long haul.

Soft. Adoring. Nimble.

He put only an inch between us, rubbing his thumb over my

bottom lip. "I know it's a terrible day, a bad reminder. But however I can make it up to you, I will. I'm devoted to you, Angel."

I didn't doubt him for even a second.

And all too soon he was gone with the darkness, people moving around me and leaving me to feel like a still stuck in a movie projector.

Liam came out when the dinner ended, asking what happened, but I'd never reveal something so private and intimate.

Closer to midnight, I snuck back up the stairs, searching the smokey corners and ceilings for any sign of him.

Fingers wrapped around my wrist, twisting me until I came in contact with a hard chest. A laugh passed my lips as Ayden pressed me back into the railing. His lips started warming up mine before leaving a trail of fire down my jaw and across my throat.

"My legs are sticky because of you," I said between pants.

"My bad. I should have cleaned up after myself." Cradling my head in one hand, he tilted it more as he nibbled the soft skin. He was going to send me into a frenzy.

He brushed over my scars, going rigid. "I can never apologize enough."

"Then don't," I finished. "Just love me now. Here. As I am."

We both loosened as I melted into his soul, tethered for eternity. I wasn't ashamed of the fight I put up for his sake. Never.

I simply allowed his hot kisses to light a flame.

Maybe people could see us up here. Maybe it was risky. I didn't care.

I'd let him consume me if that was what he so much as wanted. I'd bend to his every desire, every whim.

A drug I wouldn't kick. The kind that took away the pain and bad thoughts but left you with a few symptoms you could withstand. The very kind a doctor prescribed—and maybe Heaven had been that doctor.

The night closed out, and somewhere along the way, I came to terms with whatever would happen. I'd never stop loving Ayden Dyer. I'd never stop seeing him.

He was mine, and I was entirely his.

"I think it'd be good for you, Matt, to meet Ayden's family and see they're like anyone else."

Matthew grumbled—something about falling angels choosing their fate.

Which, fair, they had. Fallen angels were not born. They were made, and in the rare case like Ayden, they were forced into it.

And *that* was the unfair part.

He'd rightly made his decision and they stripped it away from him.

His dad was the first to swing open the door, and the second he caught sight of Matt, he slammed it shut. Nevermind the fact that his own son was standing beside him.

"He does not like you," I whistled.

Matt shook his head, spinning on his heels, hands balled into fists. "It was a bad idea. Come on, we should go." Ayden grabbed his sleeve, whipping him back around.

Ayden didn't bother knocking this time. "It's my family. What are they going to do, kick me out? It's Dad's fault." He walked in to find his dad scowling. "You can't just slam the door on us like that."

"It's my house, I can do what I want." He crossed his arms like a toddler throwing a tantrum.

Matt's eyebrows shot up for a second. "And how did you attain this house, exactly? Oh, that's right. You slept with a human. Your name can't even be on the lease, can it?"

That opened up a can of worms, in the sense of more questions *and* an actual can of worms.

Ayden's father lunged for the Archangel just as his mom emerged. "Leo! You need to put your differences aside for once and think about our kids. Is that understood?"

He mumbled, fixing his shirt. "He's in our house."

"And what if Ayden hadn't been poisoned? You gonna kick him out because he was an angel? What about his girlfriend?"

Matt lifted his chin, triumph plastered on his face. "You chose to go to Hell. That was *your* decision."

"That's enough," his mom's voice boomed. "Both of you. We're here now. No use in changing the past. It's Christmas for Heaven's sake. Let's go eat."

And eat we did.

Mostly. Liam scarfed it down. Ayden took a bite here and there. Matthew pushed it around on his plate with a fork. His father didn't even pretend as his arms rested on both sides of his plate, eyeing Matt with much hostility.

"It's delicious, Mrs. Dyer," I said. "Thank you."

She smiled at me. "You might as well call me Audrey."

Esme and Arabella both exchanged looks before shooting one at Ayden who stopped mid chew.

My gaze darted between us. What was that about?

Matt put his fork down, folding his hands together. "We need to talk."

"Why?" his father asked, head tilting forwards.

"Because your son was wrongly kidnapped and poisoned. I don't particularly like you or agree with what you did, but I'm well aware that God's Word is the final say. Ayden had made Heaven, even if I didn't agree entirely at the time. Now, God's been missing and if we can find Him, we can hopefully restore the order and get your son back up in Heaven. He'll be safe, protected, and loved, even." He glanced at Ayden. "Not summoning Nephilim in a cemetery on Halloween night and getting himself into trouble."

"Ayden!" his mother shouted. "What's bloody wrong with you?"

My boyfriend swallowed his food. "I had to make a reckless decision at some point. Besides, with this poison running through my soul or whatever, it's a lot harder for me to just say no."

Biting my bottom lip, I leaned back. "That's how I feel when you walk around looking like a snack."

Liam choked on his food while the parents made a face. Esme and Arabella laughed it off between the disgust while Matt muttered something incoherent.

Ayden, however, twisted his body and smirked. "Oh? She speaks."

I shoved another bite of potato in my mouth. "At least now you get it."

His mom pointed her two fingers at us. "You two haven't..."

My cheeks tinted as I shook my head. "No, no. Not that."

He snorted. "But I do know what you taste like." Warmth spread through my core.

Matt dropped his fork.

"To be fair, Ayden, I want to. But you've said you're not ready."

"Wait, wait, wait," Esme leaned her elbows on the edge of the cherry table. "*Ayden* was the one who turned *you* down?"

I nodded. "That's correct."

Her eyes shot to him. "Ayden."

He cast his gaze at the plate. "Sex has always been strictly about pleasure for me, about that self-gratification. It was about gaining control of my body again. But it never meant anything else. Angel does mean something. I don't want this to be another one-night-stand." He stabbed a roasted potato. "I want it to *mean* something. Is that so bloody wrong? When Angel and I have sex, I want it to be different. I want to focus on what it feels like when you love someone."

Arabella rested her chin on her hand, sighing. "That's so sweet. Our baby brother wants to make love."

Matt patted his mouth with a napkin. "That's actually very romantic, and honorable."

"I can take my time when it happens." He glared. "I can truly savor the woman I've fallen for. And once I discover that, we can go crazy with ideas. Try everything. I can fuck her brains out."

Arabella grumbled. "And you ruined it."

He rambled on, "Not that she has brains anymore. Literally speaking. I'm not calling my wife dumb."

The table froze. My heart must have started beating again because it was pounding in my ears as I melted into this chair. My limbs went numb.

Wife.

We weren't even engaged. We were barely girlfriend and boyfriend, seven months in the making.

But Ayden Dyer called me his wife.

What were we supposed to say to that?

He wanted to marry me. He saw a future with me. And he wanted it all *now.*

To Ayden's prayers, nobody responded. We all glossed over the event and continued our Christmas dinner.

"I'll do it," his father broke the silence. "I'll help you find God, only because it'll help my son and my daughters when that time comes. My wife, too, if it dare comes to it." He reached over, sliding his hand over hers, wrapping his fingers around her palm.

Wife. There was that word again.

I couldn't keep it out of my head. My vision blurred, savory and sweet scents—as well as metal clinking against ceramic—both wavering. The world shifted. Tilted, in fact.

He wanted to *marry* me right now.

Hugging myself, I peered out over the monstrous branches powdered in snow. Another year since my murder, and there'd be many more to come. Would I ever get used to them? Would I get used to the world moving on as if I'd never existed in it at all?

Someone laid a blanket over my bare shoulders, and I glanced down at the hand decorated in two rings.

A year ago we stood here. A year ago Ayden found me out here on this balcony, reeling from the idea of being dead. Little did we know we'd end up here again, in the same spot, three hundred and sixty-five days later.

Turning around to face him, I fixed his collar. "So I hear you have a smart wife you want to screw. This is news to me."

He rubbed his neck. "Yeah, that was a slip-up."

A slip-up. But it meant something right?

My head lowered just in time for Ayden to grab my chin and lift it until I found his sparkling green eyes. Always so bright, so full of roguery. Hope and wonder. A man looking for a place to belong.

It was with me. In my arms. My heart. I'd wrap him up in my soul and keep him safe and warm forever.

"Yes." His thumb rested against my bottom lip. "Yes, you heard right."

My soul leaped. I studied every fleck in his irises. The brown, the dark green, and the one hidden just to the left of his pupil in his right eye. The unchanging one. Always solid, always firm, promising me I had a home even if I didn't have a body.

"You've really made tonight bearable," I said in a quieter tone. "I haven't thought about my death much at all."

"Good," he muttered in a low voice. "I like it when I can distract you from these terrible things."

A chill hurried up my spine. "It's best I don't wallow. You keep me occupied."

"Then allow me to fulfill that." He leaned in, pressing his lips to mine.

I pulled away, whispering, "What about Matt, or Liam?"

"Let them find us. I don't care anymore."

And he kissed me as if we'd just discovered each other after a century of searching. Desperate. Yearning. Every heartache pouring out.

He wrapped his arms around my waist, pressing me deeper into him. I lifted my arms around his neck, tangling my fingers in his tufts and letting him know that if he ever asked, I'd say yes without hesitation.

I wasn't sure about much these days, but he'd always been concrete. Solid. A person forever rooted in my soul.

Besides, his lips moved the way the ocean waves crashed against the shore—smoothly—taking what they wanted.

He had all of me, and now he knew that without any doubt.

No longer my drug, nor the treatment. He became the *cure*.

Saint

As I rounded the corner, Liam struggled with something. Someone?

I pulled back, poking my head around just enough to watch him grab someone by the throat, then rip him back. He stumbled, a soul peeling from its vessel.

"Come with me, and you'll be safe," he told them.

The body dropped with a thud as their glass eyes pierced through me. *My first customer.*

I covered my mouth to keep myself from gasping.

"No way!" The soul fought in his grip. "You killed me!"

"I'm saving you!"

"From who?" they screeched.

Liam tightened his grasp. "From Heaven! It's corrupt."

Whipping away from sight, I pressed my back to the wall.

Liam had been playing us this entire time. He was using us, *still* ripping souls. He may not have said it, but he wasn't working for God. He'd been working with Lucifer and his angels. He knew where God went. And if he knew I knew...

I ran back the other way, to Matt's office. I didn't knock—again. When did I ever? "Matt!"

He glanced up from his desk, Naeva perched on the edge to the side of him. She peered over her shoulder.

Why had he let her in? She must not have told him what she was doing to Ayden, and that she had told him and Sunny a lie to erase me from his mind.

I'd smite her if I could.

But now wasn't the time.

"It's Liam." I ran my hands through my hair. "He's ripping souls from their bodies, telling them Heaven is corrupt, that he's trying to save them. You think it has to do with what happened to Ayden and him? And where God went?"

Naeva furrowed her brows. "Liam, the same one I shot?"

I nodded frantically.

Matt stood. "I'm not sure, but there's one way to find out. We need to have a chat." He circled his desk as Naeva slid off, tailing him. "We can't go in blind." He gave us both wary looks. "If he is behind all of this, then we need to be prepared. That means it's an automatic boot from Heaven. We lock him up until we get answers and restore order up here. Then Lucifer can have him all he wants."

Not a foolproof plan, but still a *plan*.

The three of us marched back to the cloud in which I saw Liam. "He was here. He brought a human up here and ripped their soul. I saw it."

"He brought them *up* here?"

Another nod.

Matt narrowed his eyes. "Another mark against him."

Dread bubbled in my chest. If he wasn't here now, where had he gone?

Ayden's gaze moved between the three of us. "You sure?"

"Are you questioning me?" I furrowed my brows. "Matt didn't!"

"No, no." He shook his head. "If he's still using his power and for the wrong reasons, then I may know where he is."

"You do?" Naeva stepped forwards. "Where?"

"In Hell, of course. I may be Nephilim, but there's a lot that Lucas and Levi don't let me in on. They don't trust me. They must be letting him in on everything."

"Which means he would *definitely* know where God went," I finished.

It was Ayden who got us in. I'd been too familiar with the burning hallways and scattered bones (mostly for decorative purposes). Matt had seen it before, and it didn't put terror in his feathers even an ounce. Naeva, though, was the one grabbing onto his arm. She wasn't comfortable in such a place.

I couldn't just bury the hatchet after she had tried to set my boyfriend up with Sunny.

He led us past the cells, past the dead-ends.

When a familiar pit came into view, I tapped my fingers to my thighs. The pit in which I saw Ayden's form. The pit they threw me in after I'd lost my wings. The blazing agony of my soul melting and oozing blood.

"Hey," Ayden mumbled and his fingers wrapped around my wrist, tugging me to his side, arm around my waist. "I've got you. You're safe now."

We entered the luxurious, gothic cave, or so I was calling it.

"Ah, Ayden, our good foe." Levi grinned. "You brought more foes. Victims."

He lifted his chin, tucking me behind him.

I appreciated the sentiment but I wasn't some damsel for him to coddle. I stepped out on my own.

However, I allowed him to guide this conversation. He knew them best.

"Where's Liam?"

Well.

Maybe that was a mistake.

"Liam?"

"We know he's been here. He's been ripping souls. He's telling them Heaven is tainted, and he has to be taking them somewhere other than up there." He circled Levi. "So, where is he?"

"The man who got into Heaven and refused to sell his soul is working for us?" He tilted his head to the side, eyebrows knitted together. "This is news to me."

"I'm not buying that." Ayden crossed his arms, stopping at his feet. "I know you too well now. You think everything is some joke. You like to play games and fuck with us. If Liam was asked to sell his soul then refused, he's not going to just get away with it. He doesn't slide under the radar with you, does he?"

Levi's eyes went wide. Crazy. A man who took joy in this little facade. "Nothing gets past you, does it, Ayden boy?" He shook his head, clicking his tongue. "Here's the deal—"

"No deal. We're not here to make fucking deals."

"Oh, you'll like this deal. Trust me." His grin widened. "If I were to confess—"

"You just did."

"If," he started again, "I were to confess and tell you everything about Liam's little plan, then we get something in return. One night with your precious Angel."

Ayden lunged forwards. "No!" He shoved his finger in Levi's face. "You said I'd like this deal."

He frowned. "Oh, did I? I thought you liked to share. Not that you've tied the knot or consummated the relationship." An ugly cackle erupted. "Joke around a little with me, will you? I'm just trying to have some fun. Don't be so serious." He patted Ayden's shoulder who shook him off. "Fine." His eyes darkened. "We'll tell you about Liam's plan and about God, because that's why you came, right?"

I swallowed as Matt narrowed his eyes. "And?"

"And in return..." Mischief swirled around in his eyes. "Ayden stays one of us."

"No!" This time I lurched forwards, but Matt grabbed my waist and held me back. "No, he can't do that! Ayden, tell him!"

Ayden glanced back at me, desolation swimming. "Angel..."

"Ayden, don't you fucking dare agree to this!"

He took another step towards Levi. "What do I have to do?"

"It's binding." He swiped a curved knife. "Blood binding."

"Ayden!" I screamed, kicking my legs. "Matt, let me go!"

"I can't do that, Eliana," he said quietly. "Ayden would definitely kill me for it."

Ayden placed his palm up. "Then do it. But you have to uphold your end of the deal."

"Oh, we take those seriously." He grabbed his hand, slicing the blade into his palm. Blood oozed. "You realize you're giving up everything for this."

"I know."

I yelled. I kicked. I started to cry.

Levi grabbed his hand, shaking it. "That's it then. Welcome to the dark side. No getting out of this one." To prove his point, a dark glow seeped from between their palms, sealing his fate.

Matt loosened his grip and I slipped from his arms, falling to my knees as my wails grew.

Levi began to circle us. "Liam's been with us since the beginning. Even before Naeva shot him. He's a good liar, isn't he?" He gave a proud smile. "He never sold his soul, so he did get into Heaven. But by the time he made it to Heaven..." He shrugged. "God was missing. So the very One who could stop Liam, the One who would know he was lying, He wasn't around. Liam's been ripping souls and bringing them to us, and it's easy for people to trust him because he *is* an angel after all. White wings don't lie, do they, Ayden boy?"

I collapsed onto my calves, tears staining my cheeks.

"Believe it or not, God came looking for you."

"What?" he breathed.

"That's how we captured Him. After we poisoned you, He came here looking, to set things straight with Lucifer. Well, here we are. It's a lot easier to capture a god when you were once one of His army."

"Then release Him," my boyfriend said.

"Ah, ah, ah. That wasn't part of the deal. I said I'd tell you about Him, not release Him. The rest of that is up to your friends. You better figure out how to fall out of love because your relationship ends here."

"Angel wouldn't break up with me."

"There's no way they're going to make an exception for Nephilim and a *Virtue*. Lucifer was once God's favorite and look how that turned out. What makes you so special?"

"Then we'll find Him ourselves." He turned as Levi grabbed his arm.

"Nice try, but you're not going anywhere."

Matt grabbed my arms, lifting me from the ground. He attempted to set me upright but my legs gave out again. "We'll find Him."

Naeva rushed over, lifting my arm around her shoulders as she slipped one of hers around my back. I could hear the thoughts brewing in her mind about how she was right and Ayden wasn't any good for me. I didn't want to hear it. It didn't change that she shot a man working for the Devil. She made him fall *in love* with me.

She'd been just as culpable.

Matt helped her drag me back up to earth, and I had no energy left to fight them.

Ayden sold himself to Hell without even considering how I'd feel, or how I'd survive without him. What the fuck was the point of any of this?

JUDGE

"We tried, didn't we?" I whispered. "We tried to help him and in the end, he still turned around and chose wrong."

Matt tapped his foot. "Who are we talking about here?"

"Liam, who else?"

"Well, Ayden did just sign his soul away in blood."

My face sunk, color draining. "Don't remind me."

He leaned forwards. "Eliana. We'll get this sorted, okay? There's not much we can do for him now until we go to the Heavenly Court. To do that, we must go find and save God."

I snickered. "Saving God, never thought we'd have to say those words."

He shrugged. "Me either. But we do what we do."

"Is it true, then? God went down to meet with Lucifer to save Ayden? All this time we thought nobody cared what happened, that we didn't really matter..." I dropped my gaze, fiddling my fingers.

"There's always more than we know, more behind the scenes that we can't see. It's just in your nature to jump to the worst conclusion. It's not your fault exactly. It's Adam's and Eve's." He grabbed my hand, rubbing it. “But that means we have to go back down there.”

The words I dreaded hearing.

“Ayden’s father, Leo, told me where they’d keep God if He were to ever be taken. I know who we need to see.”

That sounded far worse.

Matt and I went back down, and when I turned to ask him how we’d get in, he opened it himself. “What? Archangels have to have some neat features.”

We slipped down in the fiery den, through halls and—

He turned left instead of right.

“Where are we going? The lair is that way.” I pointed.

“We’re not going that way. We know that’s too easy, that He’s not there. It’d be a trap.” He waved me to follow, and I did.

I grumbled. “And how do you know your way around?”

He chuckled. “Eliana, dear, I was here when Hell was created.”

That was true, too.

We dragged on for what felt like centuries, the air growing stuffy the deeper we went. Dim lighting from torches on the walls. The heat suffocating us.

“Here.” He stopped and I collided with his back. “This is where Lucifer is.”

I widened my eyes. “Matt! Why are we getting involved with him?” I yelled in a whisper.

“Because he took God. We used to be friends, once. I can’t promise to get through to him, but I can read his tells. Come on.” He turned the silver knob and it swung open.

“Welcome! Matthew, always a surprise.” Lucifer turned to us. Dark hair slicked back. Clean-shaven. Dark eyes that were only a shade lighter when appearing to humans. He was too much like all the rest. Perfectly put together much like a businessman, but also indistinguishable. Bland. “Although, you have been letting yourself into my home a lot lately. Unannounced. Without knocking. Don't they call this breaking and entering? Isn't that a sin?"

Matt growled. "Only if you're not a kidnapper."

"Even then, I'm pretty sure I have rights." He wiggled his finger.

"So you admit you took God."

Lucifer dropped into his chair, sighing. "Such a fickle thing you are. If you must, Matty. I didn't take God. He came down here to yell at me about Ayden, but it's not on me. Ayden was mine from the start. He's Nephilim. He has always belonged to me."

"Ayden belongs wherever he decides. His soul chose Heaven. I highly doubt God yelled at you. Your idea of yelling is far-fetched."

"How would you know? You were never the favorite." He tapped his fingers together.

Matt scoffed. "And yet I'm the one in Heaven. You were thrown into a lake of fire."

"And now I'm Lord."

"You're Lord of the Flies, don't get it twisted. We all know how it ends."

"Do we? I'm the one who has God." He tilted his chin.

"For fuck's sake," I mumbled.

The pits of his eyes lit up in flames. "Eliana! How lovely to see you. You're a very bad girl, aren't you?" He twirled his finger as he pointed it at me.

I curled my lip. "Ew, don't say it like that."

"You used to be so loyal, obedient, and naive. You've *grown*."

"Don't mistake my disobedience for loyalty to you, nor should you assume I'm switching sides. I'd never. It's your fault, too. You took God, making me believe Ayden was disposed of and forgotten."

"You abandoned your faith. I'm hardly to blame for such things." He dismissed me with the wave of his fingers.

Matt stepped between us. "Where is He?"

"Who? Ayden? Well, he did bind himself, by blood might I add." His eyes darted from Matt's toes to his hair.

His fists balled up, his jaw clenching. "Don't play dumb with me."

He gasped. "Me? Play dumb? Never!" He shifted in his seat. "Wait." He grabbed a stone off the table beside him, turning it over to reveal buttons. He pressed one. "Levi, bring in our special guest of the night."

Matt and I held our breath as we waited for either Ayden or God to be dragged in.

Neither.

"What the hell is this?" I seethed. "Get him out of here!"

Sam's eyes met mine, a conniving smile flickering. "Eliana. Fancy seeing you here."

What a fucking prick.

I never wanted to see him again.

I'd once felt remorse for what I did, but seeing him now, I knew he never regretted it. Why should I?

Walking through the never-ending halls of the university, I kept my head down. Unfortunately, it got me into some trouble.

I ran into someone, dropping my bag. "I'm so sorry." I picked it up.

I glanced back at the guy, but he raised both eyebrows in surprise. I lowered my head and quickly walked away. It wouldn't have turned into one of those romance books. That wasn't me. That wasn't my *life.*

After I made it to the girl's bathroom, I peered into the mirror, reapplying my red lipstick to make sure it was as bold as red could be. My mascara and eyeliner had always stayed on no problem but finding a lipstick that didn't fade over the course of hours had been a challenge all in itself.

The door opened and I stepped back, looking at the boy who had just run into me. "This is the girl's b-bathroom," I stuttered.

He shut the door behind him, facing me. "This is college, Eliana. I came to talk to you."

How did he know my name?

He closed the gap between us. "You don't have many friends, do you? Socially awkward—I like that."

That was an understatement.

"Why are you in here?" I scanned the bathroom for any kind of escape. Who was I kidding? He was blocking the door.

"To see you, remember?" He reached out, grabbing my wrist and yanking me against him. My heels echoed as I stumbled forwards. Before I could protest, he leaned down to kiss me.

This was not how I pictured it. In a girl's bathroom? With a stranger?

I placed my hands flat against his chest, shoving him away from me. "Please, don't kiss me. I don't want you to kiss me. I don't know you." I didn't consent to this, nor did I ever imply I wanted this in any shape or form.

His eyes darkened. "I know you do." He tried to kiss me again, but I was firmer this time, pushing harder. "Oh, Eliana, don't you want to kiss a boy before you die? Don't you wonder what it's like to be touched?" He grabbed my hips, digging his nails into the fabric of my skirt. "You can't stay a virgin forever."

As my eyes widened, he lunged for me.

I screamed. Once I managed to get his filthy hands off me, I tripped, and he landed on top of me. Adrenaline coursed through me, giving me enough strength to throw him off. The rest of him smelled just as putrid as his breath.

I scrambled for the door. He grabbed hold of my ankle and dragged me across the floor. I kicked, plunging my heel into his eye. He yelled out, his hand shooting up to cover the horror.

Grabbing the door handle, I yanked on it only to realize it was locked. How the hell...?

He threw himself against me, knocking me into the wall. I fell to the floor, blinking a few times, my vision swimming along the tile walls.

Everything slowed, as if I was walking through a strobe-lit room. His face closed in, and that awful odor overpowered me.

I'd remembered seeing him somewhere before this, and then it clicked. Liam. This guy was friends with Liam, but Liam would never condone this.

What was his name? Spencer? Simon?

"Sam, please..." I struggled to move my limbs, but they weighed me down.

His fingers left bruises on my cold skin as he unbuttoned my shirt. I couldn't let this happen to me. This couldn't happen to anyone after me. "Stop," I pleaded. I knew better. He wouldn't listen to a girl. He wanted one thing and I couldn't beg away his sick desires.

He pulled down my underwear while lifting my skirt. He began to undo his belt, the buckle ringing in my ears. I wasn't going to let him win.

I brought my knee up into his crotch, sending a fit of pain through him. "Bitch!"

I crawled away and stood up, flinging my underwear off before I tripped. I grabbed onto the sink for support before feeling the right side of my head. When I brought my fingers into my view, blood coated the tips.

Sam pushed me against the counter, trapping me. He attempted to lift my skirt once again, but I shoved back with everything I had left, knocking him against the stall door. It flew open, and he stumbled backwards. A loud cracking sound bounced off the walls.

I turned around, inhaling every ounce of oxygen left in this room as my body shook from the fear settling itself in my bones, making home. Sam lay on the white, plastic floor as a pool of crimson formed around his head, more of it dripping down the bowl of the toilet.

I'd killed him. I'd killed a man.

"Who would I be if I were to keep two enemies apart?" Lucifer wiggled his fingers.

"We are hardly *just* enemies. He targeted me. I defended myself."

"Ah, yes. Victim and criminal. My bad." He rolled his eyes.

The door burst open as Ayden nearly stumbled. "Bloody hell."

"And look who has decided to join the party!" Lucifer clapped. "Now we can begin."

EPISTLE

"The gang's all here," Lucifer commented.

"What, are we *Scooby-Doo* now?" I spat. "Don't answer that."

He grinned, teeth and all. "You're here for one reason. Let's not sugarcoat it. You want to get God out and take Ayden with you."

I'd love to take Ayden. I'd fight like hell to get him back up into Heaven. But Matt made it clear we had to do this a certain way.

"We came for God. That's all. We swear it." I put my hands up, palms facing him.

"I'd never lie to you," Matt added.

Sam spoke up, "Careful. Eliana might slam your head into a toilet."

"Keep your fucking mouth shut," I screamed at him.

Lucifer lifted a finger. "No, Sam's right. We should hear him out."

Grating metal to my ears.

I didn't want to hear what the bastard had to say. He'd twist the story.

I was the victim.

Nobody ever saw it that way though. Society. A college campus. The dean. The court system. Everyone was quick to tell me I could have stopped it by not wearing a skirt or looking nice for myself. By wearing pants instead. I'd been *asking* for it.

They'd say that assault wasn't as bad as murder, and I didn't need to go to such extreme lengths.

But assault was violent. It was abuse. It stripped a person of everything they were—their dignity, their sanity, feeling safe.

It stripped the criminal of their humanity.

I would have rather died, my head cracked on a toilet, than to ever feel violated every time I took my clothes off. To feel so unsafe in my own skin...

Didn't I deserve that basic right?

Sam fixed his appalling shirt. "I've seen the stories, heard the fantasies. Girls love it when a man wants them. Why else do they wear makeup and skirts? Why have big boobs, or any at all? I saw an opportunity to help Eliana gain experience. Poor girl had never been pursued by a man. She was applying her lipstick. *Red*, might I add. Wearing those heels."

I kicked, plunging my heel into his eye.

My eyes watered as I scrunched up my face in disgust—anger.

"She started attacking me."

"You attacked me first!" I shouted, prepared to charge at him before Matt grabbed my arms to hold me back.

He frowned. "She threw me into a stall and killed me. She just got so violent when I was only trying to help."

I growled. "Fuck you."

"I tried. You killed me for it."

I yanked against Matt's grasp, unable to get free. Archangels certainly had more strength than a Virtue. "Matt, let me have a go at him! He deserves it!"

"I'm certain he does. But wasting all your energy on him won't help Ayden."

I slowed.

Matt let me go when he was certain I was able to control myself. I wouldn't have blamed myself if I lost it though.

He released a sigh. "Sam, you ended up here for a reason. That was no mistake."

He pointed to Ayden. "Ayden ended up in Hell, too."

"He was kidnapped."

"And Liam?"

Liam. Fucking Liam. Him and his shitface friend.

Lucifer chimed in, "Liam only got into Heaven because he didn't sell me his soul. By then, God was all mine. What could he do? Liam was part of my plan to infiltrate Heaven and bring all the souls down here. It was intentional on my part, not God's."

Ayden wiggled in Lucas' grasp.

Lucifer glanced at Sam. "You'd like to have some fun, wouldn't you?"

Sam's eyebrows shot up. "Indeed."

Lucifer pinched the bridge of his nose. "Bring in the chains. The ones fresh from the fire." Levi did as he was told.

I leaned close to Matt. "So? What's his tell?" I spat.

Matt shook his head. "He's not bluffing yet. He has plans for us first."

I didn't like the sound of that.

Wasn't whipping me and cutting off my wings *enough*?

As Levi dragged in heavy chains carrying a faint orange glow, Lucifer grabbed a hold of them. He tossed them towards Matt as they flung around him and practically glued him to the wall. He fought against the restraints, hissing and cursing under his breath, the metal searing his soul.

Ayden yanked against Lucas but Lucifer threw another pair of chains his way with the same result.

"Investing in these was a bright decision on my part," he said.

I backed away, not sure where to go first. What was I supposed to do?

"Lucas. Levi," he ordered.

They rushed at me as I turned to run for the door, only to be thrown against it as they grabbed my arms and pinned them behind my back. I started to thrash, to scream. Matt and Ayden did the same, too.

But nobody got loose.

They dragged me back over to Lucifer who commanded them to tie my hands. And when they did, they shoved me onto my knees which nearly cracked on the stone. Lucifer loomed over me. "Ayden is supposed to be one of my favorites, but you took that away from me. I had a good deal going with Liam. Sure, he works for me, but I almost had his soul. I *crave* souls, Eliana. You keep taking what's mine. I'll be pleased to watch Sam take what's yours." He stepped back, gesturing to Sam whose eyes widened in hunger.

I started to throw my entire weight against Levi and Lucas, screaming and shouting.

The closer Sam got, the more nauseated I'd become.

I turned away from him as he lowered himself to my level. As he grabbed my chin, I spat on him. A slap echoed, leaving a tingling skipping along my cheek.

"That was rude," he said. As his eyes narrowed, his hunger became clearer. If I could still throw up, I would have. All over him, too.

I did dry-heave in the process.

I barely registered Matt and Ayden in the background, shouting profanities and attempting every escape known to the supernatural.

My mind only lingered on Sam ripping my good shirt, buttons

flying across the room and bouncing off walls. I tried desperately to tune out his grimy fingers running all over me. I couldn't just wash him off, either. He'd always be there—a *stain.*

"I swear to God I'm going to fucking rip you apart," Ayden seethed.

Sam brushed over his threat, fingers trailing sickness down my stomach.

Ayden yelled some more, growing in size and fighting for his shadows to reach out and either grab me or Sam. Whoever was closer.

But he couldn't.

"My chains are built against Nephilim, too," Lucifer added. "Since men like your father can't resist the female body." He rested his chin on his knuckles.

I closed my eyes to fly to another reality. I attempted to throw some other scenes up in my head, to keep myself stable. I couldn't do even that. I couldn't seem to block him from my mind.

Then his fingers disappeared.

I opened my eyes to find almost a monstrous creature tearing Sam to shreds. Head. Limbs. Dick. Balls. Every inch of him now strewn out before me as some kind of prize—or some kind of offering.

A creature blinding. Unrecognizable. Large wings, a sword. No face. Just hands and a sword.

Then the light dimmed.

When I lifted my gaze, Matt panted, pushing his hair back. "That's what I think of Sam, Lucifer."

Lucifer stared at the remains of a soul.

Matt stepped closer. "You're going to tell me where God is right now or so help me, I will tear you apart myself, even if He forbids it."

Forbids it? Would God forbid that?

Lucifer glanced at his fingers, the same way Selene always did. "I don't really do fights, Matt. War is not my thing. I've got an army to do all the dirty work for me, but I've also got a reputation to uphold." He fixed the collar of his suit jacket. "Ayden already bonded himself to me. Nothing you can do about it. Now that you know about Liam, there's not much we can do about that either. You can have God back. My work here is done." He waved his hand.

Matt shot daggers back at Levi and Lucas who let go of me and backed away. The Archangel was there to fix my shirt and help me to my feet.

A stone door slid away in the back corner, behind the side table. It toppled over as God climbed out.

A tomb. A fiery furnace. Ironic, and fitting. Predictable, too, had we put any thought into our search.

Matt rushed over to make sure He was fine as He grumbled something in return, between the two of them. "We're leaving now."

Lucifer waved using all five fingers, grinning as we exited. Chains fell, Ayden's hands slapping the stone as he dropped. The door closed between us, and I whipped my head forwards again. I ached to run back in and take him home, but we had to do things differently. I couldn't say goodbye. I couldn't kiss him. I couldn't shout my love for him. I simply had to leave in silence as if I barely cared at all.

Deep down, I was swimming in rage and sorrow.

Ayden Dyer—the air in my lungs, the beat of my heart, the ghost of my wings. Maybe it was wrong of me to admit how much I needed him around, but wasn't that the entire point of love? Wasn't the point of finding someone to spend forever with to not be able to live without them? Why have them around if not?

"We'll get him, Eliana," Matt whispered. "We've got God now."

When I glanced at Him, He nodded and rested a hand on both our shoulders. "Thank you both for coming back. Whatever you need, I'm here."

That was the hope I had to hold onto as I twisted my fingers in my own palm.

That hope didn't last all that long though.

The second I got back up to Heaven, the second they left me on my own...

Alone.

The world crushed me beneath its boot, and I gave in, crumbling to the cloud as it offered a warm hug. As soft as silk, as sweet as a chocolate chip cookie.

My Ayden gave up his freedom.

And they stole *mine*.

Reaching behind my back, where my scars burned against my fingertips, I wailed, falling face first into the white fluff. I gripped it. I succumbed to the numbness. I allowed the shame to swallow me whole.

I became everything I swore to my guardees they were not.

Weak.

Worthless.

Nothing.

The isolation—the vacancy rooted itself in the pit of my soul, growing and festering. Rotten. Damp. I attempted to disintegrate it in my hands but to no avail.

I decomposed all over again.

"Eliana," a rough voice drifted under my chin.

Lifting my gaze, I met Matt's empathetic eyes. My cheeks inflated, tears leaving their stain while snot bubbled, running down my nose.

"Hey, hey," he reassured. But as he reached forwards, I broke down into another fit of cries.

His arms wrapped around me anyway. He tugged me into his chest, pressing my face to his shirt, to promise me that he was here and he *heard* me.

"I want my wings back, Matt," I sputtered. "I'm useless without them."

His embrace solidified, and so did his understanding. "You're not useless. You've never been useless. You're more important than you'll ever know. You've proven to us that we can save anyone, even Nephilim. You're brave, Eliana. You're strong. You stand firm, and you always have."

"I've caved!" I cried out. "Lucifer said my faith wavered."

"No," he said with grit. "No. You've always been you. You were right to question things because it shows that you're grounded. You have never been the woman who blindly follows. You know when it's the right time to take a step back and examine the natural order, the law. You never stopped fighting for Ayden, and we need that tenacity. You keep us in check. You keep things running smoothly. We'd never get anywhere without you."

"I can't fly," I sniffled.

Grabbing my face, he directed my eyes back to him. "You've soared farther than any other Virtue has been willing to go. Hold onto that. You matter more than you will ever be able to fathom." Did I?

My mind began to wander, to dig its grave.

Calling my name to get my attention, Matt uttered words I never thought he'd ever say to anyone, let alone *me*.

"Thank you for everything you've done."

I stepped foot into the library. The memory of it was now darkened by his presence, but it was mine. I'd take it back however I needed to.

As I began dusting shelves and spines, the bell dinged. "Oh, we're not open yet," I said as I spun around to face the customer. I had locked the door, right? How did they get in?

"Not even for me?" Ayden cocked an eyebrow.

I recalled the way he broke into that library just to figure out what my first name was. Now it made sense.

"Why are you here?"

He shrugged. "Why are any of us here? God wanted to have some fun writing stories." When I shot him a look, he laughed. "Okay, I just came to return the books." He set them down. "That's all."

Anxiety swirled in my chest. "Oh."

"I loved them." He flashed a smile. "Truly loved them."

My chest warmed as I hurried over to stamp the dates. "Really? Ayden, that makes me happy to hear." I brushed my fingers over the covers. "Which book was your favorite?"

"Definitely book three."

"Which part?"

He leaned against it. "The chase scene toward the end. When she's having to run through tunnels and such to escape the zombies."

I didn't have the heart to tell him that was the most boring part. "That lasted like five chapters."

He grabbed my hand. "But it was worth the outcome, right?"

His green eyes seeped into mine.

"It was," I spilled out in a small, hopeful tone.

"I should go. Assuming God hasn't made His decision yet." He turned towards the door.

"No, but He will. He was grateful, Ayden. He was grateful that we set things right again, and He's going to come through for us. He cares about you. That's why He went missing in the first place. You do matter." My face softened. "Please don't question your worth."

A smirk captured me. "Never." He slipped out of the glass door, allowing me to lock it behind him.

I grabbed the books, checking their condition when something stood out. "Wait." I grabbed *The Dark and Hollow Places*, flipping through the pages. Writing in the margins. None of it my own either.

Glancing back up at the door where Ayden disappeared, I scanned the buildings. Dropping my gaze onto the pages again, I stopped on one, reading out what he'd written, *'Eventually the bloke will realize love is good for him, like I did.'*

Pages upon pages of notes, of Ayden's raw thoughts on something that spoke to me growing up. He'd seen me. He'd truly picked me apart and understood me in ways I've begged anyone to understand me, and I hadn't fully expected or asked him to.

Reading the final annotation, tears sprung to my eyes, one single drop rolling down my cheek.

'She was forced into a cruel world, begging to be loved and seen by anyone willing to stop. She shouldn't have to beg, it's a basic human need. Maybe I'm not the best influence, but I'll love her the way she deserves. I stopped to smell the roses, just like Catcher did Annah. I don't regret any of those choices I made.'

PROPITIATION

Ayden snickered, gazing off towards the window. "I can't stay much longer. I won't lie to you, Angel. You do something to me. My cock aches."

I gagged, the image twisting into pure grime from the bottom of a shoe.

"What? You think I'm not having these thoughts? You know I am." As he faced me again, his brows knitted together.

Swallowing, I averted my gaze. "I hate that word. I despise that word with a passion. Please, for the sake of our love, don't say it again."

His brows furrowed. "Cock?"

I stepped away from him. "Are you trying to *poison* me? What is wrong with you?"

"Why is that word so bad? Americans like to demonize lots of words, don't they?"

"Whether it's Americans or not, that word is awful. Penis is fine. Even dick is okay! But the mere sound, the emphasis on the *K* makes me sick." Which made zero sense since I'd just told him *dick* was okay.

"I'd rather hear you drop the *F-bomb* every minute for eternity if it meant you'd never say that word again. It's vulgar. It's giving me mental images I don't want. It doesn't turn me on. It doesn't make me want you. It makes me want to punch you and then chop your balls off. And am I possibly the only woman who feels that way? Maybe.

"That's never bothered me, however. You know I've never needed to follow the popular opinion. I've been well aware of my own emotions. Right now they are telling me that you need to fulfill your sexual needs more than you need me at all. That is what that word means to *me*. Men think it attracts us. Hell, women think it attracts us. But as for I, as for *me*, I have always been repulsed."

He cracked a smile I hadn't seen in days. "I'll keep it in mind."

"And before you ask if there's a female alternative that I feel the same way about, it's exactly the word you think it is. The *C* word. *C U Next Tuesday*."

"Cunt?"

"Ayden!" I rushed up and shushed him. "You can't say that! And yes I will completely blame that one on Americans. The word is just as vulgar and offensive."

Ayden wrapped an arm around my waist and pulled me against him. He pressed a kiss against my palm, and I lowered it. "You're so cute when you're worked up." He grabbed my wrist, kissing my fingers. "I miss you."

Reality settled—the air growing heavy. "Things weren't supposed to turn out this way," I whispered. "You were supposed to spend forever with me." Yet we'd had to waste so much time just fighting for him to come back.

Sliding his fingers across my wrist and up my neck, he placed a knuckle under my chin. "And I will. No matter the cost."

My lips quivered. I could lose everything just being with him now, in the rare event God didn't take our side. But did I care? "No matter the cost," I repeated.

His lips crashed against mine as he grabbed my face in his hands. Hot, salty tears made their way between our desperate pleas for love. He tasted of longing, scandals, and impurities. He tasted like petals detached from the stem—fallen. Alone. Hoping for a place to belong again after losing everything they'd ever known.

When I pulled away, I wiped away the tears with the back of my hand, sniffling. "You should go. I have to go to court. I'd say I'll let you know the results but I assume you'll know when it's over anyway."

We said our goodbyes, and Matt came down to get me. Liam couldn't be trusted, and surely he knew that now. Although he tried to talk to me regardless.

We entered the courtroom looking as pristine and bland as ever. The room, not us.

I wore a button-up tucked neatly into a black skirt. Matthew put on his best gold suit.

He was *definitely* a favorite.

We took our seats as it began.

"Now that order has been restored, things have been set in motion," the judge started. "We have brought our case to God and despite the events that unfolded, He has determined that things were not right with it. You not only brought Him back to us, but your persistence was admirable."

I chewed my lip, folding my fingers under the table.

"Our decision was not made lightly but with careful consideration. Ayden Dyer was wrongfully kidnapped after he earned his place. Due to these circumstances, we are ruling in his favor. He will be reinstated as one of Heaven's angels."

I broke out into a cry, covering my mouth. Matt rubbed my back.

"As for Liam Brown, he has been conspiring with Lucifer and harming souls. His wings will be stripped from him and he will be sent down to Hell to pay for his sins."

Liam slumped in his chair across the aisle.

Naeva told us she couldn't reverse the arrow. She had tried, but they figured it would be a fitting punishment for him to rot in Hell, be hopelessly in love with me yet never get to see me again, and *knowing* I was with Ayden. I didn't disagree with that.

When we left the courtroom, Matt grabbed Liam by the arm. "We'll be back."

I believed it.

For a time.

But when hours passed, the sun set, and darkness fell over the city, I couldn't wait longer.

I leaped from the cloud.

I didn't stick the landing but I couldn't exactly break a bone when I had none to begin with.

Heading to the portal, I stood at the entrance, but nobody entered or exited. It didn't even open. So I checked the cabin for Ayden, but it was empty. Nobody showed up.

Something was wrong.

I was on my own.

Hurrying back to the portal, I lifted rocks and boulders. It wasn't like a hidden library behind a bookshelf though.

"Hey," Naeva's voice echoed from behind me.

I whipped around. "Why are you here?"

"To help, of course."

I scowled.

"What did I do this time?" A frown disgraced her.

"Excuse me? You lied to Ayden, lied to Sunny and promised to fix this before trying to erase his memories. You keep trying to pair

Sunny with Ayden and letting her know where he is so she can steal him from me," I spat.

Confusion swept over her features. "I did what?"

I opened my mouth to accuse her some more, but I didn't have the energy for this right now.

So she added, "I messed up and I'm truly sorry. I was in the wrong and sometimes it doesn't pay to follow orders. Please, *let me help.*"

Releasing a sigh, I straightened. "Matt took Liam to Hell, and to grab Ayden. They should have been back by now. I can't get in." I pointed to the empty cave in the ground. To any passerby it'd look like a small cave that led nowhere. But in our realm, it was a portal. Most caves were.

"Liam is down there, right?" she asked for confirmation, as if I hadn't just told her that exact thing.

"Yes...?" I wasn't sure how else to respond. Why did it matter whether he was or wasn't? Her question had taken me off guard.

Naeva stepped over a small shrub and shot an arrow at the cave. Fire exploded as the door opened up.

I stared at her with wide eyes. "What?"

"Oh, right. My arrows aren't just for love. Well, they are. In a sense. I'll explain later."

As in, she'd never explain later.

Then we descended into the pits of Hell.

Navigating the halls on our own wasn't as bad as it had been, although the thought of Matt being trapped down here did scare me.

Naeva was still on edge.

We rounded a corner, but her fingers wrapped around my wrist as she pulled me back. "I'm sorry, Eliana. I'm sorry I screwed up with Liam."

"I know. I know. Now's not the time."

"No, I need you to hear it now. I screwed up big time. And yes, I know about your secret."

"Secret?" I furrowed my brows.

"Your secret," she whispered. "I said *someone* intentionally, because I know everything about everyone. Romance is my department. I promise it's safe with me." She patted my shoulder.

"Well, well, well," a familiar voice bounced off walls. "If it isn't Eliana and..." Selene's eyes narrowed. "Naeva."

She nodded, chin lifted high. "Cupid, essentially. Wait, was I not supposed to say that?" She shot me a look. Then she paused, gaze falling back on Selene. "How do you know my name?"

Selene redirected her attention to me. "Did you come looking for Ayden?"

"And Matt," Naeva interjected. "How did you know my *name*?" she repeated.

"Once upon a time I was you, Naeva." Stepping back into the shadows, things shifted accordingly. Black curls, a silk dress. But those brown eyes were still too dark.

Realization slammed into me. "Oh my fucking shit," I breathed. "It was you!"

Naeva's eyes darted between us before she got it. And that was when the rotted woods took root in her soul.

"It's just a trick of the shadows." Selene stepped forwards, humming as she glanced at her nails. "Ayden and Matt wanted to leave. That was a no-go."

I growled. "God said Ayden belongs to us." Not *with* us, but to me.

"Oh Elli, no he doesn't. He made his deal. Don't you remember? It's binding by blood. Of course God doesn't know about that. But what He doesn't know won't hurt Him. Or I suppose it will in this case."

I lunged for her, Naeva ripping me back. "No! He's ours!"

However, she wanted to tear her apart instead.

"I don't think so. I'm here to make sure you don't leave with him."

"I don't suppose your arrows work for us now, do they," I mumbled to Naeva.

"No, sorry." She closed the distance. "We came here for a reason. God said he comes with *us*. You won't get in our way." Spacing her feet, she bent her knees a bit as she prepared for the attack.

Selene positioned herself, lifting her fists. "Try me."

Naeva tackled her to the ground, biting, hitting, punching. Shoving her thumb in her eye. None of it made a mark. "Eliana, run!"

I immediately sprinted past them and down the halls, recalling the way Ayden led us last time. I'd thank Naeva later.

Bursting through the black door, I faceplanted, scraping bits and pieces of my soul. I groaned as I climbed back to my feet.

"Ah, Angel." Levi planted himself in front of me, hands clasped behind him. "What a nice surprise."

"Where are they?"

"Oh, you mean your boy toy?"

I slapped him, the sting only prevalent in my hand. "Levi!"

He sighed. "I can't help you there. You must know that."

"You took them!"

He put his hands up. "I did no such thing. Matt came here with Liam and tried to take Ayden against the blood oath he made to us. The very oath that Matt witnessed and knows is against the law."

"Is it though?" I spat. "God said Ayden is ours."

He shook his head, wiggling his finger. "Only because God doesn't know about the blood oath. Those are binding for eternity. It's no different from the Mark, now is it?" he paused, clicking his tongue. "No, it's not."

Naeva stayed back and I was stuck in here with Levi, no sign of Matt or Ayden. We'd stupidly split up with no plan. And what could we do about it? They could hurt us here, but we couldn't hurt them.

Somehow, I had to slip by and figure out where he went.

"So." I coughed. "You like games?"

Levi crossed his arms. "I'm not a moron, Eliana. I see right through you."

"What?"

"You're going to entice me with a game I can't refuse to find your friends. Sound familiar?"

I pressed my lips into a thin line.

"But I'm not some *witch* who picks up on deals like that. I don't make any more deals. I got what I wanted."

"My boyfriend. Ayden. Because you're in love with him."

"If that's what you want to believe. But you'd know a thing or two about feelings for the same sex, wouldn't you?"

I sighed. "Why does everyone seem to know but me?"

"Hard to miss the way you look at Selene." He chuckled. "I kid! Liam told us."

Right. The liar broke a promise.

I sidestepped him when he jerked forwards.

"What, you scared?" His maniacal laugh echoed between chandeliers, absorbed by the glass. "You should be. Just you and no army."

I wasn't strong. I had no wings, and nothing else other than already being dead.

But maybe I wasn't in total shit. I was smarter, wittier, more intelligent. I had to use that.

And knowing fallen angels, they had weapons stashed around here. I couldn't use them against him, but it'd distract him enough while I found an escape route.

I screamed when he came at me. Running to the couch, I launched myself behind it and dropped to the floor, eyes dragging under the sofa until I spotted a machete.

"That'll do," I mumbled, fingers wrapping around the hilt.

"Oh no you don't!" he shouted as I screamed again. I rolled onto my back. He attempted to straddle me, reaching for the blade. I sliced at him.

Nothing happened.

I plunged it through his chest. I kneed his balls. I scooted just far enough until I brought my foot to my chest and launched him backwards. "Fuck you, Levi!"

I scrambled away, using the couch to hoist myself to my feet. I swung the blade too hard while he came for me again. He dodged every hit. So I stumbled, tripping over the rug behind me. A rug made of black bear fur.

Oh they were sick.

Levi stomped his feet on each side of me, reaching for my legs. I swung again, sending a foot to the chest.

I recalled every piercing scream. Each tear. The agonizing suffering as he hacked away my wings. The deal he made with Ayden, taking him away from me.

Like that, I summoned exactly why I despised them.

I needed to watch them burn like I'd promised.

Yelling in his face, I sent my foot to his chest one more time. He landed back on his ass as I jumped to my feet. "He will always be mine. *Never* yours. You can't fucking have him." I kicked his head, enough to stun him, but not enough to do damage.

I leaped out of the way as he swiped his arm. I fell back against a table, wincing as the edge drilled into my back. My arm came down as I grabbed hold, using it to lift myself. The fireplace shifted.

"No!" he shouted.

Before he could stop me, I sprinted for it.

Levi was hot on my tail, wings flapping just as I dropped and skidded into the passageway hidden behind it. He flew above me, halting when I hit a wall. I rolled away and hurried to my feet. As he chased me, I dodged and ducked, slicing the machete back and forth.

My toe hit a stone and I crashed to my knees. A cry escaped as a stabbing pain exploded in my thigh. Levi ripped the curved knife out, blood splattering the stone.

Still, I pulled myself up and pushed on.

I whipped around a corner, following the dark halls and allowing my subtle glow to be the light that guided me.

A door at the end opened up.

"Close it! Close it!" I yelled.

Whoever they were, they didn't listen.

I barreled into the darkness, rolling across the floor. My machete clattered to the ground. I covered my face with both arms, expecting them to capture me.

Levi yelped.

Hush.

Slowly peeling them back, I searched for any sign of life. "Hello?" my voice croaked.

Soft tendrils slid under me, lifting me from the ground, ice biting at my soul. I sucked in air from the sudden change in temperature, closing my eyes. The darkness tucked me into its chest, and I curled into it, burying all my fears. "Ayden," I let out a breathy whisper.

As the darkness shrunk around us, he materialized from it, arms wrapped around me. "I got you, Angel. I got you."

I threw my arms around him, pressing him so tightly against me as if I could absorb him into my soul and sneak him out. If only. "We need to find Matt and Naeva and leave. We did it, Ayden. God said you belong up there."

"Angel," he started.

I yanked myself away, gasping. "Don't you dare. Don't you dare argue. If you love yourself at all, you'll do this. For you. You need to prove to me that you love yourself just as much as I do."

"I know where to look." He stood, pulling me, leading me out of the bare room.

I winced with each step, biting back the pain.

We snuck through the halls and moved quietly. When we slipped into a room, we turned to find Matt unconscious, tied to a chair.

"Oh that's going to be fun," Ayden mumbled. Thankfully, he untied him with no obstacles. "I'll carry him. We should hurry."

"Naeva."

"What?"

"Naeva came with me. She was distracting Selene."

"Shit. Okay, well, we get you and Matt out. I'll come back for Naeva."

I started to argue, but a sharp pain shot through my leg.

Nevermind that.

He threw Matt over his shoulder like he weighed the same as a sack of potatoes. Did he *work out*?

Or was that the strength of being Nephilim?

He led the way as I trailed close behind. He took the halls less traveled, growling at any fallen angels attempting to threaten him. It scared them off fairly easily.

The sun blinded me as we emerged. Ayden lowered Matt. "Stay here."

I wasn't going to be able to get far on my own anyway.

He vanished back into the portal.

I lay back on the grass. I hadn't noticed the sun set.

A starless sky, dead quiet woods.

A passage of time I barely noticed...

"Angel," he whispered.

I opened my eyes to the mesmerizing shade of green—a glittering river under a bright sun. "Ayden."

"Why didn't you tell me?" He frowned.

"Tell you what?" I sat up in time to hear him hiss "careful" before grabbing my shoulders.

A dull throbbing in my thigh brought me back to reality.

He lifted my pant leg before finding it wouldn't go much higher. "Oh, fuck this." He grabbed my hips and slipped them down to my knees. "What happened?"

My blood stained the grass.

"Levi, in the tunnels. I didn't want to slow us down."

He pulled back, removing his white shirt and tearing strips. He tied a few around my thigh, knotting it well. "Come. We've got to get to Heaven."

The gesture was thoughtful, although my wound had stopped bleeding since we stepped back onto earth. Some habits did die hard.

Matt came into view, arms folded, pacing. "Now. Before they come back."

Ayden scooped me up before I could protest. Matt was the key as the three of them flew me into the clouds. With his help, Ayden broke that threshold.

My boyfriend dropped me off to get my wound turned into a scar while he and Matt went to the Great Hall.

Naeva stayed with me, sitting at my bedside as they peeled back the blood-crusted fabric. "Since the potion I used on Liam was for you, I can use my arrows to also *find* him, including opening whatever doors I need to if he's behind one that's locked."

They placed a hand over my gaping laceration, light slipping through their fingers as it fused itself, leaving behind a nasty scar. Another for the books.

She went on, "He was in Hell, right? And my arrows can open the path that led us to him."

I supposed she did explain.

And she got her revenge on Selene for impersonating her.

We left the room, Matt leaning against the wall near his office.

"It's a perk." She shrugged, a little hop in her step as she returned to the Archangel and left me outside the double gold doors.

The wait itself was agony.

It only lasted ten minutes, but that was a lifetime in my eyes.

I stood outside, glancing up at Ayden as he exited, ready to ask how it went. But I didn't quite get there, the white wings behind him as stark a difference as my change from a white gown.

"As good as new," he said, spinning for me to see.

We could *finally* go back to the way things were before.

I brushed my fingers over his feathers as we lay in the bed, crickets chirping outside the window. "Did you mention the blood oath?"

"And ruin my chances of getting back into Heaven? Never. Besides, it's because of my oath that we found out what happened which ultimately restored order in Heaven. I think it's a fair trade," he said with a chuckle. A shiver scurried down his spine, feathers ruffling.

My fingers—and gaze—snagged on something. A single black feather tucked lower on the left wing, beneath white ones. I rubbed it between my thumb and forefinger. "What about your power?"

Ayden lay back, hooking his hands behind his head, chest on full display. "That's the best part. I still have it."

"Really? How?" I propped myself up on my elbow. "You're just a regular angel, right?"

He shrugged, eyes roaming over the ceiling. "Maybe. Maybe not.

It could have something to do with what I am, or my oath. What I know is that I can access Heaven and Hell. I have my powers. And I'm with you."

My mind wandered to the black feather, wondering if because of the blood binding that he couldn't rid himself of every drop of poison.

I glanced back as a wisp slid around my waist, tugging me closer to him. It'd been mostly white, a black tip that faded into the rest.

With a sigh, I rested my cheek against his shoulder. "Good. I quite like your powers if I'm being honest. I *must* admit that." I traced his chest down to his stomach, fingers bringing out the *V* disappearing into his jeans.

With a laugh, he wrapped an arm around my back. He winked. "If you stay with me, Love, they're all yours to play with."

What an asshat.

But he was all mine to mess with.

And *they* burned for their sins against us.

Epilogue: Bronze

Ayden

She was still angry with me. I could see it all over her face. Even if things turned out okay in the end, she'd never forgive me or trust me again.

I still had to try.

The red and white chequered blanket was laid out on the grass as the beginnings of spring peaked. Dew on the grass, chilly breeze, buds starting to sprout.

The cliff overlooked Salt Lake, where we first met. Where we fell in love.

Crossing her arms, she shot me a glare. "What the hell is this?"

I chuckled. "This isn't Hell; it's earth, dear Angel."

I smirked a little, arm sliding around her waist as I pulled her into my chest, whispering in her ear, "This is our first date after the madness."

I pressed a soft kiss to her temple and sat down, pulling her with me. "I thought it would be nice to watch a sunset but then I thought that was boring. We can't eat much food because we're dead. However, I thought I would do something I love, to create something you love, so I baked this cupcake for you." I pulled out a red velvet cupcake. Many people hated them. Angel had a thing for red. After all, it was her *favourite* colour.

"Ayden, this is the most romantic thing you have ever done." As she took a bite, she closed her eyes and moaned. "Wow, that tastes like Heaven. And I intended that pun." She flashed me her pearly whites.

I leaned inward and took a bite of her cupcake. "It does."

"Ayden!" She gasped, pulling it out of my reach.

Clearing my throat, I said, "This is not exactly traditional and I'm sorry, but we're dead." I grasped her chin, pulling her eyes back to me.

"What do you mean? Angels still go on dates in Heaven."

I leaned in, mumbling against her lips, "They do, Angel, but angels don't have wedding rings." I slipped my fingers between hers. "I have no ring to offer you for your hand in marriage. I still want to be with you nonetheless. I wish to spend forever with you, in love and putting up with my shenanigans. Will you marry me and become my Mrs. Dyer?"

She scrambled back from me. "What?"

I furrowed my brows. "Did I say something wrong?"

"Ayden, this better not be a joke."

I was taken back. "Am I supposed to joke about this?"

She lunged forward, grabbing my collar and shoving me back into the ground as she landed on top. "Yes!" She kissed me hard. "Yes, I'll marry you. Under one condition."

"What's that?" I held her waist.

"We elope first and hold a ceremony later. No more waiting. Just be my husband." And nothing could go wrong there.

I pressed my fingers into the bare skin peeking out from her shirt. "If that's what you want, Love, then call me your husband."

She grabbed my hand, pulling me into the cabin. Gold rings shimmered on our fingers. She shut the door behind us, pressing me against the wall and kissing me.

I flipped us around. Still, the vibe wasn't right. "We need candles. And petals." I pulled away, looking for anything left behind. Under the couch, in the drawers.

"Ayden," she called out.

"It has to be right."

"Ayden," she whined.

I looked at her. "I'm not going to give you anything less."

She shouted, "Ayden!"

"What?"

"Stop, please. I don't need rose petals and candles and soft music." She closed the gap, grabbing my hands. "Of course you assume that I want that, but I know the first time isn't always perfect. I just want *you*. That's all I care about."

I tugged her against me, grabbing her face. "There's pressure. A lot to live up to. It's your first time."

"Whether I was experienced or not, you'd still have to show me your best," she joked. "But seriously. Just be yourself. And we have all of eternity to try everything."

My tongue weighed heavily. My palms would be sweating if they could. I'd had sex many times with so many women. Why was this time different? I didn't get clammy like this.

I led her back into the bedroom, kissing her before another part of me suffered with anxiety.

The back of her legs hit the edge of the bed and she fell back, laughing. "Are you okay?"

"I'm great." I grabbed her thighs, pushing her higher up on the mattress and climbing on top. "Let's hope we don't break the bed." I got a laugh in before I kissed her again, running my hands over every inch of her body. I gripped the dress, pulling it up her legs before inching it up her stomach. When I got it over her head and tossed it to the side, I took a moment to admire the fact that she wasn't wearing anything. How many times had I been in her presence without knowing it was always one piece of clothing standing between us?

"What?" She unbuttoned my shirt.

"You really don't like underwear."

"I see no point in wearing it when I'm dead. I told you that."

I helped her get my shirt off, then shimmied out of my pants.

She pulled my briefs down, mumbling about me wearing them in the afterlife.

I pressed more kisses to her throat, her shoulders, her collarbone, and every bit of her I could that was exposed to me. I didn't want there to be any part left untouched.

Our hands explored one another, no longer shy about what we could have.

Digging my fingers into her hips, we fit together perfectly. Maybe it was cheesy to say.

I buried my face in her neck, nestled between her thighs, chest to chest. It'd been nothing like the other times. This moment between us would forever patch up a piece of me that'd been hanging on by a thread for a long time. Angel had stitched up the areas of my heart that nobody else had access to.

She loved me whole and showed me my worth, regardless of my grandpa stripping it from me at such a young age.

She warmed the ice once encasing me, melting my insides, turning me into mush.

The things she did to me, the way she showed me emotions I never thought I'd feel again...

I adored her.

And now—*now* I could call her my wife forever.

The gasps and pleasure were a bonus.

There were pros to waiting until death to have sex. She didn't bleed. She didn't feel any pain. We skipped all the hard stuff and went right for the best parts, and when I slowed, she threw her body weight against me until we flipped over. I let her have her fun, too. She'd waited plenty.

After a few rounds, I pulled her into my chest, kissed her head, and stroked her hair. "So, Eliana Dyer," I whispered with a grin. Her eyes lit up as she lifted them to meet my hooded gaze. "What's next?"

Also by Monica Shantel

THE FEATHERS AND FLAMES TRILOGY

Beauty of a Crimson Soul

Beauty of a Burning Flame

Beauty of an Undying Love

THE TO BELIEVE DUOLOGY

To Believe in Peter Pan

To Believe in the Demon King

STANDALONES

Blissful

37 Nights

The Goddess in the Shadows

Tainted

THE QUEENS OF ORSADIA DUET

Seven Deadly Sins

One Poisonous Queen

ACKNOWLEDGEMENTS

I want to say thank you to Ashly, my ride or die, for always supporting my writing and going with whatever shenanigans I've come up with. I want to thank my mom. I want to thank God for loving me even when I'm struggling to see the light in anything.

I want to also thank my beta reader, Vivian. Without you, this book would be a mess. You are appreciated more than you know. I want to thank my sensitivity reader, Wendy. You provided valuable input that I could never see on my own. I want to thank all my readers and my author friends who have gotten me this far. Ben, Morgan, Joe, Juliet, and of course Vivian again. All of you have helped me through dark times and I wouldn't see the importance of my stories.

Last but not least, I want to thank Zoey, my dog, for putting up with endless hours of writing and ranting. She's always a great listener.

ABOUT THE AUTHOR

Monica Shantel has always had an interest in artistic and creative hobbies of sorts. At the age of twelve, she began building stories to escape reality and find hope in life. Her debut novel is Beauty of a Crimson Soul. Her style can be described as pushing limits and striking emotional responses. She takes the time to touch on dark topics and aims to shed light on the impact trauma can have on people. In the same breath, she also offers hope with the romantic and platonic side of things as a way to keep her head up even in the worst of times. When life lets us down, her goal is to give people a piece of ambition.

<u>Keep up with Monica:</u>
Instagram: @lxstinneverland
Backup Instagram: @authormonicashantel

For more information, visit:
www.monicashantelbooks.com

www.ingramcontent.com/pod-product-compliance
Lightning Source LLC
Chambersburg PA
CBHW020341310726
48979CB00015B/2454/J